WATCHING
OVER
HER

WATCHING OVER HER

JEAN-BAPTISTE ANDREA

TRANSLATED FROM THE FRENCH BY FRANK WYNNE

atlantic·*fiction*

Published in trade paperback in Great Britain in 2025 by Atlantic Books, an
imprint of Atlantic Books Ltd.

1 2 3 4 5 6 7 8 9

A CIP catalogue record for this book is available from the British Library.

Trade paperback ISBN: 978 1 80546 273 6
E-book ISBN: 978 1 80546 274 3

Printed and bound by CPI (UK) Ltd, Croydon CR0 4YY

Atlantic Books
An imprint of Atlantic Books Ltd
Ormond House
26–27 Boswell Street
London
WC1N 3JZ

www.atlantic-books.co.uk

This book is supported by the Institut français
(Royaume-Uni) as part of the Burgess programme.

Product safety EU representative: Authorised Rep Compliance Ltd., Ground Floor,
71 Lower Baggot Street, Dublin, D02 P593, Ireland. www.arccompliance.com

To Berenice

There are thirty-two of them. On this autumn day in 1986, thirty-two are still living in this monastery at the end of a rutted track that would make any traveller blench. Nothing has changed in the past thousand years. Not the steepness of the path nor the vertiginous drop. Thirty-two stout hearts – it takes courage to live on the edge of an abyss – thirty-two bodies that were strong in their youth. Some hours from now, they will be thirty-one.

The monks are gathered in a circle around the dying man. There have been many such circles, many farewells, since the walls of the Sacra were first built. There have been moments of grace, moments of doubt, moments when bodies steeled themselves against the looming darkness. There have been and will be other departures, so they wait patiently.

This dying man is unlike the others. He alone has never taken the vows. Yet he has been allowed to stay here for forty years. Each time the subject has been mentioned, each time the question has been raised, a man in purple robes has come – never the same man twice – and it is he who decides. *He stays.* The dying man is as much a part of the monastery as the cloisters, the columns, the Romanesque capitals, whose conservation owes much to his talent. So let us not complain; he has paid for his sojourn here in kind.

From beneath the wool blanket, only his hands emerge. They are balled into fists either side of his head: an eighty-two-year-old child in the throes of a nightmare. His skin is sallow, like parchment stretched so sharply over jutting bones that it might break. His forehead gleams, made waxen by his fever. It was inevitable that one day his strength would fail. A shame that he never answered their questions. But a man is entitled to his secrets.

Besides, they feel as if they know. Not everything, but the most important facts. Sometimes their opinions differ. To stave off boredom, the monks find they are as gossipy as fishwives. He is alternately a criminal, a defrocked priest, a political refugee. Some say he is being held against his will – a theory that holds little water since they have seen him leave and come back of his own volition; others claim he is there for his own safety. Then there is the most popular theory, and the most clandestine, since in a monastery, romance must be smuggled in: he is there to watch over *her*. She who waits, in her marble shroud, a few hundred metres from his spartan cell. She who has been waiting now for forty years. All the monks in the Sacra have seen her once. All would like to see her again. They need only ask permission from the abbot, Padre Vincenzo, but few dare to do so – out of fear, perhaps, of the impure thoughts that are said to come to those who come too close to her. And monks have more than enough impure thoughts without finding themselves pursued, in the inky darkness, by dreams with the face of an angel.

The dying man struggles, opens his eyes then closes them again. One of the monks swears he sees a flicker of joy – he is mistaken. Someone gently dabs a cool flannel over his brow, his lips.

The dying man is still struggling, and for once, all the brothers agree.

He is trying to say something.

Of course I'm trying to say something. I've witnessed man's first flight, and I've seen him fly faster and faster, further and further. I've seen two world wars, the crumbling of nations, I've picked oranges on Sunset Boulevard – surely you know I have stories to tell? I apologise. I'm being ungrateful. Since I first decided to hide out here, you have clothed and fed me when you yourselves had nothing, or so little. But I have been silent for too long. Close the shutters – the light hurts my eyes.

He's getting restless. Close the shutters, brother, the light seems to be troubling him.

The shadows that watch over me in the harsh light of the Piedmont sun, the voices that grow muffled as the long sleep looms. It's all happened so quickly. Only a week ago you could still see me out in the vegetable garden or up on a ladder – there was always something that needed repair. Age has slowed me, but since no one gave me long to live when I was born, it is quite impressive. Then one morning, I just couldn't get up. I could see in their eyes that my turn had come, that soon the bell would toll and that I would be carried out to the little garden that faces the mountain, where a sea of poppies grows over centuries of abbots, illuminators, cantors and sacristans.

He's in a very bad way.

The shutters creak. In the forty years I've lived here, they've always creaked. Darkness, at last. The darkness of the cinema – which I witnessed being born. At first, nothing but a barren horizon, at first nothing. A dazzling plateau that, as I stare, is filled with shadows by my memory, with forms that resolve to become cities, forests, men and beasts. My actors move towards the front of the stage. Some, I recognise; they haven't changed. The sublime and the ridiculous, inseparable, smelted together in the same crucible. The currency of tragedy is a rare alloy of gold and glitz.

It's only a matter of hours.

A matter of hours? Don't make me laugh. I died long ago.

Another cold compress. He seems to be a little calmer.

But where is it written that the dead cannot tell their stories?

I l Francese. The Frenchman. I have always loathed the moniker, although I have been called much worse. All my joys, all my pains are rooted in Italy. I hail from a country where beauty is ever imperilled. If she should slumber five short minutes, ugliness would ruthlessly devour her. Here, genius grows like a weed. People sing as easily as slaughter, paint as willingly as they play false, let dogs piss against church walls. Not for nothing was a scale of devastation named for an Italian, Mercalli, a scale that quantifies the devastation of an earthquake. One hand tears down, the other builds up, and the emotion is the same.

Italy, kingdom of marble and of manure. My country.

Yet, the fact remains that I was born in France in 1904. Fifteen years earlier, my parents, scarcely married, had left Liguria to seek their fortune. By way of fortune, they found themselves dismissed as wops, were spat upon, were mocked for the way they rolled their Rs – though, to my knowledge the word *roll* begins with *R*. My father barely escaped the massacre of Aigues-Mortes in 1893, which took the lives of two close friends: *brave* Luciano and *old* Salvatore. They were never again mentioned without these qualifiers.

Families forbade their children from speaking their mother tongue, to avoid the charge of 'being wops'. They scrubbed them with Marseille soap in the hope of bleaching their bronzed skin a little. But not the Vitaliani. We spoke Italian, we ate Italian. We thought Italian, which is to say larded with superlatives, frequent invocations of Death, copious tears and hands that were rarely still. We cursed as one might pass the salt. Our family was a circus, and we were proud of it.

In 1914, the French government, which had showed scant enthusiasm for protecting Luciano, Salvatore and the others, declared that my father, without a shadow of a doubt, was a good French citizen, worthy of being conscripted. Especially since some bureaucrat, in error or in jest, had shaved ten years from his age while copying his birth certificate. With no smile, no spring in his step, he went to war. His own father had lost his life during the Expedition of the Thousand in 1860. Nonno Carlo had fought in Sicily with Garibaldi. It was no Bourbon bullet that killed him, but a prostitute of doubtful hygiene in the port of Marsala, a detail that the family passed over in silence. Whatever the cause, he was just as dead and the message was clear: war kills.

It killed my father. One day, a gendarme appeared at the workshop above which we lived in La Maurienne. My mother still opened the workshop every day in the hope that it might be some commission which her husband could fulfil on his return, since sooner or later he would have to return to stone carving, restoring gargoyles, making fountains. The gendarme adopted an appropriate countenance, which turned ever more doleful when he saw me, cleared his throat and explained that there had been shell fire, and, well, that was that. When my mother, with great dignity, asked him when the body would be repatriated, he mumbled, explained that there had been horses on the battlefield, other soldiers, that a shell could cause great damage, and so, it was impossible to tell who was who, nor even what was man and what was horse. My mother, thinking he was about to cry, offered him a glass of Amaro Braulio – I have never seen a Frenchman drink it without a grimace – and did not weep herself until many hours later.

Of course, I do not remember all this, or only badly. I know the facts and titivate them with a little colour, those same colours that now slip through my fingers in the tiny cell on Mount Pirchiriano that I have occupied these past forty years. Even today, my French is very poor – or was, some days ago, when I still had the power of speech. No one has called me Il Francese since 1946.

Some days after the visit of the gendarme, my mother explained that, in France, she could not give me the education I required. Already her belly had begun to swell with a brother or a sister – that was never born, or at least not alive – and she covered me in kisses as she explained that she was sending me back to the old country because she believed in me, because she could sense my love of stone despite my tender age, because she knew that I was destined for great things, that it was for this that she had given me my name.

Of the twin burdens of my life, my Christian name was the easier to bear. Yet I passionately despised it.

My mother would often go down to the atelier to watch her husband work. She realised that she was pregnant when she felt me quiver to the sound of the chisel. Till then she had spared no effort, had helped my father shift vast blocks of stone, which perhaps explains what follows.

'He shall be a sculptor,' she said.

My father grumbled, told her that it was a dirty trade, the hands, the back, the eyes wore out more quickly than the stone, and that unless a man were Michelangelo, he should spare himself the grief.

My mother nodded, and decided that she would give me a head start.

My name is Michelangelo Vitaliani.

I rediscovered my country in October 1916, accompanied by a drunkard and a butterfly. The drunkard had known my father and initially managed to avoid being conscripted because of the state of his liver, but given the turn events were taking, his cirrhosis might not protect him for much longer. They were conscripting children, old men and cripples. The newspapers claimed that we were winning, that the Hun would soon be history. In our community, news that Italy had joined the Allies the previous year was welcomed as a promise of victory. Those coming home from the front sang a different tune from those who still felt the urge to sing. Ingegnere Carmone, who like the other Eyeties had collected salt from the salt marshes of Aigues-Mortes before opening a grocery shop in Savoie, where he drank much of his stock of wine, had decided to go home. If he was going to die, better to do so in his own house, his lips red from a bottle of Montepulciano to allay his fears.

His country was the Abruzzo. He was a kindly man and agreed to drop me off at Zio Alberto's on his way. He did so because he felt a little sorry for me and also, I think, for my mother's eyes. Mothers' eyes are often something, but my mother's were a curious almost violet blue. They triggered more than a few fistfights, until my father stepped in to put an end to things. A stonecutter's hands can be dangerous, even I won't deny that. The competition quickly lost out.

On the platform of La Praz station, my mother shed great violet tears. My uncle Alberto, who was also a sculptor, would look after me. She swore that she would come and join me as soon as she had sold the stonemason's studio and earned a little money. A matter of a few weeks, a few months at the most – it took her twenty years. The train blew, belching out black smoke I can still taste to this day, and carried the drunken *ingegnere* and her only son away.

Grief does not last long when you're twelve, whatever people say. I didn't know where the train was headed, but I knew I had never been on a train – or if I had, I didn't remember. My excitement soon gave way to anxiety. Everything was moving too fast. The moment I tried to focus on some detail – a fir tree, a house – it had disappeared. Landscapes are not meant to move. I felt queasy, but the *ingegnere* was snoring with his mouth open.

Fortunately, there was the butterfly. It fluttered into the carriage at Saint-Michel-de-Maurienne and landed on the window, between the mountains and me. After a brief struggle with the glass, it surrendered and never moved again. It was not a beautiful butterfly, one of those splendours of colour and gold that I would see later that spring. Just an ordinary butterfly, grey, with a bluish tinge if you looked hard enough, a moth stupefied by daylight. For a moment, I considered pulling its wings off, like any boy my age, but then I realised that by staring at this, the one still element in a whirling world, I no longer felt nauseous. The butterfly stayed there for hours, sent by a friendly power to reassure me, and this was my first inkling that nothing is really as it seems, that a butterfly is not merely a butterfly but a story, something vast lurking within a tiny space, an intuition that would be confirmed some decades later by the first atomic bomb and, perhaps even more so, by what I will leave behind when I die in an underground vault within the crypt of the most beautiful abbey in the country.

When Ingegnere Carmone woke up, he told me all about his project, because he had a project. He was a communist. *Do you know what that is?* It was an insult I had heard a few times in the village in France – people always wondered whether so-and-so was *it*. I said, 'Ha, of course I know. It's a man who loves men.'

The *ingegnere* laughed. 'Yes, in a way, a communist is

a man who loves men. Besides, there is no wrong way to love men, you understand that?' I had never seen him so grave.

The Carmones owned a vast estate in L'Aquila, a province twice blighted by geography. Firstly, it was the only province in Abruzzo with no access to the sea. Secondly, it was ravaged by earthquakes at regular intervals, like the Liguria of my ancestors, except that even that bitch Liguria had access to the sea.

The estate afforded beautiful views over Lake Scanno. The *ingegnere* planned to build a tower on a gigantic ball bearing to house all the local proletariat, for a modest rent that would allow him to live decently – especially since, being a good communist, he planned to keep the top floor for himself. Two teams of horses would alternate every twelve hours so that the building revolved throughout the day. In this way, every resident, without exception, could enjoy a view of the lake once a day, with no profiteers and no exploited workers. Electricity might one day replace the horses, although Carmone admitted that the project would never get that far. But he liked to dream.

The ball bearing also offered the advantage of separating the building from the ground in the event of an earthquake. Even after a tremor of Force XII on the Mercalli scale – he taught me the name – his tower would have a thirty per cent greater chance of withstanding the shock than an ordinary building. 'Thirty per cent doesn't sound like much, but then Force XII is no laughing matter,' he explained, rolling his eyes. 'It's colossal.'

I let myself drift off, my eyes riveted on my butterfly, and we rolled into Italy as the *ingegnere* tenderly spoke to me about devastation.

Italy and I embraced like old friends meeting for the first time. In my hurry to get off the train at Turin, I tripped over the footboard and ended up spreadeagled on the platform. I lay there for a moment – it never occurred to me to cry – in the rapturous bliss of a priest at his ordination. Italy smelled of cordite. Italy smelled of war.

The *ingegnere* decided to hire a hackney carriage. It was more expensive than walking, but my mother had given him some money in an envelope and, as he put it, just as the wine must be drunk, money must be spent. Speaking of which, we'll just go buy ourselves a little carafe of red from the river Po before we set off, if you don't mind.

I didn't mind. I was astounded by what I was discovering: soldiers on furlough, soldiers heading back to war, porters, train drivers and a whole host of sleazy people whose professions or aspirations seemed mysterious to the boy I was then. I'd never seen any sleazy people before. I felt as though they were kindly returning my insistent stare, as if to say *you're one of us.* Maybe they were just staring at the blue protuberance growing in the middle of my forehead. I made my way through a forest of legs, utterly transfixed by other smells: creosote and leather, metal and rifle barrels, the smell of darkness and of battlefields. And then there was the noise, the deafening roar of a foundry. It shrieked and squeaked and clattered, a form of *musique concrète* played by illiterates, a far cry from the concert halls where one day jaded celebrities would flock to pretend to enjoy the real thing.

Though I did not realise it, I had arrived right in the midst of futurism. The world was speed, the speed of footsteps, trains, bullets, changes of fortune or changes of alliance. And yet all these men, this great throng, seemed to be holding back. Bodies exulted as they raced towards the train carriages, the trenches, the barbed wire that ringed the horizon. And yet, between two movements, two surges, something seemed to scream *I want to live a little longer.*

Later, after my career took off, one collector proudly showed me his latest acquisition, *La Rivolta* by the Futurist painter Luigi Russolo. That would have been in Rome, on the cusp of the 1930s, I think. The collector considered himself a well-informed amateur who was passionate about abstract art. He was a moron. Someone who was not there that day, at Torino Porta Nuova station, cannot possibly understand this painting. They do not realise that it is not abstract. It is a figurative painting. Russolo painted what was blowing up in our faces.

Needless to say, no twelve-year-old would put it in those terms. At the time, I just looked around, wide-eyed, while the *ingegnere* quenched his thirst at a cheap taverna at the end of the platform. But I *saw* everything. Proof, if it were needed, that I was not quite like other people.

When we left the station it was snowing lightly. Hardly had we left when a carabiniere stopped us and asked to see my papers. Not my companion's, just mine. His fingers numb from the cold and the little carafe of red from the Po, Ingegnere Carmone gave him my permit. The carabiniere eyed me with a suspicion that he donned every morning with his uniform and took off every night – unless, of course, it was innate.

'So, you're a *piccolo francese*?'

I did not like being called 'French'. I liked being called 'little' even less.

'*Piccolo francese* yourself, *cazzino*.'

The carabiniere almost choked. *Cazzino* was the favourite insult of the backyards where I had grown up, and a carabinieri does not choose a profession where he gets to wear an elegant uniform only to be insulted about the size of his manhood.

Being the talented engineer he was, the *ingegnere* took my mother's envelope from his pocket and greased the administrative cogs that had seized up. Soon we were on our way. I refused to get into a hackney carriage and pointed to a tram. Carmone grumbled, looked at a map, asked some questions and discovered that the tram would set us down not far from where we wanted to go.

Sitting on the little wooden bench, I travelled through the first big city I had ever seen. I was happy. I had lost my father, I had no idea when I would see my mother again, but I was happy and intoxicated by everything that lay ahead, this block of future I had to climb, to carve out for myself.

'Tell me something, Signor Carmone?'

'What's that?'

'What is electricity?'

He stared at me, stupefied, then seemed to remember that I had spent the first decade of my life in a little village in Savoie that I had never left.

'It's that right there, *figlio mio*.' He pointed to a street lamp topped by a magnificent gold globe.

'So, it's like a candle, then?'

'But one that never burns out. Electrons are flowing between two pieces of carbon.'

'What is an electron? Some kind of fairy?'

'No, it's science.'

'What is science?'

Snowflakes whirled around us, light as a lady's gown. The *ingegnere* answered my questions without a whit of impatience or ever being condescending. Soon, we passed a vast building still under construction: the Lingotto where, a few years later, Fiat cars would go up onto the roof via a spiral ramp to the test track where they would make their first circuits after being assembled – an industrial Sacra di San Michele.

The houses became sparser, roads gave way to tracks, the tramway pulled to a halt in what looked like a field. We had to walk the last three kilometres. I'm grateful to this guy, Carmone, for going so far with me, despite the cold, despite the era. We ploughed through the mud, and it seemed to me that already my mother's eyes were beginning to fade in my memory, to look less violet. But Carmone led me all the way to Zio Alberto's door.

We had to sorely abuse the bell and pound on the door before Alberto deigned to open it, wearing a dirty vest. He had the same misty eyes as the *ingegnere*, criss-crossed with a lattice of thin red veins: the two men shared an immoderate love of the grape. My mother had written to let him know of my arrival, so there was not much to explain.

'This is your new apprentice, Michelangelo, the son of Antonella Vitaliani. Your nephew.'

'I don't like being called Michelangelo.'

Zio Alberto looked down at me. I thought he was going to ask me what I liked to be called, to which I would have said 'Mimo' – the nickname by which my parents always called me, the name I'd be known by for the next seventy years.

'I want nothing to do with him,' said Alberto.

Again, I've forgotten a detail. And this is a small but important detail.

'I don't understand. I thought Antonell— that Signora Vitaliani had written to you, that it was all agreed.'

'Oh, she wrote to me. But I don't want an apprentice like that.'

'Why not?'

'Because nobody told me he was a dwarf.'

'*C'è un piccolo problema,*' said old Rosa, the neighbour who attended my mother's labour one stormy night. The stove clanked and clattered; a strong headwind fanned the flames and painted the walls with a deep red glow. A few of the local matrons, who had come to witness the event and were curious to catch a glimpse of the firm flesh that made their husbands fantasise, had long since fled, making the sign of the cross and whispering *il diavolo*. An impassive old Rosa carried on humming, sponging and encouraging my mother. The cholera, the cold, plain bad luck and a knife that would never have been drawn but for too much drink had taken her children, her friends and her husbands. She was old, she was ugly, and she had nothing left to lose. So the devil gave her a wide berth; he knew trouble when he saw it. He went for easier prey.

'*C'è un piccolo problema*,' she said, pulling me away from the belly of Antonella Vitaliani. Everything hinged on the word *piccolo*: it was clear to everyone who saw me that I would remain more or less *piccolo* all my life. Rosa laid me on my exhausted mother's breast. My father took the stairs four at a time. Rosa would later say that when he first saw me, he frowned and glanced around as though looking around for his real son rather than this rough draft, then shook his head. *I see, it's like that, is it?* Much like when he tapped into a hidden crack in the heart of a block of marble and the work of several weeks dissolved into dust. You can't blame the stone.

And it was to stone that my difference was attributed. My mother had had no respite from hauling blocks of marble into the workshop that were so huge they would have made the local strongmen red in the face. And, the neighbours said, poor little Mimo suffered as a result. Achondroplasia, some would later claim. They would call me a person of small stature, which, to be honest, was no better than Zio Alberto's 'dwarf'. People said I should not be defined by my height. If that was true, why talk about my height at all? I've never heard of a 'person of average stature'.

I never resented my parents. If stone made me what I am, if some dark magic was at work, it gave as much as it took. Stone has always spoken to me, all kinds of stones, limestone, metamorphic rock, even gravestones, on which I would soon lie to listen to the stories of the dead.

'This is not what was agreed,' muttered the *ingegnere*, tapping a gloved finger to his lips. 'It's very vexing.'

By now, it was snowing hard. Zio Alberto shrugged and tried to slam the door in our faces, but the *ingegnere* blocked it with his foot. He took my mother's envelope from the inside pocket of his old fur jacket and handed it to my uncle. It contained almost every centime of the Vitaliani savings. Years of exile, of drudgery, of skin weathered by sun and salt, of new beginnings, years of marble dust beneath their fingernails, and sometimes a trace of tenderness like the one that had seen me born. This is why those grubby, crumpled banknotes were so precious. This is why Zio Alberto opened the door a fraction.

'This money was intended for the little man. I mean Mimo,' Carmone corrected, and flushed crimson. 'If Mimo agrees to give it to you, he would not be your apprentice, but your partner.'

Zio Alberto nodded slowly. 'Hmm, a partner.'

He was still hesitant. Carmone waited for as long as he could, then sighed and took a leather pouch out of his pack. Everything about the *ingegnere* celebrated wear and tear – he was a piece of shreds and patches, his aesthetic was the passing time. But the leather of this pouch, fresh and supple, still seemed to quiver with the rage of the bull that had last worn it. Carmone ran his cracked glove over the pouch, then reluctantly opened it and took out a pipe.

'This is a pipe that I bought at great expense. It was carved from the stump of the heather plant on which the Hero of Two Worlds, the great Garibaldi himself, is said to have sat during his noble and fruitless attempt to bring Rome into our kingdom.'

I had seen dozens of such pipes sold to gullible Frenchmen in Aigues-Mortes. I had no idea how Carmone had come to buy this one, how he had allowed himself to be duped. I felt a little ashamed for him and for Italy in general. He was a naïve but generous man. This gesture cost him dearly, and I know he did it sincerely, to help me – not because he was in a hurry to get home or afraid to burden himself with a twelve-year-old of unusual proportions. Alberto agreed, and the deal was sealed with a shot of hooch, whose bitterness caused the very air to smart inside his hovel. Then Carmone got to his feet, one for the road, and soon his flickering silhouette disappeared into the snow.

He turned one last time, raised a hand in the yellow phosphorescence of a dying world, and smiled at me. The Abruzzo was far away, he was no longer a young man, and these were harsh times. I never visited Lake Scanno, for fear of discovering that there was not, and never had been, a tower there set on a ball bearing.

I owe much to those women who are termed 'fallen women'; my uncle Alberto was the son of one – a courageous girl who used to lie beneath men at the port of Genoa, without anger or shame. She was the only person of whom my uncle spoke with a respect, a fervour, bordering on veneration. But the saint of the alleyway was far away, and since Alberto could neither read nor write, his mother became more of a myth with each passing day. As for me, I wrote tolerably well, to the delight of my uncle when he realised.

My uncle Alberto was not my uncle. We did not have a single particle of blood in common. I never truly managed to get to the bottom of the story, but apparently his grandfather owed a debt to mine, an unpaid loan whose moral burden was passed down from generation to generation. In his perverse way, Alberto was honest. Having been petitioned by my mother, he agreed to take me in. He had a small workshop on the outskirts of Turin. Being a bachelor with little taste for extravagance, a few commissions here and there were sufficient to support him – or had been until I arrived. The war – a progressive endeavour much praised by many zealots at the time, who did not favour the term 'zealot', preferring 'poet' or 'philosopher' – had popularised materials that were not only less expensive than stone, but also lighter and easier to produce and work with. Steel was Alberto's sworn enemy, which offended him even in his sleep. He hated steel even more than he did the Austro-Hungarians or the Germans. Excuses could be made for the *Crucci*, as the Huns were called here. They had much to be angry about – their national cuisine, their ridiculous pointy helmets. Whereas there was no excuse to create things out of steel, and he would have the last laugh when the whole world collapsed. Alberto had not realised that the whole world had already collapsed. And, to its credit, steel played an important role – it made some magnificent cannons.

Although Alberto looked old, he wasn't. At thirty-five, he lived alone in a room adjoining his studio. His being a bachelor was surprising, especially since, after a shower, washed cleaned of the marble dust and dressed in his only suit, he was quite handsome. He always visited the same brothel in Turin, where he treated the girls with a respect that was legendary. In the southern regions of the city, between the Lingotto and San

Salvario, the expression 'to do it like Alberto' was popular in the early 1920s, only falling into disuse when Alberto moved away, taking with him his marbles and his slave – that is to say, me. Being his partner, I still laugh about that.

I have often been asked what role Zio played in what came later. If 'what came later' refers to my career, then none; if, on the other hand, it refers to my last sculpture, then it undoubtedly contains a few shards of him. No, not shards, *fragments* – I would not want anyone to think that Alberto had ever glittered. Zio Alberto was a bastard. Not a monster, just a poor bastard, which amounts to the same thing. I remember him with no hatred, but no sadness.

For almost a year, I lived in his shadow. I cooked, I cleaned. I hauled, I delivered. A hundred times I was almost crushed by a tram, knocked down by a horse, beaten up by some guy who mocked my size and I retorted that at least I had no problem with size downstairs in the *piano di sotto*, ideally in front of his girlfriend. Ingegnere Carmone would have been thrilled that the atmosphere in our neighbourhood was so electric. Every interaction was a potential lightning strike, a rapid discharge of electrons whose result was always unpredictable. We were at war with the Germans, the Austro-Hungarians, our governments, our neighbours; in other words, we were at war with ourselves. One side wanted war, the other craved peace, tempers flared, and the side that craved peace wound up throwing the first punch.

Zio Alberto forbade me from touching his tools. He once caught me correcting a small holy water font commissioned by the neighbouring parish of Beata Vergine delle Grazie. Once or twice a week, Alberto would go on a monumental drinking binge, and the most recent one had left its mark. The font was crude, offensive; a twelve-year-old could have carved something better, and did so while his uncle drank wine. When Alberto woke, he caught me in flagrante, chisel in hand. He gazed at my work in astonishment, then beat me and insulted me in a Genoese dialect I didn't understand. Afterwards, he promptly went back to sleep. When he opened his eyes to find me crippled and bruised, he pretended not to remember what had happened. He went straight over to look at the font, decided that he was not dissatisfied with his work and magnanimously offered to deliver it himself.

Alberto would regularly dictate a letter to his mother and allowed me to write one to mine at the same time – he generously paid for the stamp. Antonella did not always reply, being constantly on the road, chasing some work that would keep her going for one week, then another. I missed her violet eyes. My father, the man who had guided my first faltering chisel strokes, the man who had taught me the difference between a file, a rasp and a riffler, was fading away.

In 1917, work commissions were scarcer, Alberto's moods were darker, and his drinking binges more violent. Columns of soldiers could sometimes be seen marching in the twilight, and the newspapers talked of nothing else but war, the war, yet we felt only vague unease, a sense of disassociation from our surroundings, of never being in the right place. Somewhere over there, a foul beast was sullying the horizon. But we led an almost normal life, the life of sluggards and slackers that imparted a little taste of guilt to everything we ate. At least until 22 August, when the bread ran out and there was nothing left to eat. Turin exploded. The name of Lenin appeared on the city walls; barricades were erected. A revolutionary stopped me in the street on the morning of the 24th and told me to be careful because their barricades were *electrified*, which, more than anything else, told me how much the world was changing. The man referred to me as 'comrade' and patted me on the back. I saw women confronting sheepish soldiers at the barricades, clambering over armoured cars, baring their angry, triumphant breasts knowing they would not shoot. At least not yet.

The rising lasted three days. No one could seem to agree on anything, other than the fact that they were sick of war. In the end, the government got everyone to agree using machine-gun fire, and fifty deaths cooled the revolutionary fervour. I hid out in the studio. One evening shortly after calm had returned, and with it a little bread, Zio Alberto came home in a happier mood than usual. He pretended to lash out at me, chuckled when he saw me dive under the table, then ordered me to take up my pen and dictated a letter to his mother. He stank of cheap wine from the corner taverna.

Mammina,
I have safely received the money order you sent me.
Thanks to it, I'm going to be able to buy the little
workshop I mentioned to you at Christmas. It is in
Liguria, so closer to you. There is no more work here in
Turin. But in Liguria, there is a castle that is constantly in
need of repair, and a church the authorities are very keen
on, so at least that means work. I've sold my place here,
just signed a contract with that rat Lorenzo, and will soon
be leaving with that little shit Mimo. I'll write to you from
Pietra d'Alba. Your loving son.

'And give me a beautiful signature, *pezzo di merda*,' concluded Zio Alberto. 'A signature that proves that I'm a success.'

It's curious that, when I think about that time, I wasn't unhappy. I was alone, I had nothing and no one. In northern Europe forests were being razed and tilled, and sown with shrapnel-filled flesh and a few shells that, years later, would blow up in the face of some innocent rambler; a devastation had been invented that would make Mercalli pale, since he had given his poor scale only twelve degrees. But I was not unhappy, as I realised every night when I prayed to a personal pantheon of idols that changed throughout my life and later came to include opera singers and football players. Perhaps because I was young, my days were pleasant. Only now do I know how much the beauty of the day owes to the prescience of night.

The abbot leaves his office and begins to descend the aptly named Staircase of the Dead. In a few moments, he will be in the annexe, at the bedside of the dying man. The brothers have sent word to say the hour is at hand. The abbot will place the bread of life upon the dying man's tongue.

Padre Vincenzo moves through the church, paying scant heed to its frescoes, passes through the Zodiac gate and comes to the terraces at the summit of Mount Pirchiriano, from which the abbey overlooks Piedmont. Before him are the ruins of a tower. According to legend, once, with the aid of Saint Michael, a beautiful young peasant girl named Alda took flight from here to escape enemy soldiers. *Vanitas vanitatis*: when she attempted to perform the feat again to impress the villagers, she was dashed onto the ground below. Just as the part of the tower that bears her name was in the fourteenth century, toppled by one of the many earthquakes that shake the region.

Further on, a few stone steps sink into the ground, barred by a chain and a sign that reads 'No Trespassing'. The abbot straddles this with an agility commendable for his age. This is not the way to the annexe where the dying man awaits. Before joining him, the abbot wants to see *her*. She who sometimes troubles his sleep, because he fears a break-in, or worse. You never know what could happen, like the time, fifteen years ago, when Fra Bartolomeo surprised someone just outside the last grille protecting her. The man, an American, tried to pass himself off as a visitor who had lost his way. The abbot instantly smelled a lie, a stench he knew all too well: the smell of the confessional. No tourist could wander into the bowels of the Sacra di San Michele by accident. No, the man was there because he had heard the rumour.

The abbot was correct. Five years later, the same man reappeared with an authorisation duly signed by the Vatican. The gate was opened and the list of those who had contemplated her was increased by one. Leonard B. Williams was a professor from Stanford University in California who had devoted his life to the prisoner of the Sacra, attempting to unravel her mystery. He had published a monograph and a few articles about her; then, silence.

His work, though brilliant, languished on forgotten shelves. The Vatican had shrewdly played its cards, opening that gate as though it had nothing to hide. For years, calm returned. But over the past months, monks had been reporting tourists who were not tourists but snoopers. They were instantly recognisable.

The pressure was mounting.

The abbot spends long minutes descending, making his way through the labyrinthine corridors. He has made the journey so often that he could find his way blindfolded. He is accompanied by the tinkle of a bell – the sound of the bunch of keys he carries. Those damn keys. There is one, and sometimes two, for every door in the abbey, as though mystery lurked behind each one. As though the sacred Eucharist, the greatest of all mysteries, were not enough.

He reaches his goal. He can smell the earth, the humidity, the scent of billions of atoms of granite crushed under their own weight, and even a little of the lush surrounding slopes. Finally, he comes to the gate. The old gate has been replaced with a five-point lock. On his first attempt, the remote-control box doesn't work. Padre Vincenzo struggles with the rubber keypad. *It's always the same, people talk about progress, it's 1986 – why can't these idiots make a remote control that works?* He regains his composure. *Lord, forgive me my impatience.*

Eventually, the red light winks out; the alarm is deactivated. The last corridor is monitored by two state-of-the-art surveillance cameras, no bigger than shoeboxes. It is impossible for anyone to get in without sounding the alert. And even if an intruder should manage to get in, what could he do? He could hardly steal *her*. It took ten strong men to carry her down here.

Padre Vincenzo shudders. It is not theft that he fears. He has not forgotten the crazy man Laszlo Toth. Again, he chastises himself: *'Crazy' is hardly a charitable term, let us say 'unbalanced'.* The abbey had come close to tragedy. But just now he doesn't want to think about Laszlo, about the Hungarian's grim face and gleaming eyes. Tragedy was averted.

We keep her locked away in order to protect her. The irony is not lost on the abbot. *She is here, don't worry, she is in perfect condition, the only problem is that no one is allowed to see her.* No one except the abbot, the *padre*, the monks who ask to see her, the cardinals still alive who had her locked up here forty years ago, and perhaps a few bureaucrats. At most, some thirty people in the whole world. And, of course, her creator, who possesses his own key. He would come and go at will to tend to her, to wash her. Because, yes, she had to be washed.

The abbot opens the last two locks. He always opens the top lock first, a little quirk that betrays a form of nervousness, an idiosyncrasy he would like to cure, and he vows – as he did on his previous visit – that next time he will open the lower lock first. The door opens soundlessly – the locksmith who vaunted the quality of the hinges did not lie.

He doesn't turn on the light. The original fluorescent strips were replaced with softer lighting at the same time as the gate, which was for the best since the fluorescent lights were damaging her. But the abbot prefers to contemplate her in the darkness. He steps forward, runs his fingertips over her out of habit. She is a little taller than he. Here, in the centre of the circular room, this primitive sanctuary with its Romanesque vaults, she stands, bowed slightly over her plinth, lost in a dream of stone. The only light comes from the corridor; it carves out two faces and the curve of a wrist. Having stared at her until his eyes were strained, the abbot knows every detail of the statue that sleeps in the shadows.

We keep her locked away in order to protect her.

The abbot suspects that those who put her here were trying to protect *themselves.*

The city of Savona provided Italy with two popes, Sixtus IV and Julius II. The little village of Pietra d'Alba, some thirty kilometres north, almost provided a third. I believe that I was in part responsible for this failure.

If someone had told me, that morning of 10 December 1917, that the history of the papacy might be swayed by the young boy trudging behind Zio Alberto, I would have laughed. We had been travelling almost non-stop for three days. The whole country had been waiting anxiously for news from the front ever since the savage defeat that the Austro-Hungarians inflicted on us at Caporetto. Some said the front lines had stabilised not far from Venice. Others claimed the opposite, that the enemy would land and slit our throats while we were sleeping or – worse – force us to eat cabbage.

Pietra d'Alba appeared, carved out of the sunrise atop a rocky peak. Its position, I would realise an hour later, was an illusion. Pietra was not perched on a crag, but on the edge of a plateau. So close to the edge, in fact, that there was barely space for two men to walk abreast between the village walls and the cliff edge. Beyond this, fifty metres of sheer void, or rather of pure air, redolent with resin and thyme.

You had to walk through the whole village to discover what had made its reputation: the vast undulating plateau that stretched towards Piedmont, a fragment of Tuscany displaced by the whims of geology. Meanwhile, to east and west, Liguria kept vigil, reminding visitors not to get too comfortable. There was the mountain, and slopes blanketed by forests of a dark green almost as black as the animals that roamed within. Pietra d'Alba was beautiful, with its stone of faded pink encrusted with a thousand dawns.

No matter how exhausted or ill-tempered, a visitor immediately remarked upon two noteworthy buildings. The first, a magnificent baroque church, owed its proportions and its red and green marble façade – unusual to find so far inland – to its patron saint. San Pietro delle Lacrime was built at the place where Saint Peter paused on his way to convert the country louts and boors that would become the French. According to legend, on the night he spent here, he dreamed of his threefold denial of Christ and wept. His tears had seeped into the rock and created the wellspring that now fed a lake a little distance away. The church had been built in 1750 right above this spring, which was still visible in the crypt. Donations poured in, since the waters were said to have miraculous properties. But there had been no miracles, unless it was that the waters transformed this plateau into a little piece of Tuscany.

At Alberto's insistence, the driver dropped us outside the church. My uncle had insisted on coming from Savona by car, as a conquering hero, not like some yokel in a cart. It was a publicity stunt before such things existed, but it fell flat. It seemed as though the village had thrown a wild party the previous day, to judge by the banners still draped over the fountain, serving as a scarf for a lion, and the confetti lifted and whirled by a playful breeze. Alberto asked the driver to sound his horn, but this merely startled a few doves. Furious, he decided to make the rest of the journey on foot. The workshop he had bought was outside the village.

It was as we left Pietra that we saw the second building. Or rather it saw us, because I felt as though, despite the distance, it was appraising us, deeming any visitor unworthy unless he was a prince, a doge, a sultan, a king or even a marchesa. Every time I came back to Pietra d'Alba after a long absence, the Villa Orsini had the same effect on me, forcing me to stop in my tracks at precisely the same spot, between the last village fountain and the point where the road plunged towards the plateau.

The villa stood on the edge of the forest, some two kilometres from the last houses. Behind it, the steep untamed foothills came to rest against its walls in a spume of vivid green. Here was a land of lofty heights and springs, whose paths, it was whispered, shifted even as you walked them. The only people to venture there were lumberjacks, charcoal burners and hunters. It is to them we owe the story of the shifting paths, invented to salvage their pride when they emerged, haggard and dishevelled Little Thumblings, a week after losing their way.

In front of the villa, for as far as the eye could see, stretched an ocean of orange, lemon and melàngolo trees. This was the Orsini gold, shaped and polished by a sea breeze that breathed its unimaginable gentleness from the coast up to these heights. It was impossible not to pause and gaze at this vibrant, pointillist landscape, a firework of tangerine, melon, apricot, mimosa and sulphur flowers that never faded and contrasted with the dark forest behind the villa, an illustration of the family's civilising mission as emblazoned on its coat of arms. *Ab tenebris, ad lumina.* 'Out of darkness, into light.' The sense of order, the conviction that everything had its place, which was invariably in the ambit of the Orsini family. The family deferred only to the pre-eminence of God, but were happy to manage His affairs in His absence. As a result, the two notable buildings in Pietra d'Alba were irrevocably linked and would remain so to the very end, twin brothers who rarely spoke but held each other in high regard.

I remember wandering along the rows of orange trees that morning, and the curious eyes that followed us. I remember discovering Alberto's studio, an old farmhouse flanked by a barn, separated by a large expanse of grass with a walnut tree right in the centre. I remember thinking how much my mother would like this place, when I had earned enough money to send for her. Alberto looked around, his fists on his hips, his eyelashes rimmed with hoarfrost. He nodded contentedly.

'All that's left now is to find some good stone.'

In 1983, Franco Maria Ricci wanted to devote a few pages of his magazine *FMR* to an interview with me. Since he was something of a madman, I agreed. It was the only interview I ever gave. Contrary to what I expected, Ricci did not ask me about *her*. But she was there at the heart of his piece, as unobtrusive as an elephant.

The article was never published. People in high places got wind of the interview. The print run of the magazine was small and all copies were bought directly from the printer before they could be circulated. Issue 14 of *FMR* in June 1983 came out a week late and a few pages short. It was probably for the best. Franco sent me a copy that had survived pulping. It will be found in the little trunk under my cell window when I depart. The same trunk with which I arrived in Pietra d'Alba seventy years ago.

In the interview, I say this:

My uncle Alberto was never a great sculptor. This is why, for so long, I too was mediocre. Because I turned a deaf ear to the lone voice inside me and believed him when he said there was such a thing as good stone. There is no such thing as good stone. I should know, because I spent years searching – until I realised that I need only bend down and pick up the stone at my feet.

Old Emiliano, the former stonemason, had sold the workshop for a pittance to Alberto, who gleefully rubbed his hands every time he mentioned the deal. He had rubbed his hands in Turin, rubbed them all through the journey, rubbed them when he set eyes on Pietra d'Alba, the workshop and the barn. He did not stop rubbing his hands until the first night we spent there, when he felt someone crawl into his bed and press two icy feet to his.

Alberto had allowed me to move into the barn, which was his way of saying that the studio and adjoining bedroom were his home. This arrangement suited me perfectly: at thirteen, what boy has not dreamed of sleeping in the straw? Hearing the scream shortly after midnight, I came running and found Alberto about to come to blows with what at first I thought was another man.

'What are you doing here, you little bastard?'

'I'm Vittorio!'

'Who?'

'Vittorio! Paragraph 3 of the contract!'

I can still hear his timorous voice, dancing between two registers, high-low-high. This was precisely how he introduced himself: *Vittorio, Paragraph 3 of the contract*. To dismiss the proffered nickname would have been criminal.

Paragraph 3 was three years my senior. In this country of squat men, who lived close to the land to be tended, he was remarkable because of his height. It was the only thing he had inherited from his father, a visiting Swedish agronomist. His reasons for visiting the region were never known, but while here, he had knocked up a local village girl and did not hang around when she told him the news.

It took a moment for us to realise that Paragraph 3 had worked with old Emiliano, and had always curled up against his master to sleep. There was a local saying that, in winter, a man offered the choice between a sack of gold and a roaring fire did not always choose the gold. In these parts, warmth was rare, both in men's homes and in their hearts. As far as Alberto was concerned, two men sleeping together was unthinkable – in fact, he had never heard of such a thing. Paragraph shrugged and said he would sleep in the barn, which only served to further annoy my uncle – who was beginning to regret not carefully reading the contract sent to him by his solicitor. I reminded him, a little maliciously, that he couldn't read, but he wasn't offended. The solicitor should have warned him. Indeed, thinking about it, Signor Dordini could have told him in person on the night they spent drinking with the men from the carpenters' guild. An exchange of letters later confirmed that Paragraph was part of the fixtures and fittings, and the workshop had been sold for a song with the stipulation that the young man continue to be employed for a further ten years – this was Paragraph 3 of the contract.

In all my life, I have rarely met a man with so little talent for working stone as Paragraph. But he proved a great help to us. He was extremely hard-working, earned little and for the most part was content to have a room and board. Alberto discovered a certain fondness for the boy when he realised that he now had a second slave: a version of me who was more muscular, less insolent and, above all, completely talentless.

The following day, a convoy arrived, a ragtag assortment of carts and sweaty horses appearing in the violet dusk. These were Alberto's tools sent from Turin. The drivers had a drink with my uncle then set off straight away.

We were ready for our first clients. In the village, there had only ever been two: the Church and the Orsini family. Alberto decided to pay his respects to both, but worried about the protocol of whom to visit first. In the end, the Orsini family prevailed. The Church was a little too fond of pleading poverty for Alberto's liking, who kept muttering that he had bills to pay, though this was a lie. His mother had bought the workshop for him with hard cash, and he was not paying us. Shortly after the Angelus was tolled at six o'clock, all three of us arrived at the tradesman's entrance of the villa. A maid opened the gate, studied our motley crew and asked our business.

'I am Maestro Alberto Susso, lately of Turin,' my uncle said with a flourish. 'Perhaps you have heard of me. I've taken over the stonemason's workshop from old Emiliano and have come to pay my respects to their excellencies the Marchese and the Marchesa Orsini.'

'Wait here.'

A major-domo appeared to take the place of the maid, but quickly decided that we would report, not to the household staff, but to the secretary of the Marchese, who was next to come to the gate. Behind the perimeter wall, we could see a lush green garden and the dark glow of a pool steaming in the morning air.

'The Marchese and the Marchesa are not in the habit of receiving tradesmen,' explained the secretary. 'Speak to the major-domo.'

He spat the words with a disdain that rained down around us, the same disdain that has showered nascent revolutionaries the world over. The kingdom of heaven was less well-guarded than the Villa Orsini. I paid little heed to the secretary, fascinated as I was by the garden, in which I could see several statues. Servants were busying themselves between two of the statues, taking down a banner similar to the one I had seen in the village fountain when we first arrived.

'Has there been a birthday celebration?'

The secretary stared at me, one eyebrow perfectly arched. 'No, the family were celebrating the young marchese leaving for the front. He has enlisted with a French regiment, to the glory of his family and the Kingdom of Italy.'

All of a sudden, I started to cry. The secretary and Alberto looked bewildered, and competed with each other in embarrassment and disbelief. They would have felt more at home under the Austro-Hungarian bombardments in Caporetto. Even Paragraph, who was entering the world of men and leaving the land of childhood, stepped aside and studied the gatepost with unusual interest. The maid who had first greeted us abandoned protocol for a moment. She pushed the pompous secretary aside and knelt down in front of me.

'Well now, what's the matter, little man?'

I didn't take offence. I assumed that 'little man' referred to my age rather than my height. I had no idea why I was crying over someone I had never met. At the age of thirteen, what could I possibly know about the griefs we bury inside us? All I could say was: 'I just want him to come back.'

'There, there,' murmured the maid, resting my head between her ample breasts, which she had generously placed there for the purpose, and I am ashamed to say that I felt better.

A week later, with great pomp and ceremony, the whole village filed into the church of San Pietro delle Lacrime. Alberto had insisted on being present – *It's good for business, it's important to be seen* – but we were seated in the last pew. The nave was thronged. People had come from Savona and Genoa. In the front row, the Orsini family. Just behind them, the *magnifici*, the noble families of the region: the Giustinianis, the Spinolas, the Grimaldis.

The young marchese, the hero of Pietra d'Alba, was also present, at the crossing of the nave and the transept, wreathed in a glory he didn't care about. This was his funeral mass. When I was crying in the maid's bosom, he had been dead for two days, having died on 12 December 1917. Not on the front lines, having led his men and triumphantly captured an enemy position at the cost of his own life. No, the young marchese had died as most men do, stupidly, in what would (when the army finally acknowledged it, some decades later) be known as the biggest railway disaster ever to occur in France.

On 12 December, eager to report to his commanding officer, the young marchese boarded the Bassano train bound for Modane, where he changed to take ML3874 heading for Chambéry with a troop of young men on furlough. As it descended from the hill of Saint-Michel-de-Maurienne, the engine had been unable to curb the weight of three hundred and fifty metres of rolling stock, five hundred tonnes of steel and young men happy to be heading home for Christmas. Their joy weighed heavily; the automatic brakes had been deactivated – *We'll use the hand brake* – but this had not been enough to brake its speed. The carriages derailed, ploughed into each other, creating a tangled heap of metal in which girders as thick as a man's arm were twisted like wire before the whole thing burned. The young marchese, who had been thrown from the train by the impact, was one of the few fatalities to be found intact. Most of the others, more than four hundred, were a mass of flesh fused with steel.

Ever since, the people who were powerless to unravel the tightly woven web of fate have been wondering *what if?* What if the young marchese had not gone to war? For the *magnifici*, it was easy to avoid being drafted. What if he had not caught this particular train in his haste to get to the front sooner? But Virgilio Orsini had caught the train. He had voluntarily enlisted. So there was nothing left to do but weep. At least, the villagers wept; the Orsini family remained dignified, the corners of their mouths downturned, as was appropriate, but their chins held high and their eyes staring into the distance away, towards the future of the dynasty.

The great organ resounded as the coffin was carried by men in uniform out into the light, and the villagers dispersed. Because of my height, the size of the crowd and my position at the back of the church, I did not see a single member of the Orsini family that day other than as dark, distant silhouettes. After the congregation had dispersed and I thought I was alone, I paused to study a statue that had caught my attention.

'Do you like it?'

I was startled. Dom Anselmo, the newly appointed parish priest of San Pietro, was staring at me, his eyes blazing. The priest, a prematurely balding man in his forties, had that unsettling mixture of fervour and gentleness that I would later see in many others.

'It's a *pietà*. Do you know what that is?'

'No...'

'It refers to a representation of the *mater dolorosa*. A mother at the foot of the cross weeping for her son. This one is the work of an anonymous seventeenth-century master. So, do you like it?'

I studied the mother's face more closely. I had seen a lot of sorrowful mothers, not just my own.

'Well, go ahead. Speak, child.'

'I don't think she is really sad. It's a sham.'

'A sham?'

'Yes, and Jesus' arm is too long. And the Virgin's cloak

could not possibly fall that far, otherwise she would trip over it. Nothing about it is *true*.'

'Ah, so you're that little French boy who works with the stonemason.'

'No, Father.'

'Aren't you his apprentice?'

'I am, but I'm not French, I'm Italian.'

'What is your name, my son?'

'Mimo, Father.'

'Mimo is not a name.'

'Michelangelo, but I prefer Mimo.'

'Well, Michelangelo, I think you're an intelligent boy. However, in this case you have committed the sin of pride. Indeed, it is blasphemous to suggest that the Virgin might trip over her cloak. Almighty God did not leave Our Lady subject to such contingencies. She is *grace*, not disgrace. Would you like to attend confession?'

I readily agreed – the priest seemed surprised. My mother was always going to confession, and I had often asked to go too, but she felt I was too pure. Being eager not to disappoint, I took some of Alberto's sins upon myself, which shocked Dom Anselmo to the core but allowed him the pleasure of interceding with the Almighty on my behalf. While he was giving absolution, I was distractedly thinking about the Orsinis and wondering what they might look like. Whether their faces were noble or ugly.

I was fascinated by them, as though I could already sense the chaos roiling beneath the appearance of order, the new world rumbling below the surface about to overthrow the old.

After confession, Anselmo led me out through a door in the ambulatory to the sacristy, which opened onto a baroque cloister with a garden, surrounded by a low stone wall, filled with palm trees, cypresses, banana trees and bougainvillea. The bell tower that watched over this little Eden protected it from the winter wind and the summer sun.

'Father?'

'Hmm?'

'What are contingencies?

'Aleatory, unforeseeable situations that occur on a daily basis.'

I pretended to understand. On the far side of the garden, set against the outer wall of the cloister, was a gurgling fountain in the form of a folded shell. Three cherubs perched on dolphins, each carrying an amphora under his arm, had filled the basin for three hundred years. A fourth dolphin had lost its cherub. Anselmo dipped his fingers in the water and traced the sign of the cross on his forehead.

'This is the place where Saint Peter wept,' he explained.

'Are those really his tears?'

The priest smiled. 'I don't know. What I do know is that this is the only wellspring on the plateau. Without it, Pietra d'Alba could not exist, and neither could the fruit trees. That in itself is a kind of miracle.'

'Does it work other miracles?'

'There is no record of any. But you can try.'

I dipped my hand in the water – I had to stand on tiptoe in order to reach. I did not truly believe, but you never know: *I want to grow tall*. Nothing happened. Which was all the more unfair because at that very moment an Austro-Hungarian man (in other words, an enemy) by the name of Adam Rainer was about to undergo the very transformation I had wished for. The only person known in history to have been a dwarf and then a giant. I don't know which fountain he dipped his fingers in.

Anselmo pointed to the dolphin that had lost its rider. Actually, he explained, the fountain was never finished; the sculptor died at the age of thirty.

'Could your master make us a fourth cherub? We have just received a generous donation that will enable us to undertake a number of projects.'

I promised to ask and then took my leave. Night was drawing in. Before heading down the hill, I stopped on the outskirts of the village and gazed at the Villa Orsini. I sensed a movement at the window, but I was too far away to see clearly. The table would have been laid beneath the lofty ceilings of the dining hall, everything would be made of gold and silver, but could anyone be hungry after burying their son? Perhaps they were simply sitting, sobbing, not touching their food, weeping tears of gold and silver.

Zio Alberto was already nodding off when I got back. There was an empty bottle in front of him. *It's been a bit of an emotional day*, he said, *I mean, Jesus, dying at the age of twenty-two is bloody ridiculous.* I proudly told him about Dom Anselmo's offer; it was a mistake I never made again. He flew into a rage and slapped me, and it was only thanks to a frown from Paragraph, who was eating in a corner of the studio, that I wasn't beaten as I had been in Turin. Zio Alberto, beside himself, accused me of doing business behind his back. *Do you think I'm not capable of bringing in money? If you're so good, go ahead, carve your own fucking cherub.*

Then he fell asleep. Choking my tears, I picked up a hammer, placed a chisel against a block of marble that seemed about the right size and gave the first of a long series of blows.

The following morning Alberto left for several days to visit neighbouring villages and brought back several contracts. When he returned, he came straight into the studio and studied the cherub I was finishing. He looked tired but sober, which only meant that he had been unable to find anything to drink.

'Did you do this?'

'Yes, Zio.'

I would like to see that cherub again. No doubt I would laugh at my youthful mistakes. But, all the same, I think it was acceptable.

Alberto shook his head and held out his hand. 'Pass me your rasp.'

He moved around the cherub, holding the chisel, seemed about to correct one detail, gave up, another detail, gave up, then he looked at me again. 'Did you do this?'

'Yes, Zio.'

Without taking his eyes off me, he went and fetched a bottle, pulled the cork out with his teeth and took a long slug. 'Who taught you to carve like that?'

'My father.'

At thirteen, I was precocious, though the term did not yet exist. It was a simpler world. You were either rich or poor, alive or dead. This was not an era of nuance. My father had made the same face as Zio Alberto when, aged seven, I said 'no, not there' as he placed his chisel on a trumeau he was carving.

'Well, you've got a little skill, I'll grant you that, but back in Turin I could find lads just as talented on any street corner, so don't go getting big-headed. And this workshop is like a pigsty. You'd better not think about going to bed before you tidy up.'

Then he picked up my work, turned it around and affixed his monogram. The first work by Mimo Vitaliani, *Angel Holding an Amphora*, is signed Alberto Susso.

I took to my straw bed in a foul mood. A little later, Paragraph joined me, stumbling up the ladder to the attic. He swore and huffed as he crawled over to my corner. He had had a few glasses of Zio Alberto's *piquette*.

'Bloody hell, the boss, he ain't very happy about this business with the angel. Keeps saying you're too big for your breeches.'

'I can't help it – I've got a callipygian arse.'

'Huh?'

'Nothing. Goodnight.'

'Hey, Mimo.'

'Hmm?'

'What do you say we go to the cemetery?'

Few words hold such a promise of adventure as 'cemetery', at least when you are thirteen. I propped myself on one elbow. 'To the cemetery?'

'Yeah. Everyone's got to run all the way round all on his own. First one who chickens out has to kiss the Giordano girl.'

Giordano was the local innkeeper. His daughter was a voluptuous fourteen-year-old beauty who was fascinated by everything. Kissing her was no punishment, quite the reverse, but her father rarely left her side, and a loaded rifle rarely left his.

To get to the cemetery, you had to walk back towards Pietra d'Alba and turn right, just before the steep climb up to the village, where a path cut across the main road. A short walk through the forest led to the shady terrace and the cemetery, which was surprisingly large for a village of five hundred souls. But many illustrious families in the region considered the place charming, far from the stigma of the coast, and chose it as their eternal resting place. Among the humble graves, lavish mausoleums stood as testament to the unalloyed power of their occupants, despite the fact that they had lost what was most precious to them. This paradox troubled no one. The dead are hypocrites.

The short trek through the forest sorely tested my nerves. It had been raining all day and steam was rising from the ground. The little path looked a trench, set between steep embankments barely constrained by bulging walls. With a cocky air intended to mask the fact that he was terrified, Paragraph kept asking me if I was scared. As was I. I had visited many cemeteries with my father; I had even accompanied him on his own journey to the cemetery – an empty coffin in which we placed a few objects he loved. But my father was no longer here to hold my hand.

As we approached the entrance, a dark figure emerged from the undergrowth. I almost fainted.

'Don't worry, that's just Emanuele.'

Even more than Emanuele's uniform, it was his uncanny

resemblance to Paragraph that first struck me. Clearly the Swedish agronomist had every reason to decamp since he was leaving behind not one but two sons. Emanuele had unexpectedly appeared some minutes after his twin, just as his mother – who had been cursing God, men and Sweden – was beginning to get her colour back. His face was blue; the umbilical cord was wound around his throat. He owed his life to the breath of the midwife, the breath of an old woman on her last legs. Their mother named Vittorio and Emanuele in honour of the King of Italy, and even wrote to the palace in Rome to tell him so. She received a reply from an obscure seneschal assuring her of the monarch's gratitude, which she had framed and would exhibit for almost forty years in her small haberdashery.

This turbulent birth left Emanuele with severe scars. His movements were jerky, sometimes uncontrolled. He could speak only with great difficulty – only his brother and mother could understand him. But though he could barely tie his shoelaces, to everyone's surprise, he learned to read unaided. His two great passions were picaresque adventure novels and uniforms.

I never saw Emanuele wear anything other than a uniform. He was not at all a sectarian in his choices and cheerfully mixed elements of civilian, military (including rival factions) and religious (including rival factions) regalia, not to mention eras. The fuss over the Swedish agronomist and later the

King's letter had transformed a dreary love affair into an epic tale and, from Savona in the south to the Piedmont border in the north, almost everyone knew Emanuele and regularly sent him new uniforms – rarely complete but very numerous – as elderly relatives died and attics were emptied. The war had been a boon that made Emanuele as happy as the great industrialists.

That night, he was wearing Second Empire epaulettes, the leather and felt cap of a Bersagliere adorned with a golden cockade and rooster feathers, a postman's jacket fastened with a broad Askari belt, and the trousers and boots of a carabiniere. As he vigorously shook my hand, he launched into an incomprehensible tirade, to which his brother replied: 'No, no, don't talk shit.'

The cemetery gate was always left open. No one went in there at night, and no one came out either. Paragraph was the first to run the circuit. He disappeared between the tombs. Here and there, the tall cypresses that kept vigil over the dead blotted out the moonlight. The clear lines and certainty of day gave way to blurred borders, a world of shadows and grisaille where everything moved. Five minutes later, he reappeared, hands in pockets, whistling. But from his flushed cheeks it was obvious that he had been running like a madman. Emanuele was next to make the run, and he too came back calm and collected, as though he had not exerted himself. Now it was my turn. I hesitated.

'Go on, then,' said Paragraph. 'There's nothing to worry about. I think I heard a creak like a mausoleum being opened, but that's all. Or are you going to back down?'

My diminutive size made it impossible for me to back down. I always had to make twice as much effort as others. I stepped into the cemetery. I got the impression it was chillier within the walls. I thought I heard a noise and froze. The scent of cypresses reminded me of the smells that wafted from the workshop of a luthier who had been our neighbour back in Savoie. This reassured me a little. I set off at a run, keeping my eyes on the ground. The sounds became clearer and sharper, ricocheting in the icy air: creaks, sighs, rasps. The exquisite scent of cypresses faded, overwhelmed by the dark, leprous stench of dead things.

I had to stop again to catch my breath. Before me, a moonbeam cut a pale slash across the face of an angel with a trumpet sitting on the pediment of a mausoleum. Seeing that the door was ajar should have sent me scarpering. But some invisible force prevented me from moving. Behind the cypress trees, the moon slowly creaked along on worn-out cogs and shifted to illuminate the interior and a polished black slab of granite. Then I saw it.

With infinite slowness, the figure rose, peeling itself from the slab, and took a faltering step towards me. Her head bowed, her face hidden by a black veil, she stood on the threshold and stared at me with spectral eyes, deep set into cavernous sockets. She was no taller than me. Her skin was ashen, but her lips were full and crimson with life, from the blood of the living creatures on which she fed every night when she left the cold embrace of the tomb.

Much braver men than I would have fainted. So that is what I did.

When I came round, I found myself alone; the door of the mausoleum was now closed. An ill wind bowed the backs of the cypress trees that cackled in the darkness in some cryptic, malevolent language of wood that I wasted no time listening to. Feeling a clammy hand on my forehead, I screamed, but it was only a wet chestnut leaf. When I was finally able to get to my feet, I fled. Emanuele and Paragraph were nowhere to be seen.

I ran to my bed and hid beneath the covers, fully clothed and shivering.

My attic-mate appeared, his hair matted with straw, his eyes heavy. 'Where did you get to? We waited for ages.'

'Did you see her?'

'Who?

'Her! The dead woman!'

'You saw a dead woman?'

'She came out of a mausoleum, all dressed in black. I swear!'

Paragraph looked at me and frowned, then burst out laughing. 'You, my lad, you've got a hankering to kiss the Giordano girl.'

The wind raged all night. I didn't get to sleep until dawn, when my fears were allayed by daylight. Three hours later, I was woken by a kick.

'What the hell are you doing snoring? What do I pay you for? Shift your arse, we've got work to do.'

Zio Alberto clambered down the ladder. I quickly followed, and briefly plunged my face into a drinking trough fed by a tributary of the miraculous spring. In the hinterlands of Liguria, wind – like fire and water– was the source of both life and destruction. That night, it had destroyed one of the statues on the gable of the Villa Orsini, sending it hurtling onto a section of roof. There was no other damage beyond some water in the attic, since it had rained during the night between the raging gusts. A carpenter would come and deal with this later. But, for the Orsini family, the more urgent task was to replace the statue and restore the symmetry of the façade. A steward from the villa had appeared in the early hours to tell my uncle.

My uncle... I never could bring myself to call the old bastard anything else.

Workers were already busy in the groves of citrus trees. Thousands of kilometres away, on the far side of the Atlantic, in a country I never imagined I would one day visit, men were making their fortunes from a black oil that spewed out of the earth, a viscous liquid like coal tar that would be used to win the wars it provoked. In Pietra d'Alba, fortunes were made from the colours that shifted with the sun, a delicious bitterness or a sweet sensation on a cold morning. I miss the world of oranges. Nobody ever fought a war over an orange.

After we had been ushered in through the large gate, I finally discovered the Villa Orsini. I had never seen a lawn before, let alone a topiary hedge. Two great tiered terraces softened the steep slope in front of the house, with a stone staircase running through the middle. The first terrace was carpeted with grass and planted with laurel trees as spherical as pebbles and short conical yew trees, like pieces of an unfamiliar board game abandoned by giants. To the right of the terrace closest to the villa was a boxwood labyrinth, while on the left was the ultramarine blue pool. The major-domo was waiting for us on the front steps. Above the lintel, fashioned from rough stone with a vestige of polychrome, was a banner emblazoned with the Orsini coat of arms. *D'oro, all' orso di verde sormontato da due arance dallo stesso.*

Or, a bear Vert surmounted by two oranges Or. That was the beginning of the legend of the family to which I owe my name, my deepest sorrows and my greatest joys, the family to which I owe, in short, the life that is now ebbing away.

No one knew where the Orsinis came from. There was no trace of them in the history of Genoa's noble families. Yet here they undeniably were. The Villa Orsini was built in Pietra d'Alba in the late eighteenth century, and its opulence quickly made people forget its previous absence. Anyone who asked the villagers would be told that it had always existed.

Out of boredom, jealousy or a taste for fable, a thousand legends sprung up about the Orsini family. That they were originally from Sicily, members of the Onorata Società striving to seem legitimate. But the honourable society in question, later known as the Mafia, and which insiders called Cosa Nostra, didn't even exist when the Villa Orsini was built. Alternatively, they were descended from the Beati Paoli, a medieval quasi-mythic Sicilian sect that stole from the rich to give to the poor. And in frequenting the rich – if only to rob them – they had allowed themselves to be seduced by the siren call of wealth. Ridiculous, others said, growing citrus fruits did not make them Sicilian. Besides, their coat of arms included a bear, and the very name Orsini contained the word *orso* – bear. This 'real' truth – the version most popular in the valley – was that the Orsinis were descended from a family of *orsanti* – breeders and entertainers from the Abruzzo, who sold their trained bears around the world, from men with dancing bears in the Ariège to circuses in America. When this story was first told in the bar of Pietra d'Alba, there were howls of derision: no one had ever heard of a family growing rich by breeding bears. True, admitted the teller of the tale, but that is not how the Orsinis made their fortune. One night, while camping near Pietra d'Alba, on their way to sell their bears, they stumbled on the buried treasure of the Knights Templar. Or maybe it was the Cathars. Or some nobleman heading to the Crusades, who thought it prudent to bury his fortune before setting off to fight the infidel. In short, a treasure so vast that, in little more than a century, it had made their name synonymous with wealth and elegance.

Now, I warily trod over just such myths and legends. The steward led us through a long, rather clammy corridor used by tradesmen to a trapdoor that opened onto the roof. The secretary to the Marchesa had insisted on accompanying us. The villa was composed of two nested structures: the visible one, with its anise-green stucco and pedimented windows, a blend of classic and Palladian architecture, and within this, another slightly smaller structure. The space between the two, a mere sixty centimetres wide, was a labyrinthine warren of tunnels leading to reception rooms, bedrooms and the family living quarters. Tradesmen and servants were expected to use these narrow passageways, lest their presence offend the sight of a member of the Orsini family.

The rooftop still glistened from the previous night's downpour. A third of the fallen statue was buried beneath the hole it had punched in the roof tiles. Even as a team of three, it took Alberto, Paragraph and me a long time to get it upright again. It was the figure of a woman draped in a toga, her right hand gracefully resting on her left shoulder. One of her arms had been broken in the fall. Paragraph and I briefly argued about whether the woman was fastening her toga or taking it off. Whatever the case, she was heavy – words that no woman likes to hear, so I tactfully dropped my voice to a whisper when I said she weighed more than a dead donkey.

'We're going to have to work out a way to make her more secure,' Zio Alberto said. 'As for the arm, there's a bit of repair to do, but no one will notice from a distance.'

We spent the morning scrabbling up and down, fetching tools and hoisting sacks of lime and mortar. Or rather, Paragraph and I did the scrambling while Zio Alberto barked orders, perched on the eaves with a bottle in his hand because the open air made him thirsty. Working had the advantage that it made me forget my spectral encounter the night before. After two hours in the sun, I was all but convinced I had imagined it. By midday, we had replaced the statue on its pedestal and reinforced the seal. I criss-crossed the rooftops as necessary. I may have been only thirteen, but Zio made me work like any other labourer. He would watch as I ran myself ragged, his dark eyes glittering, his lip quivering, as though he was constantly about to say something, but never did. It was a tic that followed him all through his life – I never discovered what it was he wanted to tell me.

Ours is a dangerous craft. Had the war not killed my father, the tin oxide and oxalic acid we used to polish marble would have finished him off. Tin, my arse! We used powdered lead. It would not surprise me if, after my death, the postmortem revealed on my lungs the stain that has blackened the fate of so many stonemasons. During the years I spent in society, I once had a conversation with Riccardo Cassin, a brilliant mountaineer. Whether because both of us spent our days grappling with rock, or because he too was fatherless, we became friends. And because he was a modest man, he tried to persuade me that my profession was the more dangerous. We both run the same risks, he said. You can fall just as I can.

It was late afternoon when the accident occurred. I had just mixed up the ten kilos of mortar required to securely mount the statue. My stomach was churning, and I felt a vague nausea. I had walked for miles across that rooftop in the cold, bright sun, with nothing to eat or drink except the sip of wine generously offered by Zio Alberto. I stopped mixing to watch the distant figure of a postman riding past on his bicycle. Someone was running behind him, but froze every time the postman turned around and waved his fist. For a long minute I watched, spellbound. From the sunlight glinting on the pursuer's clothes, I thought I recognised Emanuele.

'Hey, Paragraph!'

'What?'

'Look over there. Isn't that your—?'

Just then, without warning, my legs gave out from under me. As I toppled head first, I instinctively grabbed the bucket. *Whatever you do, don't let go, or Zio will thrash you for wasting all that good mortar.* The weight of the bucket dragged me down, and as I plummeted, I heard faint cries that grew more and more distant, and seemed to matter less and less. I slid down the steep roof, was launched from a ventilation outlet and bounced off the zinc gutter. For a split second, my fingers clutched at the guttering, but there was no point, I was too exhausted. I let go and, arms splayed, I tumbled ten metres into the void.

I was unconscious only for a moment. Having traced a perfect arc, I slammed into the façade with full force, fully awake. The rope broke my fall. Unlike Zio and Paragraph, who considered the use of ropes unmanly, I always took precautions when working at height, something I learned from my father who summed it up with the maxim: *When someone builds a cathedral, it rains sculptors.*

Paragraph's distraught face appeared over the gutter, just above. Zio joined him a few moments later, more out of curiosity than concern. Seeing me hanging at the end of my rope, Paragraph burst out laughing. 'You scared the shit out of me!'

'Pull me back up!'

'Not possible. You can get in through the window on your right. I'll swing you.'

Paragraph pulled on the rope and, as I swung, I managed to grab the sill of the window – it was open. He gave me a thumbs-up and disappeared. I felt the rope slacken and I fell into a bedroom painted in acid green tones and redolent of sleep and orange blossom. To pull myself upright, I grabbed a table with a bowl of oranges on it, which tipped towards me. By some miracle, I caught the bowl, then set off to hunt for the fruit that had rolled under the furniture. Still trembling, I sat on the edge of the bed. My every movement was a defilement, my very presence a sacrilege. In all my life, I had never touched a mattress so deep, nor seen a bed canopy. The bed was made, but the sheets were rumpled, as though someone had been lying on top of them. I could not stay there.

On the bedside table lay a half-open card. It began with the words 'Happy Birthday' in cursive copperplate. The steward had made it abundantly clear that under no circumstances were we to enter the house. He had said nothing about the penalties for reading the correspondence of its inhabitants, but I imagined they would be unpleasant. Nonetheless, fascinated by the beauty of the handwriting, I picked up the card and I read and reread the few lines: 'We hope you like your present.' I sniffed the paper – smelled an exotic feminine scent mingled with that of oranges. So this was what it meant to be a member of the nobility. People who sent each other cards written in ink, in elegant handwriting, just to say happy birthday.

Clutching the card to my chest, I lay back and daydreamed that I was the intended recipient. *Dearest Mimo, we hope you like your new suit and the horn knife you so wanted.* I was the one who would spend tonight sleeping on this cloud of feathers, wool and horsehair. For a few moments, I was a part of this world, even if it was mere pretence.

Just one minute. Have mercy, one little minute that would hurt no one, stolen from a century where everything was moving too quickly.

S lowly, Padre Vincenzo climbs back up from the depths of the Sacra. The steps feel steeper than they once were. He is short of breath, his muscles ache; it has come time for him to think about his successor. He has worked tirelessly for his congregation, has protected the secret entrusted to him as best he can. He wishes he could say *There is no other treasure in this place than the faith of the men who live here* without lying. His retirement will be well-earned. He will finally be able to do all the things that he has dreamed of. For example... Nothing comes to mind. It is probably just his exhaustion.

He steps into the cell where the little man has spent the past forty years of his life. There is no disdain as he thinks 'little man', especially since whenever he finds himself in the presence of Michelangelo Vitaliani, it is the abbot who feels dwarfed, as though the sculptor casts a vast shadow.

Even supine, even clinging to the last vestiges of life by a spider's thread, Michelangelo Vitaliani is intimidating. Oh, he has been cantankerous and downright rude, but the two men rub along well. The circle of monks moves away. They make for a reassuring sight; one day, the abbot knows, he will have a circle of his own. They will not let him pass away alone.

Suddenly, he remembers! When he finally hangs up his robes, gives his thousand keys to his successor, he would like to visit Pompeii. Take a tour of the Amalfi coast. People say the colours are glorious. But what if something were to happen to him? What if he were to die there, like those men who retire only to drop dead soon after? He wouldn't have his circle. No one standing vigil, holding his hand and helping him enter the darkness. Perhaps he will simply stay here. It's not so bad.

He kneels down beside the bed. Only a few days earlier, Vitaliani was still hale and hearty for a man of eighty-two. In a single night, impending death hollowed his cheeks, the worn-out cogs began to show; the machine will soon grind to a halt.

'Brother, is there anything you wish to say?'

On the brink of death, many men divulge some secret. For decades, the sculptor's secret has shaken the corridors of the

Vatican, troubled the sleep of cardinals. The man's lips move. They are dry despite the ice regularly applied by a novice. The abbot bends towards the mouth; the voice is distant, almost ghostly, barely an echo. When he stands up again, he surveys the room, his brow furrowed.

'Did Signor Vitaliani play music?'

'No, padre, why?'

'I think he just said: *violin, violin, violin.*'

Viola. Viola. Viola.

I was fast asleep when I caught a whiff of something.

I was sleeping like a baby when I felt a presence. The same scent of orange blossom, but stronger now. I moaned, but the presence remained, insistent, so I propped myself on one elbow. The birthday card lay on the floor, where it had fallen as I slept.

I suddenly realised what I had done. I had fallen asleep in a bed. A bed belonging to the Orsini family. Yet this was nothing, a mere peccadillo, compared to what awaited me when I turned.

It was *her*. The dead girl I had seen the night before was standing by the bed, wearing a green silk dress. She haunted me, never to leave me again. I opened my mouth to scream, then knit my brow. It seemed strange that a dead woman would change her dress or smell of orange blossom.

'So you are the boy I saw in the cemetery lasty night,' she said, peering at me.

The dead do not speak, or at least not to make small talk. The conclusion was obvious: this was no ghost. She was a girl of about my age. I did not know whether to beg forgiveness for falling asleep on her bed or to faint with relief.

'You are not going to faint again, are you? You gave me quite a scare last night.'

'I gave *you* a scare? I thought you were dead.'

She stared at me as though I were insane. 'Do I look dead?'

'Not now.'

'Besides, it would be absurd. Why would you fear the dead?'

'Um... because they're dead?'

'Do you think it is the dead who start wars? Who lurk by the wayside? Who rape and steal? The dead are our friends. You would do better to fear the living.'

I gazed at her, speechless. I had never heard anyone talk this way. I had never spent much time talking to a girl, except for my mother, who was not really a girl, she was my mother.

'I've got to get back on the roof, signorina.'

'What are you doing in my room? How did you get in here?'

'Through the window, signorina.'

'Why did you do that?'

'I tried to fly, signorina. It didn't work out.'

Her reaction surprised me. She gave me a smile, a smile that would last for thirty years, a smile to which I clung as I crossed many an abyss. The girl took an orange from the bowl and handed it to me. 'For you.'

I had not eaten many oranges in my life, as one quick look made her realise. Just then, the door opened.

'Darling, we're waiting for you to—'

My first meeting with the Marchesa, a tall, lean woman whose raven hair was drawn back into a severe bun – an austerity belied by the lock of hair that had escaped and tumbled over her shoulder, too soft, too shiny to be an accident. The Marchesa stared at me, unsettled by my presence, by this creature daubed in mortar, sweat and lime that marred her home. A drop of blood trickled from my forehead, where I had hit the façade, and, with deliberate slowness, fell onto the dark parquet floor.

'What is he doing here?'

'He fell from the heavens, Mamma. Well, from the roof.'

The Marchesa tugged on a bell-pull hanging by the canopy. 'Tradesmen are not permitted to enter the house unless expressly working there. The boy is fortunate to be dealing with me rather than your father.'

A panel opened in the wall – a hidden door – to reveal a servant in black livery. The Marchesa gestured towards me.

'This... young man lost his way. He is working on the roof. Ask Silvio to show him the way back.'

As I passed, the Marchesa snatched the orange from my hand. 'And you can give me that, you little thief.'

As the wood panel slid closed behind us and we were plunged back into the labyrinth of passageways around the villa, I heard the distant voice of the Marchesa. 'Dear God, what was that repulsive little creature?'

Obviously, this remark hurt my feelings. My mother had always told me I was handsome, that my height made no difference. But as a dear friend of mine used to say, nobody listens to their mother.

By the time I got back to the roof, Zio Alberto was asleep, leaning against a chimney, drool trickling from the corner of his mouth. Paragraph had started work on repairing the arm of the statue. I rushed to help, so as not to look as though I was skiving. He had prepared a lumpy mixture with too much water and not enough powdered marble. We needed to start again.

'I think I saw your brother,' I said as I stirred another bucket of mortar. 'Just before I fell off the roof. It looked like he was running after the postman.'

'Oh, yes. Emanuele follows Old Angelo everywhere, because he loves the uniform. Angelo pretends to be angry, but actually he is very fond of my brother. From time to time, if his legs are aching at the end of his round, he even gives him a few letters to deliver.'

The sun was setting when Alberto woke up. His mouth was dry; he spat on the roof tiles and complained that he was thirsty. Then he disappeared, leaving us to bring down the tools. It took us half an hour to load the cart, then I went back up to inspect the roof and unhook the rope and pulley we had used to lower our equipment. I made one last tour of the gardens and was about to head back when I was startled to come face to face with the girl in the green dress. She had this curious talent for *appearing*. With her flushed cheeks and the twigs in her black hair, she looked as though she had just stepped out of the forest that abutted the rear wall of the villa.

'I'm sorry, my mother says she does not want me to speak to you any more. A well-bred young girl does not consort with tradesmen. She tells me that I am lucky I wasn't raped.'

'But I—'

'You have to understand, we do not come from the same social class. We *cannot* be friends, and that is an end to it.'

'I understand.'

'Tonight, ten o'clock, at the cemetery?'

'Pardon?'

'Shall we meet tonight, at ten o'clock, in the cemetery?' she said with exaggerated patience.

'But I thought your mother said...'

'No one listens to their mother.' She set off at a run, then suddenly stopped. 'What is your name?'

'Mimo, signorina.'

'I'm Viola.'

I made my way back to the cart like a sleepwalker, clambered into the back and did not say a word on the journey home. Even Alberto noticed that I seemed troubled.

'What's the matter with you?' he said, his voice a little slurred.

'Nothing.'

But something had happened to me, and her name whirled inside my head like those melodies that our old folks used to sing when they had had too much wine, those country tunes that made their eyes look twenty-one again.

Viola. Viola. Viola.

That night, in bed, by the glow of a storm lamp, I wrote to my mother. Every day, I would write to tell her about my life. Then I would burn the letter. I only ever posted one a month. I did not want to worry this woman who always called me 'my little man' at the top of her letters. She had worries enough about me, about money, about what I did or did not eat. All her letters were written in different handwriting because, like my father, my mother was illiterate and had to ask for help. The last I heard, she had left Savoie for the north of France, where she had found work on a farm. *My employers are very nice. Soon, I'll be able to take a holiday.* I would reply: *Zio Alberto treats me well. I'm saving up so I can send for you.* We lovingly lied to each other.

The village bell tolled nine thirty. I did not know what to do about Viola's invitation, having never been invited anywhere, let alone a cemetery. Paragraph's wisdom would have been useful, but he disappeared as soon as we got home. I suspected that, despite the risks, he had gone to flirt with the Giordano girl. Like me, he had had a dreamy look as we came home in the cart, and there was precious little to dream about in Pietra d'Alba. Out of a sense of politeness, I set off, debating whether I should carry on or turn back, and just when I had decided that it was utterly perverse to disturb the dead a second time, the yawning gates of the cemetery appeared out of the darkness. The village bell tolled again. At that moment, Viola emerged out of the forest from a point where I could see no path. She passed without even looking at me, then, after a few steps, she stopped and, seeing that I had not budged, gave me an exasperated look. 'Well, are you coming or not?'

She headed for the mausoleum she had appeared from the night before. Viola could never stay still. It was becoming difficult to watch her, to describe her. She was beautiful, in her own fashion, that is to say the polar opposite of the Giordano girl. Her femininity lay not in her curves but in the sensual austerity of their absence, the angular movements that made it seem as though she was constantly avoiding invisible obstacles, all knees and elbows. The eyes beneath the tousled shock of raven hair were almost too big, her features chiselled deep into the bone. Her deep gold complexion lent credence to the theory that the Orsini family hailed from the Mediterranean.

'This is our family vault. Virgilio is here now.'

'Is that your brother, signorina?'

'Stop calling me signorina – it's annoying. Yes, he was my brother. Virgilio was very clever. I've never met anyone so intelligent.'

'My father also died in the war.'

'Bloody war,' muttered Viola. 'What do you think about it?'

'About the war?'

'Yes. Personally, I think the entry of the United States will change everything – our defeat at Caporetto was a temporary setback, mostly due to the weather and the fact that Cadorna was unprepared. But I'm wary of the promises that led to us joining the Triple Entente. I mean, it's all very well for the French to offer to restore our former lands, but I suspect that Wilson will have a thing or two to say about that. It could end badly, don't you think?'

'Um... I suppose.'

'*Um, I suppose?*'

'I don't really know much about the war.'

'Well, what are you waiting for, a visit from the Holy Ghost?'

'How do you know so much?' I asked, a little offended.

'The same way everyone knows. I read the newspapers. I'm not supposed to – my mother insists that it mars a young woman's complexion. But as soon as my father throws out his *Corriere della Sera*, the gardener lets me read it before he burns it, in exchange for a few lire.'

'Have you got any money?'

'I steal it from my parents. It's in their best interests not to have an ignorant daughter. Would you like me to lend you some books?'

'Books about what?'

'What subject do you know a lot about?'

'Sculpture.'

'Well, anything other than sculpture. Although... What are Michelangelo Buonarroti's dates?'

'Umm...'

'1475 to 1564. You know nothing about sculpture. Actually, you know nothing about anything. I'll help you. It's easy for me, I remember everything I see and hear.'

I rubbed my eyes – everything was moving too fast. Deep down, Viola was a futurist. Talking to her was like hurtling down a mountain road at breakneck speed. I always came away exhausted, terrified, elated or a mixture of all three.

In the chill night air, our breaths condensed into vaporous balls. Viola smoothed her dress.

'What about your mother?' said Viola. 'Where is she?'

'Far away.'

'What does she smell of?'

'Huh?'

'Every mother smells of something. What does yours smell like?'

'Nothing. No, actually, she smells of bread. And vanilla, when she makes *canestrelli*. And the rosewater my father gave her for her birthday. And a little sweat. What does yours smell like?'

'Grief. Well, I'd better be getting back.'

'So soon?'

'If I am not back in time for midnight mass, there will be a hell of a row.'

'What midnight mass?'

'Christmas mass, you idiot.'

My second Christmas away from my family. This time, I had thought it best to forget the whole thing.

'What did you ask for as a present?' asked Viola.

I had to improvise. 'A knife. With a handle of carved horn. And a miniature automobile. What about you?'

'A book about Fra Angelico. Not that I'll get it, they always give me clothes, as though I don't have enough. Do you like Fra Angelico?'

'I love him.'

'You don't know who I'm talking about, do you?'

'No.'

'Will you walk me back as far as the road?'

She held out her hand and I took it. Crossing the unfathomable abyss of conventions and class barriers just like that. Viola held out her hand and I took it, a heroic feat that no one ever talked about, a silent revolution. Viola held out her hand and I took it, and this was the precise moment that I became a sculptor. Not that I was aware of the change, of course. But it was in that instant, when our palms were joined amid this dark conspiracy of owls and brushwood, that I had an inkling that there was something to sculpt.

We agreed on a signal. A short distance from the crossroads where the village road met the path that led to the cemetery there was a hollow stump. We would use it as a letterbox. To let me know when she had left a message, Viola would cover a lantern with a red veil and hang it in her window, which I could see from the workshop a kilometre away. She promised to meet me soon. We would meet in the cemetery, where no one would think to come in the middle of the night. We would not be disturbed. When we came to the crossroads, she gave a little wave and said *Ciao, caro*. Then she turned right, and I turned left.

Every night, before going to bed, I would stare at the dark mass of the Villa Orsini. Night after night, Viola's window in the west corner of the building remained empty. Gradually, the remnants of 1917 washed up on the shores of 1918; there was a party in the village square to celebrate the transition from a world at war, where men were slaughtering each other, to a world at war, where men were slaughtering each other. There was talk of soldiers being shot for fraternising with the enemy, for mutinying, refusing to go to the front, for mutilating themselves. In Pietra d'Alba, the war seemed very distant, even though the tracks of the hearse that had carried Virgilio Orsini to the cemetery were still visible.

Delighted with the cherub that Zio Alberto had signed, Dom Anselmo entrusted us with some small jobs in the church cloisters, where the salt sea breeze ate into the limestone. Between Christmas 1917 and late January 1918, we undertook several replacements, cleanings and restorations. Alberto had started the year in fine fettle – he had met a comely widow on New Year's Eve and even tempered his consumption of wine. Two weeks later, the widow demanded payment 'for her kindnesses', while the locals laughed at him behind his back. He had stumbled on the only *grande horizontale* for miles around. Granted, she was no longer in her youth, but she was so skilled in her trade that it was rumoured a *conte* or a *barone* sometimes travelled from Savona to enjoy her many kindnesses. The following day, when Alberto arrived in the cloister, his complexion was waxy, his breath acrid. I was carefully working on a statue of a saint. He grabbed the hammer and chisel from me, but his hands were shaking. Despite his efforts, his sweating and his swearing, his hands kept dancing a jig. He dropped the tools and headed home, muttering to himself. After that, we rarely saw him in the church. I was free to sculpt to my heart's content, while he pretended to dispense advice. During my breaks, I studied the pietà that stood at the cross-section of the transept, mentally refashioning it, correcting the flaws, attempting to work out precisely where the *anonymous master* credited on the plaque had gone wrong.

Viola's window remained hopelessly mute – until one February night when, walking back to the barn, I saw a red glow flicker in the darkness. This was our signal. I took off at a run and did not stop until I reached the crossroads. Inside the hollow stump was a package wrapped in cloth. My heart hammering, I raced straight back to the barn and opened it to find a message and a book. The note read: 'Thursday, eleven o'clock. You must read this before you come.' The green card book cover was imprinted with the image of an apostle flanked by two monks and bore the title *Old Masters, Vol. 17, Fra Angelico, Published by Pierre Lafitte & Co.* The moment I opened it, I felt my head spinning – whether from my midnight run or from the contents of the book, I still do not know. I had never seen so much colour, so much sweetness. I was young, arrogant, I knew that I was gifted. With a hammer and chisel, I was more than a match for stonemasons three times my age. But this Fra Angelico knew things that I did not. I took an instant dislike to him.

On Thursday morning, the sky was stormy. As we worked inside the church, each lightning flash illumined the great stained-glass window, spattering us with garnet, gold and purple. If the downpour continued, I was not sure whether I would be able to meet Viola. We had not reckoned on this eventuality. Would Viola come, regardless of the weather? I knew nothing about the etiquette of nascent friendships.

Luckily, a strong west wind swept away the clouds. At eleven o'clock, I made my way through the darkness to the cemetery gate. Five minutes later, Viola emerged from the forest at precisely the same spot as last time. She greeted me with a little nod, as though we had last seen each other an hour earlier, and she walked straight past me. I followed her as she weaved her way between the tombs to a bench where she sat down.

'When did Fra Angelico die?' she asked.

'He died 18 February 1455.'

'Where?'

'Rome.'

'His real name?'

'Guido di Pietro.'

Finally, she smiled at me. With Viola, the cemetery seemed a little less threatening, even if I still flinched every time a twig cracked.

'You've read the book. Good for you. You're already a little less stupid.'

'I thought I'd never see you again. I watched your window for weeks, but there was no red light.'

'Oh, yes. I was very angry with you.'

'Um... what did I do?'

She looked at me in astonishment. 'You really don't know?'

'Um... no.'

'You start almost all your sentences with *well* or *um*. It's coarse.'

'Is that why you were angry with me?'

'No. Last time, when we went our separate ways at the crossroads, you remember? You left without looking back. That's why I was angry with you.'

'I don't understand...'

Viola sighed. 'Whenever you say goodbye to someone you love, you take a few steps, then turn around so you can see them one last time, maybe even give a wave. I turned around. You just kept walking as though you'd already forgotten me. So I decided never to see you again. Then I thought about it and realised it was probably because you were a boor and an ignoramus.'

I nodded vehemently. 'Yes! Yes, that's why. Thank you so much for coming back. And thank you for the book. From now on, I'll turn around, I swear.'

'All you have to do is put the book back in the hollow tree and I'll give you another one. I took this one from our library, but I can't take more than one at a time, because I'm not supposed to go in there. Mamma says it's a waste of time for me to be reading rubbish about dead people. Speaking of dead people, shall we go?'

'Where?'

'To listen to the dead, you idiot. Why do you think we're here?'

Viola was a tightrope walker precariously balanced on an elusive wire strung between two worlds. Some would say between sanity and madness. More than once, I had to fight, sometimes physically, with people who said she was insane.

Listening to the dead was Viola's favourite pastime. It had all started, she explained, when she accidentally fell asleep on a gravestone during her grandmother's funeral when she was five. She had woken up with a head full of stories that were not hers and which, therefore, must have been whispered to her from below. *Demonic possession*, declared Dom Ascanio, who had been Dom Anselmo's predecessor at San Pietro delle Lacrime. *Childhood hysteria* was the diagnosis of the doctor in Milan to whom her parents took her some weeks later. He recommended ice baths. If the ice baths did not work, a harsher treatment would have to be considered. After her first ice bath, Viola, who was not insane, insisted that she was cured. And it was then that she started going out at night, sliding down the sandstone drainpipe at the back of the house next to her bedroom window. She would lie on the gravestones, choosing them at random or because she had known the deceased. By her own admission, the dead had never spoken to her again. But she wanted to be there in case one of them should need to confide in her. Who would listen to them otherwise? She was simply trying to be helpful. The night I had taken her for a ghost, she had come to lie on her brother's grave. The two of them lay there in complicit silence, just as they had before. They did not need to talk in order to communicate.

Viola did not take offence when I flatly refused to lie down on a tombstone. She simply said: 'What are you scared of?'

'Ghosts, like everyone else. I'm afraid they'll haunt me.'

'Haunt you? You really think that you're that interesting?'

She shrugged and walked off towards her favourite grave – a small limestone slab, partially overgrown with moss – and read out the name of the owner for me: *Tommaso Baldi, 1787–1797*. Little Tommaso was now part of local legend. In 1797, a villager claimed to have heard the sound of a flute rising from somewhere deep below his cellar. At first people thought he was mad, but in the days that followed, other residents of Pietra d'Alba swore they heard an ethereal flute coming from beneath a street or the floor of a living room or from the church crypt during mass. A group of circus acrobats arrived in the village, utterly exhausted. They had spent days searching for one of their troupe, little Tommaso, who had got lost in the forest. He had gone off to practise his flute, as he often did. No one had seen him for a week.

The village men launched a search party. They scoured the woods, looking for a cave or a hollow where the boy might have got lost. They heard the sound of the flute in the distance, then drifting up from beneath the fountain, and once more on the outskirts of the village. Then nothing. The following Saturday, a dog led his master into a clearing. There, they found a boy lying on the grass, his lips curled up to reveal his pale gums, his body terrifyingly emaciated. He was clutching a wooden flute that no one could wrench from him. He was hurriedly carried back to the village, his eyes wide open and burned by the sunlight. Shortly after midnight, the boy regained consciousness. In a faint whisper, he told the troupe that he was sorry, that he had lost his way in the great city beneath the earth; then he breathed his last.

Viola firmly believed that the boy had not been delirious, that some secret and mysterious continent lay beneath our feet. Unbeknownst to us, we were walking over temples and palaces of pure gold, where a sallow people with white eyes lived beneath a sky of soil and clouds of tangled roots. Who would not want to discover a new continent? Viola spent a lot of time lying on Tommaso's grave – it was so short, her feet stuck out over the edge – in the hope that the dead boy would show her the way.

I sat on a nearby bench while she demonstrated. For nearly half an hour, she did not move, seemingly impervious to the cold. Now that my imagination was no longer overwhelmed by Viola's presence, by the pizzicato of her speech and the ideas that teemed from her, it filled the darkness with other noises. The rustle of something crawling between the mausoleums, *danses macabres* just beyond my field of vision. Back in the village, the bell tolled midnight. I could feel lidless eyes watching from behind branches. I almost wept with relief when Viola finally got to her feet.

'Did he speak to you?'

'Not this time.'

As we headed back, I stopped when we came to the gate. 'You always appear from out of the forest. Are there paths through there?'

'None that you could use.'

And that was all. She ignored my puzzled look and said nothing until we reached the crossroads.

'I'll bring you more books – I don't care if someone catches me in the library. Read them, even if you don't understand them. By the way, how old are you?'

'Thirteen.'

'Me too. What month were you born?'

'November 1904.'

'Me too! Imagine if we were born on the same day? We would be cosmic twins.'

'What does that mean?'

'It means we could be linked beyond time and space, by a bond which we cannot understand and which nothing can break. I'll count to three, and then we'll both say our birth date. One, two, three...'

'November 22nd,' we said as one.

Viola jumped for joy, she threw her arms around me and led me in a little dance. 'We're cosmic twins!'

'That's really amazing – the same year, same month, same day.'

'I knew it, I just knew it. I'll see you soon, Mimo.'

'You won't make me wait two months, will you?'

'One doesn't keep a cosmic twin waiting,' Viola said gravely.

She turned right, I turned left. Her joy made my footsteps lighter, the darkness brighter, and I felt less angry with myself for lying to her. I was born on November 7th. But I remembered the date on the birthday card I had read over and over before falling asleep in her room. I did not believe that a little white lie that made someone happy was a lie at all. Perhaps it was something I could discuss with Dom Anselmo. A perfect opportunity to confess.

As I walked away, I made sure to turn back three times. Once for the time I had missed, once for this time, and a third time because I could not help myself.

O nce our various jobs at the church were completed, Zio Alberto's workshop experienced a lean period. Work was scarce, and so Zio had to take to the road, touting for business in the neighbouring villages and valleys. He even contacted the Orsini family, who, via the seneschal, informed Alberto that they would call on him when needed.

With no work to be done, Paragraph and I kept ourselves occupied as best we could. Zio's reserves of stone were depleted but for a magnificent block of marble that he had reserved for some potential large-scale commission. As a result, I amused myself sculpting bas-reliefs in the surrounding countryside, wherever a rockface permitted. Some of these studies may be there to this day – perhaps they still surprise ramblers at the bend in the path. As for Paragraph, he spent his time restoring old pieces of furniture brought to him by the villagers, and so discovered his vocation: he was as gifted at carpentry as he was terrible at sculpting. I saw Viola three times during the spring of 1918, always at the cemetery. Despite her best efforts, she could not persuade me to join in her necromantic experiments – I refused to lie on a gravestone. Besides, the dead never talked to her. If they had, I would have run for my life.

Viola was the youngest of four children. Virgilio, the eldest, the only member of the family she loved unreservedly, had died in the famous train accident at the age of twenty-two. I wish I had known him. 'He was a little like you,' she told me one day. 'When I told him something, he believed me.'

Next came her brother Stefano, who was twenty. Whenever she talked about him, Viola always peered around as though fearful he would jump out of a bush. Tall and loudmouthed, with a passion for hunting and automobile racing, Stefano was their mother's favourite. At eighteen, Francesco, the youngest son, was a serious young man with a pallid complexion, whom I had unknowingly encountered many times in the church while we were working in the cloisters. He often talked to Dom Anselmo or spent long hours praying in front of the pietà I had been so critical of. Viola seemed to have a certain fondness for Francesco, one she always qualified with a mocking 'he'll go far'. Francesco was destined for the priesthood, much to his parents' delight. And he did go far, even if he was thwarted by me.

As for the Marchese and the Marchesa, they were shadowy figures in Viola's life. Two adults far removed from her concerns who happened to live in the same house, sometimes passed her in the corridors and spoke in a language she did not understand. They were not cruel, she explained. They never laid a hand on her, even when she did something stupid. At ten, she almost burned down the house in a failed experiment to produce perfume by distilling mimosa flowers. For reasons she still did not understand, the mixture had exploded, and Viola hid in a lean-to while the curtains burned. When the fire had been extinguished, the servants found her and brought her to her stern father, who forbade her from going into the library again because the chemical experiment that had led to the fire came from a book that she had borrowed. Viola promised to obey him, while privately deciding she would do no such thing. Especially since her experiment had been a partial success – the explosion that had singed her eyebrows had left her smelling of mimosa for a week. If it was simply a matter of adjusting the formula, why stop now?

'Could you make a perfume for me?' I said one night while she was lying on the grave of some Genoese nobleman.

'Oh, I'm not doing perfumes any more. I'm studying other things now. The internal combustion engine, electricity, clockwork movements and some basic medicine. And art, obviously. I want to be like people during the Renaissance who knew everything about everything.'

'And when you know everything about everything?'

'Then I will study the things we do not know yet.'

Viola was the victim of a curse that her parents had initially found amusing: she remembered *everything* – things that she had read or heard or seen only once. When she was five, they would drag her out of bed in the middle of the night, when they had had a little too much to drink, to show her off to visiting guests. How enchanting to see a skinny little girl with big eyes reciting poems by Ovid that she had only just read. It became a problem when Viola developed a thirst for knowledge, when she wanted to understand. For that, she needed to read more. One book invariably led to another, *a vicious circle*, in her mother's words, that had culminated in the incident of the exploding perfume. The Marchesa, who could no longer smell mimosa without picturing her curtains being consumed by crimson flames, in which she was convinced she had seen demons, had every acacia tree in the grounds torn out.

Gradually, the stream of books increased. Sometimes when I replaced the books I had read the week before, I would find three new ones in the hollow stump. The moment I went to bed, I devoured them, soaking up names, dates, capitals, theories and concepts like a sponge that has been left out in the sun. I hid my excursions from Paragraph, who was far from stupid. One night, he caught me engrossed in an impenetrable work of engineering. True to my promise, I read the book from cover to cover. To my surprise, I always learned something new, even in the most esoteric treatise. Viola was careful to alternate books that were accessible and difficult, illustrated or not. Sometimes she even slipped in a novel, having diagnosed me with an 'acute imagination deficit'.

'What are you reading?' said Paragraph.

'*A Treatise on the Expansion of the port of Genoa by the engineer Luigi Luiggi, born 1856.*'

'Is that what you've been spending your nights doing? Emanuele wondered why you don't come to the cemetery any more. I didn't realise that you wanted to build ports.'

'I don't want to build ports. Viola lent it to me.'

'Viola? Who is Viola?' Paragraph blenched. 'Viola Orsini?'

'Yeah.'

'*Viola Orsini?*'

'Yes. She's a friend.'

'The girl who turns into a bear?'

Paragraph had often amused me with countless legends about the Orsini family. They were so rich, he told me, that when one of them sneezed, servants would steal his handkerchief to extract the gold dust. But it was the first time I had heard this particular story. And unlike the others, which fascinated or amused Paragraph, this story terrified him.

'You shouldn't see that girl.'

'Why not?'

'Because she's a witch. Ask whoever you like. Ask around the village.'

I would later notice that the villagers deliberately avoided Viola as much as possible without offending the family. The story of the bear dated from a few years earlier. A group of foreign hunters had spent a few days in Pietra d'Alba. 'Foreign' was generally taken to mean 'anyone not from Liguria, Piedmont or Lombardy'. The hunters were described as Croatian, Black, French, Sicilian, Jews or – worse – Protestants depending on whether the storyteller was a racist or a fantasist. The one thing on which everyone agreed was that there had been hunters and they were coarse and rowdy: they got drunk every night; they had wandering hands and were quick to grope the village girls. On the day before they were due to leave, only two men went hunting. They encountered Viola wandering alone in the forest and, mistaking her for a roe deer, almost shot her. Curious, they watched from afar as Viola picked up pebbles, gauging their roundness by holding them up to the sun. They had followed her, with no ill intentions, simply because she was pretty. 'Pretty, isn't she?' commented one of the men. 'Don't be a fool, she can't be more than twelve or thirteen,' said the other. 'That's old enough,' the first man quipped. 'Besides, if she is walking alone in the forest, she is fair game.' He jumped on the little girl, who shrieked. 'Shut up! I'm not going to hurt you,' he said, trying to sound reassuring as he unbuttoned his trousers. Viola miraculously managed to free herself and darted into the undergrowth. 'She acts like your wife,' said the second hunter with a snigger while the other plunged into the dense vegetation after Viola. 'That little slut is going to get what's coming to her,' he muttered, holding up his trousers with one hand. Stumbling into a clearing he let out a howl that could be heard in far Savona.

He had come face to face with a bear. The animal reared up on its hind legs – it was a full head taller than the man – and let out a deafening roar, spattering him with spittle that smelled of raw meat.

'All right, so a hunter ran into a bear,' I said, rolling my eyes. 'That doesn't mean that Viola turned into a bear.'

'Wait, I haven't told you the whole story.'

What Paragraph had not yet told me, and what had terrified the hunters even more than an encounter with a she-bear, was the fact that the beast was wearing Viola's tattered dress. Her hat lay nearby on a carpet of pine needles. The she-bear roared again. The huntsman, still holding up his trousers with one hand, used the other to reach for his dagger. But, with a nonchalant swipe of her paw, Viola – since it had to be her – slit his throat. The wide-eyed huntsman dropped his trousers and blood gushed from his throat. 'He died with his balls hanging out,' said Paragraph. Half-crazed, his friend raced back to the village to tell his tale. At first, no one believed him, especially since no trace of the missing man was ever found apart from an empty shoe. It was the abject fear of the survivor that persuaded the villagers. No one could feign such terror, not even an actor, not even Bartolomeo Pagano, the great Genoese actor who held Italy spellbound in his film roles as Maciste the Strongman. The hunter who survived could not possibly have invented such a tale. And, when the villagers came to think about it, the source of the Orsini family's fortune was deeply mysterious, and they had a bear on their coat of arms... The whole thing reeked of sorcery. Hence, the mere sight of Viola caused people to stiffen imperceptibly and their lower lips to quiver – something they quickly hid so as not to offend Signor and Signora Orsini, who were oblivious to their daughter's shapeshifting. Since the family was the biggest employer in the region, it was considered best to keep this detail from them.

I laughed at Paragraph, who seemed to believe this tale. Emanuele came to join us, wearing a hussar's jacket open over his bare chest, a pith helmet and knee-length canvas breeches. When Paragraph asked his brother to corroborate the story, Emanuele launched into a long speech that I did not understand, at the end of which Paragraph looked at me triumphantly. 'See? I told you.'

I have never encountered anything like the sweetness of springtime in Pietra d'Alba, where dawn lasted all day long. The stones of the village would capture the pink glow and transfer it to anything reflective: roof tiles, metals, the mica embedded in rocky outcrops, the miraculous spring, even the eyes of the villagers. The pink did not gutter out until the last villager fell sleep, because even after dark, it lingered in the eyes of a boy gazing at a girl beneath the lanterns. In the morning, the process would begin again. Pietra d'Alba: the stone of dawn.

Zio Alberto came back after two weeks, a pattern that would recur in the years that followed. He had been as far as Acqui Terme, in the heart of Piedmont, vainly touting for work in the villages along the way. No one needed a stonemason. On the other hand, many people suggested he enlist and defend his country. Only in Sassello, on his way home, did he have a stroke of luck. A featherless, emaciated stroke of luck, but in a time of famine, it was better than nothing. The Basilica dell'Immacolata Concezione entrusted him with four cherubs and two ornamental urns in need of restoration, together with an ex-voto. Zio arrived home with his cargo of fallen angels in the back of the cart and refused our help to unload them. He immediately set to work, did a preliminary sketch for the first angel and, so pleased was he with his work, spent the rest of the night drinking. The following day, Paragraph and I had to take over because Zio Alberto was ill. My uncle spent the whole week lying in bed, beleaguered by dark thoughts that he tried to dispel with mutterings in a dialect that few people spoke now, except perhaps in the alleys of the port of Genoa. Surprisingly, during times like these he remained sober. I can confidently say that Zio Alberto drank only when he was happy. But somewhere in his drunkenness, his happiness cracked, allowing long sinuous shadows to pass through. At such times, he would lash out at me. I learned to dodge the blows, and as he did it purely out of habit, with little conviction, it did not really hurt. Sometimes a bruise or two, but who didn't have a bruise?

It took two months for me to finish restoring the angels. Paragraph dealt with the ex-voto, which was almost impossible to bungle. But he somehow managed to snap it in two and had to start all over again.

When I presented the finished angels to Zio Alberto, feeling particularly proud of my work, he studied them.

'Your name is a curse,' he said. 'You act like you're Buonarroti, but you're just a *pezzo di merda*, nothing more, who sculpts like a *pezzo di merda*.'

As he rained down blows on me, I curled up in a corner and I found myself thinking: 'Michelangelo Buonarroti, 1475–1564.'

I'd grown up in a world filled with grunting. Talking was at best a luxury and more often a futility.

We grunted our thanks, grunted our satisfaction, grunted just to grunt. And when not grunting, we rolled our eyes or gesticulated. No words were needed for 'pass me the salt'. This was my father's way and Zio Alberto's too. It was a male thing. Viola, on the other hand, often said 'as it happens' or 'notwithstanding'. She opened up a world of infinite nuances. If I remarked 'it's windy', Viola would say 'that's not the wind, that's the libeccio'. She knew the names of all the winds.

On Midsummer's Day, 24 June 1918, she asked me to meet her at the cemetery. It was the best night to see will-o'-the-wisps. As always, she stepped out of the forest from a specific point I had studied in broad daylight and where I swear there was no path. I immediately told her how reluctant I was to hunt will-o'-the-wisps, especially when it came to lost souls.

Viola clapped a hand over my mouth. 'Forget the will-o'-the-wisps. I've made a momentous discovery.'

'Really?'

Viola had taught me that only boors say 'Oh?'

'I've just realised that I can travel through time,' she said. 'In fact, I've just come from the past.'

'What do you mean?'

'Well, I've just come from a second ago. If T is now, then one second ago, at T-1, I was not yet here. And now I am. Ergo, I have travelled from T-1 to T. From the past to the present.'

'You can't really travel in time.'

'Yes, I can. I just did it again. I just did it a second ago.'

'But you can't go back.'

'No, because the past is of no value. That is why we travel from the past to the future.'

'You can't travel ten years into the future.'

'Of course I can. Let's meet here at the same time ten years from now, on 24 June 1928. You'll see, I'll be there.'

'Except that it will have taken you ten years to get there.'

'So what? When you came from France, it didn't matter whether your train took a minute or a day. You travelled from France to Italy, didn't you?'

Still puzzled, I looked for the weak point in her logic. But Viola did not have weak points.

'I will also be here on 24 June 1928, so I will also have travelled into the future. *Quad erat demonstrandum*. Come on, the dead are waiting.'

'Is it true that you can turn into a bear?'

She had taken a few steps towards the cemetery. She came back towards me, looking serious. 'Who told you that?'

'Clau— Vittorio.'

'Is that Emanuele's brother?'

'Yes.'

'I'm very fond of him. We all played together when we were little. Until the age of five, a member of the nobility can play with anyone without infringing protocol. What else did he tell you?'

'That a hunter tried to... to rap—'

'Yes, I know what he tried to do,' Viola interrupted, her face suddenly hard.

'So, is it true, the thing about the she-bear? I mean, I know it's impossible, but—'

'I will tell you the truth, because I would never lie to you. Promise that you will never lie to me.'

'I promise.'

'And that this has to be secret.'

'I promise.'

'I don't really like people telling stories about me. But in this case, Vittorio's right.'

'You can transform yourself into a bear?'

'Yes.'

'You're making fun of me?'

'Why ask the question if you don't believe me?'

'All right, then, I believe you. You can turn into a bear. Can you show me?'

With a gentle smile, Viola tapped me in the middle of my forehead. 'Use your imagination. If you do, you don't need me to show you. And when you don't *need* me to show you, then maybe I will.'

It took me eighty-two years – eight decades of bad faith and a long agony – before I realised what I already knew. Mimo Vitaliani cannot exist without Viola Orsini. But Viola Orsini exists without the need for anyone else.

D on Vincenzo pauses, hesitates before the wardrobe in the corner of his office, the one to which no one but he has access. He turns away and goes to stand at the window from which he likes to gaze out at the mountains – how many times has he done so in all his years as a monk? A light drizzle has begun to fall. Directly below his office is the flagstone-tiled roof of the cell he has just left. He expects at any moment to have someone come and say, 'It is finished, padre, *consummatum est*,' but Vitaliani is tenacious. Who knows what visions roil beneath the brow that is just a little too big, what joys and sorrows rack the limbs that are a little too short? The abbot has this strange impression that his guest is trying to tell him something; that he wants to say something now that he can no longer speak, perhaps *because* he can no longer speak.

Despite himself, the abbot goes back to the wardrobe. The reassuring lustre of the wood is deceptive; this ancient armoire, like these venerable walls, is not all it seems. The wardrobe is actually a safe, whose key he constantly keeps with him. He has been through the contents a hundred times without finding anything to justify such a precaution. Granted, some of the documents it contains raise questions. That in itself is problematic. The Church does not appreciate questions – it has already answered all of them.

When Don Vincenzo first took up his post, he was surprised to learn that these files were kept not in the Vatican, but in the Sacra. Because, he was told, it was safer. Knowledge can be a powerful weapon, one that the countless men who scheme within the Holy See could use for political ends. Had used for political ends. Had not these self-same files put an end to the meteoric career of Cardinal Orsini, once tipped for the Cathedra Romana? It was shortly afterwards that they had been transferred here to the Sacra. There was a certain logic to the decision, since *she* was also here.

The abbot decides to open the wardrobe, as he has done many times in recent years. He slides the key into the tamper-proof lock and activates the complex, silent mechanism. Inside, it is all but empty, something that has always seemed somewhat ridiculous. Some cardboard box-files occupy a single shelf. There are only four of them and they look like those used by clerks or accountants. A banal casing for something so explosive it deserves tooled leather, gilding, brass fittings, all the trappings that the Vatican adores. Then again, the casing of a stick of dynamite is no different.

The box-files all bear the same inscription. *Pietà Vitaliani.* They contain almost everything ever written about *her*, which is precious little. There are the early testimonies and official reports, initially written by clerics, later by bishops and later still by cardinals. There is, of course, the detailed study made by Professor Williams of Stanford University. Vincenzo remembers he once thought it *a lot of fuss about nothing*. He knows what has been said about the statue. He has read and reread the statements, listened to his own monks at confession tell him about the strange dreams that tortured their sleep after they had seen *her*. But since the statue had no effect on him – perhaps he lacks imagination – he did not take it seriously. He found her beautiful, very beautiful; he knew a lot about sculpture. As for the rest? Idle gossip.

Until the Pentecost of 1972, when he first heard the accursed name: *Laszlo Toth*. A name that would thereafter give him sleepless nights and anxious days when he would lay his hand on his chest a dozen times to feel the cord and the key to the tamper-proof lock.

Summer 1918, an inferno. The scorching sandstorm blasted the plateau such that the vegetation withered and so did the men. Endless days when the sky did not turn blue but remained stupefyingly white. Cannon breath, some called it. The cannons had been fired so much, had grown so hot, that what you felt when you got up in the morning, your forehead in a vice, streaming with sweat at the slightest movement, was war itself. In this apocalyptic atmosphere, the men walked around bare-chested while the women clutched at their dresses just a little too late to stop the wind from lifting them, which further fuelled the torrid heat. There were many births in 1919.

Money was scarce, food was rationed. Paragraph did more and more woodwork and shared his earnings with me as though it were the most natural thing in the world, giving me a loaf of bread or a piece of cheese when Zio Alberto was not looking. Alberto called us bloodsucking leeches while he drank away the money my mother had given me, or what little remained. He decided that, through my pen, he would write to his own mother.

Mammina,
Business is not going particularly well here, but we are
making do. But the greatest expense are these leeches,
who don't do a bloody thing – what have I done to God?
But don't go thinking I'm complaining or asking you
for money. Like I said, I'm getting by. We simply have to
tighten our belts a bit more. After all, there's a war on.
Your loving son.

Late July, a dust cloud obscured the horizon but did not disperse, as it usually did, at the bend where the road turned towards the Orsini estate. It rolled on towards us, and Zio Alberto was overcome by a strange agitation. He plunged his head in the water trough, smoothed his hair and changed his shirt. We stood in the middle of the road, squinting into the sun. Rising and falling, an automobile gradually took shape among the orange groves. A Züst 25/35, a genuine automobile with a long golden bonnet and conquering mudguards, emerged from the haze and came to a halt in front of us. The chauffeur got out and opened the passenger door for a plump woman in a fur coat. It was thirty-five degrees. As the woman walked towards us, the driver took a rag to repair the insult the dust had done to the gleaming bodywork.

'You always were the handsomest man,' said the woman, pinching Alberto's cheek.

I realised it was his mother, because while Alberto was not ugly, he certainly was not, and never had been, the handsomest man. Mammina, as she insisted we call her, was no longer just a girl who plied her trade down at the docks. She managed an establishment that enjoyed a goodly reputation – at least in certain circles. War had made her queen of a demi-monde whose dark streets she had spent long years walking.

Her chauffeur quickly produced a picnic from an ice box. Mammina's international clientele, who often paid in kind, ensured it was a veritable feast, a culinary journey stretching from Samarkand to Turin. I had caviar for the first time, a barefoot kid who had not yet turned fourteen. Zio kept to himself, regularly spitting into his hand so he could slick back a rebellious lock onto his forehead. Naturally, his mother had invited Paragraph and me to join them, and he had not protested.

'Do you need money, *caro*?' she asked, stifling a burp after a bowl of strawberries.

'No, no, Mammina, everything is fine.'

'But what if it would please Mammina?'

'Well, that would be different. If you insist, I can't refuse.'

His mother snapped her fingers. The chauffeur fetched an overnight bag from the car, from which she took a large envelope stuffed with lire – I thought Alberto would start drooling. Before she handed it to him, she took out a few banknotes for Paragraph and me. 'For the little ones. Just look at them, skinny as rakes. And you, boy, you're not very tall. If you don't eat, you won't grow any bigger.'

'He's a dwarf, Mammina,' said Zio.

'He's a handsome lad is what he is,' she said, giving me a wink. 'Tell me, are you fond of a fig?'

'Yes, signora, but you can't really get them here, except in the church garden.'

They all burst out laughing, even Zio Alberto. Paragraph was rolling in the dust, and this is how I learned that the fig she was talking about did not grow on trees.

Mammina got to her feet, reeling a little from the two bottles of Val Polcevera she had drained. 'Well, I had better go, the house isn't going to run itself. *Ciao tutti!*'

She waved a beringed hand as she walked back to the automobile. I raced over to open the door for her, while the chauffeur crank-started the Züst.

Mammina smiled, leaned towards me and whispered, 'What a gallant young man. If you ever visit Genoa, come see me. We'll look after you. Courtesy of Mammina.'

When the automobile disappeared, in a final blaze of

bronze, Zio turned and held out his hand. We handed over the money his mother had given us.

During this time, Viola was dreaming. She had not mentioned anything about it, but I found her increasingly distant. She no longer interrupted me, no longer answered her own questions – there were even *silences* between us. I assumed that I had done something wrong, even though I made sure to turn back every time we parted. We saw each other more often, sometimes two or three times a week. We had become inseparable. I was amazed at how easy it was for her to sneak out, but nobody at the villa seemed to pay her any heed. Her father was preoccupied by the orange groves, which were threatened by the looming drought. He consulted obscure meteorological archives, sent daily letters to Genoa and somewhat reluctantly – given his contempt for local superstitions – began to perform ancient rituals for summoning rain. As for Viola's mother, she spent all her time charting, planning and mapping the progress of the Orsini family on the chessboard of Italy's noble families. Her son Stefano, now the eldest, was one of her pawns. He regularly travelled around the country visiting 'gracious families' and meeting with 'important people', because the war would not last forever and she had to plan for the aftermath. Francesco, the youngest, was enrolled in the seminary in Rome. Amid all these absences, Viola could come and go as she pleased.

Her only fear was being caught in the library, which was her father's sanctum sanctorum.

But still the books kept coming. And with them, my world expanded. For the first time in my life, when sculpting, I found myself thinking that my gestures were not orphans. They had been refined by thousands who had come before me and would be further refined by those who came after me. Each hammer blow came from afar and would echo down the ages. I tried to explain this to Paragraph. He looked at me wide-eyed and then advised me to stop sucking deadly nightshade berries.

At first, I was perplexed by Viola's sudden mood change; later, I grew worried. Towards the end of the summer, in an attempt to atone for my imaginary sins, I agreed to lie on a gravestone. She looked surprised and she laughed with her old insouciance. She found two graves set close enough for us to hold hands. Plagued by superstitions and by irrational fears, I had to force myself to lie down – was I inciting my own death? But then the sky took hold of me, and the cypress trees, like abandoned paintbrushes amid a glaze of stars. I felt Viola's hand in mine. Again and again, I let go, for the sheer pleasure of taking it back.

'Are you scared?' she said after a long silence.

'No. I'm not scared when I'm with you.'

'Are you sure?'

'I'm sure.'

'Good. Because that's not my hand you're holding.'

I let out a howl and jumped up from the gravestone. Viola laughed so hard she had tears in her eyes.

'Very funny! Can't we just spend some time together like ordinary people? Do you have to be so weird?'

Viola's tears continued, but she was not laughing now.

'What's the matter? I'm sorry, I didn't mean it. It was funny, honestly! Did you see the way I jumped? You really got me!'

She took several deep breaths then raised her hand. 'It's not you. It's me.'

'What do you mean?'

Wiping away tears with the back of her sleeve, she sat up on the grave and hugged her knees. 'Don't you have dreams, Mimo?'

'My father always said there was no point. Dreams don't come true, that's why they're called dreams.'

'But you do have dreams?'

'Of course. I'd like my father to come home from the war. That's a nice dream.'

'What else?'

'I dream of being a great sculptor.'

'Why can't you make that come true?'

'Look at me. I work for an alcoholic, I sleep on a bed of straw, I've never had any money, and most people laugh when they see me.'

'But you are gifted.'

'What makes you think that?'

'Dom Anselmo told my brother Francesco. He knows you do all the sculpting in the workshop.'

'Who told him?'

'Vittorio tells everyone.'

'Vittorio talks too much.'

'Dom Anselmo says that you have a gift. An abnormal gift.'

The first compliment I ever received came with the word 'abnormal' carefully attached.

'I have big dreams for you, Mimo. I want you to create something as beautiful as Fra Angelico. Or Michelangelo – after all, you are named after him. I want the whole world to know your name.'

'Do you have any dreams?'

'I'd like to go to university.'

'To university? To do what?'

Viola took a piece of paper out of her pocket and handed it to me. She had been waiting for this question all night.

The article is still in my trunk, under the cell window, tucked into the issue of *FMR* that was never published. The paper is yellow now. I have not opened it in a very long time – it will probably crumble to dust when someone touches it. It's an article from *La Stampa*, dated 10 August 1918. Gabriele D'Annunzio had just led the 87th air squadron – known as La Serenissima – on a flight over Vienna. An impossible flight for a squadron of biplanes – more than a thousand kilometres, lasting seven hours and ten minutes – that had taken the Austrians by surprise. But rather than bombing the city, D'Annunzio had dropped leaflets urging the residents to surrender. *We Italians do not make war on children, on old people, on women. We are making war on your government, the enemy of national liberty, on your blind, stubborn, cruel government that can give you neither peace nor bread and feeds you hatred and illusions.*

D'Annunzio was not a pilot; he was a poet and an adventurer. It was to Natale Palli that he owed his safe arrival and his return. The same Natale Palli who, some months later, would fall asleep in the snow on Mount Pourri after crash-landing and trying to walk back to the valley. He would never wake. He would forever be part of the legend of those who first slipped the surly bonds of earth. And Viola, quite simply, wanted to do the same.

Since childhood, Viola had longed to fly.

'You want to fly?'

'Yes.'

'With wings?'

'Yes.'

'I've never seen an aeroplane in my life. I have never seen a person fly. How do you plan to go about it?'

'I'll go to university.'

'Have you talked to your parents?'

'Yes.'

'And they agreed?'

'No.'

Viola was exhausting. The sky was streaked with strange clouds that trailed their shadowy fingers over the cemetery.

'How do you expect to fly if you have to study and they refuse to let you?'

'My parents are old. I don't mean old in years; they are from a different world. They don't realise that in the future people will fly the way we ride horses now. That women will have moustaches and men will wear jewellery. The world of my parents is dead. You are afraid of zombies, but it is their zombie world you should really fear. It's dead but it keeps moving, because nobody has told it that it's dead. That is why it is so dangerous. It is collapsing in on itself.'

'Can we go somewhere else? Those clouds are strange.'

'They're not "clouds", they're altocumuli. I'm never going to persuade my parents to let me go to university by pleading. "I never went to university," my mother says, "and look where I am today." She was born a baronessa and ended up a marchesa. Some ambition! No, I have to show them, prove to them that I'm serious. I want to fly *now*. Well, as soon as possible.'

'How?'

'I've been studying aviation for two years. I've read everything I can find. I've pored over Leonardo's sketches of flying machines, and I think we should be able to make a simple wing mechanism. It doesn't have to go far – as long as I can fly a hundred metres, maybe two. That will shut them up. People will hear about me. I'll be allowed to attend a men's university.'

'Can't you choose something else? Something simpler? I mean, you can already travel through time and turn yourself into a bear, isn't that enough?'

'It's all part of the same thing, it's all connected.'

'I don't understand.'

'I just need you to help me. You'll understand later.'

'I'm a sculptor, Viola. I'd like to help but...'

'You said Vittorio is a wood-turner? The mono-wing I have in mind is built from wood and fabric. The only important thing is to find the balance between lightness and stability and come up with a system to steer and counterbalance. A series of ropes and pulleys,' Viola said, as I stared at her, bewildered. 'The problem with da Vinci's designs is that they require superhuman strength to operate. A strange mistake from someone who understood anatomy. But our wing will be easier to build, because I'm light – I am light, don't you think?'

'Very light. But this plan of yours... it's completely insane.'

'That's what the newspapers said about D'Annunzio. They called his air raid "the crazy flight". So will you help me? Will you help me fly?'

'Yes,' I sighed.

'Swear.'

'I swear.'

'Again.'

'I already swore I would – what do you want me to do, cross my heart?'

'Adults cross their hearts all the time, but it doesn't stop them from betraying and stabbing each other. We are going to do things differently.'

She took my hand and placed it on her heart. It was one of the most extraordinary feelings of my life. Viola didn't have breasts, she never really would, but their absence filled my palm just as surely as some of the women I would later know. Then, she placed her hand on my heart.

'Mimo Vitaliani, do you swear before God, if He exists, to help Viola Orsini fly and never to let her down?'

'I swear.'

'And I, Viola Orsini, swear to help Mimo Vitaliani become the world's greatest sculptor, on a par with Michelangelo whose name he bears, and never to let him down.'

For an instant, Viola and I are the same size. We are almost fourteen. We are exactly the same height. It will not last: she knows it, I know it; *we* know it – I like saying 'we'. A second from now, Viola will still be growing, soaring skywards. And I will be left here on the ground. So, for an endless moment, we stare into each other's eyes, amazed by this fleeting equality in the darkness of a cemetery and the colours baked in the heat of the day. I almost find myself believing that nothing will ever change. But already forces are at work, cells are multiplying, bones are extending, and molecule by molecule, Viola is growing away from me.

A saint is weeping. He is not yet a saint – but that is a minor detail. Standing on a plateau very different from the valleys he has traversed, he sheds tears of exhaustion or perhaps relief. He has not wept since the night they took away his closest friend, the man for whom he was prepared to die. He was prepared to die, but not on the night he denied his friend three times before cockcrow.

His tears trickle into a cleft in the rock. And because he is no ordinary man, because the friend he betrayed was no ordinary man, Pietro's tears pass through the rock, the *pietra* whose name he bears, and are transformed into a miraculous spring. Soon, this plateau, on which nothing grows but stone, will be filled with people and orange groves. A more scientific proposition would emphasise the constantly shifting bedrock of limestone karst that is conducive to wellsprings erupting where there were none, but science doesn't detract from the miracle, it merely phrases it in a poetry all its own. The result is the same: the hydrography of the plateau is essential for understanding Pietra d'Alba. Water has patiently shaped the destiny of the plateau and those who live here. Asked to explain its purpose, the inhabitants would say 'drinking and irrigation'. In fact, the correct answer is 'jealousy and devastation'.

In Pietra d'Alba, as elsewhere, he who understands water understands Man.

The morning after Viola and I made our solemn oath in the cemetery, I went looking for Paragraph to tell him that we would need his help. He was not at the workshop. He didn't appear until two hours later, dressed to the nines – which in his case meant a clean shirt – and accompanied by Anna, the little Giordano girl. He had formally asked her to accompany him for the day. Accompany him where, I asked, and they both laughed – of course I didn't know, I was 'Il Francese'. I grabbed Paragraph by the throat, 'Just try calling me Francese again!', and we rolled around in the straw under the impatient eye of Anna, until Paragraph sent me sprawling over a hay bale. There were no hard feelings, and the two of them invited me to go with them.

'Go where?'

'To the lake, idiot.'

After coursing underground for five kilometres, surfacing here and there, including the drinking trough in front of our barn, the miraculous spring spilled into a lake at the foot of the eastern valley slope. The lake belonged to the Orsini family. Each year, on 15 September, the family invited the whole village to swim there. It was quite simply a beautiful day. Except that in Italy, and all the more so in Pietra d'Alba, nothing was ever simple.

I never had the opportunity to see Caruso perform on stage – he died three years later in his native Naples. But via the magic of the nascent technology of sound recording, I would later hear him sing the role of Pagliacci, a man betrayed by his wife who attempts to hide his sorrows beneath the face of a clown. *Vesti la giubba.* Put on the jacket, put on a smile to hide the pain and all will be well. I could not help but wonder whether Leoncavallo had known the Orsini family. Whether he had bathed in their bloody lake before writing that aria. *Ridi, Pagliaccio, e ognun applaudirà.* Laugh, Pagliacci, and everyone will applaud.

The annual swim on 15 September was the laugh of a sad clown. A painted face put on to entertain the hoi polloi. For if the lake belonged to the Orsini family, with its glassy green surface and ten metres of shoreline, it was bordered on every side by fields that belonged to their sworn enemies, the Gambale family from the neighbouring valley.

True to their reputation, the villagers of Pietra d'Alba vied with each other to explain the feud. The Gambale family had been tenant farmers of the Orsinis and shamelessly stolen from them. The Orsini family had irrigated their orange groves with the blood of the Gambales. There was talk of rape, murder and betrayal. But the cause mattered little; the feud was as ancient and as impossible to wear down as the rock that formed the valleys. The Orsinis owned the lake but could not draw water from it to irrigate their groves because the Gambales would not give them right of way across their land. The Orsinis could access their lake only via a path that they owned, which meandered through the forest. The only solution would have been to pump the water through a system of pipes along this tortuous path, which, as Viola explained one day, was 'technically possible, but economically stupid'. Pump maintenance, power supply and the steepness of the slope made the operation too complex. To irrigate their orchards, the Orsinis had to make do with a resurgence of the miraculous spring on their property and reservoirs to collect rainwater. What was even more absurd was that the Gambale family, who grew flowers in the neighbouring valley, had no use for the lake. They left the fields that surrounded it fallow, their sole function to taunt the Orsinis. The only way that the Orsinis could retaliate was the annual swim on 15 September, when the whole village would troop through the forest. A squadron of Gambale labourers, armed with rifles, were posted in the surrounding fields to make sure that no one trespassed on Gambale lands, and the villagers kept to a ten-metre stretch of beach. The Orsinis responded with several platoons of labourers whose job it was to keep an eye on the Gambale workers. The tradition had existed for barely twenty years, yet, miraculously, things had never got out of hand.

The parched summer of 1918 served only to inflame the wound. The Orsini branch of the miraculous spring had dried up and, despite endless negotiations, the two families had been unable to reach an agreement. Given that the whole world was at war, it seemed only natural that a war would be waged here too. The Gambales vowed that not a drop of Orsini water would cross their land, and if the wind should blow it towards them, they would plant a hedge of tall cypresses. In retaliation, the Orsini, supported by the noble families in the region, let it be known that anyone who bought flowers from the Gambales at the markets in Genoa and Savona would lose their aristocratic clientele. Flowers rotted in warehouses; orange groves dried up and shrivelled. But the honour of both families was preserved. And on 15 September, the villagers laughed, dived, splashed and lightly fondled each other under the water.

By the time we arrived, the Orsini family was already enthroned. Needless to say, they did not bathe, but benevolently surveyed the scene, with only the occasional gesture of favour or disapprobation. Viola, squeezed into a turquoise dress, stood sulking in the background. I had known her for some time now and assumed that she hadn't told me about the annual swim because she was ashamed. From the dizzy height of my thirteen summers – and I use the word 'height' with the scorn I have experienced all my life – I did not yet understand the turmoil that roiled beneath the surface.

Shedding my clothes as I went, I raced to the lake and dived in, oblivious to the peculiar body I had been lumbered with since birth. The water must truly have been miraculous, because once submerged I looked like everyone else. With only my head sticking out of the water, I was tall, powerful and muscular. Despite the blazing heat, the water was still cool.

From the shade of their large parasols, the Orsini family watched us as they sipped their wine and ate fruit. Viola lurked on the edge of the forest, on the threshold of a childhood that, with every passing second, she was leaving behind. Her father, the Marchese, was a towering figure whose long face was made longer by a curious coiffure – a tall tuft of grey hair cropped short at the sides. Stefano, the eldest son, a stocky boy in a tight-fitting suit, constantly clenched and unclenched his fists, as though to exorcise some force that could find no outlet. He sported a moustache that his mother would force him to shave off a few months later, on the grounds that it looked 'Southern Italian'. The great tragedy of his life was that he had the dark curls of a little girl, something he attempted to disguise with a patient and liberal application of hair oil. Only Francesco, the youngest son, was missing, caught up in the spiritual ecstasy of the Vatican, six hundred kilometres away.

I was not yet familiar with Pagliacci, Leporello, Don Giovanni. I knew nothing of the lessons to be learned from opera. I did not yet realise that we laugh merely to heighten our tragedy – a lesson that Alberto, after his inimitable fashion, had tried to instil in me: *don't get too big for your breeches*. It was Alberto I saw emerging from the forest as I swam past the young girl smiling at me. Paragraph and I had suggested that Zio come with us, only to be dismissed with a wave of his hand as he slumped in his armchair, macerating his dark thoughts in the middle of the workshop. Even from a distance, I could see he was in good spirits. He walked towards the Marchese, making a series of exaggerated bows that clearly infuriated Stefano, who grabbed him by the collar and dragged him in front of his father. Zio Alberto handed something to the Marchese and gestured. The two men shielded their eyes with their hands and stared out over the lake. And, fool that I was, I waved.

Instantly, Stefano raced down to the shore and jabbed a finger towards me. 'You there!'

I stepped out of the water and, as everyone stared, my imagined body shrank to its abnormal size. Stefano viciously grabbed my ear and dragged me over to his father, enthroned on a wicker chair on a little hill. I instantly recognised what was in his lap. It was the most recent book Viola had lent me: a late but sumptuously illustrated edition of *De historia stirpium commentarii insignes*, a history of herbal plants by the sixteenth-century Bavarian botanist Leonhart Fuchs. The beauty of the woodcut illustrations left me speechless. So much so that, though I could not read a word of Latin, I had not returned the book to Viola straight away.

'I found this among his things,' said Alberto. 'And I realised that he must have stolen it from Your Lordship's library when we were working on your roof, given that I have no books in my house, and I don't know anyone who has.'

'Is that so, my boy? Did you take that book home?'

Viola, standing on the edge of the forest, turned pale.

'Yes, signor.'

'Your Lordship,' corrected Stefano Orsini, giving me a kick.

'Yes, Your Lordship. I meant no harm. I did not intend to steal it, merely to read it.'

By now, the whole village had gathered by the lake's edge to watch the spectacle. A dank curiosity that smelled of mud. Even the Gambale family had inched closer to see what was going on. The Marchese stroked his chin. His wife feverishly whispered into his ear, but he cut her off with a curt gesture.

'It is far from shameful to wish to rise above one's condition through the acquisition of knowledge,' he observed. 'What is reprehensible, on the other hand, is appropriating the property of others, albeit temporarily. The deed must therefore be punished.'

He had said these last words louder, so that they would be clearly heard by the Gambale family. Signor and Signora Orsini had a whispered conversation about the nature of the sentence: forty strokes of the cane were demanded by the Marchesa and Stefano, while the Marchese favoured ten. I think he was flattered by my interest in the library he had patiently created and which was regularly supplied by merchants from around the country. According to Viola, her father rarely went into the library. But for the *magnifici* – the noble families of Genoa – the size of one's library was no laughing matter.

Since an example had to be made in front of the Gambale family, they finally agreed on twenty lashes. I was wearing only a pair of canvas trousers that clung to my legs, and Stefano abruptly stripped me. With tears in her eyes, Viola smiled at me before turning away. Stefano snapped a soft branch, stripped the bark, spat into his hands and laid into my buttocks and my lower back. Luckily the only trees around were pines, which make for poor switches. I took the beating without so much as flinching, struggling as I was with a greater agony: that of my body being exposed to the avid gaze of this rural coliseum, as though my body had not already punished me a thousand times over. Stefano gave me twenty-five lashes, pretending to lose count. I never took my eyes off Zio Alberto. At first, he smiled triumphantly, then I saw his jaw twitch, and, as the last blows fell, he looked as though he was being beaten.

Silence descended, the exhausted silence that follows coitus. *All that fuss for nothing*, people thought, while also thinking, *Let's do it again.* Everyone stood frozen. It was left to me to make the first move; my exit from the stage before the curtain fell would liberate my audience, leaving them free to cough, to scratch, to slump back in their seats before the next act.

Clenching my teeth, I pulled up my trousers. I confess that, for a second, I felt like crying. *Laugh, Pagliacci, and everyone will applaud.* But then I met Stefano's mocking gaze and decided I would have my revenge. I could have joined the Gambale family, stabbed one of the Orsinis, chopped down their precious orange trees at night, poisoned their water. But Viola was right: this world was dead. Mine would be a twentieth-century revenge; my vengeance would be modern. I would sit at the tables of those who had scorned me. I would become their equal and, if I could, surpass them. My revenge would not be to kill them, but to grace them with the same condescending smile they gave me that day.

It is possible that, when it comes down to it, I owe my career to the fact that I bared my arse to the people of Pietra d'Alba.

O ne of the most beautiful statues ever created – some would say the most beautiful – smiles upon all those who visit her. On 21 May 1972, she smiles on Laszlo Toth, a Hungarian geologist who has just paused in front of her in the Vatican. There is something extraordinary in this moment, in the look they exchange. As though she *knows*. And her smile, that Pentecost Sunday, is all the more troubling.

It is difficult to imagine that she was once just a mountain. The mountain later became the Polvaccio quarry. A block of marble taken from it was given to a man with a rough face, scarred by a fight with a jealous colleague. True to his philosophy, the man chiselled away the stone to free the form already within. And from the stone a woman appeared, exquisitely beautiful, bowed over her son who lies in her lap, abandoned in a death-like sleep. A man, a chisel, a hammer, some pumice stone. How little was required to create the greatest masterpiece of the Italian Renaissance. The most beautiful statue of all time had lain hidden within a rock. Michelangelo Buonarroti searched and screamed but never found another like it in a single block of marble. His later pietàs look like rough sketches of his first.

In the half-light of the basilica, Laszlo gazes at the *Pietà*. He is smartly dressed today; this is a momentous occasion. He has slicked back his shoulder-length hair and run a comb through his goatee beard. Granted, wearing a bow tie, he looks a bit like a lunatic. But he is not a lunatic, quite the contrary. He has been in Rome for only a few days, during which he has written several times to the Pope, requesting an audience. Pope Paul VI is inexplicably silent. Laszlo wants the audience simply to share an important piece of news: he is the risen Christ. What pope worthy of the name would not want to hear such news?

Then, in a gesture that some of the witnesses describe as abrupt and others as quietly composed, he takes a geologist's hammer from his pocket and, shouting, '*Io sono il Cristo!*', leaps onto the *Pietà*, a work of preternatural beauty that has smiled upon visitors for four hundred and seventy-three years, and hits it fifteen times. Fifteen hammer blows – it takes a long time before dumbfounded witnesses manage to neutralise him, something that takes at least seven men. The

Virgin in Michelangelo's *Pietà* has lost an arm, her nose, a fragment of one eyelid and is battered and bruised. If many in the crowd don't have the presence of mind to react, they have the presence of mind to pick up the marble fragments and take them home. Overcome with remorse, some will send the fragments back – but they are not the majority.

Laszlo Toth is deemed not to be responsible for his actions and isn't jailed, but extradited after two years in an Italian hospital. Where the general public is concerned, the case is closed. Meanwhile, experts ponder the connection between Laszlo's belief that he is the risen Christ and his attack on the *Pietà*. The Pope slighted Laszlo, who was perhaps angered by this. But the marmoreal Virgin and her dead son did nothing to harm him. Unless one believes that he was in the presence of absolute genius, closer to God than Laszlo Toth will ever be. Unless he considered the *Pietà* to be unfair competition, proof of his imposture – for who could be closer to God than His own son? – and wanted to destroy it.

So begins a part of the case unknown to the general public. Interest wanes – after all, the victim was carved from stone and no one is going to spend their time reading an investigative report, especially when a few senior officials at the Vatican contact senior officers in the *carabinieri* and politely suggest that certain pages of the report are irrelevant. Pages which reveal that Toth had not just arrived in Italy, but had been living in the country for ten months. That he had spent some considerable time in northern Italy, visiting churches around Turin. A detailed record of his travels suggests that he was circling the Sacra di San Michele, as though searching for something whose exact location he did not know. As though he, too, had heard of *her*, the work that so troubles those who see it.

The *Pietà* in the Vatican is restored and cleaned – only careful scrutiny reveals the joins, and because of the Hungarian geologist, the sculpture can only be admired now through bulletproof glass. The incident has been relegated to history. But experts believe that she was not the original target. That in his attempt to eliminate anything that contested with his claims to divinity, Toth had set his sights on the *Vitaliani Pietà*. And when he could not find it, attacked that of Michelangelo. A second choice.

If this is indeed the case, if there exists a work of art more divine than that of Michelangelo, then it can be considered a weapon. And the men of the Vatican are doubtless thinking: *We were wise to hide her.*

Viola and I are fifteen years old. Paragraph and Emanuele, standing opposite, are eighteen. And then there is Hector. This is our time. The time of youth and its dreams of lightness. Time to fly.

It is warm for October. I can taste salt air. The libeccio blows in from the sea, up the vertiginous rockface to the walls of Pietra d'Alba, all the way to the rampart walk on which we are standing, mere centimetres from the void. A night of pirates and of conspiracies. Months of working through the night, of studies and of infinite patience. The maiden flight of our mono-wing. I refused to allow Viola to try it, deeming it too dangerous. We argued in front of Paragraph, who looked petrified, no doubt fearing that she would turn herself into a bear. But Viola did not turn into a bear and agreed to give up her place. Because we have

Hector with us. A brave lad, always cheerful, always ready to help. Hector feared nothing, not even jumping fifty metres into the void. He was of the calibre of pilots who, less than fifty years later, would fly machines that were part-aeroplane part-rocket at six times the speed of sound. A mere fifty years separate Gabriele D'Annunzio's biplane and the North American X-15. The futurists were right – this was the century of speed.

We exchange one last look, wish Hector good luck.

Hector takes wing.

After my public thrashing, the hollow stump stood empty for a few days, then once again began to fill up with books. Viola insisted her father would never notice a few missing books in a library of three thousand volumes. The important thing was that I no longer keep them at Zio Alberto's place. One night, Viola led me to a deserted barn deep in the forest on the western slopes of the plateau. The way she moved through the forest was strange: she flowed like a wave between the tall green sentinels that soundlessly let her pass, while they regularly pricked and prodded at me, sounding me out – *Who is this?* – and Viola would patiently retrace her steps to free me from my prison of brambles, sweetbriar or wild asparagus. 'Leave him alone, he's with me.' And, gradually, I was allowed to move freely through the thick forest. I almost missed the ominous peace of the cemetery.

The barn consisted of three roughly built stone walls set against a rocky outcrop. The tiled roof was still intact, except for a hole caused by a falling rock which Viola had patched with branches and some oilcloth. This would be our headquarters when not at the cemetery and where I would leave books. Most importantly, it was here that we would meet to work on our common project: a flying machine.

Nothing would have been possible without Paragraph. By now, my friend had opened his own woodworking studio in Zio's barn, and business was brisk. Zio did not say anything, a high-mindedness born of the percentage Paragraph paid him. From that point, I did most of the sculptural commissions. Alberto hated me, I hated him, but we had to lean on one another if we were not to fall. Without me, the studio was finished. Without him, I would have to leave Pietra d'Alba, and Pietra d'Alba meant Viola. So I endured the bullying, the humiliation, the taunts of '*pezzo di merda*' and 'your mother calling you Michelangelo was a cruel joke'. I did not even care about the monies he deducted from the wages he never paid. Perhaps, in our own way, we were happy – like half the couples in the village and far beyond.

As I expected, when I told Paragraph about Viola's project, he laughed in my face. 'Are you insane? I'd never work for a witch.'

'She said she would be very grateful. It would not be a difficult job for you – you have a gift for turning wood.'

'Tell her to find someone else. And, honestly – flying? If men were meant to fly, don't you think the Good Lord would have given us wings?'

'I'll tell Viola what you said. But from what I know of her, she'll be furious. And, as you told me yourself, the last time she got really angry with someone, all that was ever found was a single shoe...'

Paragraph gave a nervous laugh, but stopped when he saw my funereal expression. 'Do you really think she could hurt me?'

'No, of course not,' I quickly reassured him. 'But, still...'

'What is it?'

'Well, if I were you, I would probably steer clear of the forest from now on. Just to be safe. I know you like going there with Anna... And I would probably not go out at night. Or alone. If you *really* have to go alone, tell someone where you're going. Just in case. But you're in no danger. It's just a precaution. I'm off to see Viola. I'll try and explain that it's not really your fault, that you just don't want to work with a witch.'

'Wait! All right, all right, don't take it like that. I'll help. If you pay for the wood. And Emanuele has to be involved too, whether she likes it or not.'

We agreed to meet once a week in the barn. At first, Paragraph was suspicious, but he quickly grew so fond of Viola that, a month later, he confessed that he had begun to doubt the story about the bear. 'She's so small and delicate, how could she possibly have a bear inside her?' I had come to realise that Viola could easily encompass several bears, a whole menagerie, a circus with a big top, a stock of gunpowder, biplanes, vast oceans and high mountains. Viola was our creator; with a click of her fingers or a smile, she organised our lives as she saw fit.

Viola took charge of the theoretical aspects of the project, I was responsible for the diagrams, and Paragraph and Emanuele dealt with the execution. Our first mono-wing went through various models and maquettes. The extent of Viola's knowledge at only fifteen was astounding. She spoke German and English as well as her native Italian. She told us that she had exhausted the skills of several tutors and terrified her parents by insisting on more qualified teachers. It was because there were no qualified tutors in Pietra d'Alba that Viola was determined to go to university – this was the very reason our conspiracy existed. Viola devoured all the science books she could lay hands on and would talk to herself while wandering in circles after one of our scale models failed to fly. She had read and reread Otto Lilienthal's *Der Vogelflug als Grundlage der Fliegekunst*, a book about the influence of bird flight on the construction of a flying machine. In the 1890s, Lilienthal had repeatedly managed to glide almost three hundred metres. We were mesmerised by this idea until Viola explained that this was how he had died. She reassured us that it would not happen to her, since she had identified the weak point of Lilienthal's *Storm Wing*: its lift was compromised by the hole in the middle that accommodated the pilot. Our wing should therefore combine elements of da Vinci's and Lilienthal's: maximum lift without interruption to structural integrity, steered by the pilot's body movements, requiring no physical force. The wing had to be simultaneously light yet rigid. She left it to Paragraph to come up with a solution. After each meeting, Viola returned to her world, and we to ours.

It would be almost a year before the night of the full moon when we could finally gaze upon the result of our labours.

The war is over!

One autumn night, Emanuele came back to the workshop, gesticulating wildly. He had already visited all the houses in the village, and even the Villa Orsini; we were the last ones in his path. For once, we did not need Paragraph to translate his gibberish.

The war is over!

The news seemed of little interest to Zio Alberto. When I pointed out that business might pick up now, he simply said, 'You'll see, when all the men come back from the front and those still fit to work are scrabbling to find jobs, there won't be much work for us. Who needs a stonemason when you can barely afford to eat?'

It was a rare moment of lucidity on the part of Zio Alberto. But Paragraph and I did not care; we raced down to the village through the biting November cold so we could dance and cheer in the square and sing, sing *the war is over*, because everyone believed it was.

One night in the summer of 1919, some months before our maiden flight, Pietra d'Alba was woken by screams. A huge fire was blazing near the Villa Orsini. Paragraph and I hurriedly dressed and raced to see. The orange groves were burning, and a crowd had gathered outside the gate. Manure had been splattered against the walls and the gate. It took a few moments for us to realise that several *braccianti* – day labourers – had riled up the local farmers and turned them against their employer. We had heard vague rumours of riots and strikes elsewhere, but now the seething rage of militants had infected our patch of countryside. Workers demanded a share of land and better wages. Standing on the steps of the villa, the Marchese and his son Stefano, with a glint in their eyes and a rifle in each hand, did not quail before this socialist zeal. Between them, they managed to contain a crowd that could have easily swept them aside were they not paralysed by the atavistic yoke of submission. Behind them stood the Marchesa, deathly pale but dignified. Standing next to her, Viola curiously surveyed the scene, her hands behind her back, her face flushed from the burning groves. The men were intoxicated by the smell of smoke and orange zest.

Someone suggested fetching the mayor – but he had decamped to avoid having to take sides. At two o'clock in the morning, a horseman left the back of the house and rode off to Genoa at breakneck speed. Meanwhile, the rioters discussed their demands with the Marchese and Stefano. While the former was prepared to consider a modest increase in wages, the latter bellowed that the family were not prepared to part with another lira and that he was quite prepared to drag those who opposed him to hell itself. The rival groups called each other capitalist shirkers and Bolshevik vermin. Shortly before dawn, the blaze subsided, the revolution was tiring, it was time to get some sleep. Early the following morning, negotiations resumed. Some fifty trees had been burned, and the astonished villagers discovered a colour they had only read about in newspapers – ash grey. Arturo Gambale and his two sons arrived and offered to mediate. Stefano Orsini said he would rather die than talk to a Gambale. The eldest, Orazio, stepped forward and said he would be happy to help. The tense exchange was interrupted by a dust storm on the horizon.

I was there at that moment, having had a short sleep. Ever since I had arrived in Pietra d'Alba, I had thought of it as a precarious paradise, where a person might be publicly beaten but was more or less protected from the upheaval tearing the world apart. That morning, I realised my mistake.

Deep down, my mother and I were not as far apart as I had thought. Our windows opened onto the same infernos.

The cloud of dust dispersed to reveal a convoy of about a dozen motor vehicles. The moment they saw this, the Gambales fled. The convoy turned onto the road that led to Villa Orsini and hurtled towards the crowd. The first automobile hit a rioter who tried to stand in its way. He rolled on his side and never got up again.

Men, some wearing black shirts, leapt from the vehicles: this was one of the first *squadre d'azione*, militias made up of Fascists, lunatics and war veterans who felt victory had been snatched from them and who would soon sow terror throughout Italy. Over the past two years, Stefano had worked hard and, to his credit, he had made the right friends.

With the swiftness of a blade, the *squadristi* charged the crowd. The shouting continued, shots were fired and I did not hang around to see what happened. The following day, whispers in the village claimed that eight people had been killed, all of them day labourers. Their bodies were never found. Some suggested they had been dragged into the forest and fed to a certain bear. For a few days, Paragraph eyed Viola strangely, but it passed. The mayor made a public speech condemning these intolerable events that came hard on the heels of the barbarous war from which the world was only just beginning to recover. At least the war made us more dignified and upstanding men, he thundered. An investigation would be launched and justice would be done.

The war is over! The war is over!

There was no investigation.

Viola and I were fifteen years old. Paragraph and Emanuele, standing opposite, were eighteen. And then there was Hector. Hector who had just taken to the wing, brave Hector, with his big, simple-minded grin, who feared nothing. Hector flew and, encouraged by our whoops of joy, he picked up speed. Then the wing began to shake; it pitched sharply and turned over. Hector fell into the canopy and became tangled in the straps. 'Pull up! Pull up!' we screamed – but what was the point? Hector was deaf and Viola, being a talented engineer, already knew that her wing would not fly.

We didn't find his body until the next day. As luck would have it, this was a Sunday, the only time when Viola could be with us during the day, since no one paid her any notice. Her father was roaming his estate, her mother was writing her letters, while Stefano was off in some town or other, scheming with angry men like himself. No one ever knew what or who made him angry. He was born angry.

The wing had snapped into three pieces, its leather was shredded, and it now lay on the forest floor below the village. Hector was spreadeagled in the undergrowth amid the smell of humus and mushrooms. It was not a pretty sight.

His skull had shattered on a rock. We could hear a distant fanfare. Somewhere, a brass band was practising for the first anniversary of the armistice – a rough-and-ready requiem for the fallen. Hector, the fifth member of our group. It was sad to see him like this, even if among his many talents, as well as his unshakeable courage, Hector was immortal. We had built him to simulate the weight and balance of a human body. That lovable pumpkin head, which Viola had stolen from the family cellar, had watched us work for weeks from a corner of the barn. His body was made up of old clothes and crudely articulated planks.

'A year's work for nothing,' said Paragraph. Viola, with an enthusiasm that I found surprising, pointed out that the greatest experiments always begin with failure. So we would do well to learn from Hector, she said. Change the pumpkin and start over.

Zio Alberto was right: we had very little work in the early months of 1920. The victorious nations were fighting over the carrion of the vanquished. The tensions of the previous year spread like a plague throughout the country, following the same pattern that I had witnessed: demands for justice were ruthlessly suppressed by groups in the pay of the fledgling Fasci Italiani di Combattimento, founded by a former socialist in Milan. Viola and I saw each other almost every night, right under the noses of her family. When her mother came upon her in the garden one night, heading to the cemetery, Viola pretended she was sleepwalking.

At first, I thought the Orsinis were a little naïve, relics of another era, but Viola corrected me. They were dangerous. I was never sure whether she hated her family or simply felt alienated from them. The unintentional farce of the Orsinis, like that of the greats of this world, masked powerful, turbulent currents. Without a whit of embarrassment, Viola told me a popular story that circulated among the servants in the villa. Her father had once gone into one of the unused rooms in the house and found the gardener servicing the Marchesa. She described the scene in great detail; her mother was bent over a small chess table, her skirts hiked up, and the gardener standing behind her, his muddy trousers pooled around his ankles. Seeing the Marchese, the pair were petrified, but he merely smiled affably and said: 'Ah, Damiano, there you are. When you've finished, could you meet me in the orange groves? I'm afraid some of the plants are showing signs of sooty mould.'

The offhand reaction of the Marchese quickly spread around the estate. That night, at the local taverna, the scene was re-enacted in the form of a harlequinade. After a few drinks, the gardener reprised his role with a table standing in for his lover, and everyone agreed that the whole thing was hilarious.

A week later, Damiano was found covered in hoarfrost, hanging from an orange tree at the entrance to the estate, clearly visible from the road. In his pocket was a letter explaining that he had money troubles. It did not matter that Damiano could neither read nor write. That was precisely the message.

'Never trust an Orsini,' Viola warned me.

'Not even you?'

'No, you can trust me completely. Do you believe me?'

'Of course.'

'Then you haven't understood a word of what I just said!'

The year stretched out between occasional work in the studio, nights when the dead stubbornly refused to speak to us, and our efforts to rebuild a wing. Now when we were at the cemetery, Viola would only lie on the grave of young Tommaso Baldi, convinced that one day he would whisper and reveal the entrance to the subterranean kingdom where he and his flute had lost their way. Sometimes, she managed to persuade me to join her. These were the times when we were closest, huddled together, adrift on our raft of limestone. From time to time, Viola would even drift off and, feeling her sleeping body against mine, I all but forgot to fear the wrath of the dead.

The deserted barn in the forest was still our workshop. Viola came up with a new design for the wing, Paragraph a new way of bending a single piece of wood. Hector made two further test flights, died and just as quickly came back to life. Emanuele would often fall asleep in a corner of the barn, his face lit up with a beatific smile, exhausted from running around after the postman all day, especially since Old Angelo now entrusted him with more and more letters.

That year, Viola grew quickly and before long was two heads taller than me. Paragraph, having completely forgotten his fear of her inner she-bear, told her that, compared to Anna Giordano, she didn't have much of a balcony. Viola said – I still remember her exact words – that a balcony like that brought nothing but trouble, especially since it was bound to collapse in time. Paragraph asked why she couldn't talk like everyone else.

It is true that Viola did not have breasts, but she was leaving the rough edges and angles of adolescence behind. This was the polishing phase, perhaps the most important in sculpture. Her elbows and her knees no longer stuck out when she sat down in the barn to think. Her movements acquired an arabesque poetry. Her moods, on the other hand, were as jagged as the mountain peaks. She was simultaneously demanding, impatient, cajoling, furious, pleading. She was exhausting.

In the summer of 1920, Viola's mood darkened. As a group, the four of us were inseparable. Much to my annoyance, Viola could even understand Emanuele. The twins and I did everything we could to distract her, amuse her, but it was futile. One night, she deigned to explain. 'I'll soon be sixteen and I still can't fly. I'll never be Marie Curie.'

'What does that matter? You're you, Viola, and that's much better.'

Viola rolled her eyes and stalked out without troubling to close the barn door, leaving us to speculate on the virtues of this mysterious *Marrycury*.

The financial plight of the workshop deteriorated. On three occasions, a series of begging letters had allowed Zio Alberto to wring some money from his mother, but then the stream dried up. At such times, we had to rely on the munificence of the villagers, on what little we could steal from vegetable gardens or on the unexpected windfall of some urgent commission. With a determined air, Alberto would pick up his tools and announce that he was going back to sculpting. Really. He would stand in front of the block of Carrara marble that he kept in reserve and had always refused to sell, despite offers from sculptors in Genoa. For in its marmoreal veins, he swore, lay his *magnum opus*. He would circle the block purposefully, spend all day going round and round; with each revolution, his shoulders slumped, he would uncork a bottle and swig from it as he continued to spin. He would mutter to himself, hurl inaudible insults. One day when I came into the workshop to clear out the dead soldiers, I thought I heard him ranting about *that old whore*.

'Why are you looking at me like that?' he roared when he spotted me. 'You think you're better than everyone else, don't you? Just because your name is Michelangelo and you can sculpt something vaguely recognisable...'

I ducked and narrowly avoided the bottle he threw. There was still wine in it, a sign that he was seriously angry. It shattered against a dolphin Zio had started and abandoned a month earlier – a commission from Dom Anselmo that my uncle had decided not to fulfil. At heart, Zio Alberto was fiercely anti-clerical, because all through his childhood, the parish priest of San Luca in Genoa had told him his mother was a succubus, a fallen woman, a lost soul. This was perhaps the root of all Zio Alberto's difficulties. He was constantly trying to reconcile two visions of his mother, the one that he worshipped and the one that, as a boy, other children and secular and religious authorities had spat in his face. *Mammina* or *filthy whore, filthy whore* or *Mammina*. And in the uncertain moments, when exhaustion or wisdom made him think *What does it matter if Mammina is a succubus?*, he would sculpt, or visit the nearest brothel and treat the girls like queens.

Suddenly, he was calm. He ran to the little bureau where he kept his papers and handed me the inkwell.

'Here, write this down: *Mammina, winter is fast approaching, and there's a bit of a famine here in the workshop, especially with the two leeches – you cannot imagine how much the dwarf eats, I can't help but wonder where he puts it all. So here I am, asking you for a little help. This will be the last time, I promise, because 1921 will be a good year, I can feel it. I am going to get back to sculpting, I have a beautiful block of Carrara marble and a vision that it might be Romulus and Remus. It is something I need to think about. You have more than enough money to last the rest of your life, and no one knows how you earned it better*

than me since I was in the next room and, if you remember, I was
the one who cleaned your room between shifts. Your loving son.'

Two weeks later, a letter arrived from an address we didn't
know.

> *Egregio Signor Susso,*
> *I regret to inform you that your mother, Signora*
> *Annunziata Susso, died unexpectedly on 21 September*
> *1920 at the age of sixty-three. Might I request that you*
> *contact our offices as soon as possible to expedite the*
> *testamentary dispositions of the deceased, proprietress of*
> *Il Bel Mondo, who has named you as sole legatee.*

Mammina had been knocked down by a tram in the early
hours on her way home from work. She was almost sliced
in two, and her blood watered the streets to which she had
already given so much.

Zio Alberto looked at me, wide-eyed, and when he spoke
there was a quaver in his voice. 'I hope she didn't read my
letter before she died. I didn't mean to be so cruel. Mammina
was a lovely woman...'

It was a question that would haunt him for the rest of his
life, and Zio no longer had much time to sculpt.

Alberto left for Genoa the following day. That night, Viola
burst into the forest barn in a frenzy. We had been on

completely the wrong path, she said. Weight was and always would be the enemy of a flying machine that relied entirely on updraughts and physical human strength. Viola's new hero was Fausto Veranzio – a man after her own heart, since he, too, knew everything. She showed us illustrations of the Homos Volans, a crude form of parachute devised by Veranzio in 6116. Armed with my recently acquired wisdom, I reminded her that da Vinci had previously devised a similar machine. Viola laughed and retorted that da Vinci's machine also had a weight problem since, even supposing it worked, it would crush the pilot when its eighty kilos fell on him during landing. Viola was, to my knowledge, the only person who could criticise the greatest genius of the Renaissance without seeming arrogant. In fact, she was the only one, as far as I know, to criticise the greatest genius of the Renaissance.

Viola wanted to combine the concept of Homo Volans with that of Lilienthal's wing, and to do it immediately. The cellars of the Villa Orsini were stuffed with rolls of fabric acquired to upholster sofas and tailor suits, only to be forgotten as soon as fashions changed. The twins' mother, who was in favour of anything that kept her sons away from the taverna, lent us an old sewing machine. The wing designed by Viola was something between a circle and a rectangle and was controlled by a system of ropes and pulleys. It could be folded and weighed no more than ten kilos. Forty years before anyone else, my friend Viola invented a basic version of paragliding.

We spent the week smuggling out rolls of fabric by night. And since there was no work in Zio Alberto's workshop, we could spend the days cutting and assembling the wing. Viola was increasingly impatient, as though her days were numbered. Then, abruptly, around mid-October, Paragraph stopped coming. He came up with various excuses which I readily accepted, but one evening when he deigned to show up, Viola grabbed him by the collar and, though he was a head taller, she slammed him against the wall.

'We've lost a whole week's work! You'd better have a good excuse.'

Paragraph finally confessed: Anna Giordano was jealous. Viola simply nodded and told him to bring her with him the following night, which he did. Anna and Viola sized each other up. Viola realised that Anna was not a bad girl, with her apple-red cheeks and her irrepressible joie de vivre. Anna, whose cleavage had Emanuele, Paragraph and me ogling, concluded that Viola was no threat because, aside from the long hair and big eyes, she looked like a boy. Anna studied the wing and, deciding that the stitching was of poor quality, offered to help, and so became one of us.

At the beginning of November, Zio still had not come back to the workshop. I got a letter from my mother telling me that she had remarried. *He is a little older than me, but he's nice and he treats me well.* She had recently moved to Brittany. Her letters always triggered the same emotion, a mixture of joy and sadness that was increasingly tinged with anger. Anger at my mother's rudimentary French, her derisory dreams, anger at the social class that my body still inhabited but from which the real Mimo was gradually moving away, relentlessly drawn by Viola into her world, her feverish life in which the stars were only just beyond the reach of our outstretched hands.

One night, as I was heading back from the cemetery, where Viola had been lying on a family grave in the hope of increasing her chances of communicating with the dead, I saw a red light in her bedroom window. We had only just gone our separate ways. I turned back, and in the hollow stump by the crossroads, I found an envelope tied with a green ribbon. The paper was of the finest quality, with an exquisite texture; my name was written in green ink. Inside, a simple message. *Tomorrow lunchtime, at the Hanged Man's Oak.*

I only ever saw Viola during the day on Sundays, and the following day was Thursday. That night, I did not sleep a wink, and in the morning, I set off early. Which was just as well, because on the way I encountered Dom Anselmo on his way back from blessing a new orange grove at the Villa Orsini.

'Ah, Michelangelo, I have been meaning to speak to you. Your uncle is still not back from Genoa, I believe.'

'No, Father.'

'You have a gift, you know.'

An abnormal gift. I bit my lip; I did not want to run the risk of being late. 'Thank you.'

'What are you planning to do with that gift? You're wasting your time with Alberto.'

'I don't know. I'm happy here.'

Dom Anselmo smiled, then looked around. 'Yes, I suppose it is a pleasant place. We each have our place appointed by the Almighty. If yours is here, who am I to say otherwise?'

Fortunately, Dom Anselmo and his metaphysical musings headed towards the village, while I turned off towards the forest. Not west, to the cemetery, but east. I walked past the outer reaches of the Orsini estate, the fallow fields that lay closest to the village, then took the path into the forest. The Hanged Man's Oak stood at the crossway of two paths and was often used by hunting parties as their starting point. Its long, straight branches were at the perfect height for a hanging, though no one had ever made the attempt as far as was known. Having arrived an hour early, I sat down and leaned back against the trunk and did not open my eyes again until Viola tapped me on the shoulder. She looked at me mockingly and pointed to the drool trickling from my open mouth.

'Perfectly disgusting,' she said.

'Don't play the marchesa. I'm sure you snore at night. You'll never find yourself a husband or anyone to sleep with you.'

'Excellent, because I am not looking for either. Now, if you've finished sulking, I have a gift for you.'

'A gift? For me?'

She plunged into the woods, ignoring the paths as always. The trees must have spread the word, because they allowed me to follow unhindered. Summer lingered here; it clung to the branches, to the resin that oozed from the tree trunks in great amber droplets. Ten minutes later, the sky reappeared as we reached a clearing.

'Wait for me right here,' said Viola. 'I'm giving you this gift because we are cosmic twins, and it is our birthday soon. Sixteen is an important age.' As she said this, she strode towards the edge of the clearing. 'Remember: whatever you do, don't move.'

Then she disappeared, engulfed by the trees. One minute stretched into five. I was beginning to think she had left me, a trick to see whether I could find my way back, when I heard a creak. And she re-emerged from the forest.

I have only fainted twice in my life, both times because of Viola.

The first time was when I saw her appear from the family vault and thought she was dead.

The second was when she turned herself into a bear for my birthday.

The she-bear was enormous. It would have seemed gigantic even to someone who was not my height. On all fours, she was terrifying. Seeing me, she stopped, sniffed the air, then reared up on her hind legs – almost three metres of brown fur and muscle garbed in the tattered remains of Viola's dress, which had torn during the transformation. We stared at each other for endless seconds, but Viola did not seem hostile. She yawned, baring her huge yellow fangs, and that was when I fainted.

When I regained consciousness, Viola, in her normal form, was leaning over me.

'I've never seen anyone faint the way you do. In fact, before I met you, I had never seen anyone faint.'

She helped me to my feet. I was shaking all over.

'I didn't think you would really fall for it,' she said. I looked at her, wild-eyed.

She slapped me. 'Hey! You're not going to pass out again, are you? Surely you didn't really believe I could turn into a she-bear...'

Her dress was untorn. Logic regained the upper hand. I was beginning to understand the nature of the trick, if nothing else.

'Come along now. Walk slowly.' This time, she took my hand and led me into the forest. Now that I had grown accustomed to the half-light, I could make out trampled bushes and broken branches. The ground plunged steeply, then suddenly rose towards the mouth of a cave flanked by serried pines. Some had fallen to create a wall of logs. A strong, musky smell swept over me. The bear in the tattered dress sat, scratching herself, at the entrance to the cave. As we approached, she reared up on her hind legs. Viola let go of my hand and ran to bury her face in the animal's great belly. The bear raised her snout to the heavens and let out a roar. The ground beneath my feet quaked.

Eighty-two years old. I think it is fair to say I have had a long life. One marked by great art, magnificent cities, by music and by searing beauty. But nothing came close to the sight of that radiant girl between the paws of a she-bear. All of Viola was captured in that moment.

'This is Bianca. Bianca, go say hello to Mimo.'

The bear dropped onto all fours. Viola nudged her hind-quarters, propelling her towards me, then had her rear up and stand next to me. The bear brought her muzzle close to my face; she sniffed me and licked my cheek. Then she went back to the mouth of the cave, rolled onto her back and offered her belly to a warm sunbeam.

'Sit down, you're white as a sheet.'

Finally, Viola told me her story. At the age of eight, she was walking in the forest when she heard a cry of distress. When she reached this cave she found a cub. A hunter had killed a bear – presumably her mother – a week earlier. Next to Bianca lay her twin brother; he had starved to death.

'Bears often have twin cubs,' said Viola. 'A little fact that might amuse Emanuele and Vittorio if we told them. But we won't. No one can *ever* know.'

Viola read everything she could find in her father's library about plantigrade animals. She raised Bianca, even going so far as to sneak out twice in one night to make sure the cub was all right. She wept with the cub, laughed at her clumsiness and even nursed her through a mysterious fever, giving her pills stolen from her mother, pills whose purpose she did not even know. Miraculously, Bianca survived.

'When she was a cub, I used to dress her up in my old clothes. She was my only friend.'

As the years passed, Viola tried to keep her distance. Spending too much time with Bianca was putting the animal in danger. The bear would never learn to fear humans, would never learn to hunt. Bianca was now eight years old, and Viola only visited her two or three times a year. It had been on one such occasion, three winters earlier, that the legend was born. Viola had spent the afternoon playing with Bianca. Finding one of her old, tattered dresses at the back of her cave, she had put it on the bear to see just how much she had grown. Viola had laughed at the sight and headed off to find some round pebbles to fashion a necklace. It was then she had run into the hunters, one of whom tried to grab her. Viola ran, heedlessly, without thinking where she was going, and found herself back with Bianca.

'So, it was your bear that... that kill—'

'She is not *my* bear. But, yes, Bianca killed him. And do you know what? I don't care. It's the law of nature. A predator encroached on her territory. He should not have done that.'

The tattered dress the bear was wearing was not even identical to Viola's, but the hunters didn't notice. I had fallen for the same illusion. As with all great magic tricks, we were not looking in the right place.

Viola brought a finger to her lips and we looked at the bear in silence. Bianca was snoring, her eyes half-closed. As the horizon flamed red, she got up, stretched and poked her black muzzle out into the breeze. Viola went over, put her arms around the bear's neck – though they could not quite reach – and whispered to her. Bianca grunted and, swaying her hips, wandered off into the trees.

'She must have a gentleman suitor,' said Viola. 'She rarely listens to my advice any more – but I suppose that means I've been a good mother.'

'Viola...'

'Yes.'

'I've never met anyone like you.'

'Thank you, Mimo. I have never met anyone like you either.'

I cleared my throat. 'I really like you.'

'I really like you too.'

'No, what I'm trying to say is—'

'I know what you're trying to say.' She took my hand and placed it on her heart. Her breasts were as small as ever, but as moving as the hills of Tuscany. 'We two are cosmic twins. The bond between us is unique – why complicate things? I have not the faintest interest in the things that such conversations usually lead to. Did you see the moronic look on Vittorio's face when Anna came into the barn? Did you see how he stares at her when she adjusts her cleavage? Though I grant that these things must be pleasurable to make such fools of people. But I do not want to be a fool. I have things to do. And so do you. A great destiny awaits us. Do you know why I introduced you to Bianca?'

'For my birthday.'

She laughed, in that rare and unique way she had, her head thrown back, her arms wide, as though she were about to sing a high C.

'No, Mimo. What I wanted was to show you that there are no limits. There is no tall or short, no big or small. Every border is artificial. Those who realise this fact cannot help but infuriate those who create borders, to say nothing of those who heed them – which is pretty much everyone. I know what people in the village say about me. I know my own family think me strange. But I do not care. You will know that you are on the right path, Mimo, when everyone tells you otherwise.'

'I would prefer people to like me.'

'Of course you would. That is why, right now, you are nothing. Happy birthday.'

That night, when Paragraph came into the workshop, he found me standing in front of Zio Alberto's precious block of marble, with a gleam in my eye.

'What are you staring at?'

'Viola's birthday present.'

He frowned. He looked from me to the marble and back again, then gazed at me, wide-eyed. 'Oh no, Mimo. Zio will kill you. There is a masterpiece hidden in that block.'

'I know there is. I can see it.'

Something in my expression must have frightened Paragraph, because he looked at me open-mouthed, then shrugged his shoulders and stepped back, never taking his eyes off the marble. The block was a parallelepiped one metre wide and two metres high. Perfect for what I had in mind. But I only had ten days before Viola's birthday on 22 November. I grabbed Zio's best tools, the ones he had never allowed me to touch, leaving me to work with blunt chisels with split handles that left splinters in my palm. Then, without a flicker of hesitation, I struck the first blow, exactly where it was needed. Paragraph heaved a sigh.

Over the following ten days I slept barely two or three hours a night. I told Viola I was ill so that I could miss our meetings at the barn, where construction of the new wing was nearing completion. But to avoid arousing suspicion, I agreed to meet her one night at the cemetery where I immediately fell asleep on the tomb of the little flautist, Tommaso Baldi. Viola woke me with a laugh – I had been snoring like the dead. When I got back to the workshop in the middle of the night, I went back to sculpting.

In the early morning of the day before Viola's birthday, Emanuele came to the workshop in his favourite hussar jacket waving a letter. He handed it to Paragraph, then came closer to the statue, which I was polishing with a piece of pumice. I had spent two whole days polishing. The marble was smeared with blood from my burst blisters and the sweat from my forehead. Emanuele grabbed my wrist and, looking me straight in the eye, he whispered something. It was the shortest sentence he had ever uttered.

'He says you've finished,' Paragraph interpreted.

I took a step backwards, tripped over a piece of wood and fell flat on my face. I did not immediately get up, but lay there admiring the bear towering above me. It emerged from the block of uncut marble halfway up, one paw resting on the stone as though to tear itself free, the other paw reaching for the sky. Its muzzle was open in a growl, but the slight tilt of the head made it seem less menacing. I had carved only the top half of the block, sculpting the she-bear in increasingly intricate detail from the waist up. The eye of the viewer was taken on a journey from the base to the top of the snout, from brutality to beauty, from stasis to movement. People can say what they like about my work, but I believe that there was something of the divine in this marble genesis that began as nothing, a jumble of angles and absences that, when shattered, gave birth in a blaze of white to a brutal, tender, tortured world, an abandoned cub greeting another, Bianca calling to Viola with that affectionate growl. After gazing on the sculpted section, you could almost see the shape still buried within the diaphanous depths of the uncut stone.

Zio Alberto was right, the marble was extraordinary. He would kill me when he found out what I had done. But that was fine, because all I wanted was to sleep, to sleep and never wake up again.

A couple of slaps and half a bucket of cold water in the face put paid to this plan. Paragraph and Emanuele had dragged me outside to the trough.

'This is no time to sleep – he could be here any minute!' Paragraph was waving the letter in front of me.

I tried to close my eyes again, but the other half of the bucket made me choke and sit up.

'For Christ's sake, Alberto is coming back!'

'What? When?'

'How would I know? In his letter he says a few days, but he probably posted it in Genoa at the beginning of the week. So he could get here tonight, tomorrow or the day after.'

Viola's birthday was the following day, 22 November 1920: the day she turned sixteen. All my work, the stone I had to chip away, the time I would spend polishing, had been calculated based on this date. I had planned to have the sculpture, my first real work, delivered to her in the morning with the help of a few men from the village. I could not risk waiting. But despite all the marble I had cut away, the statue weighed at least two tonnes.

I grabbed Paragraph by the sleeve. 'Run to the Villa Orsini. Ask to speak to the Marchese in person, tell him you have a message from Zio Alberto. Tell him there is a gift for his daughter Viola waiting at the workshop.'

Paragraph nodded and ran off. After a momentary hesitation, Emanuele nodded and ran after him. I dragged myself back to the workshop, put the tools back in their place and cleaned up as best I could. Then I stood on the road, staring at the horizon. An hour later, the twins reappeared.

'The Marchese will come tomorrow morning.'

'Tomorrow morning? That's too late. Alberto may get home before then.'

'Mimo, we had to plead with half of the staff at the villa just to get to talk to him. When we arrived at the gate, they thought we had come to start another riot, and the son showed up with his rifle. We told them there was a valuable gift waiting at the workshop, but the Marchese has guests, so he said he would come tomorrow morning.'

Despite being exhausted, I did not get a wink of sleep that night. I got up at dawn and scanned the horizon. The air was crisp and clear, almost brittle. As the sun rose, it brought forth a fine mist from the ground that was quickly whipped away by the mistral. It was a windy day.

A small figure shimmered on the horizon, disappeared at a dip of the road, then reappeared in a flicker of gold. Emanuele. Ten minutes later, he was in front of me, panting for breath. Feverishly, he jabbed his finger towards the village, pulled a face, mimed steering an automobile, ran on the spot rolling his shoulders, then pulled the same face and mimed turning a steering wheel. I ran and woke Paragraph, who came and talked to his brother.

'Emanuele says that Alberto has an automobile and stopped off in the village square to show it off to everyone.'

All three of us stared into the rising dust, which in Pietra d'Alba served as the bush telegraph. The main road traced a line across the plateau from north to south, with only a crossroads that led off to the Villa Orsini on one side and the cemetery on the other. This long, meandering road afforded a wealth of information to those who could recognise the signs. The morning dust was that of labourers trudging to the fields; a trail denoted the speed of those moving and hence their social status. At about 10 a.m., we saw the fateful sign. A long brown trail of dust starting at the village that bloomed faster than it subsided. An automobile.

Zio drove past the barn, pulled up and clambered out of a shiny crimson car, very different from the one that had belonged to the late Mammina. He slammed the door and patted the bonnet. 'A 4-cylinder Ansaldo Tipo 4A with an overhead camshaft. Straight from the factory that barely two years ago was manufacturing engines for aeroplanes. All that's missing is the wings!'

He patted the bonnet again, then his face grew dark. 'I don't want your filthy fingers anywhere on my bodywork, understand? But if you beg me, then I'll take you for a spin.'

Zio was wearing a suit that, despite the tailor's best efforts, did not manage to make him look respectable. Hooking his thumb into the waistcoat, he whistled as he wandered into the kitchen, took out the coffee pot and set it to boil. Paragraph had vanished. I attempted to keep Zio Alberto talking, to play for time, only to realise that, even if it would save my skin, I had nothing to say to him.

'Just look at the state of this place!' he said, glancing around. 'There are going to be a lot of changes around here from now on. Now, the apartment I've rented in Genoa is really something – the other residents call me Maestro Susso. I've had it completely redecorated. I plan to do the same thing here. I'm almost impressed you didn't torch the place while I was away.'

Taking his cup of coffee, Zio headed into the workshop. I had covered the bear with an old tarpaulin, tossed negligently over the block of Carrara marble.

Zio froze instantly. 'Take off that tarp.'

'It's all dusty and—'

'*Take off the tarp.*'

Defeated, I tugged at the canvas.

Zio gave a low whistle as he circled the she-bear, studying it from every angle. He shook his head. '*Pezzo di merda...* After everything I've done for you. I take you in, I feed you, and the minute my back is turned...'

Then he began to roar. 'Who the hell do you think you are, huh? You think you're better than me, don't you? Well, I'll show you who's better.'

He grabbed a sledgehammer and took a swing at the sculpture. I'm ashamed to say that I did not stand in his way or do anything to protect it. In his fury, Zio missed the bear and hit the plinth, taking a small a chip out of it. He raised the hammer again.

'Maestro Susso?'

Zio gasped when he saw the Marchese on the threshold. Viola was with him, as was a young man in a cassock I recognised as Francesco, the youngest of the Orsini brothers. They were followed by an older man, also in a black cassock with a purple sash around his waist.

Zio quickly recovered his senses, dropped the hammer and bowed. 'Your Lordship, Father—'

'*Your Excellency*,' corrected the Marchese in a quiet voice, turning to the man with the sash. 'Monsignor Pacelli, who is one of Francesco's tutors at the seminary, has seen fit to visit us this weekend. It is an honour for the Orsini family.'

'It is an honour for me to teach such a promising seminarian,' said the bishop, patting Francesco on the shoulder.

Before Zio Alberto could say anything, I stepped forward. 'My master here asked me to sculpt this work as a tribute to the Orsini family, on the occasion of your daughter's birthday, and generously entrusted me with a precious block of Carrara marble. I decided on a bear like the one emblazoned on your coat of arms.'

Somewhat discomfited, Zio stared, slack-jawed, as the little group moved closer.

The Marchese turned to me, puzzled. 'Did you carve this, my boy?'

'Yes, Your Lordship.'

'How old are you?'

'Sixteen, Your Lordship.'

'Just like my little Viola. Look what that young man has fashioned for you, my dear.'

Viola nodded. I could immediately tell that this was one of her bad days. 'Thank you. It is very beautiful.'

The monsignor put on his glasses and stepped closer. 'Extraordinary. Especially from one so young, but then the great sculptors of the Renaissance also started young. The perfection of form and movement is simply astonishing. And the modern twist... Any other sculptor would have been tempted to sculpt the lower half of the block, the whole animal. But this is much more striking. Bravo, young man. You are destined to go far. And who knows, perhaps we can help you along the way.'

Viola slowly nodded, her mournful eyes filled with *I told you so*.

Francesco gazed at us benevolently, his hands behind his back. 'We will send some men to help transport the statue early this afternoon. The birthday celebration begins at lunchtime and will carry on into the evening. Viola will be able to admire her gift and decide on its location. It goes without saying that this generous gesture will be handsomely rewarded, Maestro Susso.'

'Perhaps the young sculptor could come to my party?' said Viola. 'He is truly talented.'

The Marchese arched an eyebrow, studied me for a moment, then looked at Francesco, who nodded imperceptibly. 'Of course, why not. This is your day after all, and anyone you choose to invite will be our guest.'

On 22 November 1920, I strode into the Villa Orsini in triumph – via the tradesman's entrance, naturally, but the gates to Paradise could not have seemed nicer. The statue had been delivered that afternoon and installed by the dew pond next to the villa, just outside the great salon. Though there were many guests, not one was of Viola's age. I did not yet realise that for a young woman in her position a sixteenth birthday party was not a celebration among friends, it was a political act.

Feeling intimidated, I sought refuge in the kitchen.

The Marchese flushed me out. 'Well, don't just stand there, boy. You are Viola's guest, so you may stroll wherever you please.'

Stroll. I usually walked only to get from A to B, to collect or deliver something. My footsteps were utilitarian. Strolling was a privilege.

I knew nothing of the social arts. I did not have the poise of those men who promenaded through the gardens, cigars dangling from their lips, talking amongst themselves, while the women tittered beneath white parasols, a little to one side. Several prelates and a few priests numbered among the guests. They walked with their heads bowed, listening intently to the secrets poured into their ears by some count or baroness. For the first time in my life, beneath the high vaulted ceilings of the Villa Orsini, I felt small. The guests looked at me curiously, sometimes amused, perhaps thinking that I was a jester, like those they had seen in the paintings of Veronese.

Veronese. 1528–1588.

Hands in my pockets, I moved from room to room, trying to look taller. Green was the colour that predominated, suffusing wallpapers, drapes, tiebacks, chandelier-chain covers and fringed armchairs in variations of lime, aquamarine and celadon. It went without saying that the new flying wing, which we had completed two days earlier and were eager to test, had the same colour scheme. I spotted Viola moving from group to group, greeting the guests with an affected grace and a cordiality belied by her eyes, which darted about, unable to find the slightest point of interest.

She was utterly bored, because these people were alive and therefore had nothing of interest to relate.

Servants circulated with silver salvers bearing flutes of champagne – none was offered to me. In one corner of the great salon, I encountered Stefano, in company with a man with a shaved head dressed in an old-fashioned, vaguely alpine costume.

'Ah, Gulliver!' he said when he saw me. 'First you steal our books, then you sculpt a statue for my sister and manage to get yourself invited to the villa. You are very resourceful, I'll give you that. I admire resourcefulness.'

I stared at him without answering, torn between fear and hatred.

Stefano leaned over and took my chin in his thick hand. 'But never forget that we have all seen your arse, all right?'

Viola suddenly appeared next to me and shoved her brother aside. 'Leave him alone!'

Gripping the sleeve of my shirt, she dragged me away from the crowd, through several increasingly empty rooms, including a shuttered boudoir with a musty smell, and into the library. I stopped in my tracks, spellbound by the bookshelves. The great room was pervaded by the scents of leather and oak. In the middle, an ancient mappemonde with Latinate names was set into an octagonal table. When I went over to examine it, Viola once again grabbed my hand and pulled me towards the wall. A wooden panel swung open and we stepped into the passageways reserved for the household staff, a world set apart that was peopled only by the kowtowing figures who were, or believed they were, born to serve. And it was here, too, that they multiplied, on some dark landing, in sweaty, feverish couplings, while their masters slept. Viola pressed me against the wall and gazed at me intently before taking me in her arms. There were no windows, no openings of any kind. A greyish glow from who knew where saved her face from the greedy shadows.

'Thank you for the bear, Mimo. It is the most wonderful gift anyone has ever given me.'

From somewhere in the villa came the clang of a bell. Viola shuddered. 'We don't have much time, so I need you to listen up. Things are moving much faster than I expected. It is my own fault; I should have recognised the signs. The pointed hints, the number of guests... I need you to know that I will never leave you. We swore an oath. I just want you to know that... what you are about to hear... it will never happen, do you understand? It will always be you and me, Mimo and Viola. Mimo who sculpts, and Viola who flies.'

I'd never seen her in such a state. She opened the hidden door again and raced out. I tried to follow, but she quickly disappeared, and I lost my way in this insidious labyrinth, watched over by the painted eyes of a gallery of ancestors. Eventually, I managed to pry open a shutter and climbed out to find myself at the rear of the villa. I made my way back to the great room, whose soaring French windows overlooked the garden. The guests had just begun to move from the grounds to the salon, in a palpable atmosphere of excitement. Night was drawing in, but a series of flaming torches lit by the servants ensured that darkness was kept at bay. *Ab tenebris, ad lumina.* The Orsinis were true to their motto. Out of darkness, into light.

Everyone was now crowded into the ballroom. On a podium, the Marchese and the Marchesa were joined by the squat shaven-headed man I had seen talking to Stefano. Next to him stood his wife, a thin woman who towered over him by a head. Between them was a boy about my age whose sharp-featured face was pockmarked by the ravages of adolescence. He wore the same thick tweed suit as his father. A servant rang a bell and silence fell.

'My dear friends,' said the Marchese, 'what a joy it is to see you gathered here at the Villa Orsini for the birthday of our daughter, Viola.'

A flurry of applause. Viola took the stage, looking pale. She had changed into a cream-coloured ball gown.

'A beautiful dress, is it not?' whispered Francesco.

He had just appeared at my side, adopting his customary position of clasping his hands behind his back. He was a young man of about twenty, whose features had neither charm nor flaw, but whose sheer ordinariness was belied by eyes that blazed and flared with a blue that was rarely seen. He had a gentle gaze, but I was never sure whether this gentleness was affected, whether it was sincere or whether it was simply the result of the long eyelashes he shared with his sister.

'No,' I said. 'It's a horrible dress.'

I still don't know why I was so candid. My nascent aesthetic sense, perhaps. Viola was a wild, coltish girl, utterly unlike the Viennese pastry that had just taken to the stage. Viola probably agreed – after all, she had given me treatises on couture and fashion that explained how nothing was inconsequential, how everything could be elevated to the level of art.

Rather than taking offence, Francesco laughed, then looked at the podium, frowned and studied me again. 'I suppose you are right. It really doesn't suit her.'

Thus was born the strange relationship that would bind us for years to come.

'My little girl is no longer a little girl,' said the Marchese. 'And tonight, we are happy to announce the forthcoming alliance of two great families. Six months from now, we will gather again to celebrate the betrothal of Viola to Ernst von Erzenberg!'

'No...' I muttered.

To loud cheers, the young man in tweed awkwardly stepped forward and held out his hand. Viola stared at him, breathing heavily, then scanned the crowd in panic. I like to think that in that moment she was looking for me. With an affectionate smile, her father nudged her towards young Ernst, his hand still extended, who did not look particularly pleased to be there either. Without looking at the boy, Viola took his hand.

'This union is all the more precious since it will make the next generation, that of our children's children, among two of the most powerful families in a country whose destiny has all too often been left to incompetents.'

I turned to Francesco. 'Surely you cannot let her marry this boy?'

'Why not?'

'She is only just sixteen! She has so many things to do.'

'Excuse me, but I thought you only met her for the first time this morning... or perhaps I am mistaken?'

'No. I don't know her. It is just... just an impression.'

'I see. Viola always makes a big impression.'

'On the strength of this union,' said the Marchese in a booming voice, 'and as a symbol of our shared ambitions, I am delighted to announce that Pietra d'Alba will have electricity in no more than two years.'

In other circumstances, I might have been amused by the contrast between the reaction of the servants, who looked dumbfounded, and that of the guests, most of them from major cities, who politely applauded. For them, electricity was no longer a miracle. They did not appreciate the technical challenge of supplying a remote village, perhaps because they did not understand electricity.

'God has preserved and enriched our families so that we, in turn, may give something back,' said the Marchese. 'So that we may bring light, and not just metaphorically, to all the souls in our care.'

'Give him time and my father will take himself for God,' Francesco whispered with a wink.

'Two years from now, the first street lamp will be lit in these very gardens. In the meantime, drink, dance and be merry in honour of our daughter Viola and young Ernst. Later tonight, there will be a fireworks display courtesy of the illustrious Ruggieri family.'

I went outside and sat in the garden. From the great salon came the distant sound of a brass band murdering a waltz. The sickening, bestial music of a street fair on the banks of the Danube in honour of the tweedy family. I understood nothing about the implications of this union. Except the fact that a married Viola would not go to university, would not fly, would no longer listen to the dead, no longer keep my head above water, encourage me to swim, to keep swimming so that together we might reach the far shores where we would be hailed like kings. Already, I felt myself foundering.

Night had fallen over the plateau and was pushing against the boundaries of the estate. I had never been so close to Viola's bedroom, except for the time I'd crashed into it. Her window dominated me, black and deserted, three floors up.

'Excuse me, Father,' I said to Francesco as he passed. 'Have you seen Viola?'

'I'm not "father" yet, I'm still a seminarian. And no, I haven't seen my sister since earlier today.' He beckoned a steward. 'Silvio, have you seen Signorina Orsini?'

'No, signor. I assume that she is with your parents.'

I was scouring the great reception rooms, determined to talk to her, when a deafening bang made the windows rattle. A fearful silence was followed by a joyous clamour as a corolla of fire spread across the sky. The fireworks display had begun. Everyone headed for the garden, dragging me along despite myself. The Ruggieri family, the world's most famous manufacturers of pyrotechnics, blanketed the night sky with luminescent dreams, flowers fashioned from light with crimson pollen and stamens of blue, red and green that made the stars pale, with the same gunpowder that, barely a year earlier, had fuelled cannon fire. Suddenly there was a spectacular burst of light and a voice shouted: 'There's someone up on the roof!'

The next firework illumined a human figure. My favourite figure. Viola was standing just below the roof ridge, swathed in the most extravagant ball gown imaginable, a palette of greens with a long train and patches of moiré that shimmered as the fireworks exploded: the flying wing, which she had obviously fetched from the barn at some point, perhaps the day before. This was her one chance, her last chance to show these people that she, Viola, was destined for greatness.

The guests stared at each other in astonishment. The scene was pervaded by the smells of cordite and anxiety. The Marchese boomed, but the end of his sentence was drowned out by a flash of golden fire. 'Viola, get down from there right now—'

Viola shouted something inaudible and ran down the roof. She pulled the ropes taut and the great wing trailed behind her. It had not been designed for such a short fall – no more than fifteen metres, or perhaps twenty if you included the natural gradient of the grounds in front of the villa, but the mistral that had been blowing since morning suddenly picked up in tribute to this brave pioneer. The canvas swelled. Viola put one foot on the zinc gutter and hurled herself into the void.

The canvas wing suddenly unfurled above her head to 'oohs' and 'aahs' from the guests, who thought she was part of the show. Beneath her green wing, Viola glided through a flurry of sparks, weaving between starburst and rockets, since those letting off the fireworks had not seen her. She glided through the darkness, gaining altitude, floating over a silent crowd. Her future fiancé, pimply and bemused, gazed at this curious patchwork butterfly of linen, velvet and satin. Twin tears of joy rolled down my cheeks and were instantly dried by a particularly fierce gust of wind. The same gust shook Viola, whipped her from one end of the house to the other, and abruptly sent her spinning. Despite her lofty perch, we heard her scream – not in fear, but in anger. There came a sound like an early morning bedsheet being snapped to dispel the night. The wing stays became tangled, and a second later, the canvas crumpled.

Viola plummeted, a furious Icarus whirling as she plunged thirty metres into a mass of green, Orsini green, forest green, and disappeared amid the trees.

The files in Padre Vincenzo's steel-clad wardrobe relating to the *Pietà Vitaliani* are divided by topic:

The Laszlo Toth affair, one folder.

Testimonials, two folders.

The Vitaliani Pietà, *a monograph, Leonard B. Williams, Stanford University Press*, one folder.

This last also contains a smaller folder entitled *The C.A. Report*. The abbot has always wondered which trickster decided to catalogue the work of an academic as little inclined to mysticism as Professor Williams next to that of the Vatican's chief exorcist, the fearsome C.A. Candido Amantini.

The biographical details unearthed by Williams are concise. Michelangelo Vitaliani was born in France on 7 November 1904 to a father who was a stonemason and sculptor. Vitaliani arrived in Turin in 1916, probably following his father's death. He was fostered by a friend, uncle or cousin of his parents, who took him to Pietra d'Alba where Vitaliani would spend most of his career, with only two exceptions: a visit to Florence, about which little is known beyond the fact that he frequented the studio of Filippo Metti, and a period spent in Rome, about which much is known. Rumour has it that he spent time in the United States, but there is no evidence to support this. Vitaliani suffered from achondroplasia. Several apocryphal sources describe him as a seductive, charismatic man. Some describe him as gentle, almost naïve, while others depict him as temperamental and occasionally violent. Such descriptions are therefore unreliable. Compared to his predecessors and his contemporaries, Vitaliani was not particularly productive. Fewer than eighty original works are recorded, compared with the thousands produced by Rodin, Moore and Giacometti. Most of Vitaliani's works have since disappeared, probably because of the political climate in which they were sculpted. It is possible that they were deliberately destroyed, either by the artist himself or by authorities seeking to purge his name from the annals of history or consign him to oblivion. This paucity of his works adds to the air of mystery, not to say fantasy, that surrounds the sculptor. Vitaliani never adhered to any movement or identified with any particular artistic trend. Michelangelo Vitaliani was to sculpture what Marlon Brando would later be to acting, Pavarotti to opera or Sabicas to flamenco guitar: an instinctive artist gifted with an extraordinary, innate talent that was mystifying – even to the artist. Vitaliani's art was never theorised, unlike that of Giacometti, with whom he famously quarrelled.

After 1948, Mimo Vitaliani vanished – thereby making it impossible to find definitive reasons for the convulsions caused by his last opus, the *Pietà*. At the time of the monograph (published 1972, revised 1981, shortly before the death of Professor Williams), no one knew whether Vitaliani was still alive, and if so, where he was hiding.

Padre Vincenzo knows the answer to both these questions. *Vitaliani is still alive, though he will not be for much longer, and he is in the cell to the right of the stairs on the first floor of the annexe.* For a fleeting moment, he considers the scoop he is holding in his hands, one that he could doubtless sell to the highest bidder, but quickly shrugs off this temptation – the devil is never idle. He will say nothing. He will leave Vitaliani to sway in the evening breeze before slowly fading, taking his secrets with him. After all, there is nothing more powerful than mystery, something Padre Vincenzo knows all too well, having devoted his life to the greatest of all mysteries.

Viola was carried into the villa through a side door as the guests were politely escorted to their vehicles or their quarters. The Erzenbergs had left immediately after the accident, without saying a word. Their message was clear: they would not allow Ernst, the pockmarked apple of their eyes, to be betrothed to a madwoman, assuming the madwoman was still alive.

According to rumours, Viola was still breathing when she was found, but a number of ladies fainted when she was brought back to the villa. She was not a pretty sight. There being no shortage of automobiles, one was sent to fetch the alcoholic doctor from the neighbouring village. Though sick with worry, I had no choice but to go back to the workshop. Paragraph, at the tender age of nineteen, choked back his tears. The following day, we heard from Anna – who did

occasional work at the villa when the Orsinis had guests –
that Viola had not regained consciousness and had just been
transferred to the hospital in Genoa.

Ever since the firework display, Zio had been looking at
me askance. Three days later, we still knew nothing. No
one had seen any of the Orsini family, and all orders came
through the major-domo, Silvio. The household staff said
nothing – even if they had wanted to, they had no news. All
that was known was that the Marchese and the Marchesa
were engaged in diplomatic negotiations intended to
restore their prestige, a purely epistolary enterprise since
the telephone had not yet reached Pietra d'Alba. Couriers
came and went within the hour in a flurry of activity never
seen before.

One morning, Zio pointed to the car and ordered me to
fetch my suitcase and join him.

'Where are we going?'

'I'll explain on the way. I need you to run an errand for me.'

Intrigued, I stuffed a few belongings into the little trunk I
had brought from France and slipped it into the back seat of
the Ansaldo. The car sped off, climbed towards Pietra d'Alba,
honked through the village and took the road to Savona.

'You're going to Florence!' Zio yelled over the engine's roar.

'I don't want to go to Florence. I want to be close to Viola.'

'What? What did you say?'

'I don't want to go to Florence!'

'You're going to Filippo Metti to pick out a couple of nice blocks of Carrara marble. The Marchese paid me three times the price of the block you used, and he paid for the sculpting. Not a bad deal, when all's said and done – though you'd better not do it again. Take all the time you need, and make sure you don't get ripped off!'

He dropped me off at Savona Letimbro railway station and drove away, leaving me with an envelope for a man called Metti.

'In here is the money order for you to give him as payment. But only if the blocks of marble are worth it. You'll also find a return ticket that is valid for any train. Don't haggle – if you need to take another day, take it. Make sure the marble has no flaws. And don't let him fob you off with French marble.'

This was a time when railway stations were beautiful. Savona Letimbro was all the more magnificent, since the sea was just a few streets away. Four years earlier, the Mediterranean had simply been a blue expanse of water to me. But, thanks to Viola, it was now covered with dotted routes that could give and take lives, spawn tornadoes and earthquakes, whose intensity Viola could recite using twelve degrees on the famous Mercalli scale. Viola knew the difference between an *Arbacia lixula* and a *Tripneustes ventricosus*. 'A black sea urchin and a white sea urchin, you idiot.' Without her, the world was a simpler place. But thinking about it made my eyes sting.

I can easily imagine what was being whispered beneath awnings, in dark corners, can picture the outraged expression hidden behind crepe fans. *The little Orsini girl would rather kill herself than marry that pimply Austro-Hungarian boy.* Firstly, the pimply boy was no longer Austro-Hungarian; for more than a year, he had been Italian, given that Trentino and Alto Adige had become part of Italy with the dissolution of the Austro-Hungarian Empire. Secondly, I knew the little Orsini girl better than anyone. We were cosmic twins. I know that when Viola was about to jump, she believed she would fly.

After an eight-hour journey, I arrived in Florence. Nobody seemed to be expecting me. I stood outside the train station, hopping about to keep myself warm. The rooftops were blanketed with sooty frost. Unlike Pietra d'Alba, where people would already be closing their shutters and huddling next to their meagre fires, Florence was intoxicatingly alive. I watched as a succession of carriages and fiacres passed in front of the Grand Hotel Baglioni.

Then something moving caught my eye. On the far side of the railway tracks, on the terrace of a café that had nothing of the splendour of the Hotel Baglioni, a small child wrapped in a thick cloak was waving. I glanced around, then pointed at myself. The little figure nodded. Warily, I crossed the tracks. The child was not a child but a man in his fifties, with a sparse grey beard that did little to hide his acne scars. But most importantly, he was like me: at birth, some trickster god had laid a finger on him to stop him growing.

'Maestro Metti?'

'Excuse me?'

'Are you Filippo Metti?'

'Never heard of him. Sit down, boy.'

'I can't, I am supposed to wait for someone outside the train station.'

'We are outside the station. You might as well sit down while you wait. What will you drink? A little mulled wine?'

'Nothing, signor.'

'You don't mind if I have another?' he said, pushing three empty glasses aside and beckoning the waiter. 'Well, sit, sit.'

With my eyes riveted on the station entrance, I perched on the edge of a chair. The waiter brought a steaming glass of something acrid and set it on the table without looking at us.

'You looking for a job, boy?'

'No, sir. I shall be leaving again tomorrow.'

'Hmm, pity. I'm Alfonso Bizzaro – and, yes, that is my real name. Alfonso Bizzaro, bastard son of a Spanish father and an Italian mother, owner, artistic director and star of the Bizzaro circus. From here, you would be able to see the big top on that patch of waste ground just behind the station if it hadn't been blown down by a gale yesterday. But what about you?'

'Mimo. Vitaliani.'

'And what are you doing in Florence, Mimo Vitaliani?'

'I'm here on business. And if I have time, I would like to see Fra Angelico's frescoes. I want to describe them to a friend who has never seen them.'

'Who is Fra Angelico?'

'A monk and a great painter of the Italian Renaissance. Birth date unknown, died 1455.'

'It is a pity that you're leaving tomorrow. I could use people like you.'

'What for?'

'For my show, by Jove. A recreation of a battle between humans and dinosaurs. The dinosaurs are actors in costume, and people like you and me play the imperilled humans. The difference in size makes it more impressive. The show is sold out every night.'

In the space of four years, Viola had completely transformed me. I only realised just how much in that moment when I, Il Francese, son of an illiterate father, found myself saying: 'Dinosaurs and humans did not inhabit the earth at the same time.'

Bizzaro looked at me strangely, then gave a low whistle. 'Well, you're pretty clever for a dwarf.'

I angrily leapt to my feet. 'I'm not a dwarf.'

'Really? What are you, then?'

'A sculptor. A great sculptor. I will be one day.'

'Duly noted. But if you change your mind before you grow up, you know where to find me. Can I leave you to settle the bill?'

He drained his glass and walked away, hands in his pockets, before my astonished eyes.

The waiter instantly reappeared and held out his hand. 'One lira.'

I had no money, I had never had any, had never needed any. Realising this, he grabbed me by the scruff of the neck.

'Mimo Vitaliani?'

A man shambled towards me across the tracks. He was still young, not yet forty, but I could see many more decades stored up behind his eyes. His right sleeve hung empty of the powerful, healthy limb that had once been there. He had just come home from the front: it was etched on his body, in the unexpected wrinkles in a man of his age, in the nightmares that roiled in his mind even during waking hours and made him draw his head into his shoulders.

'I am Filippo Metti. You were supposed to wait for me outside the train station.'

'I'm so sorry, maestro. I—'

'One lira,' the waiter said again.

Metti surveyed the four glasses on the table and arched an eyebrow. 'I can see you don't waste much time.'

'No, no, I—'

'It's all right. After all, I was late. But I warn you, there will be no drinking in my studio,' he said as he paid.

I didn't give a damn about his studio. I desperately wanted to get out of this city, to go home so I could find out how

Viola was doing, even if the trip meant I could try not to think about her, about the fact that no one could survive such a fall. I wanted to be done with Florence. As if such a thing were possible. As I would quickly realise, Florence was Viola: bruised and fanatical and gentle. She alone would decide when it was over.

Despite the cold, we wandered through the city on foot, weaving between trams and broughams pulled by horses with doleful eyes. Every building called to me, every street, every enfilade, every new perspective drew me in, lending me a lurching gait. That earned me a reproachful look from Metti. With every step, I had ten forms of beauty, ten different stories to choose from. Every crossroads was a relinquishment. The city wormed its way inside me, never to leave. The grandeur of Rome. the magic of Venice, the madness of Naples, none of these would ever make me forget Florence. It was not the most beautiful city in Italy, and yet it was. Viola again.

'Are you all right?' asked Metti.

'Yes, maestro.'

'You look as though you are about cry.'

'I was just thinking about a friend. She is in hospital.'

He shuddered and whispered, 'In hospital.'

'I'm sorry. Come on, hurry up, it's getting dark.'

'Where are the blocks of marble?'

'The blocks of marble?' he said, surprised. 'In the workshop, obviously.' He gave me a quizzical look and walked on.

We crossed the Arno on the Ponte di Rubaconte – which the Nazis would destroy in 1944, much to the delight of the Ponte Vecchio, which thereby became the city's oldest bridge. Once on the other side, we walked east along the riverbank for about two kilometres, leaving the city for fields dusted with pale hoarfrost.

At the far end of a dirt track, a rough-stone building towered over the flat countryside. A majestic archway led into a courtyard that had been transformed into a store-room with numerous windows. The place was suffused with a sense of order and symmetry, mingled with the bittersweet smell of neglect. From the first-floor windows came the chiming melody of rasp and chisel, accompanied by a counterpoint of calls, questions and orders amplified by the unseen corridors.

Metti went into the north wing, trudged up the steps to the second floor and pushed open the door to a room furnished with a bed and a copper basin filled with water. 'You'll stay here.'

'When can I see the marble blocks? I'd like to get home as soon as possible.'

'What's all this about blocks?'

'The ones my uncle is buying from you.'

Metti looked at me as if I were insane, and I met his gaze.

'I don't know anything about marble blocks, son. I arranged with your uncle to have you seconded from his workshop because I need stonecutters to work on the Duomo. He'll still be paying your wages.'

I understood. Not the whole plan, not the details, but the gist: Zio had palmed me off.

'I can't stay.'

'It's up to you. You can spend the night here. If you plan to stay, be in the cutting room just behind the main building tomorrow morning at seven o'clock sharp.'

He walked off. His body was slightly bowed, and there was a strange lopsidedness to his torso. With every step, he threw out his right shoulder, as though to compensate for his missing arm. I collapsed on the straw mattress, stupefied. Then I remembered Alberto's message to Metti. Feverishly, I tore open the envelope. It contained a second envelope marked *WIWO* – Alberto's attempt to write my name. Inside this was a single sheet of paper on which he had drawn (and the old bastard was an exceptional draughtsman, with a line worthy of a Renaissance artist) a *digitus impudicus* – a charcoal sketch of a raised middle finger so lifelike it seemed to move, which wrested from me a growl of rage. My mind suddenly teemed with a thousand thoughts. That Zio would clearly have made an exceptional painter so why had he chosen to be a sculptor? That he had not only duped me, but that it was a ruse he could not have set up in the week since he had come back. That he had not got rid of me as revenge for sculpting the bear, but had planned this all along simply because he didn't like me. Which meant there were few people on earth who loved me, one of whom was in hospital, and perhaps even as l formulated this thought she had ceased to love me.

I couldn't stay here. Viola needed me. This was Zio Alberto's stroke of genius. I couldn't stay, I couldn't leave. I had no money. Maestro Metti would pay Zio for my services but Zio would never pay me. I was a prisoner. In truth, I always had been, but every night Viola broke my chains. And so, there on my iron bed, I made a promise, a black conjuration.

Alberto Susso, you son of a bitch. One day I'll kill you.

Like so many promises, it was one I did not keep.

Florence, the dark years. It would make a good hook for a biographer, though at that time I had no idea that anyone would ever take an interest in my life; still less did I suspect that, when they did, I would do everything in my power to thwart them.

Brothers, when l have finally expired this last breath that lingers, take me to the garden and bury me beneath a beautiful white slab of marble from my beloved Carrara. Carve no name on it. Leave it soft and smooth enough for someone to lie upon. I wish to be forgotten. Michelangelo Vitaliani, 1904–1986, has said all he has to say.

The cutting room, a shed of corrugated iron, was built against the back of the main building. By the time I got there at seven o'clock the following morning, the saws were already turning. No one paid me any heed. I helped out as best I could, and before long, I was like the other six employees, a ghostly figure coated in white marble dust. Given the deafening racket, it was impossible to talk, except when the workers stopped for a smoke, sitting on a block, elbows propped on their knees, staring into space. A haggard man named Maurizio, who seemed to be the foreman, handed me a Toscano. I lit it with a practised gesture, though I had never smoked before, and choked back a coughing fit, tears in my eyes. Maurizio shot me a mocking look, though there was no malice in it. He did not merely smoke, he *breathed*, inhaling dark smoke again as soon as it left his mouth, such that he smoked the same cigar two or three times over. His tongue, his teeth, his beard and doubtless his innards were coated with a yellow crust of tobacco and marble dust. I made it a point of honour to finish my first Toscano, then promptly went outside and threw up.

I did not see Metti that day, nor indeed that week. We workers ate our meals in the old refectory – the main building that was now Filippo Metti's studio had previously been a palazzo, later a convent, only to be abandoned and used as a barn. The first floor of the north wing was the main studio where the elite of Florentine sculptors worked. Metti had been among the city's most prominent artists before he lost his arm during the Battle of Caporetto. And lose it he did. He had been leading his men on an assault that was halted when a shell exploded in a rain of earth and rubble that forced them to retreat. 'That was a close shave,' he said when they were safe in their trench. 'It could have ended badly.' At which point a soldier asked him where he had left his arm.

Stonecutting was hell, the thankless graft of galley slaves. We cut and finished the marble facings intended to decorate the façades of buildings. Sometimes, we cut blocks for sculptures, if they had not been cut at the quarry. Metti had recently been commissioned to restore part of the Duomo, one of the most prestigious contracts in the region. There was so much work that he even hired people from abroad.

In the refectory, there was a striking difference between the elite, the cheery sculptors, who were not averse to a food fight, and the 'stonecutters', covered from head to foot in marble dust, silently hunched over their plates. Arrogant though the sculptors were – and they were – they did not mess with us. The cutting room was the haunt of tough men: thugs, ex-convicts, deserters, murderers, a microcosm of all that is base in this world.

During that first week, I managed to buy a postage stamp. I wrote to Paragraph (at his mother's house, since I knew that Zio would otherwise intercept my letter), and into the same envelope, I slipped a letter to Viola. Every morning, I woke with a knot of fear in my belly to a world in which I could not know whether my truest friend was still alive. I became a necromancer; each day I scanned the world for a thousand signs and omens, and those I could not find, I invented. *Three crows on that mantel, she is gravely ill. If I can mount these stairs all the way to the landing without taking a breath, she will pull through.* Every night, after dinner, I wandered along the silty bank of the Arno, intoxicated by the smells of damp earth and the cold air, fascinated by the moonlit reflections on Giotto's campanile on the far side. I never crossed the bridge – because I felt unworthy of such beauty, because I did not want to run the risk of stumbling on some work by Fra Angelico without Viola here to see it with me. Besides, it was rumoured that there were certain dangerous streets where a man might have his throat cut for a trifle.

A week after my arrival, Metti reappeared. I recognised him by his gait as he walked across the courtyard.

'I see you decided to stay,' he said as I rushed over to him.

'Yes, maestro. I wanted to ask you... Why am I in the cutting room?'

'Because I need a stonecutter, and your uncle told me that you were a good apprentice for such work.'

'But I can sculpt.'

He planted his lone fist on his left hip. 'I'm sure you can. But, you see, I am working on highly important projects, not decorating some rural villa. If you do a good job, I promise you will be able to take lessons from my apprentices, and if you do well, you will move up through the ranks. Now, off you go.'

He went back to the sculpture in the middle of the courtyard, a statue of Saint Francis with a tender gaze. Head bowed, I went back to the cutting room, to my life as a ghost. My colleagues quickly accorded me a certain respect. I think they secretly admired the fact that I did not balk at the work despite my diminutive size. On the contrary, I made it a point of honour to take on the most arduous tasks. In exchange, they gave me glasses of beer, cigars and all the forbidden delights hitherto unknown to me. And postage stamps, which, during those first weeks, were my most precious currency.

Twelve days after my arrival, I received a letter from Paragraph. I could feel it burn in my pocket until the first break, at ten o'clock, when finally, in the warmth of a rare ray of sunshine on the threshold of the studio, I could tear it open.

Dear Mimo
Not much news. Alberto's still a dumm bastard, and Anna
still is as byutiful as ever. We miss you. No news of Viola,
even the servants dont no much. Some folks say she's dead,
some say she isnt. Ill send enny news soon as I find out.
Your friend, Vittorio.
   PS: Emanuele sez as he hopes youll be back soon
because things arent the same without you.

I decided to write directly to the Orsinis and spent the whole evening formulating a courteous request in my best handwriting, explaining that I was studying in a prestigious studio in Florence and could they *please, for pity's sake,* send me news of Viola. I tore up the letter, started over and replaced Viola with 'Mademoiselle Orsini'.

The following day, the electric saw, the pride of the cutting room, broke down. While it was being repaired, we were given an old frame saw and we had to cut the marble blocks by hand. This was the point when my height became an issue, since some of the blocks were taller than me. I tried to help with the carrying and the finishing, but on several occasions found myself wandering around the courtyard, where outgoing statues crossed paths with those being brought in to be restored. Once again, I encountered Metti standing in front of the statue of Saint Francis, at the foot of which a young man with a red scarf and a blue apron had just carved two stone birds.

Metti beckoned me over. 'Look at the birds that Neri has carved. Neri will soon be a journeyman; he'll be leading the apprentices in the workshop. What do you think of them?'

'They're very beautiful, maestro.'

Neri arched an eyebrow, wondering whether he should take the opinion of a lowly stonecutter as an insult. With a shrug, he decided to take it as a compliment, even if it was worthless. Metti patted him on the arm and Neri walked away.

'It is a commission from the Basilica di San Francesco d'Assisi,' whispered Metti. 'I was supposed to do the work myself...'

'And you would have done a better job.'

'Excuse me?'

'I lied. These birds...' I shook my head.

Metti's mouth was twisted into an almost comical grimace that nonetheless betrayed his mounting fury. 'You don't like them?'

'No.'

'Might I have your considered opinion as a stonecutter?'

I stared Metti in the eye, although this meant craning my neck. In that moment, sixteen years of mute rage rushed to the surface, sixteen years of putrid, stifled dread mingled with the panic I had felt when I saw my best friend plummet from the sky. I too was entitled to feel fury.

'You can have my considered opinion as someone who has seen countless birds,' I said, jabbing a finger towards the sculpture, 'and these two will never fly.'

'What do you mean?'

'The anatomy is all wrong. These are turkeys the size of sparrows. But turkeys never fly very far. Moreover, they pull the saint's gaze downwards, whereas surely it is the opposite that you want to depict?'

'And I suppose you could do better?'

'I believe I could.'

Furiously, he wheeled around and called to a passing apprentice. 'You there, bring me a case of tools.'

Then, to me: 'See these two small blocks? I've just come back from Polvaccio with these marble samples. Pick one of them and carve me a bird. We'll see if it flies.'

I owe everything to my father, to our all-too-short time together on this ball of roiling magma. People often thought me indifferent because I did not talk about him very much. I was accused of having forgotten him. Forgotten? My father lived on in everything I ever created – right up to my last work, my last hammer blow. It is to him I owe my boldness with the chisel. It was he who taught me to constantly be aware of where the work would be placed, since the proportions depended on whether it would be seen from face on or from below, and if the latter, at what height. And the light. Michelangelo Buonarroti sanded his *Pietà* endlessly so that it would catch the faintest glimmer of light because he knew that it would be placed in a dark niche. Lastly, it is to my father that I owe one of the finest pieces of advice I ever heard.

'Imagine your finished work coming to life. What will it do? You have to imagine what will happen in the instant after the moment you have just captured in stone. A sculpture is an annunciation.'

I settled myself in a corner of the cutting room and set to work on the block that Metti had given me. My colleagues looked at me curiously, captivated by this ugly duckling who was turning into a swan, a bandy-legged bird perhaps, but they had little to celebrate so they were not about to quibble. The grain of the marble was perfect, typical of Carrara. Ductile, supple in just the right way and not at all recalcitrant. I freed the bird that was hiding within. One wing was slightly detached from the body because a second later it was going to take wing and land on the saint's arm or his shoulder. The marble captured the power of the muscle, the transparency, the fragility of the sparrow. And because, for a saint, one sparrow was not enough, I sculpted a second, huddled against the first, half-buried in its feathers, as though the two birds had just been playfully fighting, out of boredom perhaps or to compete for the attentions of Saint Francis. I spent the last day polishing and, when I finally stepped back to look at my work, I backed into the circle of stonecutters who had gathered unbeknownst to me.

Metti appeared with Maurizio, who had gone to look for him. 'Come on, boss, come see what we can do here in the cutting room. So feel free to give us a pay rise.'

There was a burst of laughter, quickly stifled by the stern gaze of Filippo Metti. He walked over to the birds and had the same curious reaction that my works have elicited all my life: a fleeting hesitation as the viewer looks from me to the work and back again, and though never explicitly expressed, that look meant *How could that dwarf make something like that?*

He studied my work, reaching out to touch it, running his fingers over it. The more he did so, the redder his face became until he exploded: 'What do you think? You think I've got room for a new sculptor in the studio? Here, we have a hierarchy, we have a tradition that we respect. You're gifted, I'll grant you that, very gifted, perhaps the most gifted apprentice I have ever encountered, but that changes nothing. I cannot understand why your uncle told me you were an unskilled labourer, and I don't want to meddle in your family affairs. You will stay here in the cutting room.'

There was a stunned silence as he left. A moment later, he came back and jabbed a finger in my chest. 'You start in the studio this afternoon. I'm warning you, I can't pay you, I don't have the budget. Well perhaps maybe fifty lire a month over and above what I pay your uncle. I'll pay you directly.'

I watched him go out, amazed. Fifty lire, one-sixth of what a labourer might earn. But to me, it was a fortune. Enough to buy a huge pile of stamps to write to Pietra d'Alba, to Vittorio, to the Orsinis, to anyone who might give me news of Viola. Enough to one day leave this city, which was at once too beautiful and too hard, and pick up where Viola and I left off.

In the meantime, I would have to suffer a little.

I turned up at the studio, a dust-covered goblin, to the suspicious gaze of a dozen sculptors. Chief among them, Neri, who was not yet twenty. He had seen my birds and instantly despised me. Not wishing to be beholden, and since I was past the age of fairytales where bitter hatred turns into firm friendship, I instantly returned the favour. In the weeks that followed, I was subjected to some serious bullying by Neri and his henchmen. I continued to have lunch and dinner with the workers in the cutting room, which did nothing to increase my popularity in the studio, whose denizens considered themselves to be unique in possessing the rarest of traits – talent – though they had none. Except for Neri. I had been a little harsh in my assessment of his birds: they were pretty good. But mine were better.

My tools kept disappearing. My stool would collapse – one leg had been sawn through. But, being assigned the less noble tasks, I was no great threat to anyone. I carved conch shells, plants, animals and fountain ornaments. Not saints or apostles or anything approaching the divine. As for the Holy Family, or God Himself – don't even think about it; they were the exclusive preserve of Neri and two idiots I called Uno and Due (I couldn't remember their actual names), who agreed with everything their leader said.

Neri did not really matter. My anger was not directed at him but at the Orsini family. Perhaps even at Viola, since I assumed she was still alive. A girl like her was immortal. Why had I not had news? Vittorio wrote regularly, and all his letters were like the first: *Alberto is a bastard, I'm in love, nobody knows anything about Viola.*

In early February 1921, three months after the accident, a balmy spell after a particularly harsh winter brought the people of Florence out into the streets. A gentle breeze wafted down the Arno, bringing the scents of mountain pastures from the Apennines, and the studio was deserted. Neri forbade me to go out, insisting that I keep an eye on the studio, which was fortunate because, an hour later, I received a letter emblazoned with the Orsini crest. It was from

Francesco, the brother training to be a priest. During a visit to his parents' house, he had found my letter languishing on a desk. He was writing to me about his sister. Breathlessly, I unfolded the letter.

Viola had fractured her skull, a vertebra, three ribs, both collarbones and both legs, and suffered a punctured lung. She had spent three weeks in a coma.

Medical specialists from the length and breadth of Europe came to her bedside and delivered various prognoses and portents, most of them ominous, which Viola did her utmost to thwart. One morning, she woke up with nothing except some slight neurological damage: she remembered nothing about the accident and now had a slight lisp which, according to Francesco, was already beginning to fade. She was about to be discharged to go back to Pietra d'Alba where she would spend the following weeks convalescing. 'She is in fine form, but she does not want to see anyone.' Francesco had underlined 'anyone'. This was followed by a passage about my bear, which still had pride of place next to the pool. 'Archbishop Pacelli still talks about this "young sculptor of short stature but great talent".' Then, as though it were some minor detail he had forgotten, Francesco added: 'Given the extent of her fractures, it is too early to say whether Viola will ever walk again.'

Viola was alive, that was what mattered, and I could finally weep. Three crows, sitting on the mantel opposite, glowered

at me disdainfully, then took wing and flew off towards the
Arno.

That spring, I wrote every week to Viola. My poor, broken,
punctured Viola, whom I missed every hour, every minute.
The restoration of the Duomo kept everyone in the studio
busy; the whole city could hear the chink of chisel blows
when the wind was in their direction. I rarely left the former
convent, indulging in imaginary conversations with my
friend rather than drinking in the bars along the river. In
response to my constant entreaties, Metti eventually began
to entrust me with more important pieces, sometimes a
minor figure from the pantheon. On several occasions
the studio was visited by well-dressed businessmen. Metti
and Neri would give them a tour, explaining, with infinite
patience, the journey from block of stone to work of art.

The pranks and the bullying continued with a pettiness
made all the more stinging by their lack of ambition. I was
jostled, ignored, sent on imaginary errands. One night,
I found a dead cat in my bed. I complained to Metti, who
dismissed this 'childish behaviour' with a wave and ordered
Neri to sort things out. This only served to make him hate
me all the more.

This was the year I turned seventeen and the point at
which I came to be seen as volatile, or unpredictable. It
is a reputation I have carried with me all my life, perhaps

because, for a time, I encouraged it. In June, after a dozen letters to Viola, I had to accept the fact that she was not getting them. It was preferable to the alternative: that she had received them and had not replied. For a moment, I considered spending my meagre savings on a trip to Pietra d'Alba, but who was I to demand admission to the Villa Orsini? Francesco had made it clear. *She does not want to see* anyone.

One morning, I arrived at the studio to find that the statue I had been working on for a week had been decapitated.

'Who did this?'

Everyone carried on working as if nothing had happened. Uno and Due were whistling, Neri was ignoring me. I walked over to him.

'Who did this?'

'Did what?'

'You know very well what.'

'I know nothing of the sort. Do you know anything, lads?'

'No,' said Uno.

'Absolutely nothing,' said Due.

I punched Uno (or it might have been Due) in the balls. He fell to the floor, taking a workbench with him. The other apprentices separated us, still hurling insults at each other, then Metti entered the workshop and there was silence. Half an hour later, Neri and I were summoned to his office, or what served as an office: a trestle table in front of the monumental hearth in what had been the kitchen of the old convent. He idly lectured us about the rivalries common in artists' studios, hoped we would get over them and suggested we shake hands, which we did with a hypocritical smile.

'You'll get what's coming to you,' Neri hissed as we left.

'One more dirty trick, just one, and I will kill you.'

I saw a flicker of fear in his eyes. I was no longer the twelve-year-old who had arrived in this strange and wondrous country. I was a bona fide Italian, shaped by drought, deprivation and getting by. But what terrified him, like all the others who came after him, was that he assumed someone like me had nothing to lose.

A few days later, Metti asked me to accompany him on a visit to the city. I had spent little time in Florence since my arrival, aside from the occasional errand. He took me on a tour of the Duomo, up a hidden flight of steps to the great cupola. A fierce wind was blowing but beneath our feet Florence, swept clean of dust, shimmered beneath a sky of enamel blue.

'What are you thinking?'

'I'm thinking you should give me the same projects you give Neri.'

Metti sighed, half-amused, half-irritated.

We headed back down and, partially frozen, set off along the banks of the Arno. At the far end of via delle Terme, just before the Piazza Santa Trinita, a few tables had been set up in what looked like a garage. The maestro was clearly a regular, as a waiter instantly brought us two coffees and a small bottle of brandy.

'How is your friend, Mimo?'

'My friend?'

'The friend you talked about the first day you arrived. The one who was in hospital.'

'Oh, she's better. At least I think she is.'

He drank his coffee in three swift gulps, then stared at the bottom of the empty cup. 'Neri is the head of the studio. That's just how it is.'

'I have no desire to take his place. I simply want to work on projects that demand the height of my talent.'

The word 'height' made him smile. Despite himself, he glanced down at my feet, which did not touch the ground.

'Neri does not like you,' he argued.

'Neri is a *cazzino*.'

'He is also a Lanfredini,' said Metti. 'His family is one of the most powerful in the region and his father among the principal donors funding the restoration of the Duomo. I am no fool. I know that I was awarded the commission thanks to him. Because his son is head of my studio. And he deserves it,' he added before I could interrupt. 'Neri is a good sculptor. Don't make me choose between you.'

'I've got talent!'

Metti's face darkened. He poured a little brandy into his empty cup, raised it to his lips, but set it down again without drinking. 'There was a time when I, too, believed that I had talent. I have long since realised that you cannot *have* talent. It is not something a man can own. It is a vaporous cloud you spend your life trying to contain. But to contain something requires two arms.'

He stared at the ground; he seemed to have forgotten I was there. He was lost back on some foggy day during the Battle of Caporetto. Suddenly, he shuddered and looked up at me, wild-eyed, feverishly. 'Do you know why Neri is a good leader for the studio? Because he is trustworthy. He stands on his own two feet, he knows what he's doing.'

'But that is as far as his talent goes.'

'No. It's true that he has hit a wall. But the thing about walls is that you can lean against them and rest. Now, you, on the other hand, race along at breakneck speed – you don't seem to realise this is a marathon, not a sprint. You have genius. I recognise that because, without false modesty, I think it is something that I also possess. But that was... before.'

He tossed a few coins on the table, then silently shambled off with his distinctive gait. I raced to catch him up, with my own distinctive gait, and together we strolled in silence as far as the Ponte Vecchio. That day, the river had a fresh blue smell, a foretaste of the Mediterranean where it forever ended its days.

'I'll never make any progress if I only sculpt minor works,' I said as we reached the far bank.

'It is not *what* you sculpt that matters, but *why* you do it. Have you asked yourself that question? What is sculpture? And don't say "breaking stone to give it a shape". You know what I mean.'

I couldn't know the answer to a question I had never asked myself, nor did I pretend to.

Metti nodded. 'I knew it. The day you realise what sculpture is about, you will be able to make men weep over a simple fountain. In the meantime, Mimo, a word of advice. Be patient. Be like this river, tranquil, unchanging. Do you think the Arno ever gets angry?'

On 4 November 1966, the Arno would burst its banks and devastate the city.

S ummer returned, almost as sweltering as the summer of 1919 in Pietra d'Alba and barely tempered by the presence of the Arno. A fragile truce reigned in the studio. I was still restricted to restorations and minor works, while Neri was entitled to the finest stone and the noblest commissions. I began to go out more often and spent my evenings discovering the underworld circles of the stonecutters. I felt at home among these men who had no interest in hierarchies and didn't care about my birth. Between glasses of often-suspect alcohol, I witnessed brawls, score-settling, betrayals, but not one of these ne'er-do-wells ever called me 'dwarf'. After a few drinks, it wasn't unusual for one or other of them to solemnly stand up. The bar would fall silent and we would hear an aria that brought tears to our eyes. These men sang because they had something to say, and did not know if they would be able to say it tomorrow. On such nights, those dingy bars with their sticky floors, intoxicated by the song of some reprobate Caruso, were the most beautiful opera houses in the world. The Pagliaccis were demented, to say nothing of the Don Giovannis, since the singers spent their days fucking and killing. For every Caruso (who would die later that summer) and for every Di Stefano (even now being born in Sicily, his infant wail marking his vocal debut), how many singing careers were squandered in these dive bars? One false step, one wrong look and, rather than performing at La Scala, they would find themselves singing 'Nessun Dorma' to a roomful of drunks and war-wounded, drained by days with no bread. And yet I do not believe ours was the less knowledgeable audience. On the contrary, I would argue that those with loggias at La Scala, the self-proclaimed arbiters of good taste, ever ready to boo the slightest vocal slip, have never truly heard opera. Gesualdo was a murderer. As was Caravaggio. Artists sometimes have blood on their hands.

The purpose of my night-time excursions was to stop me thinking about Viola, about whom I still had no news. Some inkling, perhaps, that I would have to learn to live without her. Paragraph had confirmed that she was back in Pietra d'Alba. Everyone had heard the ambulance roaring through the village at top speed in the middle of the night. But, since then, no one had seen Viola. Not even Anna Giordano, who was now working at the villa where the Orsinis had once again begun to receive guests. Viola never went out; she never appeared in public. She was tended to by two maids, who had been with the family for decades.

If she did not reply to my letters, I assumed it was because her parents were intercepting them. So, via Paragraph, I asked Anna to deliver a letter in person. Or as close to 'in person' as possible. Once a week, Anna helped clean Viola's room, during which time Signorina Orsini disappeared into the depths of the house. After making the bed, Anna was to slip my letter under Viola's pillow. This she faithfully did, and I waited. One week. Two. Three. Autumn returned in a cavalcade of mists and the light rains that forced everyone to draw their heads in and muffled the city along the roiling river. Viola would not answer. She could not or would not, which to me amounted to the same thing.

I brooded angrily and sought to temper my bitterness with long draughts of beer. By now, I was greeted by name the moment I crossed the threshold of one of our favourite bars, accompanied by Maurizio and the other guys from the cutting room. I was given a tankard without having to order. After the third, my natural generosity would flare up and I would buy one round after another. Two months earlier, a new face had begun to frequent the bars, a lanky man with a pockmarked face known to everyone, for reasons I did not understand, as Il Cornutto – the cuckold. I knew the meaning of the word, I simply found it hard to imagine that anyone would want to cuckold such a man. I have met a fair share of crooks in my time, but he was *really* unsettling. Yet Il Cornutto was possessed of one of the most beautiful voices I had ever heard. His party piece was the immigrant song, and his biggest hit was 'Riturnella', a Calabrian song the regulars demanded by banging empty beer glasses on the bar to set the rhythm. All of us recognised ourselves in this song of exile, of a couple torn apart. Listening to Il Cornutto, it was easy to believe that he had toiled in coal mines that had collapsed, travelled aboard ships that had been wrecked, died many times over of hunger, thirst and poverty – he had that look about him. On such nights, when my head was spinning, my voice wheezy and I staggered even more than usual, I would think of my mother, of Viola, of my own rootlessness. At dawn, we would go our separate ways, swearing undying friendship, and I would be at the studio by seven o'clock, clinging to my chisel like a lifeline.

Two almost simultaneous events, randomly tossed into the crucible of the autumn of 1921, would once again upend my life. On 7 November, the day that I turned seventeen, Mussolini founded the National Fascist Party, intended to bring together the *ras*, the petty gang leaders who spread terror throughout the country. Neri clearly took this as a sign, because suddenly my tools began to disappear again, I would be jostled on my way to the refectory, someone even pissed on my bed. One day Maurizio caught Uno walking behind me, imitating my lurching gait while the others laughed. He grabbed Uno by the hair, dragged him into the cutting room, sent him sprawling on the ground then pulled him over to the circular saw and told him that next time he would be on the saw bench. Metti angrily summoned us all and upbraided us. One more offence and he would come down hard on us. I had no money – I spent almost everything on our nocturnal excursions – and nowhere to go. I had no choice but to keep my mouth shut, and so Neri – being untouchable – continued his campaign. For his part, Uno now walked straight ahead and did not speak to anyone. Though I was grateful to Maurizio, I was also a little angry. His intervention gave the impression that I was incapable of defending myself.

Then came the letter. One morning, out of the blue, on a coal-scented winter breeze. My name and address in green ink, a peppermint colour favoured by only one person in the whole world – Viola made her own ink, it was a passion that had remained with her since her days as a 'chemist'. All through the morning, I kept it under my jacket then, at lunchtime, I ran upstairs to my room, locked the door and read it.

My dear Mimo,
I have received your various letters. I'm sorry I did not write
back sooner. I hope you don't take this letter the wrong

way, but I would rather you not write to me again, at least not at the moment. In hospital, I had a lot of time to think, and I have realised that I've been selfish. I dragged you into my childish games, I have hurt a lot of people – not least myself. It is time to grow up and put such childish things behind us. I would be happy to see you again some day, for coffee at the villa perhaps, when I am feeling better. Perhaps we will laugh at our erstwhile dreams. In the meantime, as I am sure you will understand, it is inappropriate for you to write to me without my having invited you to do so. We have to grow up.
Yours sincerely,
Viola Orsini

I did not go back down to the studio until mid-afternoon. I had spent an hour lying on my bed in a stupor made worse by my hangover. Viola's letter was a forgery. She had been forced to write it. But none of these theories held water. I knew Viola well enough to know that she was capable of not just writing this letter, but of believing it too. Curiously, what I found most hurtful was that she had signed not simply her name but her surname too, in a manner so cold, so distant, so far from our shared graves and our dreams of flying.

No sooner had I sat down on my stool than Neri came down on me like a ton of bricks. 'Where have you been? You're not being paid to goof off.'

'I was sick.'

'Oh, you're sick, that much I'll grant,' he said with a mocking smile.

I should have done as I always did and kept my mouth shut, but my banks were about to burst. 'Come on, Neri, deep down, I know you like me.'

'I do not!'

'Are you sure?'

I got up and wandered over to the statue of an apostle that he was finishing, a copy to replace a damaged original, which had been transferred to the Museo dell'Opera del Duomo. 'This is one of the statues for a niche in the façade of the Duomo, isn't it?'

'So?'

'So, you've clearly never heard of perspective...'

'Excuse me?'

'This statue will be in a niche about twenty metres up. Such a distance means that you need to artificially extend the dimensions, to stretch them, if you prefer, if you want them to seem proportionate when seen from the ground. Your statue,' I said, patting Neri's work, 'has the right proportions when viewed face on. But perched twenty metres high, it will look shrunken. Like me. And since this is not your first apostle, one could say that you have scattered dwarfs all over the façade of the Duomo. That is why I think that, deep down, you like me.'

I heard giggling. Neri turned and gave the others a black look and they fell silent. He took a step forward, bent down and thrust his face towards mine. 'Go back to your work. Or go back to writing letters to your girlfriend.'

I always hid the letters I wrote. Later, some of them had seemed a little crumpled, a detail I'd attributed to my own carelessness. Neri's comment could mean only one thing.

'Have you been reading my letters?'

'What if I have? What could you do?'

If I laid a hand on him, I would instantly find myself out on the streets. There was nothing I could do: he knew it, I knew it, and he gave me a smug smile.

I headbutted him in the face.

Filippo Metti did not turn a hair when he saw me appear in his office carrying my little suitcase. He was grateful I wasn't making things difficult for him. He didn't ask for an explanation, and I didn't offer one; we had had that conversation long ago.

'What are you planning to do now?' he asked.

I had thought about this while I was packing and could see no alternative to going back to Pietra d'Alba. Nobody was expecting me, but I could live in the little barn in the middle of the forest where we had hatched our plans. I would stay for as long as it took me to decide on a future which, just now, was utterly unknown. I would go home only to leave again. I would not even attempt to see Viola, since my princess had now grown up and I had not.

'I'm so sorry,' he said when I remained silent. 'It's mid-November and I can't pay you for a full month.'

'Of course.'

I headed for the door, dragging the trunk behind me. The wheels squeaked – I had always intended to oil them but never did. It was barely four o'clock, but beyond the windows of the old kitchen it was already dark. Sitting with his hand under his chin, alone in the pool of light from the industrial bulb that floated above him, Filippo Metti looked sad.

As I reached the door, he rose to his feet. 'Just a moment.'

From a drawer in his desk, he took a few banknotes, hesitated, counted out a few more and put them in an envelope, then came over and slipped it into my pocket. 'Just in case.'

I thanked him with a nod. Neither he nor I had much time for displays of emotion. We had been born into a world of hardship, of belt-tightening, where even emotions were rationed. In the doorway, I turned back one last time, thinking of Neri's stunned expression and the bloody bubbles coming out of his nose.

I smiled. 'Anyway... it was worth it.'

'I don't think so, Mimo.'

Addio Firenze bella, o dolce terra pia, scacciati senza colpa, gli anarchici van via e partono cantando, con la speranza in cuor.

Never had Il Cornutto sung so powerfully. We all took up the chorus, carried along by his powerful tenor. When I went to say my goodbyes in the cutting room, my friends had insisted on celebrating my departure in style. One last *sbronza*, a little drinking bout. My train would not leave until morning, so why not? One bar, then two, and shortly after we traipsed into the third, Il Cornutto appeared. He sang the song especially for me and even changed the name of the city in 'Addio a Lugano', a song about exiled anarchists, about kind-hearted murderers ripped from their homeland.

Adieu fair Florence, oh sweet and pious land, these blameless anarchists are banished, but they leave with a song, with hope in their hearts.

We said our last farewells, exchanged the usual promises, and then I wandered through the freezing ice, bumping into walls, waiting for the train station to open. The future no longer looked so bleak. My drunken optimism drowned out the curses that dawn whispers to the fearful. I stopped somewhere to piss against a wall.

There were five, their faces wrapped by scarves. They had been looking for me; I did not stand a chance. I put up a good fight, much better than they expected. Alcohol numbed my pain, while my strength was bolstered by black fury, and I floored two of them before the other three overcame me. They pummelled and kicked me as I lay on the ground, then left, taking their wounded with them. It would be many years before I saw Neri again.

I could have frozen to death. Never have I been so close to surrendering my soul, allowing it to slip into the dark November night and founder in the icy river. Then I caught a familiar scent, a mixture of bread dough, roses and sweat. My mother. She helped me sit up and whispered that everything would be fine, that although I could not see her, she could see me. There were other smells – cloves, geraniums, sandalwood, immortelles, aniseed, boredom and sadness – the scents of a thousand enraged mothers, a thousand ghostly mothers whose children had been abused, all gathered around me. A few moments later, I came to, gulping air like a drowning man. I was sitting with my back against a wall. My trunk lay open, my clothes strewn everywhere. It took me a minute before I thought to rummage in my pocket for the envelope that contained my entire fortune – about a hundred lire. It was gone. I would not be going back to Pietra d'Alba.

So I followed the most precious piece of advice my parents had given me since I arrived on earth. I got up and started walking.

The big top was exactly where he had said it would be, on the vacant lot behind the railway station – a barren field bordered by the train tracks on one side and a junkyard on the other. A minute's walk from the Grand Hotel Baglioni led to this wasteland of brick, dirt and twisted metal. The tent had seen better days – probably in the nineteenth century. A weathered banner atop a pole outside the entrance was emblazoned with the name of the ringmaster, the only person I knew in Florence – assuming that being hoodwinked by him was the same as knowing him: CIRCO BIZZARO.

The open flaps of the tent revealed splintered grey wooden bleachers around a circus ring some ten metres in diameter. Two caravans that hadn't been on the road for years teetered on worm-eaten chocks a little way off. A rudimentary paddock housed a horse, a sheep, a llama – the first I had ever seen – and a stable constructed from logs. In the early hours, it looked like a moonscape, a foreshadow of the orphaned landscapes of the Great Depression. As if by design, at that very moment Alfonso Bizzaro stepped out of one of the caravans, the wild-eyed prophet of a ruined world, and staggered towards a makeshift fountain made from a jerry can fed by a pipe that disappeared into the withered grass. He had not seen me. He splashed water on his face, snorted, stretched and yawned, then gazed at the horizon.

'So, there you are,' he said finally, his back still turned to me. 'The dwarf who's not a dwarf.'

'You still remember me after a whole year?'

'A year? We've seen each other since then. You spent all night talking to me a month ago in one of the dive bars on the banks of the Arno where some lanky guy was singing. Don't you remember?'

'No.'

'Hardly surprising, I admit, given all the drink you'd been putting away...'

Dragging my trunk behind me, my pride at half-mast, I dipped my head into the cold trough and grimaced. My whole body ached.

'Someone's done a proper job on you, haven't they? Was it sculpting that got you in this state, or was it a woman?'

'Both,' I said after a moment's thought.

'I'm assuming that if you're here, it's because you're looking for work?'

'If you have any. But I don't want to be part of your degrading show.'

'Well, now. And what is it about the show you consider degrading, my little prince?'

'Mocking... this,' I said, gesturing to us both.

'Ah, but if you mock yourself, then no one else can mock you afterwards or they'll just look stupid.'

'The philosophy of the drunkard.'

He burst out laughing. Though he was barely fifty, his face was scarred by a century of abuse by the sun and cold and sundry cruelties. But his laugh was young and drew upon an invisible, inexhaustible source of joy. 'You want to talk about drunkards? You're the one in a cloud of alcohol fumes. I'm dying to spark up a cigarette, but I'm afraid of blowing the whole place up.'

'So, do you have work for me or not? I'll do whatever you want.'

'How the mighty have fallen... You'll be in *The Creation* – the struggle between man and dinosaur – and during the day, you'll clean up and help out wherever you're needed. In exchange, you can sleep in the stables, you'll be fed, and you'll be paid eighty lire a month plus tips if you make the crowd happy. Is it a deal?'

I shook his hand. He took my chin between two fingers and turned my face towards the sun, which had finally deigned to shine on the wall of the junkyard next door. My right eye was starting to throb, a taste of iron sticking to my teeth.

'Sara will look after that for you,' said Bizzaro, nodding to the second caravan. 'But you'll have to wait until she wakes up. Otherwise, she'll be in a foul temper.'

And that is how I joined the Bizzaro circus. Fortunately, no one who later took an interest in me, or sought to run me down, ever found out. If Bizzaro was to be believed, he had pitched his circus tent in Florence after years of travelling the world. He claimed to have been part of Buffalo Bill's Wild West Show during its European tours and to have personally known William Cody. He had travelled all over Europe, performed secret shows during the war and entertained princes and peasants. I never knew what was true and what was fabulation, though I later verified that he spoke six or seven languages fluently and that he was a brilliant acrobat. The act where he juggled daggers dipped in poison (in fact it was tea mixed with charcoal dust, though that did not detract from the feat of juggling daggers) drew a huge crowd. Most nights, reprobates and guests from the nearby Hotel Baglioni, tramps in search of shelter and wealthy aristocrats rubbed shoulders on the same weather-beaten benches.

The business model of the Bizzaro circus was vague. There was no troupe to speak of, just a bunch of drifters Bizzaro recruited outside the railway station. For a single night or a hundred, they would don a dinosaur costume in the show that (according to the flyers handed out at the entrance) all of Italy clamoured to see: *The Creation* in which God first made the dinosaurs, and later man, and watched them fight it out. Viola would have been horrified, which only confirmed my resolve – to spite her, though she would not know – to take the role as the first human to be chased by a lumbering diplodocus. Some nights, the back half of a fearsome sauropod would trip over because the actor playing the rear-end was drunk. These unforeseen events were the spice of the show, and those who came knew what to expect. On a few occasions, for reasons no one could fathom, the performance degenerated into a mass brawl.

The receipts from the show would probably not have been enough to keep us going, but there was Sara. Though fast approaching sixty, and despite the harsh life of the carnival, Sara looked ten years younger. A certain plumpness smoothed out her wrinkles, which appeared when she laughed – which, in her case, was often. Sara, otherwise known as Signora Kabbala – the name inscribed in large red letters on the front of her caravan – was a fortune-teller by day. By night, or between tarot readings, she practised the same age-old profession as Zio's mother. The two occupations complemented each other perfectly. She would often say to a lonely customer, 'I see a fine piece of ass in your future,' then drag him into the back of the caravan and give him his money's worth. The customer would leave delighted, despite having paid twice – for the fortune and for the fornication – and would loudly proclaim to anyone who would listen that Signora Kabbala could truly predict the future.

At around eleven o'clock, when she finally stumbled blinking into the sunlight, Sara tended to me. Not her usual services, needless to say. She tended to my wounds with some vigour, but I gave in to a pleasure I had not known since leaving France. Someone was taking care of me.

'Want me to read your future, kid?'

'No need, I'm a time traveller.'

'Are you, now?'

'Of course, I come from the past. A second ago, I wasn't here, now I am.'

'What?'

'Nothing.'

As I left the caravan, I heard her mutter, 'He's even crazier than Alfonso.'

I had become a clown, a sinister clown, not remotely funny. I, Mimo Vitaliani, in whom a few people, among them my mother and Viola, had placed such hopes. But my mother and Viola had abandoned me. Besides, they had been mistaken. There was no place for someone like me in the hallowed ranks they imagined. My detractors had been right since I was born: I belonged in a circus.

I became the third permanent member of the troupe, together with Bizzaro and Sara. Others came and went, slept God knew where, only to reappear – or not – the following day. Sara sometimes played Eve in *The Creation*, a fleshy, scantily dressed Eve who ended up being swallowed by a large-winged red animal of uncertain species. The audience loved it. At least half the people I rubbed shoulders with in those days were my size. Far from making me feel better, being with them made me uncomfortable, perhaps because it could happen only in a circus tent. It did not normalise us, it simply singled us out. The audience came to see us tumbling and tripping over each other as we tried to escape the dinosaurs who, in the Gospel according to Bizzaro, had competed with humans for dominion over the earth. Every night, when I got angry and asked Bizzaro to write something less demeaning, he would sneeringly pull back the canvas flap separating us from the crowded bleachers. And every night, I degraded myself a little more, rolling in filth that I washed down with alcohol.

In the early days, Sara and I circled each other like wild beasts, sizing one another up. She would often give me a penetrating, unsettling look, as though trying to see past the adolescent boy who spent his nights hanging out with the worst reprobates in the city, only to come back, pale as death, nursing a hangover of Dantesque proportions. I liked her soothing presence, the brusque way she ordered Bizzaro and me around, even as I openly mocked her tarot cards, her fortune-telling and all the arrant nonsense Viola had taught me to despise. We spent our days seeking each other out and avoiding each other.

One evening, after I had helped her bring some logs into the caravan, she persuaded me to stay. She opened a trunk, took out a blue cardboard box and carefully untied the ribbon around it. Inside were two strange fruits on a small bed of taffeta that bore the imprint of a dozen others.

'Have you ever eaten dates? I have a client who brings me some once a year. They come from far away, so I make them last. They're filled with marzipan. These are the last two – go on, try one.'

'But if they're your last ones...'

'Taste it, I tell you.'

I picked up a date, sank my teeth into the sticky flesh and swallowed this exotic treasure almost whole. Sara shook her head, bit into half of hers and let it melt in her mouth with a sensual delight that made my cheeks flush. I looked away. In front of me, on a small square table, was a pack of cards and a stick of burning incense.

When I turned back, the date had disappeared, and Sara was once again giving me that unsettling look.

'I can tell you are intrigued by the tarot. Ask me a question.'

'All right, then. Do you really believe all this rubbish?'

She looked surprised, then nodded. 'From the moment we are born, we do only one thing: die. Or try to stave off the fateful moment for as long as possible. All my clients come for the same reason, Mimo. Because, however they choose to express it, they are terrified. I tell their cards and invent words to console them. They leave with their heads a little higher, and for a short while, they are a little less afraid. They believe, and that is what matters.'

'Well, when you look at it from that point of view...'

'Yes. I look at it from that point of view.'

'How do you deal with your own fear of death – after all, you can't lie to yourself?'

'I eat dates.' She looked sadly at the empty box, then laid a hand on my cheek. 'Aren't you afraid of death, Mimo?'

'No. Well, not of my own death, anyway.'

'Then you are not like other people.'

'No kidding – as if no one's ever said that to me before!'

Sara burst out laughing, and in doing so joined the list of my friends, all those who found my disagreeable character amusing. I set off back to the stable, but I had hardly taken the first step than she reappeared at the door of her caravan.

'Hey, Mimo!'

'Yes?'

'Take my word for it, when your time comes, and I hope it is a long way off, you will be scared. As scared as everyone else.'

The year 1922 moved to the rhythms of the Arno in the almost monochrome setting of our fairground, where the colour of the soil was broken only by that of brick. I learned to read the immediate future in the marble of the distant towers and façades. When they shimmered, they heralded rain. When they were lifeless, a sweltering day. I rarely left the circus during the day for fear of being spotted by someone. In my nightmares, that *someone* often looked like Neri or Metti. I did not know which I dreaded more, the glee of the former or the disappointment of the latter.

At night, Bizzaro and I would prowl the city. My employer supplemented his income with petty theft and trading in stolen goods. We frequented the same bars as before, where everyone seemed to know him. Sometimes he would meet strange characters I had never seen before and converse in one of his many languages – English, German, Spanish and three or four others I couldn't identify. In those days, it was difficult to trust anyone, but I never felt as comfortable as I did among these crooks with their singular code of honour. They did not care whether you were a Fascist or a Bolshevik, a Catholic or an atheist. Afflicted as we were by rosacea, cirrhosis and madness, we were a single people, sheltered from the squalls of time, clinging to each other until dawn while all around the night pitched and reeled.

When the first days of spring came, I missed the forest scent of Pietra d'Alba, and I could scarcely get out of bed for the almost physical pain of it. I wrote a long, insulting letter to Viola, calling her a Judas and repudiating all the things we had lived through together. The following day, I ventured into town to go to the post office and beg them to give me back the letter and, above all, not to send it. They laughed in my face; the Poste Italiane had not become the pride of the country by allowing letters to linger. So I went back to my stable and wrote another letter, begging Viola to ignore the first. I gave no return address – I did not want her to know what I was doing.

Of that year, I remember very little. The days were all the same and the nights best passed over in silence, and we moved between them without quite knowing how. Bizzaro was a curious character, at once friend and father figure, yet it was impossible to let your guard down with him. It was not uncommon, on a night out after a brilliant performance, for him to suddenly refer to me as 'my dwarf', to which I would invariably reply that I was neither a dwarf nor his, and we were constantly on the verge of fighting. A drinking companion would often have to pull us apart and force us to shake hands, which we would do reluctantly, smiling as we tried to crush the other's fingers.

One morning in July, I woke with an unpleasant feeling. I had dreamed I was performing in the show, dressed as a cave man, and saw Viola in the front row of the audience. I tried to hide behind the others, but everything went dark and a single spotlight picked me out and tracked my every move. It was not the nightmare that upset me, but the fact that, in my dream, Viola's face was a little blurred. I had not seen her for almost two years and her face was slowly fading, eroded by the winds of time, by the passing seconds and the minutes, by all the days that swirled between us.

Shortly afterwards, Sara appeared in the stable clutching a metal box. 'Good, you're awake. Do you want to make a donation to Alfonso?'

She shook the box and handed it to me. Alfonso's birthday was coming up and the troupe was planning to buy him a signet ring. Bizzaro loved jewellery. He invariably wore a cheap, tacky ring or necklace, sometimes paired with a strange piece of unknown provenance that looked perilously authentic. I stuffed a few notes into the box, but I had my own idea for a gift. The boys from the cutting room, the only ones I still saw, had brought me a small block of marble, a cube measuring about thirty centimetres, and a few careworn tools. For the first time in six months, I had spent the past week sculpting.

Some days later, rather than dispersing after the performance, the troupe hung around. Sara climbed up on a table and clanged the back of a saucepan. She looked like an inverted pear – wide at the top, with surprisingly slender legs, which were very much on show. She made a little speech, thanked Bizzaro for putting up with her for so long. Bizzaro was given his ring, which everyone then admired. A few bottles of wine were uncorked and passed around – there were even some wine glasses, but everyone drank straight from the bottle.

I waited until Bizzaro was alone then tugged his sleeve. 'I've got a present for you.'

'Another one?'

I led him towards his caravan, which was never locked. The inside was always impeccable, in stark contrast to its owner – Sara tenderly cared for him though there did not seem to be any romantic connection between them. I had left my sculpture on the table. As with Viola's bear, I had taken into account the limited time available and carved only the top part of the cube. It depicted our fairground from a slightly elevated perspective, and I was proud of it. You could see the big top, the caravans and a few animals emerging from the stone. I had carved it in bas-relief rather than in the round. The viewer's eye moved over the field on a winter's morning, with that low, dense fog that obscured everything on the ground. I had carved only what emerged from the mist.

Instantly, I was greeted by that look that was beginning to irritate me, and the words that invariably accompanied it. 'Did you make this?'

'No, the Pope carved it. He couldn't be here in person, but he sends his apologies and said to wish you a happy birthday.'

Seeming not to have heard, Bizzaro stared at his marble circus, his eyes glistening.

I coughed, embarrassedly. 'So, how old are you?'

'Two thousand years old, Mimo. Two thousand years, give or take. But don't tell anyone.'

He stroked his big top with his fingertip. He swallowed several times then finally turned to me. 'So, it's true.'

'What?'

'That you're a sculptor.'

'Of course, I told you the day we first met at the train

station.'

'If you only knew the things people say to me when I first meet them at the station... The question now is what the hell are you doing here?'

I could tell he was sinking into one of his vindictive moods. There was never a good reason. I was no longer a boy; I would turn eighteen later that year, I could stand my ground and I could hold my liquor with the best of them. It was a long time since I had let people push me around. 'Do you want me to go? Because you've only got to say so.'

'No, I don't want you to go.'

'That's good. So can we go back to drinking now?'

He peered at me, stared at the downy beard that covered my cheeks, at my hair, which I no longer cut. He seemed about to ask another question, but then patted me on the shoulder. 'Good idea, let's go get a drink.'

From time to time, the carabinieri would pay a visit to the circus. They would turn over the straw in the stable where I slept and rummage through Bizzaro's caravan. They never found anything. They were much more polite when it came to Sara, contenting themselves with a courtesy visit. This courtesy was probably due to the fact that she offered them the chance to 'see the Creation' and, during their search, would sit with her skirt hiked up over her knees and her legs a little too far apart. The carabinieri would leave filled with a new-found respect for the origin of the world, which they had never imagined to be so fleshy or so hairy. Occasionally, their captain would linger for a while to carry out a 'supplementary search', the ardour of which would shake the caravan almost off its chocks. He would leave without paying, but Sara did not object. The man was indebted to her.

The Bizzaro circus was almost a free city, a state within a state, governed by its own laws and ethics. But much the same could be said about every Italian province, every village, where the great promises of the Risorgimento were slow to be fulfilled. Instead of a unified kingdom, we were still a hodgepodge of petty warlords, gangsters, caïds and brigands. On 28 October of that year, the most powerful among them, Fascists, *squadristi* and former partisans, tried their luck. A ragtag band marched on Rome, determined to intimidate the government. Despite their success in suppressing the socialist riots, they were poorly armed, diffident and, above all, unsure of what they were doing. So unsure in fact that their valiant leader, former socialist and future dictator Mussolini, stayed at home in Milan trembling in his baggy trousers, considering it safer not to join the march so that he could flee to Switzerland if things went wrong. It was an age of cowardice. Hence, the government and the King decided to let things take their course rather than sending in the army, which was primed and ready to act. Overnight, the goon from Milan found himself head of the government, and no one was more surprised than he. Across the country, every playground bully, every backroom tyrant discovered he had been right all along. I could not yet imagine the lasting impact this day would have on my destiny, but it had one immediate effect: it put Bizzaro in an even worse mood.

Sara repeatedly expressed her concern, saying she had never seen him like this. The circus was in full swing and the takings good. Sara was vulgar and bawdy and, as a result, almost mythic in her sensuality. But she was also a woman of great delicacy and, like all those who see the future, a perceptive reader of the human soul. She was right to worry, even if, in hindsight, I still find it hard to understand how one event led to another.

It was a frosty evening at the end of November. Viola and I had just turned eighteen, and despite my best efforts, I was still thinking in terms of 'Viola and I'. Bizzaro and I were at our favourite bar, a little depressed because Il Cornutto had not been seen for almost a month. Without his voice, the booze tasted bitter, but that did not stop us from drinking copious quantities. Just as I was about to drain one glass too many, my companion said 'that's enough' and dragged me outside.

Instead of heading back towards the circus, he briskly set

off northward.

'Where are you going?' Grumbling, I trailed after him, careful not to slip on the melting snow.

We were still in the centre of the city, yet these streets were unfamiliar, their names erased by icy gusts. Via de' Ginori. Via Guelfa. The storm was raging as we came to a little square with a baroque façade that seemed familiar, though I had never visited this district. Bizzaro turned left onto the via Cavour and knocked on a door. Nothing happened, so he knocked harder.

'All right, all right,' protested a muffled voice. 'I'm coming.'

Finally, a man appeared in the doorway. A man of diminutive stature like us, except that he was dressed as a monk. What with the alcohol and the cold, I felt as though I had landed in Viola's favourite gothic novel. That was the last time I thought about her, I swear.

'What the hell are we doing here? It's freezing.'

'Shut up and come in. Thank you, Walter.'

Armed with a lantern, the monk led us up a flight of stairs. When we came to the first floor, he stopped and handed the lantern to Bizzaro. The ceiling above our heads was lost in darkness. 'One hour, not a second more. And above all, don't make a sound.' He disappeared.

Bizzaro turned to me, his dazzling white teeth seeming huge in the flickering flame.

'Happy birthday,' he said.

'My birthday was a month ago, just after yours.'

'I know that,' he said, still grinning.

I glanced around; it was a bare corridor, with several half-open doors to either side.

Bizzaro handed me the lantern and said again: 'Happy birthday.'

I moved towards one of the doors, but he grabbed my arm and pointed to a door on the left. 'That one.'

I stepped inside and instantly I was assaulted and stunned by the colours before me and by the Virgin's face, as tender as anything I had ever seen. Which was not exactly true, since I had seen this same Virgin in the pages of the first book Viola ever lent me. *Illustrious painters no. 17, Fra Angelico.* There before me, an angel with brightly coloured wings was telling a young girl that she would change the destiny of humanity.

I turned to Bizzaro, speechless. He smiled, took me by the arm and led me from one room to another. Each cell contained a firework display created six hundred years earlier, an unending riot of colour.

'How did you know...?' I said at last.

'When we first met, you told me that you wanted to see these frescoes. I wasn't sure whether you had ever had the chance. From the look on your face, I assume not.'

'Thank you.'

'It's Walter you should thank. He used to work for me ten years ago, before he started hearing voices. Nice guy, though.

The museum is open during the day, but I thought seeing them like this, on your own...'

An hour later, we were back out on the street. The snow had stopped. In the moonlight, the city glowed as bright as day. A muted sadness gnawed at my belly, the ghost of more carefree days shaking its chains.

'What's with the face?'

'I'm fine. Just cold.'

For a long moment Bizzaro seemed lost in thought, the lower half of his face buried in his collar.

'When you showed up at the circus all bruised and battered, you said it was because of a woman. Is it her that's got you in this state?'

'Viola? No. I don't know. She was a friend.'

'A friend you...' He made a circle with his thumb and forefinger, and jabbed a finger in and out.

I blushed. 'Like I said, she was just a friend.'

'Why "just a friend"? Is she ugly? Is she *lesbica*?'

I stopped in my tracks. 'She's not ugly, I don't know what she is, and please don't talk about her like that.'

'Oh, come on, don't be such a sensitive little dwarf.'

'For the last time, I'm not a dwarf.'

'Oh, but you are,' he said. 'You want proof...' He gestured to me then to himself. '*Nanus nanum fricat*, dwarfs hang out with dwarfs.'

'We've just had a great time. Why do you have to ruin it?

Are you looking for a fight?'

'Me? I'm not looking for anything, I'm just telling you the truth. And do you know why? Because for all your airs and graces, for all your *I am but a man like any other*, you don't really believe it. If I called you a giant octopus from another planet, you'd laugh, you wouldn't care. But when I call you a dwarf, you get angry. Because it hurts.'

'All right, it hurts, are you finished?'

'Or what? Are you going to punch me in the face? Me, your good friend Bizzaro? Well, go ahead, don't let me stop you.'

Since he asked, and since we had been drinking, I did. His nose cracked in a gush of blood. This was far from being Bizzaro's first street brawl, so with a very professional left hook, he returned the favour. We rolled around in the snow, screaming. Yet just half an hour earlier we had been sobbing in front of the frescoes of Fra Angelico.

'Now, boys, what's going on?'

Four men had just appeared on the street. All of them wearing instantly recognisable black shirts. A militia.

'They're not kids,' said one, 'they're dwarfs.'

Bizzaro faced the man, his face bruised, his lips curled into a sneer. 'Who are you calling a dwarf?'

He stamped on the first man's foot and, when he doubled over in pain, floored him with a right cross. One of the others pulled a brass knuckle from his pocket and slipped it on. A split second later, I saw a blade in Bizzaro's hand.

'Want to play too, *Schweinehund*?' he snickered.

The blade moved so fast I didn't see it coming. There was a flash of blue and the bastard with the knuckleduster collapsed, clutching his stomach. The other two hurled themselves at us. I fought as best I could, and when I couldn't, I just took the blows. There came the sound of whistles and more shouting before we were separated by a group of carabinieri. An hour later we were all at the police station, me, Bizzaro and three militiamen – the fourth had gone to hospital, or to the morgue. Bizzaro took the rap, the militiamen were quick to press charges, and I was tossed out into the street at dawn with my nose crusted with blood, a twisted ankle and one eye swollen shut. I limped back to the circus. Beneath a blanket of snow, our field lay sleeping like a child in a manger. I was hesitant to wake Sara, but eventually knocked on her door. She opened almost immediately, dressed in a long silk nightie, with a shawl draped around her shoulders.

'*Santo Cielo*, what in God's name happened to you?'

I told her all about my birthday visit to the Convent of San Marco and Alfonso's strange mood swing afterwards. She nursed me back to health, just as she had done when I first arrived a year earlier, then poured me a drink that made me cough for several minutes.

'Is that better? I don't understand this need you all seem to have to fight. Well, I don't understand in Bizzaro's case. With you, I know what the problem is.' She poured herself a glass, drained it in one gulp and held it up. 'Hormones. They fill you up until you're overflowing and they've got to come out somehow. Are you sure you're dipping your *cazzo* regularly?'

I turned puce. She stared at me, then laughed incredulously.

'Don't tell me you've never...' She shook her head and pushed me back onto her bed. 'Consider it a gift, since it was your birthday. But don't imagine it will happen again.'

She hiked up her dress and I stared in astonishment at the Creation, majestic and purple. She tugged at my trousers, as I frantically tried to hold them up. 'Just let me get on with it, you idiot.'

She climbed on top of me and I forgot all my troubles. This being my first time, I wanted to give Sara a firework display worthy of the Ruggieri family. But there was a technical glitch, a misfire. The pyrotechnician launched the final rocket too early. I started to cry.

Sara lay down next to me, pressed my head to her breast and stroked my hair. Sara, Mammina and the millions of others who came before them. Since that grey, tender morning, I have known that when a woman lies under a man, whether on the docks in Genoa, in the back of a lorry or on a fairground, it is to soften his fall.

Thanks to her friendship with the captain of the carabinieri, Sara came back that night bearing good news. Luckily, the man Bizzaro had stabbed was not dead. But there was still the charge of attempted murder, with four witnesses. Fortunately, the captain, who despised Fascists, had tinkered with the witness statements such that the knife now belonged to the militiamen, who had pulled it only for Bizzaro to grab it during the scuffle, in self-defence. Bizzaro would probably not serve more than a few months.

The immediate result was that the circus had to close. And since they felt they needed to set an example, two officers came to place symbolic seals on the big top, under the desolate gaze of a fortune-teller, a sculptor who no longer sculpted, a horse, a sheep and a llama.

For several days, I wandered around, trying to avoid facing the inevitable. I was a dead weight to Sara, something she didn't mention out of kindness. Signora Kabbala could not make ends meet without the regular clientele from the circus. And while her extracurricular activities provided a steady income, she could not take care of a young man of eighteen who ate enough for four and drank as much at night. Nobility of spirit dictated that I take the lead, pack my trunk and leave amid the sound of squeaking wheels. But I lacked the nobility of spirit and I had nowhere to go. So I cravenly waited for Sara to throw me out.

On 1 January 1923, she blew into the stable on a glacial breeze. A month had passed since Bizzaro's arrest. I was lying spreadeagled and in a paralytic drunken stupor from the night before. Il Cornutto had reappeared shortly before midnight, just as we were about to bury the old year. He had lost a lot of weight, something I would have thought impossible had I not seen him. He told no one where he had come from or where he was going. Sixty-odd years later, I can still picture his face with surprising clarity. I see in it the mark of death, the fear of crossing the bar, now that I, too, am on that threshold. But that night, no one paid any heed – they simply wanted him to sing, and he did, though his voice was less powerful, less pure than before and broke several times. No one thought to make fun of him. We just wept all the more as we tumbled towards dawn, since all our nights were a downhill slope.

Sara stared at me reproachfully, her hands on her hips. When I tried to say something, my mouth filled with bile. I raised up a finger asking her to be patient then rolled onto my side and vomited into the straw. Finally, I propped myself on one elbow, pale and dishevelled. My voice was hoarse from having spent the night howling.

'I know what you're going to say.'

'There's someone here to see you. In my caravan.'

Ten minutes later, I went over to Sara's. I had given up on trying to wash, since the pipe that fed the trough was frozen. On the bottom step of her caravan, a young man about my age was tapping his foot. He greeted me with a nod and opened the door as if to a prince.

Despite the cassock, I did not immediately recognise the visitor sitting opposite Sara. Temporary amnesia brought on by my condition, the fact that he had lost much of his hair since our last meeting and was now wearing small round tortoiseshell glasses: Francesco, Viola's brother. He looked me up and down, smiling all the while. His gaze lingered on my long hair and my beard, still flecked with the remnants of last night's meal. He seemed perfectly at ease, while Sara nervously squirmed on her velvet bench.

'Are you sure you wouldn't like something to drink, Father?'

'No, I won't be staying long. You've changed, Mimo. When we last met you were a boy, now you're a man.'

'How did you find me?'

'I went to your old studio. Nobody there seemed to know where you were. As I was leaving, a young man covered in marble came after me, and when he was sure that I wished you no harm, told me where I could find you.'

'What do you want?'

'I'll explain back at my hotel. My secretary, the man you met outside, will surely get frostbite if I linger. I'm staying at the Baglioni. Bring your things.'

He stood up and gave Sara a little bow. 'A very good day to you, signora.'

Sara looked at him, wide-eyed, and then, just as he was about to leave, she ran after him. 'Father, Father!'

She caught him up halfway through the field. 'I am not of your faith, but bless me, Father, please.'

She knelt in the snow and I heard Francesco murmur a few words as he traced the sign of the cross on her forehead with his gloved hand. I went back to the stable, feeling queasy and stunned. Francesco looked like Viola. And that slight resemblance, that distant ghost, was enough to rip my stomach apart. I bent double and spewed a trickle of bile. Then I packed my meagre belongings into my trunk and counted up the money I had left. My fortune amounted to fifteen lire, enough to buy back a little dignity. Shortly before noon, I left the stable. Sara was nowhere to be seen; the curtains of her caravan were drawn. I headed in the opposite direction to the Baglioni, crossed the Arno by the Ponte Santa Trinita, headed up the Via Maggio, lost my way, found Via Sant'Agostino by chance and my destination: number 8 – a place frequented by many of my drinking companions – the Florence public baths. There I cleaned myself up, mortified my flesh with the coldest water and feverishly scrubbed myself to be rid of the evil engrained in the folds of my skin. I came out lobster-red and shivering, but with my chin held high. I retraced my steps, stopped at the first barber and had a haircut and a shave. Then, in a transport of oils and sandalwood-scented powder, I stared at a face I had not seen for two years. Harder, if not necessarily wiser, since a new madness shone in the eyes. But for the first time in my life, I found myself handsome. Out in the street, I lifted my shaven cheeks to the timorous sun. I did not have money to buy clothes. At the baths, I had donned my only reasonably clean suit.

Dragging my trunk behind me, I finally crossed the threshold of the Baglioni, beneath the wary eye of the same doorman who had seen me come and go outside the hotel for nearly two years. He made a move to block my path, but I glared at him and he stopped in his tracks and stepped aside. Francesco was right. I was a man now, a chain of violence and murder barely held together by a silken thread.

Francesco received me in a private room. His secretary sat in the corner typing on a portable typewriter. The ceiling disappeared into darkness. On the street side, a stained-glass window admitted a blade of amber light. The Grand Hotel Baglioni had the murky, muted splendour of the palaces of yesteryear. This was the same hotel where Pirandello, Puccini, D'Annunzio and Rudolph Valentino had stayed or would stay in the future. I should have been intimidated, but thanks to the alcohol still circulating in my blood and softening my mood, I wasn't.

Francesco gestured for me to sit. 'You're looking well, Mimo. Good to see you again. Would you care for a coffee?'

I remained standing. 'No, thank you. What do you want with me?'

I had always liked Francesco for his gentleness and his sempiternal smile, though I already suspected that he shared his sister's talent for illusion, an ability to direct the eye where he wanted it to be. I was never sure whether Francesco was burning with ambition or simply a desire to play.

'I don't *want* anything, Mimo, or nothing that can be granted to me here on earth. I am here to ask you to come back.'

'Back? Back where?'

'To Pietra d'Alba, obviously.'

'I have no home there.'

'Your uncle Alberto bequeathed you his studio.'

At this news, I slumped onto the sofa. 'Alberto is dead?'

'No, he is not dead, he has gone to live in the sun, somewhere in the south. I think he has been bored ever since he inherited a substantial sum from his mother. We approached him with a view to buying the property, but he refused to sell it to us. He wanted to give it to you. Your friend Vittorio has his carpentry workshop there, but I'm sure the two of you can come to some arrangement.'

'Just a minute. Zio is *giving* me the studio?'

'That's correct.'

That old bastard. Why he would do such a thing was beyond me. Some vestige of humanity, perhaps, had resurfaced like a burp between two swigs of booze. And I could hardly criticise, sharing as I did the same vices.

'There is not much work for a sculptor in Pietra d'Alba,' I said.

'That's precisely why I'm here. A notary could have told you that the studio now belongs to you. I came in person because we wish to employ you.'

'Who exactly is "we"?'

'We, the Orsini family. And we' – he added with a sweeping gesture – 'who serve the Lord. As you know, your sculpture made a powerful impression on Archbishop Pacelli. Monsignor Pacelli is a man of considerable influence; it is through him and his confidence in me that – though I was ordained a few short months ago – I have become a member of the Curia. I work with him dealing with external relations of the Holy See. To be brief, by the end of the decade, we hope to execute a major renovation of the Casina Pio IV, in the gardens of the Vatican, and we wish to engage a trustworthy artist to handle the sculpture. There are several works to be created and many others to be restored. It will be a major commission. You will be able to work from Pietra d'Alba or from the studios in the Vatican, as you prefer. You will of course have young apprentices to help you in Rome. Initially, we would like to offer you a one-year contract, renewable twice, at a salary of two thousand lire a month.'

'Two thousand lire a month,' I said calmly.

Six times the salary of a labourer, twice that of a university professor. More money than I had ever seen.

'Which I am sure that you can supplement with a few private commissions. Many visitors to the Villa Orsini have also been struck by your bear.'

'And... who is to pay for all this?'

'One of the Vatican dicasteries. Though it goes without saying that the whole endeavour is also a way of showing the Orsini family in a flattering light. We are acting as patrons of the arts in supporting you and offering you, despite your young age, a position that will doubtless arouse some jealousy.'

'I'm used to it.'

'Because your name will hereafter be associated with ours, you will have to abstain from any... bad habits you might have picked up during your stay in Florence, is that clear?'

'Quite clear.'

'Is it presumptuous of me to assume that you will accept?'

I pretended to consider the offer, which he tolerated with the patience of those who think in terms of eternity. 'I accept.'

'Very well, then. I am going back to Pietra tomorrow, so we shall travel together. You will take possession of your new studio, and we shall discuss how best to organise everything. For tonight, I have reserved a room for you here.' He rose to his feet and smoothed his cassock. 'Any questions?'

'No. Oh, yes, actually, was it Vio— was it your sister who suggested that you hire me?'

'Viola? No, why?'

'How is she?'

'She has been very fortunate. Obviously, such an accident was bound to leave some scars, but she is almost completely recovered. You will see for yourself. My parents are expecting us for dinner the day after tomorrow.'

I slept poorly, starting at the slightest noise, dreading that any moment my door would be flung open to reveal a baying crowd outraged by my presence in this grand hotel, demanding that I be lynched or – worse – be thrown out into the street, into the gutter where I had wallowed only the night before, a howling mob accusing me of being an impostor and insisting there was no place for impostors at the Grand Hotel Baglioni.

We set off early the following morning. After about fifty kilometres, I realised that I had not said goodbye to Sara, to my lifelong friends or to the dancing shadows of my furtive nights.

In the preface to his monograph, Leonard B. Williams writes that the *Vitaliani Pietà* has quickly joined the Seal of Solomon, the Ark of the Covenant and the Philosopher's Stone in the ranks of mythic, esoteric objects, hidden from the eyes of mere mortals, and all the more famous because they are not seen. He is quick to highlight the irony of the situation, since it is precisely the antithesis of what the Vatican hoped to achieve by burying it in the bowels of a mountain. The Vatican was merely attempting to avoid any scandal and to understand the curious public reactions to the work. Yet, if the intention of the Church had been to fashion a myth, to weave a fantasy, it could have done no better. According to Williams, entrusting the *Pietà* to the care of the Sacra and its monks was a mistake. It is in darkness that feverish dreams fester.

Before discussing the hysteria that greeted the first exhibitions of the *Pietà*, Williams devotes a brief passage to describing the work. He is quick to remind the reader that the piece was originally known as the *Pietà Orsini*, after the family who first commissioned it and, in the years following its completion, did everything in their power to disassociate themselves from the work – with notable success, since today the confidential documents about it refer only to the name of its creator, Michelangelo Vitaliani.

The *Pietà* bears many similarities to its illustrious ancestor, that by Michelangelo Buonarroti, on display in the Basilica di San Pietro in the Vatican. It is a sculpture in the round, measuring one metre seventy-six high, ninety-five centimetres wide and eighty centimetres deep. Unlike Michelangelo's work, however, the *Vitaliani Pietà* does not seem to have been intended to be viewed from below. The plinth is only ten centimetres high.

In accordance with tradition, the *Pietà* depicts the Virgin cradling her son after the descent from the cross. Here again, it echoes the Vatican *Pietà*. Christ is laid across his mother's lap. The anatomical precision is even more detailed than in that of Michelangelo. Or, rather, the precision is comparable, but unlike his predecessor, Vitaliani does not seek to make his Christ beautiful. The consequences of the crucifixion are visible in the body's rigor, brought on by a build-up of lactic acid. Paradoxically, depicting rigor in a hard material like marble is no easy task. It requires a sculptor of genius, because the stiffness is apparent only when contrasted with the serenity of the face, the half-smile that plays on the dead man's lips. Vitaliani does not seek to make his Christ handsome, yet in spite of himself, he is beautiful, the beardless cheeks hollowed out by agony, the eyes just recently closed by his mother's soothing hand. The work exudes an unsettling sense of movement, which is in stark contrast to Michelangelo's hieratic style. This is not a metaphorical impression: many viewers who have gazed at the work swear they have actually *seen* it move.

This contrast reaches its apogee in the spectacular figure of Mary. The mother looks down at her son with a tender smile, a curious absence of fear and grief, considered by many to explain the mystery and the hysteria. The Virgin is unalloyed gentleness. A lock of hair falls onto her left cheek from beneath her veil. Her expression is one of deep serenity, full of the life that has just left her son. Rather than serenity, Williams corrects himself, it is something akin to *hope* that can be seen on her features, the last emotion one would expect.

The viewer instantly knows they are in the presence of a masterpiece, says Williams, in a rare moment of lyricism in the monograph. He admits that, after his first visit, he hesitated to write about the work. And yet, in his profession, he has studied many of the great masterpieces of art. None has had a similar effect, a visceral reaction that he has been unable to analyse. In awarding him his doctorate *cum laude*, his thesis supervisor said something surprising: 'You have spent long years studying for nothing, Williams. Nothing that makes art, great art, can be explained, because the artist himself does not know what he is doing.'

Williams knew perfectly well what his professor was trying to say. Art is not reason. But Williams is not just another academic; he has instinct. And his instinct whispers to him that when he created his *Pietà*, Mimo Vitaliani knew precisely what he was doing.

'Remember what I am about to tell you,' my mother chided. I had come home from school black and blue, having fought to prove to some naysayers that I was not a half-pint but a full pint, and complained that I had no chance. I was different, said my mother, that much was true. Instead of making me tall, strong and handsome, God had made me short, strong and handsome. And my luck, too, would be different. It would never come at the first attempt; it would not be a fairground wheel where everyone always wins and in doing so wins nothing. For me, the Good Lord had reserved the very best. 'You will be a man of second chances.'

I was not far from believing this nonsense when I went back to Pietra d'Alba after more than two years. A muted, low-lying wind brought the sound of a panpipe from the plateau, a strange keening sound, modulated by the terrain, that sometimes sounded like the whimper of a dog welcoming its master. At my request, Francesco left me on the outskirts of the village, then had his secretary drive on to the Villa Orsini. I felt a pang of sadness as I passed the crossroads leading to the cemetery and instinctively rummaged in the hollow stump. The damp, misty landscape matched my mood. But behind the veil of white, the eye could distinguish the luxuriant green of the forest, just waiting for a ray of sunshine to reveal itself.

The workshop seemed at once the same and different. The stonework had been cleaned, the façade repointed and the old roof tiles replaced. The barn smelled of the fresh coat of tar that covered the wooden walls. The once-barren courtyard between the buildings had been planted with flowerbeds fashioned from stones pilfered from neighbouring fields and held together by wire. Though still bare, the black loam, which had been turned over a month earlier, would soon bring forth cosmos and spring flowers. The beaten earth I had known, muddy in winter and crazed in summer heatwaves, had been covered with white gravel.

Anna gave a terrified shriek when I went into the kitchen, only to laugh when she recognised me. Her belly was swollen, and I did not even have time to hug her before Paragraph burst in, hammer in hand. He too laughed when he saw me. They welcomed me like a member of the family and we drank thick, bitter coffee on the doorstep to ward off the cold stinging our nostrils. Paragraph was almost twenty-two, and he and Anna had been married three months earlier. I was not sufficiently expert to work out from the size of her belly whether the marriage was the cause or the consequence of her pregnancy, and I did not care. They were happy and apologised for having taken over the main house after Zio had left two months earlier. I had no intention of living there. I found it difficult to think of myself as a landowner, since only a few days earlier I had stunk of the gutters of Florence. For the time being, I would sleep in the barn. Paragraph and I would be partners, on terms yet to be defined but that might be summed up as 'nothing changes'. He would carry on his carpentry work in the barn, and I would take over Zio's studio. No contract in this region was worth a handshake.

The first thing I did was write to my mother. Of the four letters I had written during my two years in Florence, I had sent only three, having lost one of them during a drunken binge. In them I described the glories of my daily life and the praise and encouragement heaped on me. I hoped that her letters describing the quiet life in Brittany, in a village called Plomodiern in the arse end of nowhere, were more truthful. Now, for once, I could be honest: I had made it. I had a roof over my head and a job. I offered to send for her as soon as she wanted to come.

That evening, Emanuele arrived, wearing the blue stovepipe trousers with crimson facings of a Polish lancer – a genuine antique – and a khaki jacket. He cried when he saw me. Then he got down on his knees, put his ear to Anna's stomach and whispered some gibberish to the baby, which made Paragraph roll his eyes. 'That's all we need!'

The four of us dined in the kitchen on fresh bread, slightly acidic tinned tomatoes and barely salted anchovies fresh from Savona. They caught me up on two years of the history of Pietra d'Alba, where nothing of any consequence had happened. The Orsini and the Gambale families still cordially despised each other. Viola had not appeared in public since her fall. There were rumours that she was crippled and disfigured, though Francesco would have told me if this were true, as I was due to see her the following day. The much-heralded electricity had never reached the Orsini villa. Disease had decimated a third of the orange trees, and the smell of neroli was no longer as intense when the south wind blew. Nobody had died, not even Old Angelo the postman, despite his announcing his impending death to anyone who would listen.

As I had with my mother, I gave my friends a much-diluted version of my sojourn in Florence, which, in other words, meant that I lied through my teeth. Bizzaro, Sara and the others were scrubbed from the photo of those two years. I felt a little guilty, though I did not realise that, in severing their memories, I was only hurting myself. I was eighteen, an age when no one wants to be seen for who they really are.

These days Paragraph was smoking a long straight pipe and offered me a few acrid puffs as we sat and gazed at the Milky Way. Anna went upstairs to bed. I envied their complicit looks, their hands still searching for each other with no sign of weariness or habit. Then I went back to my barn, exhausted, steeling myself to travel in time to the next day.

I slept better than I had for months, on a bed of fresh straw, in the fresh scent of grass that has yellowed yet still retained a ghost of greenness. I dreamed of anchovies, thousands of them in silvery streams, coursing through the streets of Florence. A fortuitous omen, said Anna the next morning, with the supreme confidence of those who know nothing. I gently mocked her, pretending I did not believe in omens. Secretly, I began to hope that the fabled luck of the Vitaliani family – fabled for its absence – had finally changed.

Late in the morning, Francesco's secretary came to the studio. He handed me two letters. The first contained an advance of two thousand lire. I gave half to Paragraph and Anna, who initially demurred, staring wide-eyed at the banknotes. They accepted only when I told them it was for the baby, and so that they could install a new stove to heat the whole house. The second envelope contained a handwritten invitation on a card embossed with the Orsini coat of arms.

The Marchese and Marchesa Orsini, their sons, Stefano and Francesco, and their daughter, Viola, request the honour of your presence at dinner on 3 January 1923 at Villa Orsini, at 8.30 p.m.

The secretary then informed me of the various projects that awaited me this year: I was to restore two statues from the façade of the Casina Pio IV, examine the villa's extensive bas-reliefs with a view to their possible restoration and create a sculptural group on the subject of Diana the Huntress, which would be part of a fountain in an annexe. The secretary gave me the address of my studio in Rome, not far from the Vatican, above which there was an apartment that I could use. I told him that I intended to work chiefly in Pietra d'Alba, where my friends lived. As he was about to take his leave, he took a bag from the back of his car. In it was a suit in my size. Francesco had obviously anticipated my acceptance. Paragraph and Anna laughed when I put it on and spent the rest of the day addressing me as *my liege* and *Your Highness*. Aside from a few details, which Anna took care of with a needle, the suit fitted perfectly. I had never worn a tailored suit in my entire life. My clothes were a motley collection of boys' clothes and adult outfits that had been cut, shortened, darned and patched a thousand times. My entire wardrobe fitted into my trunk on wheels.

The secretary came to fetch me at eight o'clock. My friends watched me leave, mocking, waving their hands. I spent the short journey to the villa imagining all the possible scenarios for my reunion with Viola. Would she be cold, as in her last letter, more than a year earlier? And if she were, would it simply be her way of hiding her joy at seeing me again? For my own part, I had been hurt by her silence, so I resolved to be polite and distant, as befits a sculptor in the employ of the Vatican. But not so cold as to offend her should she regret our estrangement and wish to make amends.

By the time we arrived, I had considered every possibility, forgetting that Viola was mercurial, that she was not bound by the realms of possibility, the hands of hunters, by gravity and, more importantly, by what was considered normal.

'Il Signor Marchese e la Signora Marchesa.'

The hosts made a grand entrance into the lounge where we were gathered. The Marchesa wore a raspberry dress with a wide collar, while the Marchese wore a uniform with epaulettes that would have made Emanuele cry with joy. My frequent visits to the area around the Hotel Baglioni and the aristocrats who came to slum it at the circus had allowed me to develop a taste for fine fabrics. I knew that gentlemen no longer wore uniforms at dinner, lest they be considered old-fashioned or – worse – provincial. Women's fashions, on the other hand, were harder to pin down because they changed so quickly – hemlines rose and fell with the speed of those animated picture books I used to flick through as a child. But Giandomenico and Massimilia Orsini, the Marchese and Marchesa of Pietra d'Alba, wore their clothing with the elegant stiltedness of yesteryear, and not without a certain grace. They would have commanded respect wearing rags.

I was a little disappointed to find that I was not the only dinner guest – there were a dozen of us. Stefano gave me a wink and mocking smile, and then Francesco introduced me to a duke and a duchess, two secretaries from the ministry, a lieutenant-general bedecked with medals, a Milanese lawyer and an actress whose name I still remember, Carmen Boni, firstly because she was beautiful and secondly because, one morning in 1963, purely by chance, I read in the newspaper that she had been hit by a car in the middle of Paris. There were perhaps one or two others who did not leave the slightest impression on me.

I drank champagne for the first time in my life. I sipped with the same vaguely weary air as the others, the jaded expression of those no longer surprised by anything. The bubbles triggered a coughing fit that I stifled as best I could. While I tried to catch my breath, I pretended to admire a painting of a shameless nymph spying on a group of soldiers by a river. The villa had not changed since my last visit; it was still decorated in the same shades of green. But for the first time, I noticed the cracks in the cornices, the signs of wear disguised by a well-placed sofa cushion, a bluish mould in one corner of the ceiling, and the crumbling putty around the frosted-glass windows. Cold draughts insinuated themselves into the house through the slightest gap. The sound of the gramophone in the corner was accompanied by occasional squeaks and creaks. With every wall and every beam, the villa was struggling against the maw of winter. It no longer had the lithe, playful arrogance of former years.

We were only waiting for Viola. I had already drained three glasses of champagne, but a long acquaintance with Florentine liquor distilled to remedy every pain meant I was not drunk. At last, the door to the grand salon opened again. At first, I saw no one. Then a servant entered and whispered something in the ear of the Marchese.

'It appears that Viola will not be joining us this evening,' he announced. 'She is indisposed. So, without further ado, we can go into dinner.'

I caught Francesco's expression – he was frowning. He quickly smiled at me and shrugged as we walked through the great double doors into the dining room. I remember little of that dinner, except that I was sitting opposite the Milanese lawyer. He was a handsome man with a keen eye, and quite amusing, until you noticed that all his anecdotes revolved around him. He would say, 'As Bartolomeo was telling me just the other day...' and it was obvious to everyone except me that he was talking about Bartolomeo Pagano, the actor who played Maciste, a former dock worker from Genoa who had become Italy's leading man. In addition to the law practice that he had inherited, the lawyer, whose name was Rinaldo Campana, had invested in cinema. And, to judge from the cut of his suit, his wristwatch and that inexplicable air of smugness the rich sometimes exude, the cinema had repaid him handsomely.

By the end of the meal, I was completely drunk – a heavy, lumbering drunkenness that passed for solemnity. Before dessert, Francesco raised a glass and proposed a toast to me, since from that day, I would be carrying the Orsini torch. He invited the two government officials to visit my studio – if, of course, 'Signor Vitaliani agrees'. Signor Vitaliani was so drunk that he not only agreed, but was not surprised to be addressed as 'Signor'.

On the way home, I asked the secretary to drop me off on the main road, telling him I wanted to walk a little way. I had to insist, because by now it had started to rain. Once alone, I raced back to the Villa Orsini, cutting across the fields, climbed over the crumbling perimeter wall and stood beneath Viola's window. Three floors up, her blinds were open, but there was not the faintest glimmer of light behind the curtains. I threw a timid pebble at the window, but missed. A second, stronger pebble also missed. The third bounced against the façade and landed on my head. It was not a big stone, but big enough to hurt like hell. Furious, I lashed out, kicking a climbing rose that instantly showered me with dead leaves. Between rain showers, the moon reappeared, and I saw my reflection in a ground-floor window. A trickle of blood on my temple, my brown hair plastered to my forehead, a leaf stuck to one cheek. I had never been a fan of mirrors – blame my appearance – and used them as little as possible, even when shaving. But my mother was right. I was handsome; my features were unexpectedly symmetrical, and from her I had inherited eyes that were an almost mauve blue. This was the face of a strong man. The face of a man whose father had not taught him to be fatalistic. And since fatalism makes the world go round, because it allows us to cope with the thousand deaths that murder our dreams, it was also the face of a ridiculous man. Pale and drenched to the skin, a man who refused to accept a defeat that had been sounded so long ago that he alone had not noticed. I was not a fool. Viola being 'indisposed' on the very night we were to meet again was no accident. The message was clear: our relationship was over.

A bricklayer spent the next few days breathing new life into Zio's studio, which Paragraph had not reopened since my uncle's departure. The walls were repaired and whitewashed, and the few windows – all cracked – were replaced. Paragraph insisted on restoring the old oak workbench that ran along the south wall for almost five metres. Then he disappeared for two days and reappeared at the wheel of a truck that had survived the war, which he had bought at a good price with the money I had given him. He would be able to use it to deliver his orders throughout the region, and so the world shrank a little more. A merchant came from Genoa with a catalogue of sculptor's tools, the like of which I had never seen. Two blocks of the finest marble arrived, together with my first official commission, signed by some obscure Vatican secretary. According to Francesco, it was a direct but discreet order from Archbishop Pacelli, who planned to give it as a gift to the papal residence at Castel Gandolfo. The subject: *Saint Peter Receiving the Keys to Heaven*. The first statue that would really make my name.

That evening, after dinner, I went out to breathe the night air. Our plateau was an alembic, in which smells from miles around were distilled to create the world's most subtle, secret fragrance. *Winter in Pietra d'Alba*. You had only to turn your head and the fragrance would change, capricious, constantly recomposing itself as the air moved over the northern slopes of the mountains of Piedmont or those bordering the plateau. Neroli and cypress, sometimes mimosa, danced above base notes of vetiver and burnt wood. I lit the pipe that Paragraph had lent me and added a little of myself to the mix, aromas of hay, incense and horse saddle. *Empyreumatic notes*, Viola would have called it, having once seen the word in a book years earlier and remembered everything.

I had not read a book in two years. But not everything is contained within books. I had learned about intoxication, leafed through its nocturnal pages with mingled delight and disgust. All the same, I missed the smells of paper, of dry wood and dust in the Orsini library. *The Adventures of Pinocchio*, the last book she had made me read before the accident. Without thinking, I did what I had resolutely refused to do for days and turned towards Villa Orsini.

At Viola's window, the red glow of a lantern covered with a scarf pulsed softly in the darkness.

In the hollow stump, I found an envelope. I did not even remember leaving the workshop – I had simply seen the light, our signal, and now here I was, panting for breath, my lungs burning from the cold. In the envelope, a single sheet of paper, Viola's handwriting, more compact than before, sparing in the effort, but recognisable by her long descenders. *Tomorrow night, Thursday, at the cemetery.*

It was Wednesday, so she had delivered the letter this evening. With her characteristic arrogance, this was a summons that simply assumed that I would see the signal. As though I had nothing else to do but wait for her to make a move. I went back to the studio, woke Paragraph and asked him to take me down to Savona train station, from where I would take the first train the following morning.

'The first train to where?'

'Rome.'

If Viola thought that she could ignore me for two years, pretend to be ill when I finally came back, then summon me on a whim, she was mistaken. I was no longer the bewildered stateless, fatherless *francese* who had landed here on a cold night in 1917. True, it was she who had sculpted me, shaped me. But I was not her Pinocchio. I was not her creature. This time, she would be the one waiting for me. I was leaving. Just like Pinocchio, as I have only just realised now.

I had no plan. I would probably come back in a month or two, and we could start again on an equal footing, now that we had hurt each other, now that we had ridden roughshod over our friendship.

I left without realising that it would be more than five years before I returned. Or to be more precise – because I did not come back at some random time – one thousand nine hundred and ninety-one days and seventeen hours.

Wherever I've lived – with the exception of the monastery in which I am presently dying, and of Pietra d'Alba, of course – I have always felt the need to push back the dawn. To shun the daylight that will reveal the absence of Viola. I never drank for pleasure. But I drank without displeasure, like the sailors I met aboard those drunken nights, waltzing from deck to deck, creatures of pure light that burned all the brighter as the foundering rocks of morning loomed. Thankfully, we did not die, or not immediately, and lived to sail again the following night. In my memory, my nights in Florence and those in Rome are now intertwined. Purposeless nights punctuated by days without Viola. The gutters of Rome reeked as badly as those in Florence. But now I had perfume.

I was angry at Viola for creating these holes in our shared

history. For pushing me away when we were so close that not an atom could pass between us. I resented her and could think of no better way of making her understand than leaving. But I was beginning to feel guilty. In treating her like this, I was no more worthy of her friendship than she of mine. Viola was becoming a reflection of me. I raged and cursed her, and imagined that she was doing the same, up on her plateau where, at this time of year, the orange trees were dusted with hoarfrost. The same furious gestures, the same futile recriminations. We were both right; we no longer knew who was the mirror of the other. The more guilty I felt, the more I blamed Viola for making me feel guilty. I vowed not to see her again until she apologised. Like any good reflection, she would do the same, and, without realising, we left each other's lives. This vicious spiral, this tragi-comic ouroboros, is the only way to explain the years that followed.

I arrived in Rome to a blinding white sun that offered no warmth. My studio was at 28 via dei Banchi Nuovi, some fifteen minutes' walk from the Vatican, a little longer for me given my short stride. The street intersected the via degli Orsini. I was never sure whether it owed its name to my benefactors, and whenever I asked the question, they simply shrugged with a smug, mysterious air. The studio overlooked a courtyard, where four apprentices stood at attention. Francesco appeared two days after my arrival, visibly surprised by my last-minute decision, which he did not question. The marble was ready and waiting, and I set to work on my first commission, *Saint Peter Receiving the Keys to Heaven*. I entrusted the preparation work to the apprentices and the smoothing to Jacopo, a boy of fourteen, who seemed the most gifted of them. I call him a boy, but I was barely four years his senior.

My apartment was directly above the studio, a dwelling whose proportions rivalled the Villa Orsini or the Grand Hotel Baglioni. After a few days, I realised that the vast empty space was making me anxious, so I had a four-poster bed delivered, an antique no one wanted, so that I could fall asleep in a space a little more attuned to my size. This bed, floating like a raft in the middle of an empty room, beneath a ceiling on which whitewash competed with soot, earned me a certain success in love. A German client who passed through the flat one day described the décor as 'perverse Bauhaus, but Bauhaus nonetheless'.

While working on my principal commission, I supervised the restoration of Casina Pio IV, a Renaissance villa in the shadow of the dome of Saint Peter's Basilica.

Conceived as a summer residence for the pope, it had been neglected, renovated and was now patiently awaiting its new fate. Archbishop Pacelli wanted to turn it into a research library devoted to the sciences, something many of his rivals in the Curia disdained, claiming that the only science the common man needed began with *In the beginning, God created the heavens and the earth* and ended with *God saw everything that he had made; and behold, it was very good.*

In that first year, I only left my studio to visit the worksite at the Casina, to meet a supplier or to have lunch with Francesco, which we did once a month. We almost became friends, and even called each other by our first names. We shared Pietra d'Alba, after all, and being so far away from there brought us closer. Francesco had something of his sister about him – he had the same curious way of tilting his head when he spoke, the same distant gaze. The dreaminess typical of a young man of twenty-three, one might think, but Francesco was no dreamer. He had the bearing of an eagle perched atop a pine tree, watching the panicked scurrying of a dozen mice, calculating each trajectory, choosing its prey ten moves in advance. There was a sharpness to his tongue, a cutting edge that killed painlessly. He would defuse a crisis without raising his voice. I saw thugs and bullies bow down before him. But he treated me like an equal. And I can say today, without false modesty, that I was his equal. There was only one person in the world who towered over us, in terms of intellect and ambition, but we never mentioned her name.

A year after my arrival in Rome, I finally delivered *Saint Peter Receiving the Keys to Heaven* to the man who had commissioned it.

Monsignor Pacelli spent a good ten minutes in the studio circling the work. I waited nervously, my four apprentices lined up behind me. Being close to the Vatican, the sight of a prelate was hardly surprising, but the automobile waiting outside, with a grille like a wolf's fangs, and that *je ne sais quoi* that Pacelli exuded caused a small crowd to gather, despite the bitter wind that swept through Rome in February 1924.

Several times, Pacelli looked about to say something, but bit his tongue. I knew how he felt. My Saint Peter was not what he had imagined. What was the point of creating what other people could imagine? From my nights in Florence in dives and cellars where a man was either reborn or died, I had retained a somewhat suicidal temperament –professionally speaking – that has served me well throughout my career.

On those nights, all that mattered was to burn as brightly as possible. We were afraid of nothing, and the next morning everything was erased. My Saint Peter was not the bearded, rather portly apostle one might see anywhere, he had the features of Il Cornutto, because he had lived and suffered as a man suffers when he denies his best friend three times, a betrayal no one would let him forget since it was read out year upon year in every church the world over. Nor did he hold the key to heaven in that officious manner of other statues.

'The key,' whispered Pacelli after a moment. 'Am I mistaken or has he...?'

'You are not mistaken.'

Saint Peter had dropped the key. It hovered in front of him, between the hand he clenched trying to hold it in place and the floor. I had attached it to his robe with an almost invisible metal wire. The effect was striking. The man whom God had chosen to lead his Church was the man who had denied his son three times. He was a sinner. And I imagined that if Il Cornutto had been given the key to heaven, he would have dropped it in astonishment. Instead of a saint in ecstasy, a plump and pious old man half-bored to death, my Saint Peter trembled with fear at the mission he had been given, at this object that proved too heavy for his gnarled hands, which betrayed him. He watched in terror as the key fell, perhaps wondering whether it would shatter, whether he would be hit by a thunderbolt. I had no difficulty capturing the intensity of his expression. I, too, had once witnessed something precious fall.

'I cannot offer this to Castel Gandolfo,' said Pacelli.

Francesco turned pale.

Then the bishop turned to me with tears in his eyes. 'But I shall keep it for myself. I will pay for it out of my own pocket. This work is too... too daring for some. But I understand it. I understand *you*, Signor Vitaliani.'

He turned on his heel without another word. Francesco gave me a little nod, a half-smile, and fell into step.

———————

My order book exploded. Monsignor Pacelli was not shy about showing my work to friends and visitors, not that I think he did it to show off. My list of clients forced me to double the number of staff in the studio just to do the restoration work on the Casina Pio IV. Then, six months later, I had to refuse any new commissions. In total, I accepted commissions for sixteen major works, which would keep me busy for the next six years. Most were religious sculptures or works based on the coat of arms of a particular family. My apprentices would rough out the piece, then, under my supervision, Jacopo would work on it, and finally I would finish it off. Word that I was no longer accepting commissions simply made me more in demand. At last, I was desirable. I had been spat on, ignored, I had spent my life begging and now, overnight, I was the one being solicited. All because I'd learned a new word: *No*. The power of those two letters was insane. The more often I refused, and the more rudely I did so, the more people wanted the Orsini sculptor, as I was beginning to be known.

One morning, as I was leaving my studio, I was accosted by a man in a chauffeur's uniform who pointed to a brand-new car, an Alfa Romeo RL, parked in the middle of the road a little further on. Sitting in the back of the car, Francesco waved.

'Where are we going?' I said as I climbed in.

'I have no idea.'

'What do you mean you have no idea?'

'I have no idea, because this is your automobile, and Livio here is your new chauffeur. A gift from the Orsinis.'

He laughed at my bewildered expression, patted me on the shoulder and got out. That night I wrote a short letter to my mother. *Dear Maman, I will be twenty this year, I have an automobile and a driver, and I am only sorry that I cannot take you and Papa on a tour of Rome.*

Despite the long hours spent working in the studio, I found time to start reading again. There was a library not far from my apartment, and I asked the librarian to select some books, any books, for me. She was a little baffled by the request, and she did not have Viola's brilliance, but she did her best. I rarely read the newspapers, since I could hardly avoid what was happening in the world, given the endless commentary by my clients and apprentices – never by Francesco. The elections of 1924 ushered in a huge Fascist majority, which was not unexpected, given that the *squadristi* had terrorised the opposition party. No one dared to challenge the result, no one except a young deputy named Giacomo Matteotti, who called for the election results to be invalidated. In June, he disappeared, and in mid-August, his putrefied corpse was found in a forest near Rome. I remember a photo of the carabinieri carrying his body. The officer in the foreground on the left – who had surely seen it all in his career – was holding a handkerchief over his nose. Sixty years later, I can still smell that photo. The Fascists took offence that anyone would suspect them, and then in January 1925 Mussolini declared: 'If Fascism has been a criminal association, the responsibility for this rests with me.' From that point, people were even more reluctant to speak out. They invented excuses; some even said that Matteotti got what he deserved and the Fascists had a point – after all, he had besmirched their name.

I viewed these events with a certain detachment. I was an artist, and there was no way that I, from my lofty height of four foot six, could change the course of history. I delivered one statue, then another and another. My apprentices were now tackling more advanced restoration work, under my supervision, and I agreed to accept two new commissions, which I asked Francesco to assign, thereby allowing him to earn something in his own currency – influence. Twenty or so potential clients vied fiercely for the privilege of appearing in my order book.

And there were women, of course. Annabella, first and foremost, the librarian who chose my reading material. A short, skinny girl with a slightly angular face, she eventually succumbed to my advances. I think Annabella genuinely liked me. I had not touched a woman since my initiation between Sara's ample thighs, and I did not fare much better on my second time round. The most extraordinary thing about Annabella was that she was as wild between the sheets of my four-poster bed as she was pathologically shy in public. In her arms, I learned everything I know. Our relationship lasted two years. We began to see more and more of her in the studio, the lone female presence, comforting some of the younger apprentices who were homesick. Then came the day she knocked on my door, a discreet little knock as though she were afraid of being overheard. We had arranged to go to a restaurant.

'I'm late,' she said as she came in, staring at the floor.

'Not at all, it's not even seven o'clock.'

'No, I'm *late*,' she said again, laying her hands on her belly.

I must have paled, because immediately she said, 'I know someone who can take care of it.'

I closed the door. I don't remember what I said that night, except that I did not want it 'taken care of'. Not that I wanted to have a child, for fear of passing on my genes. We decided not to make a decision. I remember my craven feeling of relief when, a week later, Annabella told me that the problem had 'sorted itself out'. After that day, I stopped going to the library and claimed I had too much work to be able to see her. Annabella tiptoed out of my life as shyly as she had entered it.

Then came Carolina, Anna-Maria, Lucia and perhaps one or two others I don't wish to recall, since that would mean remembering how I broke their hearts – all except for Lucia, who ran off with my wallet.

One day in August 1925, Francesco invited me to dine at the Gran Caffè Faraglia. To my surprise, a large table beneath the vaulted ceiling was laid for a dozen guests, and all the other tables in the restaurant had been removed. A few minutes later, Stefano Orsini arrived with a group of friends dressed in suits, except for two men in *squadristi* uniforms. Noisily, they took their seats while Stefano shook hands with his brother, then, seeing me, shouted, 'Gulliver!' and waved, as though we were old friends. I stiffened when one of the *squadristi* came and sat next to me, but he turned out to be a cheerful and funny dinner companion. Later he complained about how badly the *squadristi* were treated by the press and the newspapers, telling me I had no idea what kind of vicious stunts the Bolsheviks had pulled, that the *squadristi* did not espouse violence, they were merely defending themselves. As for the Matteotti affair... They had nothing to do with it. Probably the work of some dissident element. *That said, Matteotti had it coming, though, didn't he?*

By midnight, we were all fairly drunk. The waiters danced from one foot to the other, impatient to close up and go home, but they could do nothing given the size of our party. The waiters knew it, Stefano and his friends knew it, and they ordered another round.

'Your attention, gentlemen,' roared Stefano, 'let us toast the bride-to-be!'

'What bride?' I said.

'Viola, obviously! Didn't you tell him, Francesco?'

'No. To be honest, it never occurred to me. It's true, our sister Viola is to be married. In fact, I think you know her intended. Rinaldo Campana.'

It took me a few seconds to put a face to the name. The Milanese lawyer and film producer I had met over dinner at the Orsinis' two years earlier. For a while now, I had no longer found myself thinking about Viola every day. The sight of a cemetery, the smell of spring no longer transported me back to Pietra d'Alba. But this news tore away the veil of oblivion. Suddenly, everything came flooding back. The oaths we had sworn, our hands entwined, those winter nights when the icy air we sipped was heady as brandy – everything.

Several bottles of champagne appeared. Corks were popped, and Stefano shook one of them and soaked the two *squadristi*. One gamely opened his mouth to try to catch the flow while the one sitting next to me looked furious but said nothing. It was a clear sign that Stefano's political career was advancing, as was his stoutness and his rosacea. He now worked for Public Security. More precisely, as he had boasted during the meal, for Cesare Mori, the Sicilian *prefetto* whom Mussolini had tasked with eradicating the

Mafia. He kept his hair close-cropped to hide his curls, which made him look like an overgrown baby.

Francesco, the only one of us not drinking, got to his feet and apologised – he had to celebrate an early mass the next day. 'Can I drop you off, Mimo?'

'No, leave him alone!' bawled Stefano. 'The fun has only just started, isn't that right, Gulliver? He's the glory of the family, let's take him out for a bit!'

'I'll stay.'

Francesco frowned, then shrugged and disappeared.

'And now that the saintly father has gone home to bed...' said Stefano.

He took a small silver box from his pocket and opened it to reveal a white powder. It was passed around the table. I had never seen 'coco', the newest fashion of nights out in Rome at the time. They each scooped a little onto their fingernail and snorted it. I did likewise, just so I could be normal, could be like them, tall, perfectly proportioned. Then we set off to paint the town on a night about which I remember absolutely nothing. One night less in my life, at the end of which I woke up leaning against a dustbin in front of the Colosseum, smaller than ever.

The operator connected me immediately.

'*Pronto*, the Orsini residence. How may I help?'

I did not hesitate for long. That same evening, my face still contorted from my binge the night before, I went to the Vatican Post and Telegraph Office. Over a recent lunch, Francesco had told me that the villa had recently had a telephone installed. The copper wire that braved the distance – despite the jagged branches and the playful squirrels' teeth intent on cutting through it – was yet another blow to the languid world into which I had been born. Only a few years earlier, it had taken almost a week for the Orsinis to hear of the death of their eldest son in Saint-Michel-de-Maurienne. The news had barely arrived before his stiff, battered body. Today, I was able to telephone only a few hours after learning that Viola was to be married. And that was fine by me. I was almost twenty-one, and not of an age to bemoan the fact that things were better 'before'. In fact, I was still living in the 'before' and would later miss it.

'Hello, I would like to speak to Signorina Orsini.'

'Who shall I say is calling?'

'Signor Mimo Vitaliani.' I felt ridiculous calling myself 'Signor', but I needed to impress the major-domo.

'Just a moment, I shall see whether the signorina is available.'

I listened intently, hoping to catch some whisper of Pietra d'Alba, the sound of the breeze in the trees if a window was open – which was likely, this being August. But the deafening racket outside – bells, chimes, automobiles honking on the via della Posta – kept me firmly rooted in the Vatican post office. I stood, sweating, in the telephone cabin, my clammy ear glued to the receiver, watching the comings and goings of laymen and prelates, moving like figure skaters across the polished marble of the entrance hall.

There was a rustle, a polite cough, and then I heard the major-domo.

'Signor Vitaliani? My apologies, but Signorina Orsini does not wish to speak to you.'

I was so convinced this would be his answer that I thought I heard this, though he did not say the words. I almost hung up.

'Signor Vitaliani?' he said again.

'Yes, excuse me, I am still here.'

'Just a moment, I will put you through to Signorina Orsini.'

There followed a series of clicks, and several ghostly distorted voices surged through the copper wire. Then Viola's voice.

'Hello?'

A little husky, perhaps deeper, but this voice was Viola, whole and entire, and suddenly Pietra d'Alba filled my small booth with a summer fire and the smell of fields sizzling beneath the sun. I slid down the wall and sat on the floor of the cabin.

'Viola, it's me.'

'I know.'

There was a long silence, heavy with pine resin, with unbounded joy and abject terror.

'It is lovely to hear from you, Mimo, but I don't have much time. I'm preparing for my wedding.'

'Actually, that's why I'm calling.'

'Yes?'

'I'm calling to ask...'

'Yes?' Viola said again.

'Are you sure you know what you're doing? *Really* sure?'

Another silence, brief this time.

'You can trust me, Mimo.'

Then she hung up.

Rome, my city of firsts. My first visit to the cinema later that year – *Maciste in the Underworld*, which terrified me and made me swear never again to lie on a grave. My first opera – Verdi's *Otello*, which bored me rigid. My first taste of cocaine, as we know, and my first commission from a secular authority. The Municipio di Roma suddenly contacted me to ask whether I might consider creating a statue of Romulus and Remus. Now that I knew I wouldn't be going back to Pietra d'Alba, I accepted the commission.

Francesco and I continued to see each other regularly. Viola, he told me, was married early in 1926 but had not yet been on honeymoon as her husband's business had taken him to the United States. The project to bring electricity to Pietra had been revived – doubtless funded by the lawyer's fortune. I nodded absently as I ate, and he must have assumed I wasn't interested, because after that, he rarely gave me news of his sister.

What was more surprising was that I continued to see Stefano. Not that I liked him, but he knew how to let his hair down. He was still climbing the greasy pole of government and between 1926 and 1928 held no fewer than three positions, each more prestigious than the last. He was flagrant when he boasted about this, something I understood one drunken night when he confided in me.

'You're lucky you don't have a brother, Gulliver. Virgilio, Virgilio, Virgilio, that's all we ever heard when we were little. Virgilio said this, Virgilio said that, such a little genius, and of course he was forgiven everything. But tell me, if Virgilio was such a genius, why did he go and die in the war like a fool – and not even in the war, but on a fucking train? Who fills the family coffers these days? Who is it that makes people stand to attention when they hear the name Orsini? Me, and Francesco, and Campana too, now that he is one of us. People no longer think of us as small-town hicks who grow withered orange trees. And, mark my words, the orange groves will no longer be dried up. The Gambale family had better watch their step.'

I would work from dawn until dusk, then revel until morning. In early 1927, I delivered my *Romulus and Remus*, which immediately prompted the dismissal of the municipal officer who commissioned it. There was no Romulus or Remus in my *Romulus and Remus*. And no she-wolf either. There was nothing but water. I had sculpted waves, the tempestuous roiling of the river Tiber, in the hollow of which the viewer could just make out the handle of a basket and, in it, a pair of twins. I had carved a miracle, the survival of two babies abandoned to the raging fury of a river, because here, as in Pietra d'Alba, water was the source of everything. Without the Tiber, there would be no Rome. Without the Arno, no Florence. I felt a little guilty that I had contributed to the poor man being sacked, but two months later, Margherita Sarfatti, Mussolini's mistress and his muse, saw the sculpture and declared: 'This piece utterly embodies the New Man, the Fascist artist.' The official was rehired, decorated and offered a promotion.

Rome was unusual in that it had few places to go at night, with the possible exception of the Cabaret del Diavolo, whose three underground floors represented Inferno, Purgatorio and Paradiso. On my first visit, I was thrown out for 'excessive drunkenness'. The pleonasm proved that they knew nothing about drunkenness or hell. There were few bars that opened late and fewer clubs – Rome was an elderly maiden. We would often eat in one of the city's celebrated restaurants, the Fagiano, the Gran Caffè Faraglia – our favourite, for its Liberty frescoes – or at the Hotel Quirinale or the Excelsior. Afterwards, the real partying took place in private salons where debauchery flourished. Unlike most of my fellow revellers, I was not seeking influence or fortune. I already had my share, small, but enough for me. Once again, I observed that the wealthy enjoy nothing more than being told *no*. I was not looking for new commissions, new clients. People begged just to get on the waiting list. 'I just want to drink,' I would say, and my stock would rise. It was during one such evening that I met Alexandra Kara-Petrović, a Serbian princess who instantly fell under my spell – by which I mean she fell under the spell of my fame, my automobile and my bank account, which was not as fat as people thought. I made a very good living, but it was meagre compared to that of the heirs, the opportunists and the swindlers with whom I rubbed shoulders. Alexandra was probably no more a princess than I, although she swore as much to the bitter end and was never caught out when asked about her family history and genealogy. She was unimaginably beautiful, tall and lithe. When we attended parties, I loved to watch as eyes widened and three words, so obvious they might as well have shouted them, formed in the minds of strangers. *She's with him?*

Alexandra was the complete opposite of Annabella. In public she was a tigress, in bed she was a log. She simply did not enjoy the deed, or perhaps not with me. Nor did I lust after her, though she was the most beautiful woman I had ever seen. After three or four attempts, we decided that it would be better to sleep in separate rooms and devote our energies to the things that truly entertained us: in my case, shocking polite society, in her case, spending my money, principally at a little shop belonging to Sotirios Voúlgaris, a Greek jeweller she adored. We were utterly shameless.

On more than one occasion I made plans to go and see my mother, only to put it off for a thousand good reasons – my work, the distance involved, and after all, had I not invited her to come and see me, all expenses paid? A thousand good reasons, except for the real one: I felt it was up to her to take the first step, to cross the abyss she had created between us, the gaping ravine whose jagged edges had been widening since 1916.

I could say that I regret my years in Florence, and the years I spent in Rome even more. I could pretend, unburdening my soul and earning an easier passage from old Charon, who waits for me on the banks of the Styx – the subject of one of my sculptures. But I can no more be rid of my past than a tree can be rid of the rings that mark its growth. Florence and Rome are still present in this febrile body that trembles and curses, watched over by four monks in the fading light of day. Florence and Rome are here and cannot be ripped out, any more than my heart, my kidneys or my liver – though the latter probably isn't in the best shape.

My excesses reached a point of no return in 1928. One night, Stefano told a gathering of thuggish *squadristi* about the time I was beaten by the lake, then launched into a little ditty that was taken up by the group: *Gulliver, Gulliver, show us your arse!*

Instead of leaving with all due dignity, I showed them my arse. To prove that I was just like them. That I could hold my own. I showed them my arse and Stefano roared: 'He's grown some hair, but I still recognise it!'

I regularly woke up in various parts of Rome, sometimes in an unfamiliar bed next to a woman who reeked of alcohol and stared at me with a fear that matched my own. One morning, as I stumbled along the via Appia shortly after dawn, I came across a little circus set up on a piece of waste ground wedged between two parks with crumbling brick walls. A bald man of uncertain age was training a colt in a makeshift paddock.

I called over to him. 'Hello, I just wanted to ask if you know the Circo Bizzaro.'

'Never heard of it.'

'It's in Florence, behind the railway station...'

'Like I said, never heard of it. Do you think everyone in the circus knows everyone else? Do you know every dwarf?'

He had left a hip flask on a leather strap hanging from a peg. I swung it around and sent it hurtling towards him. It was intended as a light-hearted gesture, except, with my incredible beginner's bad luck, I hit him in the face. I took off at a run, but the via Appia is long. Half an hour later, he and three of his friends drove up in a lorry, chased me across the fields and beat me up. No one said a word when I showed up at the studio clutching my ribs, my lips swollen, one eye ringed with yellow. Princess Alexandra, who was fresh as a daisy, made me a cup of coffee and rearranged our social calendar. Shortly after this episode, Francesco called me to his office to admonish me. He reminded me of my promise to represent the Orsini name with dignity. I swore to him that such a thing would never happen again. As soon as I got back, I dismissed my chauffeur Livio, since he was the one telling tales, and hired another, Mikael, an Ethiopian from the neighbourhood who was an excellent driver and asked no questions. What with my height and his skin colour, we instantly became the most conspicuous pair in Rome. So much for discretion.

During another raucous night, an inebriated baron vowed undying love for Verdi. I ventured that Verdi wrote music for circuses, and he asked how I would know unless, of course, I had worked in a circus. I defended my honour with the fierceness of those who have none and demanded restitution. The soirée was being held at the home of the widow of a wealthy industrialist, who also happened to be the mistress of an important minister. Someone came up with the romantic notion of using the old duelling pistols on display in the living room. Neither of us had ever loaded an eighteenth-century duelling pistol, so as we struggled with the weapons, each offering advice, our quarrel was forgotten, until one of the guns accidentally went off and hit the widow's arm, which, fortunately, was plump. At the sight of blood, the widow fainted. In less than a minute, everyone had vanished into the night.

I was about to deliver my last work. It had been commissioned by a *latifondista*, the owner of one of the great landed estates in Mezzogiorno. He was a man who thought ahead: the commission was for a mausoleum. Four angels at the corners of the vault watched over a gravestone that they had apparently just sealed. One of my finest works, the high point of the movement. But at the time, I was going out too much and had entrusted Jacopo with finishing the face of the last angel. The commission was a year late. I could no longer postpone the delivery, especially since the client was from Palermo and people there are shadier than average. Two days before delivery, Jacopo showed me his work. I stared at the angel in disbelief: the pinched expression, the tautness in the features. The anatomy was correct. But if Jacopo had been trying to capture the expression of an angel who had trapped his fingers under a three hundred kilo marble slab while sealing a grave, he could not have done better.

I flew into a rage, called him every name under the sun. He had disgraced the studio. Betrayed not only my trust, but that of his colleagues, of sculptors, of art in general. I screamed, red with anger, for long minutes, and several curious heads emerged from the apartments overlooking the courtyard.

When I finally calmed down, the whole workshop was staring at me with a look I recognised. It was precisely the way I had looked at Zio.

In describing the beauty of Michelangelo's *Pietà*, many people focus on the perfection of the drapery, the anatomical accuracy, the grace of the movement and so on. But whatever the experts might say, Michelangelo's genius is in the face. With a face like that, it wouldn't have mattered if his Virgin had been hunchbacked. It is the face of a woman who is all but defeated, surprised in a moment of weariness and surrender in which her soul is revealed. The surprise is everything. Michelangelo captured the split-second immediacy of photography, except that in his case it took three years to bring the image to life. Three years of armed struggle, with a simple chisel and a block of marble. This face is not merely what the eye sees. It captures everything that has gone before, everything yet to come. The time that led to this moment and all the time that lies ahead, the death of millions of seconds and the promise of millions more. But I had entrusted a nineteen-year-old boy who knew nothing of life with the impossible task of creating the face of an angel. Jacopo was gifted, but not that gifted. Not like a Michelangelo. Not like a Vitaliani.

I called Jacopo into my office and offered my apologies. Then I opened my order book. You cannot reshape a face: you either have to carve a new head or a whole statue. Carving a new head was an unacceptable compromise, a Mary Shelley monster unworthy of me. I could perhaps deliver the mausoleum with three angels and claim that this was my original design. But this was not my original design. Each angel existed and, above all, *moved* only in relation to the other three. I could deliver three angels and say that the fourth was coming. But when? It would mean postponing a commission from an industrialist in Milan, who was no less shady...

The best solution for the man I was at the time was to do nothing. At the end of the day, I met up with Stefano, resolutely determined to imbibe. But for the first time, I did not finish the first glass I was brought at Caffè Faraglia. There was a calendar on the wall directly opposite me. I stared blankly at the date: 21 June 1928.

'Hey, lads, Gulliver is looking a bit odd. Are you all right, old man?'

21 June 1928. I was not here by chance. Everything had led me to this wall. To this cheap tear-off calendar illustrated with bawdy caricatures.

'You look like you've just seen a ghost.'

'I have.'

Years of oblivion crumbled, swept away by a memory as brutal as a flood. My debasement, my indifference to success, the way I numbed myself with alcohol, cocaine and Serbian princesses, it surged past like a raging torrent. The rest of my life was at stake. If I could get there in time.

I jumped down from my seat and ran off. An hour later, I left Rome without looking back.

M ikael hurtled north along the rutted, potholed, dusty roads. Italy was marbled with roads and junctions that defied logic, paths that led nowhere, chaotic vestiges of a time when to be waylaid was a pleasure. The main thoroughfares, with their tribute to straight lines, noise and dirt, didn't appear until the outskirts of Milan. Such charm came at a price: we suffered three punctures – two tyres and the radiator. Only Mikael's peerless ingenuity made progress possible. During this trip, I learned that Mikael had held an important position in the government of Menelik II, Emperor of Ethiopia, and had fled the country following a murky adulterous affair, during which a price was put on his head by one of the kingdom's most powerful families. He had arrived in Rome in 1913 and had since lived by his wits. He had an encyclopaedic knowledge. Somewhere between

Lucca and Massa, it dawned on me that I was less intelligent and less cultivated than my driver.

On 24 June 1928, we left Savona, still heading north. Night was drawing in, and just as we came to a milestone indicating 'Pietra d'Alba, 10 kilometres', the second tyre burst. I thought I would die ten times over, the clock was ticking, but we set off again. We drove to Pietra d'Alba at top speed. On my command, Mikael stopped at the crossroads, at the bottom of the slope that descended to the plateau after the village. It was almost 11 p.m. I set off at a run.

At 11.05 p.m., I collapsed outside the cemetery gate, exhausted from the journey and gasping for breath. With my back against the wall and my head against a stone, I inhaled the fresh, familiar air. I was aware of the folly of my undertaking, but all my life I had acted on instinct. Sanity, therefore, was the wrong yardstick. I was where I had to be, that was all that mattered.

For the first time, she was late. She emerged from the wood by her usual route ten minutes later and froze when she saw me. She had not travelled as far as I, but her journey had been no less epic, no less trying. Quietly we approached each other in the small clearing outside the cemetery created by the embracing arms of the forest.

Eight long years had passed since we last met. Viola was no longer an adolescent, but a woman in her own right. Her features were stronger. I would have sworn that her sixteen-year-old face had attained a form of perfection, little suspecting the secrets that a few more strokes of her creator's chisel would reveal. Viola was an object lesson in sculpture, which made me regret those eight years away from her all the more. I wished that I had witnessed these changes, one by one, so I might analyse them and one day reproduce them.

Her hair was longer than I remembered, just as black but now impeccably coiffed, her skin just as matt. A pale scar at the top of her forehead disappeared under a lock of hair. She was tall and still very thin. She was beautiful, but not in the way of the Serbian princess. She did not have the voluptuousness of form that Stefano and his friends – and, I confess, even I – had sought out in the brothels of Rome. You had to stare at Viola, really look at her, to understand. Her eyes were a portal to other worlds, a knowledge bordering on madness.

'I wasn't sure that you would come,' she said finally.

'I never forgot. On 24 June 1918, you told me to meet you here ten years later. I realise you're right. You travel in time.'

'Yes. But I thought it would take ten years.' She stared at me, ran a hand over my three-day stubble. 'It took ten minutes. And in those ten minutes, you became a man.'

'Viola...'

Placing a finger on my lips, she silenced me. 'Will you stay?'

Without pausing to think, I nodded, her perfumed finger still resting against my lips, a scent of orange in my nostrils.

'Then we have plenty of time.'

Silently, we made our way back to the crossroads. I pointed to the Alfa Romeo waiting in the darkness. Mikael was asleep in the back seat, his feet sticking out of the window. 'Shall I take you home?'

'Thank you, I would rather walk.'

'So would I.'

She went right, I went left. After a few steps, I turned back. Further down the road, Viola was smiling at me.

'Papa, Papa, there's a gnome sleeping in our barn!'

I met Paragraph and Anna's son, Zozo, a few seconds before I met their daughter, Maria, who came to see what a gnome looked like.

'That is not a gnome, children. Actually, he is a giant. But a little giant.'

We hugged. Anna, like me, was twenty-four, Paragraph almost twenty-eight. Both had grown a little older. Their children were adorable and exhausting, and clung to me like a pair of crabs.

'Leave your uncle Mimo alone. Can't you see you're annoying him?'

'What is a crab, Uncle Mimo?'

'It's a crustacean.'

'What's a crustacean, Uncle Mimo?'

I had feared that Paragraph would react badly to my

return, having lived in the studio for so long without me. But he and Anna, anticipating this day, had built a house behind the main building. Business was good and they now had two apprentices. Anna was running the cabinetmaking business full-time. Zio's old workshop was exactly as I had left it: renovated, maintained and cleaned regularly. I had only to have my tools sent on.

'Have you got a telephone here?'

'Who do you take me for? Rockefeller?'

I woke Mikael, promised the children a ride in the automobile, so I would be rid of them, and asked to be dropped off at the Villa Orsini.

Paragraph caught up with me just as Mikael was driving off. 'By the way, I don't know if you've heard about Viola's father...'

Two weeks earlier, the Marchese had been found naked in the village square, waiting, he said, for his son Virgilio, who had talked to him during the night and said he was coming home. They had taken the Marchese home, tried to reason with him, his son was dead, but he had insisted, *No, no, it really was him, I can still recognise my son, he was riding a skeletal horse, he's coming, he's coming.* Then he lapsed into unconsciousness. A doctor came, a real doctor rather than the drunkard from the next village. A stroke, he diagnosed. The Marchesa refused to allow her husband to be transferred to hospital, so he was treated at the villa.

Silvio opened the gate and, recognising me, he smiled, something he had never done before. Out of habit, I had rung the tradesmen's doorbell, but he led me through the gardens to the front gate. The bear that I had sculpted for Viola still stood by the pool. As I passed, I could not help but criticise some of the choices made by the sixteen-year-old Mimo. There was a sense of movement, but it was exaggerated. Now, I could say much more with much less.

'I shall let the Marchesa know you are here.'

The Marchesa appeared, with only a few more wrinkles and her hair as raven black as ever. The Orsinis were not ungrateful; they knew how much of their prestige was owed to me.

'I shall fetch Viola. Do you remember my daughter, Signor Vitaliani? You sculpted that bear in the garden for her.'

Nothing was more emblematic of my success than that moment, that split second when, in the eyes of a marchesa, I passed from being a 'horrible little creature', liable to rape her precious child, to an artist worthy of the finest salons.

'I remember. I would be delighted to see her again. In the meantime, may I use your telephone? I need to call your son Francesco.'

The Marchesa led me into the 'telephone room' and left me beneath the intricate cornice mouldings. As I waited for the connection, I noticed that the walls had been redone. There were no longer any cracks or damp patches. The new putty in the windows was white and supple. An armful of freshly cut peonies in a vase were already languishing in the light that streamed through the new windows.

At first, Francesco was furious: what the hell was I thinking? I had vanished without warning, no one knew where I was, he had people scouring Rome to find me. When I told him about my plan to work from Pietra d'Alba, he calmed down. He knew as well as I did how much he stood to gain by keeping me far from the temptations of Rome. Feeling that the tide was turning in my favour, I asked him to have a telephone line installed in the studio and promised to increase my productivity. I also needed him to have some blocks of marble delivered – Carrara was not far away. Lastly, I would require an apprentice, in addition to Jacopo. I would work between the two studios, visiting Rome only when necessary. He agreed to smooth things over with my Sicilian client – I needed a few months to deliver the fourth angel. If the client was unhappy, I said I would pay him back with interest and sell his mausoleum to someone else for double the price.

'Mimo?' he asked just as I was about to hang up.

'Yes?'

'You know that my father is rather unwell.'

'Yes. I'm sorry to hear it.'

'He will pull through but... He will be much weakened. Stefano will become de facto head of the family, so you will need to report to him. But if you have any questions, if you have the slightest... doubt, you come to me, understood?'

'Understood.'

'I'll see you at the villa soon. In the meantime, rest assured that Monsignor Pacelli and I are working tirelessly for you.'

'While I work tirelessly for the Orsinis.'

'No, Mimo, your work must be to the glory of the Almighty Father, whose humble servants we are.'

'But a little of His glory reflects on your family, does it not?' I quipped, irritated by Francesco's solemnity.

Francesco sighed. 'If that is His will, who am I to oppose it?'

Viola was waiting for me in the great salon where, many years earlier, her engagement had been announced.

'Viola, this is Signor Vitaliani – you remember, the young sculptor who made the bear for your sixteenth birthday?'

'I remember,' said her daughter and smiled politely.

'Of course, silly me, after all he is very...' She almost said 'recognisable', but with the discretion that had transformed the daughter of a country squire into a marchesa, she said: '...gifted.'

'I need some fresh air, Mammina. I shall take a stroll in the garden. If you wish, you may accompany me, Signor Vitaliani.'

Eleven years after our first meeting, Viola and I finally appeared in public together. Eleven years of secrecy. Now, for the first time, the sun shone on our wounded, faltering friendship; our nocturnal relationship was blessed by daylight. When Viola stepped outside, she was dressed in a light cape and leaning on a wood cane with a silver pommel. I pretended not to notice.

'You were looking at my cane, weren't you?' said Viola as soon as we were in the garden. 'I hate it. I use it only when I have to. My legs still ache on days like today when it is cold or damp.' She shook her head. 'I fell from a great height.'

She walked ahead of me towards the rear gate through which I had entered when I first came to the villa to repair the roof. A low light mingled with the mist whose pink wisps clung to the skeletal branches of orange trees that had once flourished. Disconcerted by the silence, the wind chased its tail like a puppy on a battlefield between the black, leafless trunks. Some of the trees still bore fruit, but with every step I saw new signs of neglect: the irrigation ditches were no longer carefully marked and tended, the rows no longer weeded. Almost a third of the trees were dead. On the others, the tangled branches had clearly not seen pruning shears for a long time. I mentioned this to Viola.

'Oh, these days very little of our income comes from citrus fruits.'

'But you used to grow the finest oranges I've ever tasted…'

Viola glanced around and shrugged. 'Perhaps, but it is difficult to find labourers. What can I say, the lure of the

big city has become too great. And our foolish feud with the Gambale family makes it impossible to plan for the long term or to invest. Every other year, the crop is decimated by drought. Of course, if our two families could just be reasonable, come to some amicable arrangement, but...'
Again, she shrugged.

It was a gesture I had never seen before, one that meant *There is nothing I can do*, whereas the Viola I knew could do anything.

'So where does the money come from? I noticed that you have had work done on the house.'

'From my husband. He keeps the coffers filled. He is the head of a major law firm, but more importantly, he has invested heavily in cinema. He says it is the future. And he must be right because it makes money. All he needed was a connection to an aristocratic family, a respectability that he could not buy for all the gold in the world. Now that we are married, he has that, so everyone is happy.'

'And you, are you happy?'

Another shrug. 'Of course. Rinaldo is very sweet.'

Despite the rough terrain, Viola turned onto a path that ran between two fields and led to the forest.

'Where is your husband now?'

'In America, on business. Most of the time, he lives in Milan.'

'So you don't live together?'

'We do, but he spends so much time travelling that I am better here than in Milan. He often comes for weekends. And we are trying for a baby, which is not easy. The doctors say the country air is better for my health.'

We walked in silence for a while. Viola gave me a sidelong glance – I still could not get used to having to look up when I spoke to her.

'What?'

'Nothing,' I lied.

'I know you, Mimo. And since you've always been incapable of not telling me what you really think, you may as well tell me now.'

'I don't know... All this, it's just not like you.'

'All this?'

'Getting married, wanting children...'

'Ah, but has Mussolini not said that the role of a woman is to procreate and care for her family?'

'I don't know what Mussolini said, and I don't care. I have no truck with politics. But I am not the foolish boy you once knew. First, your family tries to marry you off to some spotty boy who – surprise, surprise! – is the runt of a preposterously rich litter. You manage to derail their plans, but a few years later you're married to another man who happens to be rolling in money. There is not a crack left in the villa, not a single damp patch...'

'I am not the girl you once knew either. Do you know what

I got from following my dreams? Months in hospital, dozens of stitches and almost as many broken bones. We have to know how to grow up. And, as I said, Rinaldo is very kind, he treats me well. He has promised that one day he will take me to America.'

'But—'

Viola stopped dead in her tracks just as we reached the edge of the forest. 'I don't need you to disapprove of my choices, Mimo. I need you to support me, or, at the very least, pretend to.'

She stepped into the forest with the same ease as she always had, but she did not wander very deep, and she stuck to the path. After a few minutes, she paused next to a pine grove and turned towards me. 'This is it.'

'What?'

'The place where I crash-landed.'

Above our heads, the pine trees tickled the clouds. Thirty metres of brown bark and imperial green.

'I owe my life to this tree,' she murmured, touching the trunk. 'Every branch I hit broke my fall and left a scar. What is curious is that I don't remember a thing. I am standing on the roof and the next thing I am opening my eyes in hospital.'

As she talked, she touched various parts of her body – reflexively, I think: her arm, her legs, her forehead. I remembered the scene as though it had happened only yesterday. Her defiant, angry cry amid the exploding flowers of light. The spiralling fall. The uncertainty of the following months, and her letter asking me not to write again. She could see it imprinted on my face.

'When I woke up after days in a coma, I asked to see you. You were the first name that came to my lips. Luckily, only Francesco was at my bedside. Nobody else knows that you and Paragraph helped me build the flying wing, that we were friends.'

'Does Francesco know about us? I always pretended I didn't know you, and he seemed to believe me.'

'Nobody knows what game Francesco is playing,' said Viola with a faint smile. 'I doubt he knows himself. As long as you don't tell him that you know he knows, you will have the upper hand.'

'You are the one who should be in politics... Why did you bring me here?'

'Because I made several bad choices. The first was to get you involved in my insane attempt to fly.'

'It was not insane! Even D'Annunzio himself—'

'Yes, I know,' she interrupted, sounding a little tetchy. 'But I'm not D'Annunzio, I'm Viola Orsini. I had a lot of time to think while I was in hospital. I was on morphine, so maybe I wasn't in my right mind, but I convinced myself that I'd let you down. I'd promised you I would fly and I had failed. I was your hero and I was afraid that you... I don't know, that you would love me less, or differently. That's why I asked you not to write any more. I didn't want you to feel sorry for me. I didn't want you to see me broken, my legs in metal callipers, the steel pins in my jaw. That was also the reason I decided not to come down to dinner on the night when you came back two years later. I panicked. Then I pulled myself together, and I put the red lantern in my window – then you were the one who left.'

I glanced around and, feeling a lump in my throat, I made as if to brush my hair back so that I could wipe my eyes on my sleeve. A tried and tested playground technique. 'Do you still see your bear?'

'Bianca? I haven't seen her in five years. I go to her cave now and then, but it's always empty. She is living her own life, and that is for the best.'

I nodded and cleared my throat. 'What is it that you want from me?'

'What did you want when you came back to the cemetery after a decade? Surely it was not just to see that I could travel through time.'

'I want things to go back to how they were.'

'But we are not the people we were. You are a respected artist and I am a married woman. But that does not stop us from travelling side by side. With no heroics this time.'

'Who dreams of a life without heroism?'

'Most heroes, I suspect.' She held out her hand. 'Do we have a deal?'

'I'm not exactly sure of the terms of this deal...'

'We shall make them up as we go along.'

I laughed and shook her hand, which seemed more fragile than ever, so I was careful not to squeeze too hard. My hands had doubled in size.

'I have missed you, Viola.'

'And I you.'

We walked back to the villa in silence. The low mist ravelled over a landscape of brown and green and orange, shot through with the characteristic pink of Pietra d'Alba.

When we reached the door of the Villa Orsini, Viola turned. 'One thing, when I sent the letter asking you not to write to me any more...'

'Yes?'

'You didn't have to obey.'

She gently closed the door. The wind picked up, whipping away the last shreds of mist. But which wind? The sirocco? The ponente, the mistral, the gregale? Or was it one whose name I did not know because Viola had never told me? I had thought that, being reunited with Viola, everything would be simpler. But what could be simple in a world where the wind has a thousand names?

I am twenty-four. I am not rich, which is simply a way of indicating how rich I will later be, because compared to the boy who arrived twelve years ago, I am a maharajah. I have an automobile, apprentices, employees and enough money to live on for four or five years if everything came crashing down. I am admitted to the Villa Orsini by the front door. Soon will come 1929, and after that a new decade which, I firmly believe, will be the calmest I will ever experience. A decade gilded by progress, by peace between nations and, even more surprisingly, between Viola and me.

Don't make me laugh.

'*P*adre! *Padre!* He started laughing.'

A novice bursts into his office and Padre Vincenzo looks up from the documents he has spent all morning studying. It happens every time he opens his secret vault – he becomes caught up in the same mystery, scrutinising and dissecting every document with the fervour of a second-century theologian, of a rabbi in a yeshiva, knowing that each word can mean one thing and its antithesis, but that there is only one truth, only one correct combination to be discovered if he is to understand everything.

The novice stops in front of his desk, gasping for breath. *Well, I suppose those stairs take it out of everyone*, thinks the padre.

'Who started laughing?'

'Brother Vitaliani.'

Although Vitaliani has never taken vows, everyone refers to him as 'brother', and Vincenzo doesn't protest.

'He laughed?'

'Yes, as though someone had just said something funny.'

'Is he conscious?'

'No. According to the doctor, his vital signs are failing.'

With a wave, Padre Vincenzo dismisses the novice and closes the window, which he foolishly left open despite the cold. From a large trunk – each of the monks has one in which they keep their personal belongings – he takes out a chequered woollen blanket and wraps it round himself. Then he opens the most intriguing file in his safe.

Witness statements.

His fire burned less brightly, and his bones creaked as he ascended the pulpit. He had lost much of what hair he had left. Only a tonsure of wiry grey tufts prevented him from being completely bald. Nonetheless, though over fifty now, he could still intimidate, with his pedantic tone, and continued to surprise people with the curious sense of humour that had led him, many years earlier, to take a liking to a little tramp of diminutive stature. The look of unbridled joy on Dom Anselmo's face as he saw me walking up the nave of San Pietro delle Lacrime warmed my heart. He hugged me and stared at me without saying a word, just nodding with satisfaction.

Sitting in the cloisters beneath a sky of Pietra blue – a colour that Technicolor or Pantone would never patent and no longer exists – we talked at length. Dom Anselmo complained that the parish finances had dried up. Ten years of peace meant that his flock thought less about death and so gave less. And the Vatican was far away. He asked me to put in a good word with Francesco, who no longer had time to visit when he came home to see his parents. Some of the architectural decorations were in urgent need of restoration. I promised to do the work, free of charge, as soon as my apprentices arrived.

On the way home I was overcome with emotion. The first day I arrived twelve years earlier was much like this. A breeze rustled through the fallow fields. As I left the village, I was greeted by the same pink, seraphic horizon. But in the meantime, I had lived a dozen lives.

From behind me I heard a scream, followed by a skid. I did not have time to turn before a riderless bicycle sailed past me and went hurtling down the embankment and I was gripped in a bear-hug and lifted off the ground several times. Emanuele whooped with joy. He pinched my cheeks and kissed my forehead. He was wearing a carabinieri parade uniform and a peaked cap from the Poste Italiane. His gibberish was as unintelligible as ever, but his gestures spoke volumes: he was now Pietra d'Alba's postman.

A month later, electricity came to the village. To the Villa Orsini, to be precise, but it hardly mattered, since it felt as though the electrons were spilling out all over Pietra d'Alba and everyone had their share. Initially, electricity consisted of a single lamp-post planted in the middle of the grounds, which was solemnly lit at 4.22 p.m. on 20 January 1929, at the precise moment when the sun dipped below the horizon. The whole village was invited to witness it but the initial excitement was followed by a certain puzzlement because, when the street lamp was finally lit, people couldn't help but wonder about the uses of this magical electricity, since any oil lamp could do the same thing. For the first time in months, the Marchese appeared in public, in a bath chair pushed by a servant. The right half of his face and body were paralysed. He gave a ponderous speech, after which Emanuele turned to us and delivered a verdict that Paragraph translated: 'I can't understand a word he says.'

That evening, there was a dinner at the villa to which I was naturally invited, being the Orsini family sculptor, a living symbol of their influence, piety and generosity. For some days now, my business was once again up and running, both in Rome and at the studio in Pietra d'Alba, where I had been joined by Jacopo and another young apprentice. The two were staying in the village, in a house that had been standing empty since the owner left for one or another of the great Italian cities. Viola and I had seen each other several times and often took long walks through the fields. We no longer talked as much as we once did. Like the orange groves, Viola seemed to be struck by the pallor of winter, and only the scent of neroli oil that clung to her hair still reminded me of the wild girl I had known as a boy. She still read as much as ever, but no longer talked about books. Occasionally I would deliberately say something outrageous: 'I hear people live upside down in the southern hemisphere,' which would rekindle the angry blaze in her eyes as she gave me a lesson in history and physics, a journey ranging from Copernicus via Newton and Einstein. Then she would stop dead and give me a grateful look, pleased to have been given a relief valve for the overflowing knowledge slowly poisoning her.

Dinner afforded me the opportunity to meet her husband again. Rinaldo Campana had just come back from the United States and regaled us all with tales of his encounters with the mixture of arrogance and charm I remembered, except that now his charm was beginning to fail. He had put on a lot of weight and became very animated when talking about money. He continued to drop names with the same nonchalance, 'Charlie said this, Charlie said that', and when asked who Charlie was, would look surprised and say, 'Chaplin, obviously.' There were two other guests at the dinner, both in black shirts, and they were joined by Stefano and Francesco, who had come back from Rome for the occasion. Sitting at the head of the table, the Marchese tried to eat with some dignity while we pretended not to notice the food that fell into his lap and soiled this man who had once hung his rivals from orange trees.

All the guests were accompanied by their wives, with the obvious exception of Francesco. The women were elegant and sophisticated, and I saw Viola cast surreptitious glances at them, and each time she would shift her posture. One of the blackshirts – whose name was Luigi Freddi – began to enthuse about Campana's plans. He suggested that Italy could take inspiration from American cinema and use its techniques to glorify the New Man of Fascism while avoiding the excesses of Soviet propaganda. In a warped way, he seemed to have a genuine love of cinema and recounted several scenes from films I had never seen. Campana listened to him intently and said that he was open to any film project that would make money 'because Fascism did not pay for the new electric power line', a remark that earned him a furious glare from Stefano and Freddi. But before long, Freddi was once again talking about his dreams of a whole city devoted to Italian cinema.

I silently listened to the conversation, doubtless influenced by my long friendship with Francesco, who did likewise, and from time to time would give me a knowing smile as he wiped his lips on his napkin after taking a sip of wine. Stefano, as always, drank enough for three men, and each time refilled my glass. Viola looked at me quizzically when she saw me drinking, then gave an imperceptible shrug, On the other hand, when Luigi Freddi spoke – melding art and politics in a way I had never heard – she quivered and constantly looked as though she were about to say something.

He must have noticed because after dessert he turned to her. 'And you, signora, what do you think of all this?'

Campana laid a hand on Viola's. 'Where are your manners, my dear Luigi? Our wives take no interest in politics. Why trouble them with our discussions?'

'True,' said Stefano. 'Why don't we go into the smoking room for a nightcap, or several – I was given the gift of some cigars that, I'm told, were rolled for Il Duce himself! We can leave the ladies to discuss the things that interest them.'

The men headed for the door leading to the next room. Francesco said that he was going to bed.

'Are you coming, Gulliver?' said Stefano.

Before joining the others, I glanced at Viola, who smiled at me sweetly. A servant closed the doors behind us just as Freddi's wife, a slim redhead, was leaning over to Viola to ask: 'The taffeta on your dress is simply *exquisite*. Where on earth did you find it?'

In the smoking room, Stefano unbuttoned his shirt collar and then his trousers with a sigh of relief. He slumped into a seat, quickly followed by Freddi and the other *squadristi*, who had had less to drink and spoke only to agree with whoever had spoken last. Campana leaned against the inlaid drinks cabinet stocked with various liqueurs and pensively puffed on the cigar one of the servants had lit for him.

After downing half a glass of whisky, Stefano cast a wry glance over the small gathering. 'Frankly, all this cinema nonsense is really just about getting to fondle a little new flesh, isn't it?'

Luigi Freddi frowned, while Campana gave a wry smile. 'Don't you believe it! I knew Rodolfo very well before he died and—'

'Rodolfo?' said Stefano.

'Ah yes, Rudolph, since that was how he liked to be known. And it has to be said that Rudolph Valentino sounds more virile than Rodolfo di Valentina. Anyway, when Rudolph married for the first time, his young wife locked him out of their hotel room on their wedding night. Turns out she preferred women.'

'I would have made her love men.'

'I doubt it,' said Campana ironically.

Stefano scowled and spilled his glass as he leapt to his feet. 'What exactly is that supposed to mean?'

'Nothing. Just that if Rudolph Valentino could not succeed...'

'Who are you to talk? You can't even get my fucking sister knocked up!'

'Gentlemen,' Freddi interrupted, giving me a worried glance.

I had seen Stefano lose his temper over more trivial matters a dozen of times. But I left him to it, because I found

Campana annoying and because I too had had a lot to drink. Besides, the lawyer could defend himself.

'I might be able to get your sister knocked up, as you so elegantly put it, if she were a little more enthusiastic.'

'You should talk about Viola with more respect. Both of you.'

Stefano and Campana turned, surprised by my intervention.

'Ah,' said the lawyer. 'I see the lady has a knight in shining armour.' He looked me up and down – a look I knew all too well, and one that did not have far to travel. 'Have you got your eye on Viola, little man?'

'Try calling me "little man" again, and you'll see.'

Without warning, Stefano laughed and shook his empty glass. 'Women – ha! – nothing but trouble! Let's not argue over a pair of tits, especially since they're my sister's!'

'I agree,' said Campana. 'It's not as though there is anything to argue about.'

Freddi saw the way I was gripping my glass. He was an intelligent man and could guess what possibilities were open to me – the one where I threw the glass at Campana's face, followed by endless other ramifications; the one where the glass cut his cheek and the one where the glass missed and I hurled myself at him to finish the job... He laid a hand on my arm and his stare had me rooted me to my chair. A waiter poured another round, while Stefano stoked the fire.

Freddi smiled at me, clearly relieved. 'They say you are a very talented sculptor, Signor Vitaliani.'

'So they say,' I muttered.

'The regime needs people like you. The people have no imagination – they need to be *shown* so they can contemplate, can touch the New Man. We are embarked upon a project with the great Marconi, the inventor of wireless telegraphy, about which I am sworn to secrecy, and I think that you too could contribute to the country's influence. Would you be interested in working for us? Il Duce can be very generous to Italy's scientists and artists.'

Perhaps because I was drunk, perhaps because I liked money, or perhaps because, in his own way, Freddi was a visionary and he did not seem to like Campana any more than I did, or perhaps for none of these reasons, I said: 'Why not?'

The next day, Viola showed up just after lunch. She burst into the workshop, where Paragraph and I were sharing a cup of coffee before getting back to work.

'I want to see Mimo. Alone.'

Paragraph calmly set down his cup and left, though not before giving me a mocking look behind Viola's back, drawing his finger like a blade sliding across his throat.

'What have I done now?'

'So you know that you have done something?' she said sardonically.

'If this is about my argument with your husband last night, I found him rude. And not just rude: crass.'

'From what I heard, you had been drinking heavily, and you are not exactly a role model. Actually, I never thought you would grow up to be a drinker, given what your uncle was like—'

'Have you come to lecture me?'

Viola opened her mouth, closed it again and sighed. Her shoulders slumped. 'Look at us. You have hardly been back a month and already we're fighting.'

'Your husband disrespected me. And he disrespected you.'

'Mimo. I need you. But I don't need you to defend me, do you understand?'

Seeing my stubborn look, a flicker of dread moved over her face. Suddenly, Viola at twelve, at sixteen, was once again standing in front of me, a creature who was simultaneously terrified and thrilled by everything. 'Don't make me choose between you and my husband.'

'It's all right, don't worry.'

'So you'll come up to the villa and apologise?'

'Apologise? I'd rather die.'

Later that afternoon, I went to the Villa Orsini and, with a palpable lack of sincerity, offered my apologies to Rinaldo Campana. He accepted them with no less palpable hypocrisy, and we parted with a handshake, despising each other more than ever.

Luigi Freddi kept his promise. In May 1929, he made the most of one of my brief visits to the studio in Rome to come and see me, accompanied by Stefano. The regime was about to begin work on a spectacular new building in Palermo, a symbol of Fascism, of the New Man everyone kept droning on about, though I could never work out what exactly was *new* about him, given that he drank, pissed, murdered and lied as much as the old man. The architectural design of the Palazzo delle Poste, a building of concrete and Sicilian marble with a thirty-metre-high colonnade, had been entrusted to Mazzoni, the interior frescoes to Benedetta Cappa, who was the wife of Marinetti, the inventor of Futurism. And Futurism was Viola. Freddi offered to commission me to sculpt a fasces five metres tall to be displayed on the side of the building, and fifty thousand lire, enough to live comfortably for a year. I had not spent six years working in Rome without learning a thing or two.

'I'm not interested,' I said.

Behind Freddi, Stefano looked crestfallen. 'But... other sculptors would kill for such a privilege!'

'Excellent. I would not wish to put you in a difficult position. Commission one of them. There are plenty of talented sculptors in this country. Or at least competent ones.'

'I don't understand. Over dinner, you said you would be interested...'

'Because I thought your government was ambitious. Why just one fasces? You need three, like the Trinity, because it seems to me that the Fascist regime wants to vie with the best in authority. Each of the fasces should be twenty metres tall, not five, otherwise your symbol will look ridiculous compared to the size of the building. As for the cost, I don't know whether you could afford it. A hundred and fifty thousand lire, not including marble and expenses.'

Freddi stared at me open-mouthed, but I thought I saw a glimmer of admiration in his eye. He could not make such a decision himself; he needed to make a telephone call.

While he went up to my office, Stefano shook his fist in my face. 'Are you out of your mind? If you fuck this up, Gulliver, I'll kill you.'

And he would have done so willingly, unhesitatingly, such was the nature of our friendship. It straddled the void, about to collapse at any moment, yet it had that fleeting brilliance and weightlessness of a mayfly. Stefano was a pig. He thought of me as a degenerate, an abnormality. We had the mutual respect of scumbags.

Freddi finally reappeared, stared at me solemnly, then laughed and shook my hand with childlike enthusiasm.

Francesco did not greet the news of this commission with the enthusiasm I had expected. What better way to increase the prestige of the Orsini family, I asked. With his hands clasped under his chin, and with a compunction that seemed a little less comical now that a few grey hairs streaked his youthful temples, he explained that relations between the Fascist regime and the Holy See were delicate. They needed each other, but necessity did not foster love. Archbishop Pacelli had only just been made a cardinal, a huge step for a man who many imagined would reach the highest heights. My decisions would be studied and analysed as expressions of the Orsini family's allegiances. And the Orsini family, Francesco reminded me, bore no allegiance to anyone but God.

I went back to Pietra d'Alba and established the working routine I would follow in the years ahead: three or four annual visits to Rome, and as many again to the sites of my projects. I would primarily work from my studio in

Pietra d'Alba, alongside Paragraph, Anna and, of course, Viola. Mikael, who was now my right-hand man, would discreetly, not to say clandestinely, take care of the smooth running of the two studios. In those days, it was easier to make your mark if you were four foot six than if you were dark-skinned.

I sent for three blocks of grey Billiemi marble from Palermo and spent four months creating detailed sculptures of the three fasces in scale models one metre high. I sent the maquettes to Rome, together with instructions on the cuts to be made to create the twenty-metre fasces, which would then be finished by my apprentices. Meanwhile, Jacopo would take charge of all commissions we received from Francesco. While these had once seemed lucrative, the fasces, which had delighted Luigi Freddi, heralded an era of extraordinary riches. Riches that seemed all the more brazen given that, since October onwards, the newspapers had written of nothing but a devastating financial crisis, one that did not seem to affect the Orsini family or any of my other clients, secular or religious. From bitter experience, I knew that such crises impoverished only the poor.

I saw Viola regularly for long walks through the orange groves. In 1930, she spent several months in Milan undergoing treatment to boost her fertility. She came back with dark circles under her eyes and heavier by ten kilos, unevenly distributed over her slender body. By the end of 1930, she was as slim as ever, and her large eyes glittered with that pale violet that made her look like my mother.

Viola seemed no more enthusiastic about my fasces and my collaboration with Luigi Freddi than Francesco. She disapproved of the Fascist regime's policies, which she knew in detail. The *Corriere della Sera* was no longer delivered to the Villa Orsini since the stroke that had left the Marchese unable to read, so I subscribed to the paper and discreetly gave it to her – which merely served to do my cause a disservice, since every issue gave Viola some new reason to rant. But I must confess that I loved to see her eyes blaze with fire, her mouth twitch, her outraged or impatient tics I remembered from a time when all Viola did was fume. And so, I tolerated her scornful looks whenever I mentioned my plans for Palermo. From time to time, we would argue.

'Just as long as you don't work for those bastards after the job in Palermo...'

'They're not all bastards, far from it. The government has done a number of good things.'

'Yes, like assassinating its opponents.'

'If you're talking about Matteotti, that is ancient history and nothing was ever proven. And, as I remember, you were perfectly happy for the *squadristi* to save the villa during the 1919 revolt...'

We would not see each other for a few weeks. Then one of us would go and loiter near the other's place – she at the studio, I at the villa – on some more or less credible pretext, and we would carry on as before. Every two months, there was a dinner at the Orsini villa during which the family's social ascent could be calculated. These dinners were increasingly attended by influential members of government. Francesco always came, but said little. On some nights, the table was decked in purple and the guests vied with each other to magnify the Lord, though they never forgot to discuss more earthly but no less important matters. Rinaldo Campana would sometimes make an appearance and sit as far from me as possible. Viola now barely saw her husband, who spent much of his time travelling in the United States, where, despite his promises, he had not taken her. As soon as the coffee was served, the couple would retire, under Stefano's mocking eye, to test the fertility of my best friend, and I would feel like throwing up.

By late 1929, the Fascist regime had created the Reale Accademia d'Italia, and Guglielmo Marconi was appointed president in 1930.

In his inaugural lecture, Marconi declared: 'I reclaim the honour of being the first Fascist in the field of radiotelegraphy, the first who acknowledged the utility of joining the electric rays in a bundle, as Mussolini was the first in the political field who acknowledged the necessity of merging all the healthy energies of the country into a bundle, for the greater greatness of Italy.' If I still remember the quote, it is because I learned it by heart and spitefully used it against Viola during one of our quarrels. Viola, who loved science, progress and speed, could not disown Marconi. And if Fascism was good enough for him, it was good enough for me, especially since Luigi Freddi had heard whispers that my name had been mentioned as a potential member of the Reale Accademia d'Italia. At twenty-six, I was perhaps too young, but if I played my cards right, I would be invited to join the lofty ranks. I, who was so short.

With her habitual rhetorical precautions, Viola told me that I was an imbecile, Marconi a moron, and between us we were lowering the collective intelligence of the nation. Mussolini had only created the Reale Accademia to compete with the Accademia dei Lincei, an institution founded three centuries earlier that even Il Duce did not dare dissolve, one that brought together the most brilliant minds in the world, among them a certain Einstein. The academicians were intelligent, but not remotely Fascist. I flew into a purple rage and did not see Viola for three months. Then came the great Palermo flood of February 1931, which inundated the site of the Palazzo delle Poste and almost caused the collapse of the first fasces, which had been completed and was in the process of being mounted. Shortly afterwards, a howling gale caused a construction crane to collapse and fall onto a neighbouring building, reviving my fears that I was cursed. I could see that Viola was torn between using my superstitiousness as a weapon, and her contempt for all forms of irrational belief. Caught between these two extremes, her brain seized up, and she did not mention that building again until its inauguration in 1934.

Yes, of course there were other women, as people constantly ask, as though it mattered. I saw them on my visits to Rome, to Palermo, but there was nothing worth mentioning about those jaded embraces. My work took up the greater part of my time, and Viola the rest.

Had we never argued, I might never have noticed the change. I might simply have accepted the subtle signs of weakness, or even decided that she had always been like this, just as Dom Anselmo was bald or Anna buxom. But our frequent estrangements meant that, when I saw her again, I would notice that she seemed increasingly absent. She would often ask me to repeat a question, start as though she had just awakened from a long sleep. Other treatments followed those in Milan, with changes to her weight and the return of the dark circles, though she still had the supple figure of a young branch, just a little more careworn. Campana began to come more often for the weekend, bringing his sister, a Milanese woman with broad hips and three boys aged between two and six. His avowed aim – as he said, when the gentlemen retired to smoke cigars – was to inspire his wife, to show her the paradigm of perfect happiness and finally stimulate her 'mournful womb', as he put it one evening, when only Francesco's presence averted another argument. Viola's belly did not swell, but remained resolutely flat, despite her husband's increasingly reluctant assaults. Then, one day, in the mid-1930s, she informed me that they were giving up on the idea of having a child. Several doctors claimed that the fall had damaged her irreparably. From then on, Campana became increasingly unpleasant, or so it seemed to me. His sister continued to visit the Villa Orsini three or four times a year. Now the point seemed to be to make Viola realise what she was missing. It was a dubious strategy, given that her three children were spoilt, stupid and unbearable.

Once they were delivered, my fasces earned me a new influx of government commissions. The ancient fasces, carried by a lictor attending a consul or magistrate, consisted of an axe surrounded by a bundle of rods, a sign of the authority of those who bore them and symbolic of the two forms of punishment they could inflict, one brutal, the other lethal. The fasces I had sculpted retained only the broad outline, blurring the distinction between axe and rods, creating a monumental symbol of a power that was simultaneously fierce and calm and whose wrath was unpredictable. It was the only one of my works that might be called modernist, if such a word means anything. The fasces were mounted on the right elevation of the building. They were admired, applauded and praised, and if they are no longer on display now, as I leave this world, it is entirely my fault. I created them and made them disappear, albeit inadvertently, some years later.

On my return from Palermo, the Orsinis organised a dinner in my honour. The revenge of the boy who had been stripped and beaten fifteen years earlier was complete. From this point, Francesco began to attend all the important dinners, including those for high-ranking officials of the Fascist regime. Pius XI had been reconciled with Il Duce, who finally recognised the Pope's sovereignty over the Vatican and Catholicism as the state religion. As a gift, Marconi had given Pius XI the first radio broadcast by a pope, whose voice was heard the world over. I attended the dinner in my most elegant suit, sporting a Cartier wristwatch. I wore only the very best, which, to my despair, invariably came from France, since Italy at the time had no interest in fashion. Cartier also triggered a rare argument with Paragraph. I had given him a watch as a gift, but he had given it back, embarrassed by the sheer extravagance of the thing, claiming he wouldn't know what to do with it, especially since the time by which wood was measured could not be calculated using such a tool. I called him an ignorant oaf.

Campana attended the dinner, separated from the table by a huge belly that spilled over his belt. His face was now a debacle of pasty, sagging flesh that starkly contrasted with his opulent suits and the brilliance of his eyes, like those of a prowling wolf. He spent the evening boasting about his latest successes, announcing that he had just discovered a young girl named Miranda Bonansea who would soon be the Italian Shirley Temple and telling us that, when it came to cinema, we had seen nothing yet. He scarcely practised law any more, making exceptions only for some sensational criminal trial, where he would turn up and do a little grandstanding knowing the verdict was a foregone conclusion. And if the verdict was not guaranteed, he could always ensure that it was, he said with a snigger and rubbing his thumb and forefinger together. Viola smiled absently. I longed to shake her awake. When Campana mentioned that he had his own private loggia at La Scala, to which he had invited his friend Douglas (Fairbanks) only the week before, I decided to needle him.

'I would love to go to the opera.'

'So would I,' said Viola immediately.

Campana gave us a forced smile and had no choice but to ask us to join him the following week, when his friend Arturo (Toscanini) would be conducting the premiere of *Turandot*. The Marchese, seated at the head of the table, gave an incomprehensible gurgle whose meaning was never known. He always presided over these dinners with his wife and was attended by a nurse who wiped away or picked up everything that fell from his mouth. A second stroke the previous year had left him considerably weaker. Only his sparkling eyes, often focused on the cleavage of his nurse, suggested there was still a spark within this lifeless shell.

Six days later, we were at La Scala in Milan. Campana had invited some friends and his loggia was full. He sat between Viola and a little blonde secretary. From their barely veiled glances, it quickly became apparent that her services were more than secretarial. Viola stared straight ahead, imprisoned behind a smile. The opera began, and it is no exaggeration to say that the story was utterly preposterous. A cruel Chinese princess, three riddles, a poor fellow who does not realise his slave girl is secretly in love with him. I leaned over and whispered to Viola: 'I'm not going to last ten minutes.'

But, ten minutes later, when Liù declared her love for the imbecile Calaf, I was in tears. I knew Viola well enough to know, just from the back of her head, that she too was weeping at the genius of Italy. Campana made the most of the darkness to slide a furtive hand along his secretary's thigh, right in front of me. On stage, Calaf was singing 'Nessun Dorma'. I pretended to shift in my seat and kneed Campana in the back, before apologising profusely and flashing him an innocent smile.

As we left the opera house, a fine drizzle cast a sad veil over the streets of Milan and the early days of 1935. Campana said his wife looked tired and suggested that she go home while he had a nightcap and talked business. I offered to accompany her, which did not seem to trouble the lawyer.

He did not see me as a threat – I was not sure whether to feel relieved or insulted.

Midway back, I ordered our driver to stop and opened the door.

'What has got into you?' said Viola. 'Where are we?'

'I have no idea, but I know it is just the right kind of neighbourhood.'

'The right kind of neighbourhood for what?'

'For getting completely hammered.'

Viola had never got hammered in her life, but she followed me. Using the instinct I had developed in Florence, and later refined during my years in Rome, it didn't take me long to find the reef of tiles and zinc to which the city's castaways clung. A tiny bar with a half-closed metal shutter, wedged between a long-closed car garage and a laundry. Viola drank her first glass reluctantly, had to be persuaded to drink a second and a third, ordered the fourth by herself, and the rest is history. For a fleeting moment, everything was as it had been: Mimo-who-sculpts and Viola-who-flies, which she did at around three in the morning, throwing herself drunkenly from the counter into the welcoming arms of a crowd of sailors who had never seen the sea.

Campana telephoned the Orsinis to complain. Viola had spent two days ill in bed and it was all my fault. He called me a 'degenerate dwarf', a moniker that Stefano delightedly took up. The degenerate dwarf didn't care; he was already back on the road. In early 1935, I accepted a series of commissions that would take five years to complete. Cardinal Pacelli wished to offer a statue of a saint to a friend who was also a cardinal. I could hardly say no to Pacelli, since I owed him everything. He allowed me to choose the saintly subject, though via Francesco, he advised me to 'consider the intended audience' and 'not to be too experimental'. A few private commissions followed, and then one of the architects in charge of the new Palazzo della Civiltà Italiana in Rome commissioned me to create ten of the thirty or so statues that would grace the ground floor. I was fascinated by the maquette of the building, another symbol of the regime's ambitions. A cyclopean white cube of six storeys, each pierced by nine arches (six for Benito, nine for Mussolini, as legend would later have it). I instantly accepted. Although the building work would never be completed, for once I would not be to blame. Lastly, I accepted a commission for the courtyard of the new aeronautical school in Forlì. The mosaics that adorned the walls, exquisite examples of the art of Aeropittura, always made me think of Viola.

In late spring, I returned to Pietra d'Alba, free of all financial worries for good. I had solved the curious equation of capitalism: by accepting only a handful of commissions, I could afford to charge exorbitant prices. There was always someone prepared to buy. The fewer works I made, the richer

I grew. Viola commented that before long I might be paid to do no work. She liked this idea, since I would be bankrupting Fascists without giving them anything in return. I reminded her that I didn't just work for Fascists and, moreover, they had done nothing to me. She told me about the problems faced by Jews in Germany, reeled off the names of towns and people, told me about places and murders, about all the things that were right there in front of me but which I chose not to see, and this triggered another of the many arguments that marked those years. Since we were cosmic twins, our grievances were perfectly symmetrical. She criticised me for contributing to the new world that was being born, for being one of its major architects. And I criticised her for doing precisely the opposite. For leaving the stage on the pretext that she had once stumbled in public.

In July 1935, at precisely the midpoint of the decade, Pietra d'Alba awoke to a warm summer morning where everything seemed to be as usual: the burnt stubble fields, the struggling, withering orange trees and the scent of neroli, less pungent but still present since it had seeped into the very stones. And the pervasive pink without which Pietra would not be d'Alba. A rippling heat haze announced sweltering weather, long hours during which nothing moved, when even the marble we worked struggled to remain cool.

Suddenly there came a commotion, a deafening racket the likes of which the village had never heard and would not hear again. A dust cloud and a black convoy swarming along the path through the Gambale family fields that separated the Orsini family lake from the villa. Five lorries rumbled along the path, axles squealing. The first three were loaded with pipes, coils and containers, the other two with labourers and *squadristi*. They moved across the roads and fields to the thunderous roar of orders and commands. Any soldier would have realised that the apparent chaos belied a precise battle plan.

After years spent patiently biding his time, Stefano Orsini was making his move.

Within three weeks, the Gambale family fields were spanned by an aqueduct that plunged into the lake at one end, while the other emptied into a purpose-built reservoir dug on the high ground behind the Villa Orsini, allowing the fields to be irrigated by gravity. The *squadristi* supervised the work and – almost for the sake of form – stood sentry during the night. Stefano was a brute, but he was not as stupid as I had thought. The presence of the *squadristi* was a pointed reminder of his position and his supporters. The message was clear and, despite their fury, not a single member of the Gambale family dared to protest. No one wanted to end up like Matteotti, a rotting body in a front-page photograph. In the final week, a pump was installed by the lake; the long cable to power it was connected to the villa's electricity supply. Stefano was not graceful in victory. He had a fountain installed in the middle of the fields simply because he could. It was sculpted by my apprentices under Jacopo's supervision. The intimate dedication ceremony was attended by the Orsini family (with the exception of Francesco, who was busy in Rome) and a handful of friends. Stefano waved away Simona, the young nurse caring for his father, and took the handles of the old man's bath chair. At sixty-five, the Marchese was not very old, but the two strokes had gradually erased his presence. Stefano wheeled his father up to the highest terrace of the villa and turned him so that he could see the orange groves. Between the trees, where there had been nothing but rock and dust, the fountain gushed while flashes of grapefruit and peach danced in the twilight.

'Virgilio would never have done all this, would he?'

Two fat tears rolled down the cheeks of the Marchese. It was impossible to know whether he was weeping for joy, for his dead crushed son or simply because he could no longer blink. Simona wiped his cheeks, putting an end to a frankly embarrassing episode in which one of the most powerful figures in Italy succumbed to a moment of weakness.

By September, the surviving orange and lemon trees were already showing signs of renewed vigour. A new shipment arrived from a nursery in Genoa and hundreds of dead, dying or diseased trees were replaced. A quiet joy flowed through the fields, the ditches, the gutters and the streets, whirling around the village square and intoxicating the villagers, who drank it in. There were impromptu celebrations. We had won a war, defeated the sun, our most fearsome enemy, and the bastard Gambales into the bargain. But the joy dissipated before it reached the workshop. When I came back from inspecting a few quarries after the autumn equinox, I found the house in darkness and the hearth cold. There was no sound, and Paragraph did not answer when I called to him.

I found him sitting under a blanket in the middle of his workshop, his cheeks covered by a beard now several days old. He smelled of booze and tobacco and clutched his cold pipe between his fingers. His eyes burned with a fever, but his forehead was dry. Panicked, I thought about the little ones – though at ten and twelve they were not so little now.

'What's happened? Where's Anna?'

'Gone.'

'Gone? Gone where?'

'To stay with cousins near Genoa.'

'She left just like that, with no warning?'

She had not left without warning. They had spent a long time talking about the widening gap between two people whom everyone believed nothing could separate. Like splinters, time slips under your skin – but who worries about a little splinter? – and eventually becomes infected. Anna saw that the world was changing and she wanted something more. She reproached Paragraph for his lack of ambition. Three days earlier, he had come home from making a delivery to a neighbouring village to find the house empty. That night, Anna telephoned to tell him where she was, and they talked with no acrimony, only the weariness of battle-scarred soldiers. Anna needed some distance; she needed to enjoy the hustle and bustle of the cities. She planned to find somewhere to stay near Savona, only an hour's drive from Pietra d'Alba. Paragraph would still be able to see Zozo and Maria as often as he liked, and bring them back to the workshop for a few days if he wanted.

'Do you think I lack ambition, Mimo? I earn a very good living. But I suppose that compared to you...'

Suddenly, I felt guilty for strutting around in my sports trousers, my linen jacket and expensive wristwatch. And because I felt guilty, I took myself to Genoa to talk to Anna. When she welcomed me, her cheeks were less rosy than usual, though Zozo and Maria were delighted to see me. Then she sent the children off to play, made me a cup of coffee and we sat in the kitchen, a little room that overlooked a bustling street. She did not have much time; this wasn't her apartment, and her cousins would be home soon. I used every trick up my sleeve to persuade her to change her mind. I reminded her of our adventures, the nocturnal missions fifteen years earlier, her first meeting with Paragraph, when their bodies were still young, when they were coming together and every night was like the first. But the more I talked, the more Anna's face hardened. Finally, she sighed.

'Mimo, you gad about from one city to another with your powerful friends, and you come back to dispense advice when you think that we need you. I know you believe that you are doing the right thing. But let me tell you something: you know nothing about us, about the winters we've spent in Pietra d'Alba. You've been gone too long. I have children, and I want them to experience something more than living like recluses. The world is changing, and I refuse to let them miss out.'

As every time that someone criticised my success, I felt my gall rising. Yes, I had money – so what? It was not as though I hadn't earned it. I deserved it! I had not changed, only the way that other people saw me.

'I do know you a little,' I said stiffly.

'Do you? Did you know that Vittorio hates being called Paragraph but he has never dared tell you?'

I headed back, defeated, vowing never again to meddle in other people's affairs. A vow I broke the very next day, when I went to fetch Viola to go for a walk and was told that she was indisposed. When I went back the next day and was given the same reply, I had a maid take a note to her. *Don't make me climb up to your bedroom.* I knew when Viola was lying. The maid reappeared a minute later and handed me a note in an elegant green hand. *I'll see you at the studio.*

She turned up in mid-afternoon, just as I was putting the finishing touches to Saint Francis, the subject I had chosen for my commission from Pacelli. She stood for a moment, framed in the doorway, then stepped inside, leaning on her cane. Although she used it less and less, on cold days she could not get around without it. It was a week before her birthday, something she had not celebrated in a long time. For a few days more, Viola would be thirty.

She had a silk scarf wrapped around her head and was wearing make-up. I turned back to Saint Francis and carried on polishing the curve of his cheek without a word.

'Mimo?'

When I said nothing, she came closer and stood on the edge of the shadows. I sculpted in the pool of light that streamed down from a skylight I had had installed the previous winter.

'Who did this to you?' I said.

Viola flinched and brought a hand to her cheek. 'How did you know?'

'I've told you a thousand times, Viola, I'm not twelve any more. And I've known my fair share of thugs – some of them have been my friends.'

Slowly, she unwound the scarf. Despite the thick foundation, the bruise on her cheek was still visible.

'It was Campana, wasn't it?'

'It's not his fault.'

She headed to the door that looked out onto the fields, went outside and sat down on a tree trunk that was destined for Paragraph's workshop, which was opposite mine. I pulled on a woollen jacket and joined her.

'I hit him first, if you must know. We had a row. I cannot bear the idea of him being seen in public with his mistresses.

Not that I care that there are other women, I'm very aware that I cannot give him what he wants. But I'm entitled to a little respect.'

'Where is he now?'

'He left for Milan this morning. He was so sorry.'

I leapt to my feet. 'I'll kill the bastard.'

Viola gripped my arm with unexpected force. 'I'm old enough to defend myself.' She pulled me towards her and forced me to sit down again. 'And believe me, if I wanted to kill him, I would do it myself.'

'I don't understand how you ended up in this situation, married to that cretin.'

'How *I* ended up in this situation?'

Her eyes blazed, just as they had done eighteen years earlier when I dared to walk away without turning back. Perhaps, deep down, the reason for our constant quarrels was a shared nostalgia for the fights we had back when knights were good and dragons were evil, when love was chivalrous and every blow was justified by a noble cause.

'I ended up in this situation the same way you ended up working for a gang of thugs, Mimo. Because people need electric lights and orange groves.'

'You could leave him.'

'Life doesn't work like that.'

Paragraph, whom I was now careful to call Vittorio, emerged from the barn. He started when he saw us, seemed to hesitate, then finally came and sat down on the tree trunk with us, staring out over the fields. He had lost weight since Anna left. His bushy beard flecked with grey contrasted with his receding hairline.

'The harvest looks like it will be good,' he said, 'thanks to the water from the reservoir.'

Viola studied the citrus groves with a serious expression. 'Stefano is a fool. Yes, there is water today, but what about a year from now, ten years from now?'

'You can't reason with Gambales,' I said, like the good village boy I had become. 'If he hadn't forced their hand, the trees would still be dying.'

'It's always possible to reason with people. Where does man's violence come from?'

'Man with a capital M?'

'There is no man with a capital M. You're all men with tiny little Ms. So, tell me – I'm genuinely interested – where does this violence come from?' Viola stared at us as though actually waiting for an answer. 'From being abandoned, maybe? But who abandoned you? Your mothers? And if so, why do you treat them and all mothers-to-be this way?'

'I suppose you think women are not violent?' muttered Vittorio.

'Of course we are. We direct our violence against ourselves because it wouldn't occur to us to make someone else suffer. But the violence we live and breathe, this violence that poisons us, it has to find an outlet somewhere.'

From the far side of the workshop came a screech of wheels and the toot of a car horn.

Vittorio jumped up. 'I'll go see who it is!' He left, just as he had always done in the past when the conversation took a serious turn.

As he rounded the corner of the barn, Viola spoke without looking at me, her eyes lost on the horizon. 'Are you familiar with *Didus ineptus*?'

'No.'

'Better known as the dodo?'

'Oh. It's a bird, isn't it?'

'An extinct bird. Whose distinctive characteristic was that it could not fly. I am a dodo, Mimo. I know you're angry that I'm not the person I used to be, the Viola who visited cemeteries and leapt into the void. But the dodo disappeared because it feared nothing. It was easy prey. I have to be very careful so that I don't disappear.'

'I would never let you disappear.'

A car door slammed and the sound of an engine faded away. Vittorio reappeared, his eyes wide.

'Mimo! Mimo!' Vittorio jabbed a finger towards the house. He had a strange expression, as though something unexpected had lifted him out of the slough of despondency in which he seemed determined to wallow. 'There's someone here to see you!'

She was waiting for me outside the kitchen door, a suitcase at her feet. It was a suitcase that I recognised, though it was a little more battered. In fact, I recognised the suitcase before I did its owner. It must be said that I had spent the last twenty years writing, less and less assiduously, to a woman in her forties, with a full head of raven hair and a body shaped by hard physical work. The woman standing before me was sixty, and her waistline had expanded. Her curly hair was artificial, as was the colour; I had learned to recognise the work of a bad hairdresser.

Slowly, I walked towards this woman who, one winter's night, had brought me into this rocky world, Mimo, the nonentity, the *piccolo problema*, now an artist whose work was coveted and fought over. And suddenly I felt ashamed, ashamed of this money that no one had ever given my father, who I genuinely believe was more talented than myself.

'Hello, Michelangelo,' she said softly, staring at the ground. 'You said I could come whenever I wanted, and I thought, now that I'm a widow...'

It was not my mother speaking, because my mother never lowered her eyes to anyone. Before me stood a woman who had given birth to a prodigy, the Virgin Mary after the Angel Gabriel's annunciation in the fresco by Fra Angelico. A woman overawed, almost frightened, by her own son.

Perhaps it was because of my conversation with Viola, but the first thing out of my mouth was not what I wanted to say. 'Why did you abandon me?'

She flinched. She had travelled a long way, she was tired, she had probably hoped for a very different welcome. Slowly, she looked up; her eyes pierced mine with a violet glow that had not faded.

'Life is a succession of choices that we would make differently if given the chance, Mimo. If you have managed to get everything right the first time, without ever making a mistake, then you are a god. And despite the love I feel for you, and the fact that you're my son, even I don't believe I gave birth to a god.'

I n those early weeks, my mother refused to live with us. She did not want to 'be in the way'. But it did not take her long to realise that Vittorio needed a woman's presence. And he seemed to come back to life when my mother took over the running of the workshop, where she had agreed to live until she found somewhere else. Her second husband, like so many men, had worked himself to death out in the fields, though in his case, he had amassed a tidy fortune and had not spent a centime. Antonella Vitaliani – or Antoinette Le Goff, as she was now called – had ample means to support herself.

We spent a few weeks getting to know each other again. It was a strange feeling, since we knew each other with every fibre of our being. But that did not preclude some awkward silences, our excessive precautions and our mutual frustration. Things got better when Vittorio, with the wisdom of Geppetto, explained.

'For all your money, your success, for all the women you have defiled in your nights of debauchery, despite the litres of alcohol you've swigged and spewed, despite the horrors you will later commit, your mother still thinks of you as six. A son who has a good relationship with his mother has given up trying to persuade her otherwise.'

I introduced her to Viola when we bumped into her in the village. Immediately afterwards my mother said: 'What's wrong with that girl? She looks as though she has swallowed the devil, hooves and all.' Shortly afterwards, I had to leave for Rome, having insisted on personally accompanying my statue of Saint Francis. We arrived in the first week of 1936.

Cardinal-purple had not changed Archbishop Pacelli: the same little round glasses he had worn all his life, the same strange contrast between those lips that rarely smiled and the sensual chin of a boxer or an actor – a chin just begging for a vicious right hook. In my studio in Rome, he studied the Saint Francis while Francesco and I waited for the verdict. It was an excellent piece of work and I had heeded all of Pacelli's instructions, or almost – and on that *almost*, everything would depend. Pacelli had asked me to curb my instincts. In other words, not to be myself. But why commission me, if not because I was *me*? I had sculpted Saint Francis with one hand close to his cheek, and a bird perched on his index finger. So far, so canonical. But, in an audacious piece of folly on my part, it was clear to the viewer that the bird's wing had grazed the saint's neck a second earlier and tickled him, because Saint Francis was giggling. No one had ever seen a ticklish saint, let alone one who giggled. At least not in religious sculpture, where saints generally look like celestial civil servants overburdened by requests for divine intercession.

Pacelli glanced at us, the corners of his lips twitching into what passed for a smile, infected by Saint Francis' giddy joy. 'How old are you, Signor Vitaliani?'

'Thirty-two, Monsignor.'

'Well, in this piece I see the same qualities I first observed when you were half that age. The same sense of movement, the same irreverence, but with that something extra that only experience can bring.'

It is customary to segment the life of an artist into periods, phases, eras, anything to reassure the buyer who might panic if he found himself in a world with no labels. Magritte had made fun of this a few years earlier with his pipe, which was not a pipe, and no one had understood, and the less people understood, the more rapturous they were in their praise. But who am I to question how the world works? Let us accept that such periods, phases and eras do exist.

If so, Pacelli's remark marked the end of my first period.

That evening, I drank. A lot and alone. I did not want Stefano to be my companion in debauchery, nor his friends who had done me no harm and who seemed very nice, but who, because of Viola, I suspected had blood on their hands. Francesco congratulated me and said that my Saint Francis was already on its way to the family home of Pacelli's cardinal friend, one more friend who, when the time came, would vote the right way.

Francesco had noticed that I was out of sorts. 'Long journey,' I said before taking my leave. Pacelli's comment went round and round inside in my head as I sat in the dismal dive bar by the Tiber where I took refuge and where no one would find me, since even the *squadristi* did not sink that low. Pacelli had intended the remark as a compliment. What I heard was that I was just as I had been at sixteen, but better. Where was the *man*? The man who could touch the secrets of the gods? Was this what being an adult was about? Making money, improving yourself a little if you could? There I was criticising Viola when in fact I had not flown much further than she.

Despite my drunken state, there was no annunciation that night. No angel came to tell me to be patient, to explain that I would touch the secret of the gods, but that it would take me a decade. Ten years. Too long. I could not bear it. Or perhaps there was an annunciation that I don't remember, because I woke up with my head in a bush on the riverbank, next to a pool of vomit that, given its contents, did not belong to me. I had not drunk so much for a long time.

I stayed in Rome until the spring. I had reached that strange point that has to be experienced to be understood, the point where the rich think themselves poor. I was earning ten times a teacher's salary; I was paid as much as a company director. But I had employees, I needed a driver, I wanted to dress properly because I liked to and because it impressed my clients. I spent every lira I earned. I constantly needed to earn more, which led me to spend more, in order to sustain this headlong rush. The equation changed only when you became *truly* rich, and it became difficult to spend as much as you earned, although during my years in Rome, I had encountered a few people who excelled at it.

I was not political. I was not religious. But while it is possible to escape the latter, the former is a perverse mistress whose fervour would one day catch up with me.

At the end of April, a few days before my scheduled return to Pietra d'Alba, there was a knock on my bedroom door. It was four in the morning. I had been living in the same apartment at 28 via dei Banchi Nuovi for almost fifteen years. The same canopy bed gliding beneath the soot-caked vaulted ceiling – for all I knew I could have been sleeping beneath a Tiepolo masterpiece. I grunted, refused to answer, until an apprentice shook me.

'Maestro, maestro! There is a telephone call for you in your office.'

'I'm trying to sleep, damn it.'

'It is Father Orsini.'

Francesco never called me at this hour. I pulled on a pair of trousers and I raced downstairs.

'Hello?'

'Mimo, can you come to Stefano's place?'

'Now?'

'Right now.'

I may not have been political, but I knew that sometimes it was imprudent to say certain things over the telephone. My first thought was to ask Mikael to drive me, but Mikael had left three months earlier. Italy had invaded Ethiopia, and he had gone home to fight alongside his family. 'Now we are enemies,' he had said, hugging me with all his might. The suddenness of his departure came as a surprise until the following morning, when the carabinieri came to the studio asking for Mikael. Apparently, there had been a disturbance in a local bar, where a man matching his description had attacked a group of stalwart Italians who had been singing 'Faccetta Nera', a popular song celebrating our soldiers, our agronomists, our engineers who had left to liberate the Abyssinians. Someone had drawn a blade, and since he had a suspicious face, it could only have been him.

Little black face, little Abyssinian girl / We will set you free and take you back to Rome, / To be kissed by our sun / You will wear a black shirt too / Little black face, you'll be a Roman ragazzina...

I set off on foot, trying to get the tune out of my head, though I had to admit it was good – the joyous triumphant brass notes made you want to invade Ethiopia. Stefano lived only half an hour from me, right next door to the Hotel de Russie. Day was breaking as I rushed into the building, just as Stefano and Viola's husband, Rinaldo Campana, were coming out.

Unusually, Campana bowed his head when he saw me.

Stefano nodded. 'Gulliver. Francesco is waiting for you up in my apartment.'

Francesco was sipping coffee in Stefano's living room, his cassock impeccable, his spectacles – almost indistinguishable from those of Pacelli – perched on the tip of his nose. He served me a cup without asking and gestured for me to sit.

'Thanks for coming. We have a little... situation.'

I waited, my lips scalded from the strong coffee.

'Our friend Campana, who's here in Rome on business, spent last night revelling with Stefano and his friends. I have upbraided Stefano countless times about these nocturnal debaucheries, but to no avail. At eleven o'clock they went their separate ways. Apparently Campana did not return to his hotel but went to – how shall I put this? – satisfy some baser instincts with a young woman he had met in a bar. A lady of the night. I do not know precisely what happened, nor do I wish to, but it seems that as part of some kind of... game that went wrong, the girl was hurt. Badly hurt. Campana fled. When he got back to his hotel, the fool realised he had left his wallet behind and immediately called Stefano.'

'He killed a young woman?'

'Killed, no, I don't think so. Seriously injured, in his words. There may be lasting injuries.'

'Well? Why don't you turn that bastard over to the police?'

'That bastard – though I do not quibble with your description – happens to be my brother-in-law. The Orsini family's resurgent fortunes in recent years, a fortune that has indirectly funded your career, have been partly financed by him personally. And we cannot afford a scandal. But there will not be one.'

'No?'

'No, because Campana spent the entire evening with you.'

I slowly set down my cup. Francesco stared at me, with his hands folded over his stomach.

'Fuck off, Francesco.'

'He spent the whole evening with you. Someone stole his wallet and the man who did so is responsible. The word of a prostitute is worthless.'

'And why shouldn't he have spent the evening with you? Or with Stefano?'

'Because Stefano is a senior figure in the government and, if all goes well, I shall be made bishop next year. Besides, we are too closely tied to him to be credible, given that he is our brother-in-law. You are the perfect alibi: you have an association with the family, so it is entirely possible that Campana would spend the evening with you. But you need have no fear of scandal by association. The case will be closed tomorrow.'

'And if I refuse?'

'You will not refuse, Mimo, if only to protect Viola. Imagine the humiliation if this should get out. And besides...'

'And besides?' I said as he fell silent.

Francesco got up, took a bottle of grappa from the cabinet, poured a little into my cup and into his own. 'I don't wish to be vulgar, Mimo, but you owe us that much.'

'What exactly do I owe you?'

'Everything.'

'I don't wish to be vulgar,' I said ironically, 'but I am commissioned because of my talent.'

'That's true, I have never denied it and never will. But you seem to forget how it all began. Who came to find you in Florence?'

'You are suggesting that I owe you a debt because you came to me in person to tell me Zio had left me his workshop? That sounds like an expensive trip.'

'Do you really believe that old drunk left you his studio? If you do, you're more naïve than I thought.'

I drained my grappa in one gulp and looked at the chess master in admiration. 'He will go far,' Viola had said somewhere in the dawn of time.

'What happened to Zio?'

'He retired to the sunny south, as I told you. He died three years ago.'

'And the studio?'

Francesco sipped his grappa, licked the shine from his lips with the tip of his tongue and set down the cup. 'We bought it from him. He made us swear never to sell it back to you. And I kept my promise, because I gifted it to you.'

'Why?'

'In the first place, because I always believed that you had talent, and that your talent would serve us well. But above all, to be absolutely candid, when she was in hospital Viola told me that you were friends.'

'Yes, I know she did.'

'I know you know,' he said with a smile. 'Well, I knew or I assumed that, one day, Viola might need help and support, and that it would be... beneficial to the family to have a friend on hand.'

'To spy on her, you mean?'

Francesco let out a long sigh. 'Don't get me wrong, Mimo, I love my sister. But she is a complicated creature.'

'On the contrary, she is very simple.'

'Would you be simple if you remembered absolutely everything you had ever read since the age of three? If you were paraded in front of guests like a circus animal, dragged out of bed at four in the morning to be exploited?'

'You have just dragged me out of bed at four in the morning to be exploited.'

'Don't try to be clever. The problem was not Viola's perfect recall. The problem was that she understood what she was reading at an age when other girls are thinking about dolls and pretty dresses. My sister is probably the most intelligent person I know, along with Monsignor Pacelli. One day, if he plays his cards right, it is likely that Monsignor Pacelli will be Pope. Unfortunately, Viola cannot be a pope, or an aviator, or any of her other crazy ideas. I am not saying that thirty or forty years from now there might not be a place for her in this world. But right now, she has a role to play within the family, though perhaps not the role she hoped for. We all have a role to play.'

'What are you complaining about? She has played it to perfection.'

'You're right. Viola has grown up. But that does not mean that we no longer need you, and this business concerns her too. Campana will tell the police that he was with you. You shall do as you please.'

Late the following morning, the carabinieri came to my office. I opened the door and looked astonished. What had I done the day before? I'd worked all day and spent the evening with my friend Rinaldo. 'Yes, Rinaldo Campana, why?' The carabinieri left, seemingly satisfied, and the affair was never mentioned again. I hated myself for helping the bastard, but I didn't delude myself that I had done it to spare Viola another humiliation. I had done it because I feared that otherwise my commissions would dry up. I had done it to preserve everything I had built up, because nothing could stand in the way of the inexorable rise that had already cost me so much. And, in doing it, I had fulfilled my wildest, most secret dream. I had become an Orsini.

*W*ell, *I went and saw the statue, and I thought it was pretty,*
obviously, but at the end of the day, what do I know? I
went because the whole city was talking about it, like I said, so
anyway, I went to see it. I don't know much about art, but it was
Sunday and I was at mass, and I thought, why not, after all I was
right there... So, yeah, I thought it was beautiful, but as I looked
at it, I started to come over all queer. I felt hot and suffocated
and I had to go outside to catch my breath. At the time, I didn't
think it had anything to do with the statue, but then I read all
the stories in the newspapers that were just like mine, and so,
since the monsignor asked, I came to tell you about it, Father.
(Testimony of Nicola S., Florence, 24 June 1948)

According to Professor Williams' monograph, religious
authorities received precisely 217 unsolicited statements,

which more than doubled after the official investigation led by the Sacred Congregation of the Holy Office. It is important to stress that the vast majority of people who walked past the *Pietà Vitaliani* saw it as nothing more than a statue. But if a hundred thousand or even a million people were impervious to its effects, how could they ignore the testimonies of six hundred people? Six hundred people who, moreover, reported almost exactly the same symptoms. A powerful emotion followed by feelings of suffocation, tachycardia, dizziness. Several witnesses claimed to have 'dreamed about her'; others suffered from a profound melancholy verging on depression. The most disturbing thing about these witness statements – which require careful analysis, something that has been done by several experts, and as is currently being done by Padre Vincenzo – is that, between the lines, one can sense something that only one witness – an accountant from Rome – dared to mention explicitly. He claims to have felt a strange *excitement*. A sexual excitement, we are led to believe, though it is impossible to confirm, especially since at the time people rarely talked about such things.

The diocese of Florence, where the *Pietà Vitaliani* was first exhibited, initially believed that this was a prank played by Vitaliani's former rivals, since the sculptor had spent some tempestuous months at the studio of Filippo Metti. Later, it was thought to be an incidence of mass hysteria. When more than forty statements were filed in the month following the exhibition of the *Pietà*, it was decided to move the sculpture. The sheer quality of the piece required that it become part of the Vatican collection, but, after only a few weeks, the same reports began to surface, many of them from foreign tourists who spoke no Italian and could not have known about the controversy in Florence.

It is impossible to draw any statistical trends from the sample of six hundred people but, extrapolating from the available data, it would appear that age, gender and geographical origin are not determining factors for whether an individual will be affected by the *Pietà Vitaliani*.

After a few months in the Vatican, the work was taken down to the storerooms to await further analysis. A number of art historians, sculptors, archaeologists and other experts were consulted, and their findings were compiled and summarised by Professor Williams. And because if you want something done properly, you do it yourself, ecclesiastical authorities called in Candido Amantini, an expert of a very different kind: the Vatican's official exorcist.

Nunc effunde super hunc electum eam virtutem, quae a te est...

11 September 1938.

...Spiritum principalem, quem dedisti dilecto Filio tuo Iesu Christo...

Francesco lies on the marble floor, his arms spread wide. Archbishop Pacelli robed in crimson.

...quem Ipse donavit sanctis Apostolis, qui constituerunt Ecclesiam per singula loca, ut sanctuarium tuum...

And I have a grey hair. Despite the solemnity of the setting, despite the presence of Michelangelo's *Pietà*, the most beautiful statue of all time, this is all that I can think about. A stupid grey hair. I am only thirty-four. Could you not at least have spared me this, Lord?

...in gloriam et laudem indeficientem nominis tui.

With a soft rustle, Archbishop Pacelli steps back, his cassock is the colour of the Passion, red with the blood shed by the Redeemer. Francesco kneels and submits to the laying on of hands of countless prelates; a mitre is placed on his head, a crosier placed in his hands, a ring flipped on his finger. He rises and takes his place on the cathedra.

On 11 September 1938, Francesco Orsini is ordained bishop in Rome. The diocese of Savona will now be led by a local man.

That evening, the Orsini family gathered for dinner. I was among them, since I now thought, ate and lived like an Orsini. The Gran Caffè Faraglia, the restaurant where Stefano and I had begun so many nights of debauchery, had been closed for some years, so we met in the private dining hall of the Hotel d'Inghilterra. The whole family was in attendance: the Marchese – despite his failing health and the fact no one was sure how much he understood of what was happening – the Marchesa, Stefano, Francesco, Campana and Viola. Viola had spent the day gazing at the city in wonderment, and I was shocked to learn that she had previously only left Pietra d'Alba to go to Milan, where she spent more time in hospital than strolling through art galleries.

My daughter of the Renaissance knew the world only through books. The Orsini family arrived in Rome on the eve of Francesco's ordination, and I took Viola to see everything we possibly could both before and after the ceremony. We had hardly begun our tour than our roles were reversed, and Viola would point to some monument and explain its history to me, and soon I found myself following her like a tourist after a guide. I had underestimated the power of libraries, which had plucked me from obscurity and even offered me a little tenderness. I had been ungrateful. How many nights had I spent drunkenly telling myself that real life was there, in the Eternal City that was whirling around me at a hundred miles an hour? Though she was far from home, Viola was teaching me a new lesson – real life was in books.

By the time we took our seats in the private dining hall of the Hotel d'Inghilterra, Viola was in a cantankerous mood. 'Have you read the paper?'

'No. I never read the newspapers.'

'I forgot: you don't do politics.' One of the few times that Viola cruelly lacked tact was when she was spoiling for a fight. She charged like a bull at a gate.

I simply smiled, because I was determined not to fight that evening. 'So, what does it say in the papers?'

'Nothing,' she said. 'Nothing at all.'

With a quick movement, she unfolded her napkin. Stefano arrived wearing the black uniform of the Moschettieri del Duce, an elite unit that served as Mussolini's guard of honour. Seeing him, Viola's mood turned darker. Stefano, who had set his sights on an appointment to the Ministry of the Interior, saw his post as a baleful musketeer as a strategic move. Despite everything, the evening got off to a good start. Dinner consisted of anything and everything that could be roasted, fried or grilled, washed down with an excellent Montepulciano because, between two earthquakes, Abruzzo found the time to produce fine wine.

Since the 'affair', Campana had been rather less effusive. He was more modest about his success, which did not make him any more likeable. He sat next to his wife, silently masticating his food, his lips glistening with grease, trying to avoid my gaze, and when he could not, giving me a pinched smile. He kept glancing at his watch, as though he needed to be somewhere else – I assumed he had resumed his nocturnal trysts. Viola ate very little. She sat staring at Stefano, and I dreaded the looming tragedy, because Viola was very inventive when it came to tragedy.

Just before dessert, she struck up a conversation with the waiter who was clearing the table. 'Excuse me, I think I detect a slight accent. Where are you from?'

'I'm German, signora.'

'German. Really. You're not Jewish by any chance, are you?'

A stunned silence fell over the table. The waiter stared at her, bewildered. 'No, signora.'

'Ah, that's good, that's good. Because my brother' – she nodded at Stefano – 'is an influential member of the government. And just yesterday, his government issued a decree restricting the rights of the Jews, especially foreign Jews, since they are doubly flawed. According to the government, the Semitic peoples are inferior to ours. But that's all right because you're not a Jew.'

The same deathly silence reigned as the waiter left the private dining room.

Stefano got to his feet, his face crimson; he closed the door and launched himself at his sister. 'What on earth are you thinking?'

The moment he grabbed Viola by the arm, I got to my feet and, a second later, Francesco, with an unexpected agility for a man of the cloth, was by her side. 'Go back and sit down, Stefano. Everything is fine.'

His brother hesitated, jowls quivering nervously, then took his seat opposite Viola. He drank a large glass of wine. 'Everything's fine, everything's fine. Of course it is. That little fool has no idea what she is talking about.'

'Really?' said Viola. 'Was the little fool wrong? Didn't your government issue two decrees this week: *Laws for the Defence of the Race in Fascist Schools* and *Measures against Foreign Jews*? Did you not ban mixed marriages? Aren't you planning to dismiss all teachers and professors of the "Hebrew race"?'

'It's only politics!'

'Viola, darling,' Campana said in a soothing tone, 'you know nothing about politics.'

'It's simply a political position to appease Germany,' said Stefano, turning to his father as though this was the person he wished to convince. 'We have nothing against the Jews. It's all nonsense. Il Duce's former mistress, Margherita Sarfatti, she was Jewish. And I have personally frequented many Jewish women with great pleasure. The government has no intention whatsoever of attacking the Jews.'

'You're a liar,' said Viola. 'You may be lying unconsciously, but you're lying. You're all liars.'

Since she had been looking at Campana when she said this, her husband suddenly sat bolt upright.

'And me,' he said, 'am I a liar?'

Viola laughed. 'Where do I start? The trip you promised me to the United States fifteen years ago?'

'Is that what you want? To go to America? Fine.'

Campana pushed back his chair and stormed out, adding to the general confusion. The Marchese retched a little. In an instant, everyone was concerned for his health; all the guests turned to him, saying what a wonderful day it had been and how proud he must be of his son Francesco – 'Aren't you proud of Francesco?' – vying with each other to talk to him as though he were a child.

Campana reappeared and sat down next to Viola. 'Be ready two days from now. Before the week is out, I promise you'll be walking down what looks very much like an American street.'

Viola had not expected this turn of events. In her eyes, I could see the timeless struggle of a child who longs to whoop out their joy, but is determined to stay angry.

'Can Mimo come?' she said, almost aggressively. 'He is rich enough to pay his own passage.'

'Mimo can come and he will not have to pay a thing.'

That night, I went home with a strange feeling in the pit of my stomach that had little to do with our forthcoming journey. Just before I left, Viola had thrust the front page of the *Corriere della Serra* into my hands.

I stood in front of my mirror, the only thing in the room apart from the four-poster bed. The same mirror that, only this morning, as I was getting ready for Francesco's ordination, had revealed my first grey hair. As I undressed, the page fell from my pocket and slid to the floor. I did not need to read the article, just the headline. *Le leggi per la difesa de la razza approvate dal Consiglio dei ministri.* I looked for new grey hairs, found two, and there were others elsewhere on my body. Slowly, over the years, I had put on weight. *The laws for the defence of race approved by the Council of Ministers.*

No, I did not like what I saw in the mirror.

Two days later, I joined Viola at the Hotel d'Inghilterra. It was cool, just the right temperature. My driver dropped me off in front of the entrance and unloaded my trunk, which was far more luxurious than the one I once trailed around

Italy. Viola was standing on the pavement, almost stamping her feet she was so impatient. Which was understandable. My clients had told me a thousand times about the wonders of the *Conte di Savoia* and the SS *Rex*, which, some years earlier, to the delight of the Fascist regime, had won the Blue Ribbon for the fastest transatlantic liner. Italy ruled the waves. Both liners set sail from Genoa.

Campana's car arrived, a brand-new Lancia Aprilia. Viola was in such a hurry that she loaded her luggage into the boot by herself.

'Where is your husband?'

'He will meet us later.'

As soon as we got in, the car sped off. We passed a group of twelve-year-olds doing gymnastics on a piazza, little Fascists in the making, in black uniforms and blue scarves. The city walls fluttered with ribbons of red, green and white that, as we slowed down, fragmented into propaganda posters urging us to Buy Italian or celebrating the genius of the nation. In a park, a group of adolescent boys, red-faced with exertion, competed for the privilege of kicking a battered leather football between two dustbins – some months earlier, Italy had won the World Cup for the second time, thanks to the magic feet of Gino Colaussi and Silvio Piola. I paid little attention to these things, since I was more concerned by the fact that we were driving south.

'I don't understand where we're going,' I whispered.

'To America!' shouted Viola. She clapped a hand over her mouth and giggled. 'Why the long face? You've been sulking for as long as I've known you, Mimo. Twenty-two years of this,' she said and scowled.

'I would just like to know what port we are leaving from, the name of the ship, that sort of thing. Did your husband not tell you?'

'No. Why don't you just enjoy life for a change!'

Then she rolled down the window and let out a long whoop, which the chauffeur, who was accustomed to such antics, pretended not to hear. We were now driving through open country, and I had mapped enough of Rome – every drunkard is a good cartographer – to know that we were not headed for Genoa or even towards the sea. Campana knew something I didn't.

Forty minutes later, the Lancia turned onto a dirt track between two fields. At the end of the road, the horizon was blotted out by a huge wall. The only thing visible in the distance was a water tower. We stopped in the middle of nowhere, in front of a towering metal door. The ploughed earth and fragments of rubble at the foot of the wall suggested that it had only recently been built. The driver knocked and the door opened to reveal a man in dirty overalls. He brought a finger to his lips and beckoned us to follow. Viola gave me a quizzical look and I shrugged. A narrow corridor ran between the outer wall and what looked like scaffolding. The building extended for a hundred metres right and left, but wooden cladding made it impossible to see what was on the other side. With a cigarette between his teeth, our guide wove his way between steel tubes, a labyrinth that only he knew. He did not utter a word. Finally, he opened a hidden door, glanced inside and, after signalling to us not to move, then stepped aside to let us through.

Viola and I stepped into Los Angeles, 1923, the height of Prohibition.

A Ford Model T flashed past, reversing up the street with gangsters armed with Thompson submachine guns sitting in the back. Two policemen in heavy greatcoats followed, puffing on cigarettes. On the opposite pavement, several corpses lay in a vast pool of blood in front of the smashed window that was emblazoned with 'Grocery Store'.

A woman came towards me with several bags slung over her shoulder. 'What part are you supposed to be playing? Haven't you been to make-up?'

'They're with us, Lizzie.'

Campana had just appeared through the shattered window of the grocery store. Stepping over the corpses outside, he inadvertently kicked one of them and apologised. The corpse politely replied: 'No harm done.' Campana was followed by Luigi Freddi, to whom I owed most of my government commissions, though I had not seen him since the inauguration of the Palazzo delle Poste in Palermo four years earlier.

Freddi greeted us warmly. 'Welcome to Cinecittà! Long time no see, Mimo. Good to see you again, Signora Campana. What do you think of our studios?'

Luigi Freddi had succeeded. His dream of competing with Hollywood was this city just outside the city, a fortress devoted completely to the art of illusion. Hollywood-on-the-Tiber, as it would soon be known, was the brainchild of this affable, well-dressed man who always had a smile on his face. But this was deceptive: Cinecittà was a weapon. The most powerful in the country, according to Il Duce himself, who had put all the resources of the Fascist regime behind the project.

'The site covers sixty hectares. We offer production teams, like Signor Campana's, seventy-five kilometres of streets. If you turn right at the end of this street,' said Freddi, pointing, 'you'll find yourselves in the Rome of twenty-three centuries ago. We shot *Scipio the African* there last year.'

'Well?' exclaimed Campana triumphantly. 'Did I or did I not lie? Are you in America or not? You can tell everyone that you walked down Sunset Boulevard. And look at this!' He walked over to an orange tree growing out of the pavement, picked a fruit and tossed it to me. 'They're real! Everything here is real – well, almost!'

A young woman with a clipboard approached and whispered something.

Campana nodded. 'Sorry, problems with an actor. If only we could make movies without them, life would be bliss. I'll leave you to it. Have fun, just follow Gerhard's instructions whenever they're actually shooting,' he said, nodding to the man in overalls who welcomed us.

Finally, I dared to steal a glance at Viola. Her eyes were shining. Not with wonder or excitement. Just black rage. Even Campana could no longer ignore it.

'Come on, it's funny, isn't it? Do you know how many people would love to be in your shoes? We're making a film about Al Capone.'

'You were supposed to take me to the United States.'

'You have no sense of humour, damn it. You're impossible to please. I go to the States all the time and, let me tell you, it looks exactly like this. Our set designer is American. So why deal with all the exhausting business of travel? But if you really want, then I'll take you.'

'When?'

'As soon as possible. That's a promise. New York, San Francisco, the real thing, wherever you want. Coney Island, the Grand Canyon, Warner Brothers Studios. We'll pull out all the stops. All right, darling?' He reached out, still charming despite the paunch that now preceded him, to take her hand. 'Am I forgiven? Tell me I'm forgiven.'

Viola sighed and gave him the gift of a smile. 'Yes.'

'Wonderful. You know something? You see that little alley

over there? We'll name it after you.' He clicked his fingers at the young woman with the clipboard. 'Call in the prop-maker. Tell him to make a Viola Orsini Street sign for this alleyway. Not a word to the director. It's not like the idiot will ever notice.'

He kissed his wife on the cheek and strode off. Luigi Freddi watched him walk away, then led us up Sunset Boulevard. What I had assumed was the sky was just a painted canvas. We emerged, as predicted, in the third century BC. Freddi took us on a tour of ancient Rome and left us in front of a lake with a floating Phoenician galley.

'Come back to Sunset Boulevard when you've finished.'

Late that afternoon, the driver dropped us back at the hotel. Viola seemed calmer, though still a little distracted. She had dinner with her family – the Orsinis would head back to Pietra d'Alba two days later – while I had dinner with the Serbian princess, with whom I had renewed my acquaintance. We had given our bodies another chance and, to our mutual surprise, experienced genuine pleasure. Alexandra no longer needed money – she had married a rich old man in 1935 – but she realised that she had no friends in Rome apart from me. The evening ended in my bed, once again with pleasurable results, which was surprising given how different we were physically – she was six feet three. I was smoking a Toscano, stark naked, enjoying the September breeze, when there came a knock on the door of the studio. It was midnight. Dreading some new antic by Campana, I threw a blanket round my shoulders and went downstairs. It was Viola. She stared at me in silence and I did the same, intrigued. Alexandra appeared on the stairs behind me, completely naked.

'Who is it, darrrrling?' she asked with that rolling R that had made so many husbands betray their vows.

'No one. Just a friend. Wait for me in the bedroom.'

Sulking, Alexandra went back upstairs.

I saw a mocking smile play on Viola's lips. 'You don't deny yourself anything.'

'You don't know how right you are – she's a princess. What can I do for you, Viola?'

'I'm sorry to bother you at such a late hour. I can see you're... busy, but I wanted to say goodbye. I'm leaving.'

'I know, I know, I know. In a couple of days. But we still have time to see each other.'

'No. I'm leaving tomorrow. Nobody knows.'

Frowning, I pulled the door shut behind me. 'What do you mean, you're leaving tomorrow?'

'It's over, Mimo. I've tried to live that life but Campana will never change. Neither will my family. So, I'm leaving.'

'Where will you go?'

'To America. I'm taking the morning train to Genoa. There's a ship sailing every three days.'

'Are you insane?'

'No, Mimo,' said my friend, looking me straight in the eye. 'I'm perfectly sane.'

'But... what will you do for money?'

'I have a little of my own. I'll withdraw some from the bank.'

'Do you have a bank account in your name?'

'No. I haven't.'

Never in my life have I come up with a plan so quickly.

'All right, I'll come with you.'

'You?'

I had her wait in my office while I got rid of Alexandra, telling her there was a family emergency, which she only half believed. But princesses do not get jealous, perhaps proving she truly was one. I made some coffee and explained my plan to Viola. I had money. We would leave together on the first ocean liner. Once she was settled in New York, I would come back and tell her family. Viola would be untouchable.

'New York...' she whispered, her eyes filled with sky-scrapers.

Clearly moved, she hugged me silently. We agreed to meet the following morning at 6 a.m. and head straight to the train station. We would have to travel with very little luggage – we would buy what we needed on the way.

As she turned to leave, I stopped her. 'Before we go to Genoa, I want to stop off somewhere. I've got something to show you, if that's all right?'

Seeing her hesitate, I added: 'You can trust me.'

Rome was still sleeping, captivated by dreams of grandeur, when the train took us north. In the first-class carriage, Viola pressed me about the mysterious stopover I had planned. I refused to say anything but persuaded her to change trains at Pisa.

I was pretending to read *La Stampa* when the train stopped in Florence, then suddenly I leapt to my feet. 'Come on! Quickly! We're getting off!'

Viola got up, confused and panicked, dropped her suitcase and burst out laughing. We barely managed to get off the train before its doors slammed shut behind us. I hailed a porter, though we each only had one bag, and told him to take them to the Baglioni.

I had left Florence with a stinking hangover, wearing foul-smelling clothes spattered with my own excesses and those of others. I returned as a conquering hero. I didn't know the doorman at the Baglioni, but the moment he saw us, he ushered us through the revolving door. I asked for two suites, one for Viola, one for me.

'We only have one suite available, Maestro Vitaliani. But we do have a very nice room that—'

I cut the receptionist off with a wave. 'That won't be necessary. We shall go to the Excelsior.'

The receptionist's manner changed instantly. 'Let me see

what I can do, Maestro Vitaliani. I think I can find another suite for you, and we can handle any other arrangements.'

I quietly nudged Viola and scowled. 'I don't understand. Is there a suite available or not? Is this the Baglioni or have I accidentally stumbled into a brothel? Because this is certainly where the Baglioni used to be.'

The receptionist forced a smile. 'I apologise for the confusion, Signor Vitaliani. I can confirm that we have two suites available. Please allow us to offer you a complementary bottle of champagne to make up for the inconvenience.'

In the lift, Viola and I burst out laughing. Then we walked along an interminable corridor, lurching and swaying aboard this ocean liner that had washed up in the middle of the city. With their dark wood panels and soft yellow drapes, our suites looked like two pompous elderly spinsters. They perched above the city, mute witnesses to the shifting mood of the times. Even in 1938, they exuded an old-fashioned charm. The Baglioni was unique in that it was born old-fashioned, the echo of a time that may never have existed.

We had no time to spare – we had to catch the 8.25 to Genoa the following morning. I went downstairs and made a few phone calls, then fetched Viola. She had swapped her travelling dress for a pair of trousers and tied her hair into a ponytail. Without that characteristic sinuousness, she might have passed for an effeminate boy to anyone who encountered us. We crossed the Ponte Vecchio and headed east along the opposite bank, a path I had trodden many times before. Viola knew nothing of my years in Florence, or at least nothing other than the flattering, mendacious portrait I had painted of them in my letters.

There was not a single familiar face left in the studio, except for Metti himself, who was in his kitchen-office, poring over the plans for a church. I hadn't told him we were coming. I studied my old master for a moment, this man who had lost his arm at the Battle of Caporetto, before I knocked on the open door. He looked up, irritated at being disturbed, and his eyes widened as he recognised me. I thought he might cry.

Finally, he came around the desk and hugged me. He had shrunk in the fifteen years since I last saw him, and his hair was completely white. He was not yet fifty-five.

'Mimo, what a wonderful surprise! And I assume that this is Signora Vitaliani?'

Viola blushed like a little girl. 'No. My name is Viola Orsini. A friend.'

'Ah, the young lady who was in hospital, perhaps?'

Viola flinched, a little on the defensive, then stared at him for a second before realising that she was talking to a brother, a fellow-traveller of stark hospital corridors and the stench of ether.

Metti joined us for dinner at the finest restaurant in town. He had followed my career in the newspapers, which had painted a very flattering portrait after I began working for the regime. Neri, he told me, had had his own workshop near San Gimignano for some years. I burst out laughing: the city of houses whose towers and turrets once proclaimed the wealth of their owners was perfect for that pretentious cretin. Whenever the conversation drifted dangerously towards my years in Florence and their procession of excesses, I quickly changed the subject.

Giotto's bell tower tolled eleven o'clock. The bronze soundwave ricocheted off the marble façades before fading away. We said our goodbyes and promised to see each other again.

After taking a few steps, Metti turned. 'So, you finally know why you sculpt, Mimo?'

'No, maestro. That is why I still call you maestro.'

He laughed, but his heart was not in it, then he left, swinging his orphaned shoulder. Thunder rumbled in the distance; the city smelled of rain. I led Viola along the via Cavour, a path I had taken only once before, but which I remembered perfectly because I had spilled a little blood there.

When we came to the Piazza San Marco, she froze at the church opposite. 'I know this place...'

I hoped Walter had not let me down. Three knocks on the door and he opened, as small and monk-like as ever. When I had telephoned earlier, the name Monsignor Francesco

Orsini magically opened the door. Rocking back and forth on our stubby legs, Walter and I climbed the staircase we had taken sixteen years earlier, with Viola trailing behind.

When we came to the top, Walter handed me a lantern and said precisely the same words. 'One hour, not a second more. And above all, don't make a sound.'

I ushered Viola into the first cell. She stepped over the threshold, stopped in front of Fra Angelico's *Annunciation* and began to cry – there was no sadness, no sobbing, she wept with joy to see an angel with the wings of a peacock and the woman-child who would change the world.

'Thank you, Mimo.'

The storm burst, hammering on the roof above our heads like lead shot. I blew out the lantern and allowed us to be guided by the lightning flashes from cell to cell. And for an hour, in a tempest of cyan, golds, oranges, pinks and blues, our friendship regained its colour.

Before leaving me at the door to her hotel suite, Viola got down on one knee – she was almost as tall as the Serbian princess.

'Thank you, Mimo. I shall never forget this night. In America, they don't really have a history. But I shall be unique because I will have this one. I'll see you tomorrow.'

Ten minutes later, I left the hotel. It was raining cats and dogs, but I didn't care. My feet found their old footprints, amid the atoms of cobblestone they had worn away, and nestled in them. The train tracks traced a blazing path with each bolt of lightning. They guided me to the fairground where the big top still stood, more patched and faded than it was before. The frayed CIRQUE BIZZARO danced in the storm. The two caravans were where they had always been. Sara's light was out, but there was a glow in Bizzaro's window, briefly obscured by a dark figure. I hesitated for a long time and then I turned back. That part of my life was over: the suffering, the poverty, all the absences I nurtured in my belly. The absence of a mother, the absence of Viola, the absence of a future, absences that I had tried to fill in every dive bar in the city. Never again.

When the receptionist saw me stumble in from the swirling lightning and the raging mistral, drenched to the bone, he asked if I was all right. I took a hot shower, wrapped myself in the silk bathrobe provided by the hotel – on me, it looked like a wedding dress with a long train – and two blankets. Needless to say, I couldn't sleep. And when, at around 3 a.m., there was a knock on the door, I went straight to open it.

Without a word, Viola came in, wearing an identical dressing gown. She nodded to the big bed. 'May I?'

I lay down again in silence. She lay on the other side and snuggled up to me. I knew I would remember this moment to my dying breath. And as you can see, my brothers, I was not mistaken.

After a few moments, Viola spoke, her voice almost inaudible, yet loud enough to drown out the roaring storm still raging outside the window. 'You betrayed me, didn't you?'

The question was rhetorical; we both knew the answer. Of course, I was hurt by the word *betray*, but arguments over semantics would have to wait.

'When do we go back to Pietra d'Alba?' said Viola.

'Tomorrow.'

In the darkness, I felt her nod.

It was strange, I felt bereft without her righteous anger and tried to justify myself. 'What would you have done, alone, in America? Do you really think your family would have sent you money? These past twenty-four hours, we have both been pretending. You knew as well as I did that this was a digression.'

'I just hoped that maybe—'

'It was madness. There are other solutions. I acted in your best interests.'

'Yes, a lot of people have been making decisions in my best interests for a long time. Who did you tell? Stefano?'

'Francesco. Just before we left. I asked him to let us have a day together in Florence. Now, try to get some sleep. We'll talk about this again.'

Lying side by side, we pretended to sleep as we waited for the dawn. Just before six o'clock, a crimson wave washed over the Arno, chasing away the dark waters of night. There came a knock at the door. I opened it to find two gorillas in dark suits waiting to take us back to Pietra d'Alba. We never talked about it again.

C andido Amantini looked nothing like the image that popular culture would later give the exorcist. Padre Vincenzo had met him once as a young priest and remembered a benignant face behind a pair of large glasses, rather than a wielder of thunderbolts and slayer of demons. But, according to Professor Williams, Amantini was the first man summoned by the Supreme Sacred Congregation of the Holy Office, before it called in scientific experts. Amantini would shut himself away and pray with the statue for twelve hours at a time, while two Swiss guards stood sentry outside the door of the storeroom where the *Pietà* was kept. According to the report, he had with him only 'a seventeenth-century bible, a box of candles and a box of white chalk'. The report does not state whether the guards saw or heard anything. After a week, Candido

Amantini finally delivered his verdict. The statue was not demonically possessed, which he found all the more puzzling because, having stared at it for hours, he too had been aware of a strange 'presence', something beyond the tons of white marble dancing before him in the flickering candlelight. But the 'presence', he said confidently, was not diabolical, since if it were, the rite of exorcism would be accompanied by the smell of burning fields, or rust, or addled eggs, as though lightning had struck somewhere nearby.

Amantini ventures an explanation that, for some, may shed light on Laszlo Toth's motives when he set out to destroy the *Vitaliani Pietà* and, failing to find it, settled for Michelangelo's *Pietà*: Vitaliani's statue brings us closer to the divine. It is possessed, yes, but by the presence of the divine. And as such, it is dangerous. God's greatness cannot be approached directly, which is why he entrusted Saint Peter, despite his failings, with the task of founding the Church, which was to serve as intermediary. If Man could connect directly with God, touch Him with his finger as Adam does on the ceiling of the Sistine Chapel, then what is the point of the Church? In his recommendations to the Supreme Sacred Congregation of the Holy Office – which belatedly replaced the Inquisition in 1908 – Amantini was categorical: while, from an artistic point of view, the *Vitaliani Pietà* is a major work, from a theological standpoint, it is inexplicable heresy. Amantini admits that he cannot explain this but recommends that the statue never again be exhibited in public.

In a footnote, Professor Williams underscores the irony that the Supreme Sacred Congregation of the Holy Office that commissioned Father Amantini is merely a new name for the Holy Inquisition that, in 1573, formally tried Veronese for his painting *The Feast in the House of Simon the Pharisee* because it included *dwarfs* – grotesque, comical characters, considered inappropriate given the religious subject. Now, almost four centuries later, the same Inquisition would criticise a dwarf for being *too* divine.

Next came the experts, the scientists and art historians. The statue was weighed, measured and X-rayed. The X-rays revealed not the slightest micro-fissure, a tribute to the quality of the marble. There was talk of possible radioactivity, of the statue emitting radon gas; this was disproved by tests. Measuring the base, it was ascertained that the dimensions of the statue corresponded to the Golden Ratio, and this Divine Proportion could be found by connecting precise points on the statue. However, nothing could be deduced from this since it was far from the first work of art to make use of the Golden Ratio. The most far-fetched theories – inclusions of meteoric elements in the stone, ionising radiation, amplification of telluric currents such as Hartmann lines or Curry lines – were advanced and roundly rejected. All the experts agreed with Father Amantini's conclusion. *We simply do not know.*

Having listed the various theories of others, Professor Williams finally puts forward his own. The solution, he believes, is not to be found in theology or in science. He argues that none of the experts truly *looked* at the statue. 'Anyone who does,' he adds, 'cannot help but be spellbound by the face of the Virgin Mary, the way in which it is modelled, the femininity and sensuality it exudes, despite the obvious signs of age.' Unlike Michelangelo's *Pietà* (in which the Virgin is unusually young to be the mother of Christ), Vitaliani's Mary is no child. She has lived. And Williams advances the hypothesis that the mystery lies in the sculptor's relationship with his model.

It was someone Vitaliani knew, Williams insists, and the nature of their relationship is the source of the mystery.

Leonard B. Williams died in 1981, having devoted the last twenty years of his life to the study of the *Vitaliani Pietà*. He would never know that he was right, and that he was completely wrong.

Although they do not know it, the Orsini family are at the height of their glory. Thanks to the waters of the lake, the citrus groves and the Seville oranges are flourishing as never before, and the family now exports much of its produce.

On 10 February 1939, in the Vatican, Pope Pius XI dies of a sudden heart attack. Since, according to some, the pontiff was preparing to make a speech denouncing Fascism, and since his doctor was none other than the father of Clara Petacci, Mussolini's most recent mistress, there are rumours that Il Duce rid himself of this troublesome pope.

On 2 March 1939, there is confusion: the white smoke streaming from the chimney atop the Sistine Chapel begins to turn black – a technical problem – so that the official news must be relayed by Vatican Radio.

Habemus papam.

At 5.30 p.m., Eugenio Pacelli – the man to whom I owe my career – is elected Pope. Taking the name Pius XII, he returns to the papal apartments that evening, turns to his housekeeper, tugs on his white cassock and whispers: 'Look what they have done to me.'

After the war, nobody wanted to hear about death. The 1920s were a time of accelerated, frenetic life, and more than once I have thought that the films of the time – with juddering, jerky images – captured that reality. In the 1930s, with the tender nostalgia that comes with distance, death was once again in fashion. Every city worthy of the name, every ambitious village, had to have its own war memorial. Despite my reluctance, I agreed to sculpt the monument in Pietra d'Alba, which was unusual in that only one name appeared on it. The military had not thought to call up the young men in this godforsaken valley, or perhaps decided not to in order to avoid offending the Orsini family. Unfortunately, their son, Virgilio, took it into his head to voluntarily enlist, thereby attracting the blinkered gaze of fate. The result was all the more tragic: a grey, martial stele that Jacopo – now officially my right-hand man – topped with a soldier hoisting a flag beneath a hail of machine-gun fire. It was impossible to look at the single name carved in the middle of an empty cartouche and not think: 'What an idiot.' What was intended as a tribute became an insult. The Orsini family hated it, the mayor hated it and, since I too hated it, I had no qualms about destroying it. I went back to working on the statues for the Palazzo della Civiltà Italiana, which would keep me busy until the end of the decade.

Since the episode in Florence – my betrayal, whether I like the word or not – Viola had not spoken to me. She didn't attend the dinners to which I was invited. If I happened to encounter her in the village after mass – I made a point of personally looking after the church – she pretended not to see me. This was easy, since she had only to avoid looking down. She stared straight ahead, into the vacancy that I would have occupied had I been of normal height, and didn't see me because I was not there. I might have taken offence but for the fact that I regularly received newspaper clippings in envelopes hand-delivered by Emmanuele from a sender whose identity he didn't feel he could betray (he stressed the word *betray* as he looked at me). The first article had arrived in November of the previous year and referred to the *Manifesto of Race*, on which Mussolini based his antisemitic laws. Then a second, about Kristallnacht, the pogrom against the Jews carried out by the Third Reich. Next came an article about the exile of Nobel Prize winner Enrico Fermi, whose Jewish wife had been banned from teaching. Fermi would go on to develop the foundations of nuclear fission for a different country. The message was clear: Stefano had lied to me. And Viola, who always intended to reform me, was discreetly letting me know that perhaps our friendship was not completely dead.

On our return from Florence, there had been heated arguments between the Orsini brothers, Campana and myself. Campana ranted and raged; he had had his fill of that 'lunatic', that 'frigid, flat-chested bitch'. With a glance, Francesco had warned me not to intervene. He was now secretary to Pope Pius XII and exuded such an air of authority that even I obeyed. The previous year, Cerletti and Bini, two medical professors in Rome, had devised something called electroconvulsive therapy. Viola was the ideal candidate, all the more so because the doctor in Milan who had seen her after her abortive escape attempt had diagnosed her with depression. And depression is no match for electroconvulsive therapy. Stefano pulled a face as Campana explained that the method had been successfully tested on pigs, and a few human subjects. With a flick of his finger, Francesco ruled out this solution. There was talk of lithium, a drug that was effective against depression. Until now, I had not opened my mouth. I got to my feet.

'There will be no lithium, no electroconvulsive therapy, nothing.' I looked Campana straight in the eye. 'You want to talk about lunatics? Fine, let's start with you.'

Campana stormed out and slammed the door. After this small victory, I was convinced that it was unfair of Viola to ignore me – in fact, she owed me a debt of gratitude. We salve our consciences as best we can.

During those years, I spent most of the time I wasn't sculpting with my mother. Our former relationship no longer worked; we had to find new ways of being together, of inhabiting the same space. We often walked side by side and rarely faced each other. She was my mother and, at the same time, she wasn't; time had eroded too much. A certain stiltedness meant I was less affectionate, but she patiently accepted this.

In 1940, war resumed as though it had never ended. I received more and more newspaper clippings, quotes from Mussolini copied out in green ink. Towards the end of the year, a Fiat 508 CM Coloniale with two little Italian flags on the mudguards pulled up outside the studio. A civil servant in a severe suit got out, followed by Stefano, who struggled to hide a broad grin. The official handed me a letter, which I immediately opened. It was a commission for a monumental group sculpture to be titled *The New Man*, which would stand in the central square of Il Duce's birthplace, Predappio. Although the official request came from the Ministry of Popular Culture, I was told that the actual decision had been made in high places. '*Very* high places,' said Stefano with a wink, to the visible discomfiture of the civil servant. The fee was set at one hundred thousand lire per year until the commission was completed, with a guaranteed minimum of four hundred thousand lire. A windfall. I wiped the green ink from my thoughts and immediately signed the contract on the bonnet of the Fiat.

That night, I made an initial sketch on the kitchen table, between two glasses of wine and two empty plates, while Vittorio cleared away the dishes and my mother sat in the corner knitting. *The New Man* would be three metres high, five including the plinth. *The New Man* would be a sprinter at the starting blocks, just after the shot, and would stand on just one foot. A technical challenge. An anatomical challenge. When I showed the drawing to my mother, she took one look at it, then went back to knitting.

'You are perfectly fine the way you are, Mimo,' she said.

'Excuse me?'

'It seems to me that this giant of yours with all those muscles, this "New Man", represents what you wish you could be. I am telling you that you are perfectly fine the way you are. But what do I know, I'm only your mother.'

Furious, I went outside, and after a few steps across the moon-white gravel, I stopped, astonished. Viola was waiting, dressed in a dark coat, little different from the apparition that had terrified me in the cemetery years before. And what stood before me was a ghost. The ghost of our childhood, her face gaunt, her great eyes red from the misdeeds of a long list of men, including me.

'Stefano told me about your latest commission. You know who it is from.'

This was the first time she had spoken to me in almost two years. Suddenly I existed, but only to be reproached. I was working like a demon, paying a dozen salaries, while the Orsinis bragged about 'discovering' me to anyone who would listen. I wasn't Gesualdo, I wasn't Caravaggio. I hadn't murdered anyone. My sculptures had not hurt a fly.

'I've told you a thousand times, I have no interest in politics.'

'I don't want you to make this sculpture.'

'You don't *want* me to?'

'No.'

'Go to hell, Viola.'

She turned on her heel without a word and disappeared into the night.

Shortly afterwards I left for France, a country I had not set foot in since my departure on that chilly night in 1916. I had been invited to a reception at the Italian embassy in occupied Paris, where the genius of our beloved country would be on display. The ambassador, keen to preserve an illusion of friendship with the Francesi, had not invited a single German just in case. It was here that my alleged confrontation with Giacometti took place. I have no idea how the American professor who once wrote about me, or rather about my *Pietà*, heard about it, but he mentioned it in his monograph. It is a legend, since in fact Giacometti and I never spoke.

I arrived at the reception early, not so much because I enjoyed socialising, but because this was business, and I knew the value of meeting people in the circles to which Francesco had introduced me. The question on everyone's lips was whether Elsa Schiaparelli would be coming. The designer of Tout-Paris did not attend. But other artists, including major figures, did put in an appearance. I was introduced to Brancusi. My fellow sculptor, who looked for all the world like a sublime tramp, had managed to gatecrash the event because his name looked Italian. We knew each other by reputation and exchanged the usual platitudes. Since my arrival, I had been surreptitiously studying a strange man with a shifty look beneath an explosive shock of hair, who seemed to be actively avoiding me. He too looked like a vagrant and walked with crutches.

Whenever our paths threatened to cross, as the social currents flowed through the assembly, he would pirouette back into the crowd.

Brancusi, who had taken a liking to me, kept refilling my glass. I elbowed him. 'Tell me, who is that over there? The man with the limp. He seems to be avoiding me.'

'Giacometti? He hates you. Come on, drink up.'

'Why does he hate me?'

Brancusi handed the barman his empty glass. 'I suspect because he admires your work.'

'Where is the logic in that?'

'It's completely logical. Why would you hate someone who will never overshadow you? To admire someone is to hate them, and vice versa. Beethoven hated Haydn, Schiaparelli despises Chanel, Hemingway loathes Faulkner. Ergo, Giacometti hates Vitaliani. And while we're on the subject, I hate you too. But we Romanians have a nice way of hating. So, what would you like to drink?'

'I think I've had enough.'

'Are you joking? Have you seen the look on your face? There are only two possible reasons for a man to look like you do right now. The first is a woman.'

'And the second?'

'A woman.'

We ended the evening dead drunk, pissing against a Nazi car on the rue de Varenne – proof that I played a little politics. Brancusi and I would write to each other occasionally until his death some fifteen years later. If someone had asked him to sculpt the ocean, he would have polished a rectangular block of marble and explained that, since it was impossible to reproduce every detail of every wave, it was enough to sculpt what they had in common. He sculpted what could only be seen by the eye of a madman, or an animal.

I spent a month in Paris, wandering around, making the most of life, and not always in the most acceptable ways. The Nazi occupation created an oppressive atmosphere, so people partied to excess behind carefully sealed doors. One morning in Montmartre, I was stopped by a German soldier and I got scared, but he simply asked, wide-eyed, whether I was Toulouse-Lautrec. I said, 'Yes, of course,' and signed an autograph.

I arrived back in Pietra d'Alba on a bitterly cold night in early 1941. I could immediately tell that something was wrong. The whole village should have been sleeping, the darkness pierced only by a few flickering lights where a shutter hadn't been closed properly. The streets should have been filled with the magnificent silence of winter nights. But the shutters were not closed. The wind whipped through the streets, rushing down the alleys, howling like a demon. On the village square, people stepped aside to let us pass. From far and wide, calls rang out.

I ran from the car to the workshop. A single lamp shone in the kitchen window, where my mother was sitting waiting for me by the stove, wrapped in a woollen shawl, staring vacantly into the gloom.

'Has something happened?'

My mother got up to put coffee on the stove. Something had happened.

Viola had disappeared.

Campana had arrived back from Milan a few days earlier with his sister and her three sons. They had come to spend Christmas at the Villa Orsini. An impromptu trip to Genoa was arranged, but Viola did not go. From Stefano, I knew that relations between her and her husband were so strained that they no longer spoke. Leaving her to take care of the three children for the evening, the rest of the Orsini family had left, including the Marchese, with his bath chair, his nurse and his drooling nets. Despite several falls, an attack of bronchitis and various other ailments, the good Marchese still clung to life.

When the family came back early the following morning, they found the boys in the living room. They were asleep, except the youngest who was crying, while the room and the beautiful green sofas were stained with the shattered remnants of things they had broken and traces of food. When questioned, the household staff confessed that they had taken the night off, assuming that Signorina Orsini was in charge. By the time I came back, Viola had not been seen for two days.

The great salon had been transformed into a general headquarters, with a table in the middle of the room that was covered with maps of the area. I had come straight from the studio without bothering to change. Campana was pacing up and down, his hands behind his back, chewing on a cigar. He didn't look at me. A search party made up of local hunters was poring over the maps, commenting on the likely paths that the young lady might have taken, occasionally pausing, misty-eyed, and recounting an anecdote about some magnificent beast they had killed there.

The Orsini brothers were in Rome directing the search from there. An alert had been sent out to the port of Genoa and to the various shipping companies. Viola would not be able to board a transatlantic liner. There were people searching for her in Genoa, Savona and Milan. For two days, they had plumbed every wellspring in the area but found nothing except Saint Peter's tears – the spring was flowing brighter than ever. The hounds had come back with their tongues hanging out. Nobody could blame them. They had not been trained for such a hunt.

The Marchese was asleep in his bath chair, oblivious to the commotion. Sitting on a sofa next to a huge tomato stain, the Marchesa tried to look dignified. She had worn mourning black ever since her husband's first stroke, and the long slender limbs that Viola had inherited from her made her look like a spider. Indeed, she had the strange beauty of a tropical spider that I had once admired in a book Viola had lent me. For some years now, the Marchesa had left her two sons to work for the family's glory, while she maintained the social web she had spent years weaving. Sometimes, she would travel on her own to Turin or Milan, and wagging tongues whispered that as a woman who was still young – barely sixty – she went there to seek the consolations that no one in Pietra d'Alba could offer. Or *dared* offer, assuming that the Marchese was not a complete invalid.

Several search parties were still braving the dark and the cold – including Emanuele and Vittorio. There was nothing I could do, so I headed back, with our last quarrel weighing heavily on my mind. When I got home, I suddenly thought of the one obvious place where nobody would have thought to look – the cemetery. I set off at a run. At the age of thirty-seven, I was no longer frightened by the cemetery. My nightmares were no longer filled with demons from *Maciste in the Underworld*. This place reminded me of Viola, of the frayed friendship we had patched up time and time again.

It reminded me of the cinema of earlier years, which I don't think was any less poignant for being silent.

The door of the Orsini mausoleum stood ajar. I warily approached and pushed it open. The interior smelled of the passing years and dust. It was empty. There were withered flowers on the altar – nobody had been here for a long time. Slowly I explored the cemetery, ending up at the grave of the little flautist Tommaso Baldi. As I stood, staring at the weathered gravestone, I had an idea that made my blood run cold. What if Viola had found the entrance to the legendary tunnels? What if she had been wandering in the dark for the past three days? She didn't have a flute.

The following day, despite my mother's feigned enthusiasm, I couldn't summon the strength to work. If Viola did not want to be found, we would never find her. Like me, her brothers knew that, after the fiasco in Florence, she would not have left on a whim, nor would she try to board a transatlantic liner under her own name. This time, Viola had made a list of everything that might thwart her plans; she had anticipated our every step, including those we had not taken. The search was over before it had begun.

By nightfall, the atmosphere at Villa Orsini had changed. Anxiety had given way to fatigue. Among those in the search party, the hope of becoming a hero, of being noticed, had faded. The hunters reeked of pessimism, their faces scratched and dirty. Campana had returned to Milan on 'urgent business'.

When I woke up the following morning, I had the terrible presentiment that Viola was dead. I was so convinced that, at first, I could not get up, I could scarcely breathe. Finally, I managed to drag myself out to the trough and plunged my whole head into the waters of the miraculous spring. According to the legend, Saint Peter had wept bitter tears. I don't know whether they were bitter, but they were bitterly cold.

Another day passed and a few far-fetched reports from various places in Italy failed to revive our hopes. My mother forced me to eat dinner, saying 'just one more mouthful' every time I set down my spoon, as though I were a child. That night, we became mother and son again.

Shivering by the fire, I thought back to all the places we used to go together. There was nowhere, really, apart from the cemetery. Nowhere.

Nowhere except...

'Where are you going?' my mother asked as she saw me leap up from my seat.

But I was already running. I had not taken a torch, grabbing only an old military greatcoat that was lying around – doubtless abandoned by Emanuele. Despite the clouds – altocumulus – the moon shone brightly enough to guide me. I reached the Hanged Man's Oak and disappeared into the forest, oblivious to the creaking black sentries that reached out their thorny branches to scratch or trip me. This time, I prevailed. Whether by miracle or by design, I managed to find the clearing and waded my way through the undergrowth to the far side.

There she was. Before I even reached the cave, I saw her lying motionless. I scrabbled up the embankment, terrified because she wasn't moving. When, finally, I reached the entrance, Viola turned to me. A cloud moved over her pale cheeks, and the moonlight revealed what I had at first taken to be a mass of shadows: the hulking form of Bianca. Viola was snuggled against the she-bear, dressed as though she were spending the night at home. Her clothes were tattered.

'Bianca died this morning,' she whispered.

I knelt down, helped Viola to her feet and hugged her. Bianca's huge head was turned towards us, her eyes were open, her tongue protruded a little. Viola had not deliberately abandoned her nephews. She had been playing with them when she heard the heart-wrenching cry of the forest. A growl so loud it shook the walls, something no witness would later corroborate. As death approached, Bianca had called out to her mother, her sister and her friend. Without a second thought, Viola set off, assuming that the servants would look after the boys. She had spent four days with the she-bear, bringing her water, talking to her and sleeping next to her. I truly believe that, had I not found her, she would have joined Bianca on that last great journey.

Viola lay down and pulled me close to her. I pulled the greatcoat over us and gazed up at the stars.

'She was twenty-five,' she murmured. 'A good age for a bear.'

'You've got to come home. Everyone is looking for you.'

'No one can know about this. I'll tell them that I heard noises in the forest and went out to look, that I became frightened and lost and have been wandering around for days.'

Neither of us moved. I sighed. 'This whole thing is ridiculous.'

'What is ridiculous, Mimo?'

'You, me. Our friendship. One day we love each other, the next we hate each other... We are two magnets. The closer we get, the more we push each other away.'

'We're not magnets. We are a symphony. And even music requires silence.'

Viola asked me to bury Bianca, and though I immediately agreed, I regretted the decision when I came back armed with a shovel. It was a Herculean task. And Hercules had the distinct advantage of not being four foot six. I stumbled home at dawn, my hands raw and bleeding, and slept until evening. Vittorio woke me with the good news that Viola had simply got lost in the forest and found her way back. I pretended to be pleased and went back to sleep.

Viola spent three days in bed recovering from her ordeal. My limbs ached so much I could not sculpt for a week. The following Saturday, Campana came back from Milan and the Orsini brothers arrived from Rome. I was invited to a festive dinner and was happy to attend. Viola and I were finally speaking to each other again, and that was all that mattered. Only later did I realise that dinner parties at the Villa Orsini invariably ended badly, and this was no exception.

There was something brewing in Campana's eyes, something I should have noticed. All the more so because I recognised the loping, sideways gait of a tiger, head bowed, as we drank a glass while waiting for dinner. Tigers usually attack from the side.

Viola, still pale, smiled at me. I congratulated Francesco on his new position as secretary to Pope Pius XII. Stefano, as was his wont, drained glass after glass. Viola's sister-in-law was there, surrounded by her brood. As a boy, I had trembled after accidentally breaking into this sanctum. Now, I no longer marvelled at the place. I was a frequent visitor who regularly breathed in the golden dust that floated in the sun's rays. When the bell rang, we went into the dining room.

Dinner was a silent affair, barely disturbed by the sound

of the boys playing in the next room, until the cheese was served. The tray had been passed around and had just been replaced in the centre when Campana banged the table with the flat of his hand, which startled even the Marchese before he quickly slipped back into a daze.

'This is intolerable.'

'What is intolerable?' said Francesco politely.

'*Her!*' roared Campana, pointing a trembling finger at Viola. 'If a car I bought turned out to be such a wreck, I would have long ago been reimbursed!'

'My sister is not a car,' said Francesco, as genial as ever.

Viola, her head bowed, said nothing.

'First Florence, now this disappearance in the forest? The woman is insane, I have always said as much. To say nothing of the fact that she cannot bear children, probably because she jumped off the roof of this house, which, I admit, should have been a warning sign.'

Crimson with rage, Campana spluttered into his plate. He jabbed a finger towards his own sister. 'And what about Eloisa's boys? Anything could have happened to them! What kind of a woman would leave children unattended, for God's sake! And I have not even mentioned *this*!'

He pulled a crumpled piece of paper from his pocket and waved it at Viola, who instantly turned pale.

Campana gave a mocking laugh. 'What exactly is this, then? We found it while searching your room after you disappeared, looking for some letter or a note. Has the signora taken to writing poetry?'

He unfolded the piece of paper and cleared his throat.

Viola looked him straight in the eye. 'Don't read it.'

'I shall read it if I feel so inclined. Perhaps it would be nice for your family to know what goes on in that head of yours?'

'I wrote it a long time ago, when I was in the hospital. It's ancient history. And, besides, it is personal.'

'*I am a woman standing…*' Campana began in a theatrical tremolo.

Viola's face was contorted into a grimace of anger I had never seen before.

'If you read it,' she said softly, 'I will kill you.'

'Oh, so you're a murderer now, too?' Campana moved away from Viola, circling the table.

'*I'm a woman standing in the midst of the fires you kindled / I am a woman standing, do you see me, burning at your stake, your auto-da-fé, your pointing fingers? / I am a woman standing, what did you imagine? That I would weep as you hissed and howled, amid the smoke / burning at your stake, your auto-da-fé, your pointing fingers.*'

'Enough,' muttered Francesco, his face grim.

'Wait, dear brother-in-law!' bellowed Campana. 'There's more to come! *Since I bit into the apple there has been something eating at me / A longing to dance, to create rockets, to heal / And so once again you burn me at your stake, you crucify me / Black cat and straitjacket, drawn and quartered, you will say I was insane, say I was a witch, or both / I have eaten of the apple, I shall eat of it again, know this / I am a woman standing, I shall never kneel.'*

Campana's sister turned away and clapped a hand over her mouth to muffle her laughter. I froze, as did everyone at the table, though their reasons were different from mine. The Viola I had believed dead was alive, dancing in this poem from my adolescence.

'I am a woman standing in the middle of the wars you provoked / I am the woman you call when all is crumbling about you / The woman you will burn again as soon as all is well, lest I see that all is not well / You will burn me, reduce me to ash and scatter me, or so you will believe / but your fire produces no heat and cannot burn / I am a woman standing, I am worth a thousand of you.'

Campana had a coughing fit, accepted a glass of water from his sister and, with his free hand, signalled for us to wait.

'And now, dear friends, the best for last, the verse I didn't understand at all – probably because I'm not poetic!'

Viola slowly rose to her feet, a mist rising from the cold cemetery ground. In a barely audible voice, she recited: *'To you who was not born, who do not yet know what it means to hurt / To fall from the clouds and rise again / When they ask you to give up, lie down, stretch out / When they seek to silence you, to coax you, to disarm you / I am a woman standing like so many before us / I am a woman standing, as you will be.'*

Deadly silence. Campana returned to his wife, threatening. 'What kind of phrase is that? *To you who was not born?* Don't tell me you had a miscarriage? Or worse, that you—'

'A miscarriage? I didn't even know you when I wrote this. This poem is the flight of fancy of a girl of sixteen. I suppose I addressed it to myself, if you must know. The one who was not born is me. The girl who did not fly. I addressed it to myself in case this girl, in some parallel universe, might hear me.'

'A parallel universe?' Campana nearly choked again, this time clearing his throat with a glass of wine. 'You're completely insane!'

'For everyone's sake—' Francesco said but Viola interrupted him with a wave. A tiny movement of her delicate hand, which could have stopped an army on the march or a herd of charging elephant. The siblings were more alike than they realised.

'You always lacked imagination, Rinaldo. Did it never occur to you that not everything is as you see it? That, yes, there might exist a parallel universe? Or that this world of ours does not exist? That perhaps we are living in the dream of a bear?'

Everyone stared aghast at Viola, everyone except me; I smiled. Campana's neck was swollen and crimson.

Viola reached out her hand and her husband unthinkingly gave back the poem. She folded it, tucked it into her dress then turned to face him again. 'I warned you.'

I did not see it coming. In a split second, Viola picked up a cheese knife from the nearest plate, and, with all her strength, she drove it into her husband.

Tragedy causes time to dilate, proof that Viola had not been teaching me nonsense. None of the dinner guests reacted, their minds still frozen in the instant that came before, in the disbelief that clung to the turning cogs and slowed them down. Then reality hit. Campana saw the knife protruding from his shoulder, the lapel of his jacket splattered with blood, together with some excellent French Roquefort that the Orsinis had specially imported and a shaving of what looked like pecorino. He staggered backwards, then screamed. His sister followed suit, then fainted. In the next room, the boys started sobbing.

As for the Orsini family, they had seen it all before. Stefano pinched the bridge of his nose. He could see that the wound was not fatal, although the two small, curved teeth of the blade embedded in the flesh must have hurt like hell.

Francesco calmly got to his feet, rang for the butler and asked him to send for the doctor. Viola looked on, indifferent, as did her father. Her mother had disappeared, holding a napkin over her mouth, as soon as the deed was done. It was impossible to tell whether Viola had intentionally aimed for the shoulder or had missed the heart.

Two hours later, Campana, Stefano, Francesco and I were gathered in the smoking room for a discussion to which the women hadn't been invited. The doctor had given Viola a sedative and put her to bed. I often wondered how I ended up in the middle of these family dramas, as though I truly was an Orsini, or whether I was there simply because I had been forgotten, because people absentmindedly looked right over my head.

Beneath his bloodstained shirt, Campana had a bandage on his shoulder. He swirled his brandy and glowered at the two brothers. 'This time, I've had enough. She's gone too far. This barren lunatic should be in jail. Or an asylum.'

Stefano sat up halfway, curling his lip, prepared to defend his sister's honour. Doubtless for the wrong reasons, out of pride or possessiveness, but to defend her, nonetheless. As usual, Francesco calmed his brother's murderous rage with a small gesture.

'Nobody is going to jail,' Francesco said softly. 'We never expected the two of you to be Romeo and Juliet, but the time has come for you to go your separate ways.'

Campana turned pale. It wasn't difficult to imagine that, in marrying Viola, he had made a number of calculations. That Francesco would never have children – at least not legitimately. That the love of revelry and wine that had turned Stefano from a thickset, handsome boy into a paunchy government official meant he was hardly likely to start a family either. So there was a small but very real possibility that a child of Campana and Viola would inherit the title. His plan was thwarted by Viola's womb. But his association with the Orsini family was a source of great prestige and, in this respect, Campana had hit the jackpot. He could boast of having a direct line to the Pope (true, always supposing that Francesco wished to open up that line) and to Il Duce (false, because Stefano quaked in the presence of Mussolini). And despite some lean years, the Orsini fortune, in terms of property alone, was still substantial. For Campana, a separation was out of the question.

He let us know this when he sprang from his armchair and shook a furious finger at us all, his glass still in his hand. 'There will be no divorce, do you hear me? Not with what I've invested in this family. Where would your citrus groves, your bloody fields, your precious oranges be without me?'

'There will be no divorce,' said Francesco. 'There will be an annulment. When she agreed to marry you, Viola was still suffering from the psychological damage brought on by her fall. Consequently, she was legally unfit to consent. The marriage is invalid, and the annulment will be arranged at the highest level. You will not have to worry about anything. Viola will go into a nursing home for a few months to keep up appearances.'

Unlike the rest of them, I couldn't leap up from my seat when I was outraged. It was an insignificant detail, but one that infuriated me. I shuffled to the edge of my seat, put one foot on the floor and propelled myself upright.

'Out of the question!' I exclaimed, a moment too late.

'For once, the midget is right,' said Campana. 'There will be no annulment. It is out of the question!'

Francesco got to his feet and smoothed his black cassock with the purple sash. Despite himself, Campana took a step back.

'Mimo, I have just spoken with our sister. She agrees. Indeed, it was she who asked me. I know a convent in Tuscany, a lovely place. You can see for yourself if you like. As for you, dear brother-in-law...' Francesco replaced his skullcap and clasped his hands, striking a curiously prayerful pose. 'You will do exactly as we tell you.'

'We shall see about that.' Campana made to leave the room.

Francesco cleared his throat. 'Let's not leave on these harsh words. Anger is a poor counsellor. You do not have to accept the annulment.'

'You're bloody right, Father. And another thing—'

'But it will be granted nonetheless,' Francesco interrupted.

'I beg your pardon?'

'There is the small matter of that sordid little... affair. Very troubling. The young woman you assaulted some years ago. I am told she lost an eye.'

Campana froze and turned around. 'I was completely exonerated.'

'Because Mimo here testified on your behalf. The same Mimo could retract his statement and say that you forced him in order to maintain the family reputation.'

'He would go to prison for perjury.'

Francesco laughed. 'For about ten minutes, yes. You, on the other hand, I am afraid, would spend considerably more time behind bars and lose many, *many* friends. And what would your sister Eloisa think? And your family? More than that, this blatant proof of your mental instability guarantees the annulment will be granted. I was prepared to offer a reasonable compromise by laying the fault at Viola's door, but since you have rejected that option...'

I had no desire to go to prison, not even for ten minutes. But I shrugged. Campana's jaw twitched. His glassy eyes bulged slightly, and he glared at the young bishop as though seeing him for the first time.

'Since the annulment will be granted regardless,' said Francesco airily, 'you simply need to let us know whether you wish to come out of this with your dignity or lose everything in the process: your reputation, your business, your family.

The end result is the same as far as we are concerned.'

Campana gave a nervous laugh. He trudged towards the door, then he turned around one last time. 'You're a bunch of fucking bastards,' he said.

Stefano, who up to this point had not said anything, got to his feet. 'No. We are the Orsinis.'

I was ridiculously happy to have been in the room when he said it.

The annulment was granted in record time, and none of us ever heard from Rinaldo Campana again. I would see his name on the credits of several movies until the late fifties, when I heard that he disappeared one evening on his way home. It was later discovered that he had fled to America, following a series of commercial flops that left him in debt to several very disreputable individuals. He succeeded where his ex-wife had failed.

Viola had asked to be sent to a rest home. In the spring of 1941, I personally accompanied her, with my chauffeur, to a convent nestled in the Tuscan hills. Two slopes of green wheat formed a U-shape around the building, which was surrounded by lush parkland. The convent, freshly repainted in pink, reminded me a little of Metti's studio – Florence was some sixty kilometres away. The Mother Superior, a gentle woman in her forties, received us in a spacious lounge, where young novices like swallows served us tea. The establishment was home to convalescent nuns, most of them suffering from 'spiritual malaise'. We were then shown to our rooms. The one assigned to Viola, at the request of her brother Francesco, was south-facing, but sheltered from the sun by a dark green cypress.

'We shall take great care of Signorina Orsini,' the Mother Superior assured me with her gentle smile. 'She will be back on her feet in no time.'

I left Viola to settle in. Back in the lounge, the Mother Superior handed me some documents to sign. Unthinkingly, I began to do so until a particular sentence caught my eye. *The establishment accepts no responsibility for any adverse side effects to the treatments provided.* I asked the Mother Superior about the treatments to which this referred and what the side effects might be. She immediately took me down to the basement and showed me, still smiling, a large area tiled from floor to ceiling under the vaults of the cellar. Pressurised water pipes snaked around our feet, with a strong smell of damp.

'This is where we give some of our residents ice-cold showers if they become agitated in the middle of the night. This natural method is ideal for treating itchy flesh, or the bite of doubt, when traditional methods have failed.'

'Which traditional methods?'

'We do use certain medicinal solutions, but before resorting to them, we recommend our guests spend a few nights in prayer and contemplation before the altar. A volunteer sister sits vigil, using a bamboo cane to prevent the praying guest from falling asleep. As Saint John Climacus writes, "He who distrusts all dreams is a wise man." The devil is made manifest and profits from the sleep of reason to whisper things against nature into our ear. Insomnia is a powerful defence.'

I asked the Mother Superior to wait for me in the living room and went upstairs to Viola, who was hanging her clothes in her wardrobe. 'We are leaving.'

Viola asked no questions. With a sigh, she packed her belongings back into her suitcase and we went down to join the Mother Superior.

'How should I address you?' I asked. 'Sister? I would not want to make a mistake.'

'Reverend Mother,' she said, frowning at the sight of the suitcase.

'Reverend Mother, this convent of yours is not a rest home.'

'You are correct. It is a battleground where we fight a war against the doubts dripped into our ears by the Evil One and against the temptations of the flesh. But with victory comes peace.'

'I admire your logic, Reverend Mother. It is like watching a convoluted clockwork mechanism. A clock so convoluted it forgets to tell the time.'

'I am not sure I understand—'

'Viola will not be staying.'

'Excuse me?'

'Viola. Will. Not. Be. Staying.'

'Listen... *signor*,' said the Mother Superior, stressing the honorific as though I scarcely deserved it, 'I do not know who you are, but you do not look like an Orsini.'

'Because the Orsinis are tall?'

She ignored my question. 'As such, I do not take my orders from you. Monsignor Orsini requested that I care for his sister, and I will accept no counter-order unless it comes from him.'

'He will give no counter-order.'

'Excellent, then the matter is settled.'

'Not quite. Let me be clear, Reverend Mother. I can leave here without Viola. But I should first let you know that an ugly, deformed creature such as myself, abandoned at birth by Almighty God, keeps extremely bad company. I am more sorry than anyone, but I cannot change who I am. So if I leave without Viola – look me in the eye when I say this – I will be back in two days. I will raze this convent so that there is nothing left but ashes. Don't worry, you and your flock will not be harmed – I am not a brute, believe me, though I am tempted to give you that icy shower that dispels doubt. But be warned, I will make sure there is not one stone left piled upon another.'

Viola looked at me in amazement, but it was nothing compared to the expression on the Mother Superior's face.

She quickly composed herself and, without a word, led us to the front door.

In a departure from his usual soft-spoken reticence, Francesco shouted at me down the phone when he received a formal complaint from the Mother Superior. I told him to take an ice-cold shower and hung up.

I saw little of Viola in the two years that followed. I had my own problems and, moreover, on her return from the convent, a remarkable transformation took place. Overnight, Viola, who had never paid much heed to her appearance, began to dress in beautiful gowns by the greatest Paris couturiers. She insisted on accompanying her mother on her social tours and played the gracious hostess when her parents entertained. Compliments soon came back to my ears about the young marchesa, *an exquisite creature, a true lady and a marvellous hostess,* who had *all her mother's qualities* and *would have made a wonderful wife,* if, at thirty-seven, she had not been considered too old to remarry.

Of the great wardrobe of personas Viola used to escape herself, this seemed to me the least dangerous. I was not concerned by it and simply ignored her rather stilted politeness when I encountered her. As 1941 progressed, it became increasingly clear that the Esposizione Universale – the 1942 World's Fair in Rome – would not take place because of the war. The Fascist regime claimed it didn't matter, that our genius was on every front was clear from the power of our weapons. Though it may not have mattered to the regime, it mattered to me. The Palazzo della Civiltà Italiana, built especially for the Esposizione Universale, never opened. The magnificent, empty shell dominated Rome for years. Fascism had not just built a monument to its glory; unwittingly, it had built its own tomb. As for me, I was left with ten statues on my hands – three years of work, supplies and apprentices' wages – which were never paid for. Having not had any money worries in almost twenty years, and all but forgotten that I had ever been poor, I suddenly found myself having to lay off half my staff overnight. I had to crack the whip at the studio to meet the outstanding commissions while travelling the length and breadth of the country looking for potential customers. For the first time in my career, I suddenly worried people would think me old-fashioned. But my work seemed to please everyone. Everyone except me, now that I realised I was merely a sixteen-year-old sculptor who was actually thirty-seven.

One night, as I tossed and turned in a feverish sleep, I heard the bedroom door creak. My mother laid a hand on my forehead and whispered *hush, hush*, then sang a lullaby. Though I did not remember it, I must have heard it in some distant past in Savoy, because a feeling of well-being washed over me.

'You don't always have to run,' she whispered.

The following day, she greeted me in the kitchen as though nothing had happened. To this day, I am not sure that I did not dream it.

Some months later, once I had stabilised the finances of the studio, I rehired two apprentices. As a result of the war, I no longer had any secular orders, except for the colossal statue of *The New Man*, for which I had chosen a marble block of astonishing purity. By now, to the irritation of my rivals, the most beautiful marble in Italy was reserved entirely for me. I was ruthless with suppliers. The size of the block meant that the statue would be a little smaller than anticipated, but when I saw the quality, I knew this was it. A shiver ran down my spine when I touched it. It *spoke* to me, something that had not happened for a long time. I was sure it did not have the slightest crack or fissure. It gave itself to me, without resistance.

I did not set to work immediately, which was slightly unscrupulous, since I was paid by the hour. But I was no more unscrupulous than those who had not paid me for my work on the Palazzo della Civiltà Italiana. Having forgiven me for my insolence, Francesco introduced me to a new client, a former priest who had made his fortune in aviation. The man wanted to build himself a spectacular monument in the Cimitero Monumentale di Staglieno, the cemetery of cemeteries, Genoa's largest necropolis. A city of the dead so splendid it rivalled that of the living, and was so beautiful, legend had it, that some were so impatient to be interred here that they lost their fear of death. The client, on the other hand, wanted to be sure that I would personally sculpt the work, forcing me to temporarily move back to Rome, since he often dropped by unannounced to check. A few months later, flying a prototype of his own design, he crash-landed in the Mediterranean and his body was never found. The mausoleum was given to his family. I have no idea what they did with it. Perhaps it still stands in Staglieno, empty or occupied by someone else. But, being an honourable man, the aviator had paid me in advance.

Shortly before Christmas 1942, I was seized by a curious presentiment. An oppression, a flickering on the edge of my field of vision. I told Stefano, who laughed at me, and Francesco, who muttered *hmm*. I called my mother, whose voice was faint and frail, and all I could talk about was myself and this strange feeling. She was worried that I was working too hard. I was not insane, nor was I working too hard. It did not happen every day, and I could not work out a logical pattern. But I was sure of myself.

Wherever I went in Rome, someone was following me.

E ver faster, ever faster.

In the early 1920s, it had taken me two days to get to Rome from Pietra d'Alba. Ten years later, it took a day. Ten years after that, half a day. Rockets were just around the corner. Five years from now, someone would break the sound barrier. The *sound barrier*. I had grown up with horses and carts, and suddenly people were breaking the speed of sound as though it were nothing, with not so much as a by-your-leave.

The feeling that I was being followed disappeared as soon as I went back to Pietra d'Alba for Christmas. My mother was in bed, suffering from a chest infection that left her gasping for breath when she spoke. The doctor examined her and, with a worried frown, informed us that there was 'an orchestra in her chest, and not a chamber orchestra'.

Vittorio tended to her day and night, his second mother, her second son. In the six years she had lived at the studio they had become close. Even Anna, who saw her regularly when she brought the children to stay, had grown fond of her. Vittorio and Anna had officially separated the year before. One night, after a little too much wine, Vittorio sighed. 'I wish I could make a pyre of all my mistakes and burn them, so I could go back to being the man she used to love.'

Christmas Eve at the Villa Orsini was an intimate affair: the immediate family, me, two dowagers vaguely related to the family, both deaf as posts, and two elderly bachelor cousins, one of them senile. Viola played the role of the young marchesa perfectly, moving between the guests, laughing at their corny jokes, her cheeks pink with pleasure, as though she were living in a dream. The Christmas presents were piled up by the fireplace, and Viola hugged her mother affectionately when she got a brooch mounted with a round-cut orange diamond flanked by two emeralds depicting their favourite fruit. I was surprised when Stefano reached into the pile, pulled out an envelope with my name and tossed it to me. In it was a card adorned with two gold embossed fasces: an invitation to a ceremony at the Reale Accademia d'Italia on 23 March 1943 addressed to Stefano Orsini.

I smiled and handed it back. 'I think it's for you.'

Stefano arched an eyebrow, studied the invitation, then shrugged. 'I must have got them mixed up.'

He pretended to rummage in his pockets and finally took out another envelope and handed it to me with a twinkle in his eye.

My heart skipped a beat. The envelope contained a copy of a decree dated 21 December 1942. *On the personal recommendation of the Minister for Popular Culture, for his contribution to the Italian intellectual movement in the arts, sculptor Michelangelo Vitaliani has been appointed as a member plenipotentiary of the Reale Accademia d'Italia.*

Tears welled up in my eyes. Just like when I had cried, at thirteen, at the gates of this villa, they discreetly looked away and gave me time to collect myself. In these circles, a man did not cry unless he was a woman. My official investiture was to take place at the event on 23 March, Stefano informed me. Champagne was uncorked, we made a toast and then a few more.

I had avoided looking at Viola, but she came over and brushed my wrist with her gloved hand. 'Congratulations. I am delighted for you.'

Over dinner, one of the elderly aunts woke up and began talking about the position of the Holy See with regard to Nazi Germany. The champagne had had its effect.

'You,' she said to Francesco, 'for all that you're a bishop now, I used to change your nappies and I've seen your *cazzino*. You

tell us what is happening in the Vatican. Because I refuse
to support that pig Mussolini, still less that pig Hitler, but
I pledge my faith to God, so I would like to know what He
thinks.'

Francesco, in his habitual velvety tone, assured her that
His Holiness was much concerned by the horrors of the war
and condemned them in the strongest possible terms.

'Why does he not say so, then?'

'He has done, Zia.'

'Yes, but without naming names!'

'His Holiness cannot always express himself... freely,' said
Francesco, glancing at his brother. 'He must be circumspect.'

Viola leaned over and laid a hand on her aunt's, as she had
done when she congratulated me. 'Come now, Zia, let's not
talk politics.'

'Exactly,' added Stefano, flushed with anger.

The less senile of the cousins went and sat with the aunt,
who quickly dozed off again. Dinner ended in a somewhat
tense silence, after which the guests withdrew: Stefano to
the garden to smoke, Francesco to his room to write letters.
I lingered because Viola was still standing by the fireplace.
She took a silver box from her pocket and swallowed two
pink pills with a glass of water.

'Are you sick?'

'Oh, Mimo, are you still here? No, I'm not sick. It's just a
little pick-me-up the doctor prescribed for when I get tired.'

'And it must be exhausting having to play the perfect marchesa.' I sighed and buried my face in my hands. I had had too much to drink.

Viola, however, did not seem to notice and simply handed me the pillbox. 'Would you like one? You'll see, they're very relaxing.'

'I apologise. I didn't mean that.'

'Really? I think it is precisely what you meant to say.'

'Perhaps, but the words were poorly chosen. I know that you disapprove of many of the decisions I have made in my career. But you must understand... the Accademia... It is a validation.'

'And I am very happy for you.'

'The fake Viola is happy for me. The true Viola would kill me if she could.'

'There's no true or fake Viola. There is only me.'

'Do you know what I think? I think all these disguises you've adopted over the years are just to piss me off.'

Viola let out a short, incredulous laugh, then put her hands on her hips. 'Well, Mimo, it seems you did not read the books I used to lend you. It is such a pity, because you might have learned how Giordano Bruno was burned at the stake for defending his heretical theses, including the idea that the earth does not revolve around *you*.'

This remark was greeted by a faint giggle. We started – the Marchese was still sitting, unnoticed, in a corner of the room. Almost immediately, his eyes clouded over again. Viola rang the bell, a maid hurriedly appeared and ushered the patriarch out of the salon.

'I deserve this,' I said, waving the letter of my appointment to the Accademia. 'I earned it, and no one can take it from me.'

'No one is trying to take it from you.'

'That's a lie, Viola. You despise the current regime. But it has been good for me.' I stepped forward and launched my lethal weapon. I gestured to my stunted body. 'You have no right to criticise. You have no idea what it is like to be me...'

Viola gestured to herself. 'And you have no idea what it is like to be me.'

She turned back to the fire, with that satisfied smirk of a fisherman who, having hooked a particularly stupid fish, tosses it back because he cannot be bothered with such small fry.

To everyone's relief, my mother recovered, and I was able to leave for Rome. It was snowing in the Eternal City. It was bitterly cold, especially in my ill-heated apartment. But I refused to allow anything to dampen my spirits. In less than three months, I was to receive the highest artistic distinction that Italy could bestow. The accompanying publicity would guarantee new commissions.

A week later, the same ominous feeling suddenly returned. I was convinced that I was being followed. I tried various subterfuges, darting into a narrow alley, ducking into a building and leaving by another door, and for a few hours, a few days, the feeling would fade. I decided to call Stefano, who held a senior position in the Ministry of the Interior.

'Who do you think you are, Gulliver?' he said and snickered. 'Do you really think you are important enough to be followed? Besides, why should the government spy on someone who has just been ennobled by Il Duce? A loyal supporter of the regime?'

But he promised to investigate and let me know. That night, he showed up at the studio and swore that I was mistaken. I was not being followed, or at least not by his services. Over the next days, the feeling dissipated. Determined to make the most of my impending appointment to the rank of Royal Academician, I booked Le Jardin at the Hotel de Russie to hold an evening in my own honour a few weeks before the event – if you want a thing done properly, do it yourself. Francesco assured me that several cardinals would attend, and I knew Pacelli would have come had his duties permitted. My recently widowed Serbian princess had taken a new lover, 'someone who is a little more present', she said. I was not sure whether she was referring to my frequent visits to Pietra d'Alba or to my increasing distractedness when we made love. But she was happy to grace my little event with her beauty, accompanied by a bevy of aspiring suitors, many prepared to do anything to please her, including commissioning a work from me they neither needed nor wanted. Stefano, as usual, turned up with his more or less unsavoury friends, who at least had a sense of fun. The two groups remained distinct and, in the great, vaulted conservatory, looked like two football teams, Vatican reds on one side and Fascist blackshirts on the other. A *sfumato* of women, each more beautiful than the last, hovered on the edges, blurring the boundaries and giving a sense of fluidity, but the two groups did not mingle. Champagne and various spirits flowed freely. I even saw a little cocaine being passed around among the Fascists.

Princess Alexandra Kara-Petrović did not refrain from openly flirting with me, which made me incredibly desirable to a number of the women present, and no doubt a few men too. If he can attract a woman like her, they thought, and if he is about to be appointed to the Accademia Reale, he must have something. I didn't enjoy these attentions as much as I would have ordinarily. Since realising that I was being followed, I was constantly on my guard.

Luigi Freddi put in an appearance, with a young actress on his arm. My height sometimes put me in an embarrassing position. Although, on several occasions, Stefano had praised my unique view of the world, I didn't necessarily appreciate talking to a woman's bosom, especially when, as with the actress, she pressed herself against me while we conversed. I stepped back, she stepped forward, and it was shortly before midnight, while we were engaged in this strange tarantella, that the concierge came to find me.

'Signor Vitaliani, our security guards have intercepted an individual attempting to break into the hotel. He claims to know you, but has no invitation. We suspect he is a freeloader or perhaps a journalist.'

'What does he look like?'

The concierge shuddered. It was almost imperceptible – but I could read expressions in marble, so human flesh... 'Perhaps it would be better if you were to see him for yourself.'

We went up to the first floor. The concierge went over to a window and lifted the curtain. Outside the entrance, a man was standing in the cold below us, stamping his feet and blowing on his fingers. Suddenly, I knew that this was the man who had been following me for weeks, because it couldn't be any other way. I also understood why the concierge had looked embarrassed when asked to describe him: he looked much like me. It was Bizzaro. A little grey, a little stooped, but there was no doubt it was Bizzaro.

With the same smile that Saint Peter addressed to an over-zealous guard two thousand years earlier, I said: 'I have never seen this man before in my life.'

I got home at three in the morning, much more sober than I had expected. I insisted on going back on foot, and my chauffeur followed – penance, perhaps, for leaving Bizzaro out in the cold. I had watched from the upstairs window as the security guards threw him out. He spat at their feet before storming away in the heavy snowflakes, his shoulders hunched, his hands in his pockets. His presence did not bode well. He had not politely turned up at my door. He had followed me. He had tried to gatecrash an event at which I was not expecting him. And Bizzaro was capable of anything, from taking a friend to visit the Convento di San Marco in the dead of night, calling the friend a dwarf a minute later, then knocking out a Fascist. Perhaps he wanted to blackmail me. I was a wealthy man; my face regularly appeared in the society pages of the newspapers.

You have not lived until you have seen Rome bedecked in snow. The cold heightened every smell. The scents of night – expensive perfumes, sweaty bodies – were followed by those of day – metal street lamps, coffee percolating behind the misted window of a café. I arrived home chilled to the bone and collapsed on my bed, fully clothed, without even turning on the light. In the corner, the stove was still smouldering – I had lit it before going out. Why was I lying to myself? Yes, I was worried about Bizzaro, but it wasn't fear that prompted me to ignore him. I had turned him away for the same reason I did not visit him in Florence, when I was there with Viola. Bizzaro and Sara had seen me lying in the gutter. I simply didn't want to be reunited with someone who had known the worst version of me, lest I discover that version was the *real* me. Because if it was, then the Mimo Vitaliani of today, with his Tank wristwatch and elegantly tailored suits, was nothing but an impostor.

I had an appointment with a supplier in a few hours, so there was little point trying to sleep, but I allowed myself to doze. I sensed the smell of burning, carried on a warm breeze from the plains of Anatolia. Faint and dreamlike at first, then more intense. This was no dream: something in the room was burning.

'So, Mimo, you don't recognise old friends any more?'

I started so violently I fell out of bed. As my eyes adjusted to the gloom, I saw Bizzaro sitting in a corner by the window. He sat on the floor near the stove, just beyond the orange halo. He was smoking a pipe, the flickering stove reflected in his pupils, giving him an eerie look.

'Bloody hell, you nearly gave me a heart attack! How did you get in here?'

'Through the door, like everyone else. Your security leaves a little to be desired.'

I pulled myself together. It was just a joke between old friends, after all. I was Mimo Vitaliani; nothing could happen to me. I came back from the kitchen with two glasses of plum brandy, pushed one towards him and sat on the floor with him – there were no chairs in the room anyway. 'I'm sorry about earlier, but tonight was...'

'That's all right, Mimo, I understand.'

'It's been a long time. How have you been?'

Bizzaro laughed. 'You really want to do this? Talk about the good old days?'

'All right, then. Why have you been following me?'

'Because I wanted to see who you were hanging around with before I talked to you. Some of your new friends, the ones who dress in black, they scare me. I needed to know just how close you were to them.'

'What do you want from me?'

'I don't want anything from *you*. I just need your help. Or rather, my sister does.'

'You have a sister?'

'Of course I have a sister, you moron. A sister you know very well – Sara.'

'Sara is your sister?' I stared at him in disbelief, bruised by the guilty and disturbing memory of the last moments I had spent at the circus. Of Sara, who had comforted me like no other woman. 'You never told me she was your sister!'

'I never told you that she wasn't.' Bizzaro puffed on his pipe.

I waited, but he didn't speak. 'What's happening to Sara?'

Slowly, he took a piece of paper from his pocket, unfolded it and slid it towards me. An almost illegible notice, stiff with glue from where it had been pasted up somewhere and torn down.

'What is this?'

'Directive no 443/45626. In which your friends order the internment of non-Italian Jews and stateless Jews. Sara has been arrested. She's been in Ferramonti di Tarsia internment camp for the past six months. A hundred or so barracks built on an old swamp in the middle of nowhere, in southern Italy. She's lucky – there are much worse places.'

'I didn't know that you were Jewish.'

'Of course we're Jewish. Surely you didn't think my name was really Alfonso Bizzaro? I was born Isaac Saltiel, near Toledo. The question is whether, if you had known, it would have made any difference to the choices you've made. I've followed your career, Mimo. I barely recognised you when I saw your photo in the *Corriere della Sera*. Look at you – you were right, you're not a dwarf. You've made it.'

'Did you come here just to insult me?'

The old belligerent spark appeared in Bizzaro's eyes. But where it once would have kindled a pure, volatile flame, now it met only saltwater and immediately guttered out. Bizzaro slumped in his corner.

'No,' he muttered. 'Actually, I wish that was the reason, but I need you to have Sara released. You have all the right contacts, don't lie. The camp she is in is bearable, but it's still an internment camp. And it won't stop there. The crackdown is going to get more brutal. I know, because I've seen it before.'

'What do you mean, you've seen it?'

'I've seen *everything*. I am the original wandering Jew, Mimo. I am two thousand years old. Two thousand years during which I have been tortured, broken and killed, two thousand years of people spitting in my face, of ghettos, of fleeing into the night. Wherever I live – and I have lived all over the world, in Venice, Odesa, Valparaiso – they hunt me down. I have died a thousand times, but I am always reborn and I remember everything.'

'You're completely insane.'

'Perhaps, my friend, perhaps. So, are you going to help me?'

'Why weren't you arrested?'

'I nearly was. We had been warned, but at the last minute Sara changed her mind. She did not want to run any more. "Let them come," that's what she said. And come they did. They wouldn't have missed it for the world.'

He took one last drag on his pipe, looked me straight in the eye, then turned it upside down and banged the bowl, emptying the ashes onto the floor, with no regard for my parquet. 'Well, are you going to help me or not?'

'And if I refuse? Are you going to blackmail me? Tell everyone that I performed with drunken dinosaurs? Pull out a knife and stab me?'

'Oh, I'm too old for knives these days. If you refuse, I'll leave alone and heartbroken. I will simply tell you that the day may come when your conscience is worth more than your wristwatch. And when it comes, you will realise that it is the one thing in the world that your money cannot buy back.'

S tefano had to close the door of his office because I was
shouting so loudly.

'You lied to me, you fucking bastard! You're going to get
that woman released from that fucking camp of yours!'

He barked at me to calm down and said he had done
nothing wrong, and this was true. Nobody ever does anything wrong; the beauty of evil is that it requires no effort
whatsoever. You need only stand by and watch.

'This is a delicate situation, Gulliver. If this person is in a
camp—'

'My name is Mimo.'

'All right, Mimo. If this person is in a camp—'

'Listen carefully: I've done more than enough for your
family when you needed it, you know what I mean?'

Stefano peered at me. His face had grown even heavier.

Instead of looking menacing, he looked like a pig dozing in the sun. 'Are you blackmailing me?'

'Of course I'm blackmailing you. Are you a complete moron or what?'

He gasped – I had never spoken to him like this before. He took a deep breath. 'I'll see what I can do. As long as this person has not committed a crime—'

'She *has* committed a crime. She's a Jew.'

He clicked his tongue irritably. 'Don't you think you are exaggerating a little? These internment camps are not at all what you imagine. Here, look at this.'

He turned around, took a file from a cabinet and slid it across the desk. A photo slipped out of dancers at a ball. All of the couples were men.

'The island of San Domino, in the Adriatic. We put fifty homosexual degenerates in a camp there back in 1938. Well, let me tell you, we had to close the camp because the bastards were having so much fun. Dressing up as women, buggering each other... And all at the expense of the princess! So maybe this Jewish girlfriend of yours is no worse off.' He laughed. Then, seeing my expression, his face darkened. He had met enough murderers to recognise one.

'I have made choices, Mimo. I don't regret any of them. I've got nothing personally against Jews, believe me. I don't even care about guys who fuck each other. They've done me no harm. But Italy is bigger than any single individual. And orders are orders: you can't accept the ones you like and ignore the ones you don't.'

He gestured for me to leave. 'I'll call you when it's done.'

On 3 March 1943, Sara stepped off the Naples train at Rome-Prenestina station. Bizzaro and I were waiting on the platform. I was shocked when I saw her. Not because she had been maltreated at Ferramonti, but because the sixty-year-old woman who had taken me in was now eighty. She was still beautiful, her hair was pure white, and she had lost weight. She was no longer a fairground fortune-teller, a comfort woman, she was Pythia, an oracle with a distant gaze and a scent of mystery and laurel.

She hugged her brother, smiled when she saw me and took my hands in hers. 'Mimo, you haven't changed a bit.'

'Neither have you.'

We looked at each other for a long time, in silence. Bizzaro cleared his throat, picked up the suitcase he had brought with him and led us to a different platform. The last of the passengers were boarding as he helped his sister onto the train.

'Where are you headed?'

'It's better for everyone if you don't know.'

The contrast with Turin station, where I had first arrived in 1916, was striking. Almost half the trains were now electric. There was less smoke, less noise. Departures were less violent. From the carriage, the High Priestess of Delphi blew me a kiss and said goodbye. Bizzaro lingered on the footboard. I thought he was about to thank me, but he simply said: 'I'm not criticising your choices, Mimo. "If you can't beat 'em, join 'em", as some of my friends say. You've earned your place at the Accademia.'

'Thank you.'

We talked for a few more minutes until the whistle sounded. With a pneumatic sigh, the train juddered into life. Still, Bizzaro stood on the footboard, and I walked, then trotted along the platform. This was not an electric train. A belch of oily black smoke that smelled of 1916 passed between us. The noise grew louder; the train creaked and screeched and squealed along its tracks. I had to run to keep up with Bizzaro.

'By the way,' he shouted. 'Forget that story about the wandering Jew the other night! I had a bit to drink to warm myself up!'

Out of breath, and out of platform, I watched a part of my youth disappear, trailing a long fuming serpent.

Two weeks later, crowds of dignitaries flocked to the Villa Farnesina, the seat of the Accademia Reale d'Italia. I personally greeted everyone as they arrived. I was still a minor, insignificant figure. An hour from now, I would be an academician with a monthly stipend of three thousand lire, a uniform that would make Emanuele green with envy, the right to travel first class, free of charge, on our beautiful Italian trains, and I would be addressed as 'Excellency'. Despite my few grey hairs, I was not yet forty.

The Orsini brothers were in attendance. Viola was not. I saw Luigi Freddi pass by with a different beauty on his arm, and various luminaries I didn't know. At the cocktail party before the ceremony, I was surprised to see Neri among the guests. Clean-cut, square-jawed and smiling, he had aged well. He congratulated me warmly; the past was ancient history. Neri had prospered and he had come here to show his face, in the hope of one day being invited to join our illustrious institution.

Just as he was about to walk away, I tugged on his sleeve. 'There's still that little matter of the money you owe me.'

'I owe you money?'

'Of course you do. Think back: Florence, 1921, you and your henchmen beat me up and robbed me. Granted, things worked out well for me, but that is not the point. That envelope contained one hundred and fifty-seven lire. Adjusting for inflation, let's call it two thousand.' I held out my hand.

Neri stared at me in disbelief, but he could tell I wasn't joking. People were beginning to stare, so he took me by the shoulder and forced a smile as he led me away. 'Come on, Mimo, that's ridiculous, we were just kids.'

'Two thousand lire.'

He gritted his teeth, took a deep breath – that old anger still simmered just below the surface. 'I don't have that kind of money on me. A thousand at the most.'

'That's a very handsome wristwatch.'

'Are you insane? It's a Panerai. It's worth three times what you're asking for.'

'Let me be very clear, Neri. Either you pay me right now or, as a member of the Accademia, I will personally ensure that that you never become one.'

Neri was white to the lips. He gave a little snicker, then removed his watch. 'Does that make us even?'

'Not quite.'

I carefully set his watch on the ground and crushed it with the heel of my shoe. 'Now we're even.'

I confess that I've always been a vindictive son of a bitch.

Dinner was served. For the first time in years, I was nervous. The academicians in their regalia were daunting. Not to mention people from the Ministry of Culture, in sober suits, and a few members of the carabinieri, without doubt here to ensure our safety in this cut-throat social whirl. A hulking figure seated a few tables from me, next to Luigi Freddi, stood out from the crowd. He took up enough space for two men. Between courses, I went over and tapped him on the shoulder in disbelief. This was the best evening of my life.

'Excuse me, aren't you Maciste? I mean, aren't you Bartolomeo Pagano?'

The giant turned and smiled at me. He was a giant weary from picking up bad guys and throwing them through windows, sending demons back to hell. He got to his feet. In that moment, there could be no more comical sight in all of Italy than the difference in height between the country's most famous actor and its most famous sculptor. Pagano held out his hand, bowing slightly. I could see that the effort was painful.

We exchanged a few pleasantries, then I slipped away. In a marble bathroom, I stood in front of the mirror, trembling, and rehearsed my speech. From the far end of the corridor came the sound of applause and creaking chairs. This was my turn. The president of the Accademia greeted the personalities present, made them laugh with a few good words and finally announced the order of the day: me, my plucking from the mud in which I had been born. Shyly, I made my way through the crowd, blushing as I accepted hugs, pats on the back and handshakes, then mounted the stage. I don't know whether the Villa Farnesina had been chosen as the venue to intimidate, but that was the effect it had. The reception was taking place on the first floor, in the Hall of Perspectives. The trompe-l'œil frescoes by Peruzzi gave the impression that the two terraces on either side opened onto Rome. The effect was staggering, vertiginous and all the more striking because there were no views from this room, still less of a terrace, just solid walls. My head was reeling, perhaps from over-rehearsing the speech I had learned by heart. *Thank you, dear friends, thank you. You can imagine what this award means...* The president of the Accademia handed me a velvet box of midnight blue containing a gold medal. I didn't hear what he said. Finally, I found myself in front of a hushed, attentive crowd of people, who twenty years earlier would not have given me a lira.

'Thank you, my dear friends, thank you. You can well imagine what the honour being bestowed means to a boy like me, who was born a long way from these coffered ceilings and gilded mouldings. Sculpture is a brutal, physical art, which is why I never thought I would one day stand here before you, since, as I am sure you can see, I am not exactly built like my childhood idol, Signor Bartolomeo Pagano, who has honoured us with his presence this evening.'

Applause. Pagano half rose, waved and nodded his thanks. 'I will not tire your patience with a long speech. I would simply like to thank all those who have travelled with me on my journey, a quest that has one thing in common with the arts celebrated here: just when you think you have found what you are looking for, you realise you haven't. The grail is always right there in front of you, elusive. The moment we move towards it, it takes a step back. All that keeps us going is the hope that it is retreating more slowly, and we may one day grasp it. So each work of art is merely a draft of the next. I would first like to thank my father, who taught me everything I know, and my patrons, the Orsini family. And it is with a message from the Orsinis, and from myself of course, that I would like to conclude, borrowing some words from a friend. "*Ikh darf ayer medalye af kapores... in ayer tatns tatn arayn!*" Forgive my Yiddish pronunciation. Literally:

"Take this medal and put it in your father's father." Or in more modern, if less poetic, Italian: "You can take your medal and shove it up your arse!"'

There was a stunned silence. The shockwave was so intense that I think the earth shifted slightly from its axis. Then an indescribable howl of protests and catcalls. Maciste calmly stared at me in surprise, his arms folded.

'Mimo Vitaliani and the Orsini family salute you, friends! We will never again work for this murderous regime!'

I was stopped before I got through the door. Out of the corner of my eye, I saw two men drag a stunned Stefano towards the exit. Nobody hit me, but after that everything went black, no doubt because, for the first time in a long time, I had just blazed in the second before.

I t had been Viola's idea. When I had called her to apologise, to admit that she had been right all along and tell her that I intended to refuse the nomination to the Accademia, she cut short my telephonic self-flagellation.

'You want to redeem yourself, Mimo? Then you need to do something.'

Of all the great political or military coups in history, and I am including the battles of Thermopylae, Trafalgar, Austerlitz or Waterloo – depending on which side you are on – and the Appeal of 18 June in 1940, Viola's was perhaps the most brilliant, if only because it came not from a warrior or a charismatic leader, but from a young woman whose legs had never really healed. Viola, who was now reading every newspaper she could get her hands on, explained that, given the setbacks we had suffered in Africa, the Allies would soon land in Italy. At which time, it would not be a good idea to be a Fascist. She had tried to explain this to Stefano, but it was futile.

'He has been pickling himself in stupidity since he was a boy,' she grumbled. 'And with age, he's turned sour. He used to be a cucumber. Now he's a gherkin.'

Personally, I believed – and Viola could hardly fail to see it – that the gherkin had spent his whole life desperately trying to fill the gaping void left by the death of his elder brother, in whom the family had placed all their hopes. But the upshot was the same: someone would have to force Stefano's hand.

Viola had asked me to speak in the name of the Orsini family. Stefano was certain to be arrested, as was I. Francesco, on the other hand, was untouchable. Stefano would not rot in prison long – Francesco was extremely influential.

'But in your case, it will be very different, Mimo. The regime has used you. You have eaten at their table. They will not let you off so lightly. I can't force you.'

Soldiers are overgrown children, just a little more mortal. By February 1943, preparations were being made for the Allied invasion of Sicily known as Operation Husky. In July, the first wave of the invasion was launched under the name Operation Ladbroke. Everything, absolutely everything, that Viola predicted happened, and the Orsini family owed her their survival. September 1943 saw the launch of Operation Baytown, followed by Operation Slapstick and Operation

Avalanche. I couldn't help but wonder whether these people made up operational names every time they had to take a piss. The whole of southern Italy was occupied; Mussolini was deposed and imprisoned only to be liberated by the Nazis when they captured Rome.

The country was divided into three, and the reason these details have stuck in my memory is because in prison we had little to do but rehash them. Part of the liberated south was placed directly under Allied administration; a second part was entrusted to the provisional government based in Brindisi, under Allied supervision, with a view to preparing for the post-war period. The north fell under the Republic of Salò, Mussolini's latest idea, which was propped up by the Germans. At this point everyone took a well-earned rest.

The night I made my grand gesture, Stefano and I were both imprisoned in Regina Coeli, a former convent and Rome's largest detention centre. Regina Coeli – Queen of Heaven – a glorious name for a prison. The Orsini family were placed under house arrest by the Germans. Francesco remained in Rome and kept a low profile, all the while using his long fingers to tinker with the cogs of the future and turn them in his favour. As soon as Stefano was arrested, the Gambale family reappeared, like worms that slither from under a stone on the first days of spring. In a single night, the aqueduct was destroyed. Seeing the vast pools of water in the fields, blazing in the light of dawn, some people said that the orange trees were bleeding. Then the soil absorbed the water, grass grew over the ruins of the aqueduct, ivy crept over the pump, and that was that. The Gambale family did not dare do anything more, especially since, as Viola had predicted, Stefano was released just three months later. He returned to Pietra d'Alba having opportunistically become an ardent anti-Fascist.

'At first, it seemed like a good idea,' he told anyone who would listen. 'But later, all the horrors… In good conscience, I could not stay quiet. The Orsini family could not remain silent.'

For daring to bite the hand that had fed me, an example was made of me. I became Il Francese again, a foreign agent in the service of those who had always wanted to destroy the Italian nation. My sculptures – or at least all those that the government could lay their hands on – were destroyed or dismantled and sold on the sly who knows where. The Palazzo delle Poste in Palermo is no longer flanked by my fasces – only photographs remain. My studios in Rome and in Pietra d'Alba were looted and ransacked. Vittorio, Emanuele and my mother watched as a gang of thugs ravaged the space, pissing and throwing paint on the walls. Before my speech to the Accademia, I had made sure to pay each of my employees six months' salary, and I had stored the perfect black marble originally intended for *L'Uomo* in a safe place, since there would be no *New Man*. I had also entrusted Vittorio with a sum of money, in cash, that would allow me to live modestly for a few years after my release. Aside from that money, within a week of my imprisonment I had nothing. Twenty years of my career disappeared, something that might have made me question the wisdom of my decision, though I never did. I had chosen my route a long time ago, and on that route there was no turning back. If it led through a forest fire, I had to follow.

I received a prison sentence utterly disproportionate to my 'crime' – which was no more than a speech – but I was fortunate not to be maltreated while in Regina Coeli, protected as I was by Francesco, who was already planning his next move. When, in a reprisal for the via Rasella attack by partisans, the Nazis came to Regina Coeli and took two hundred prisoners and massacred them in the disused Ardeatine quarry, I was not among those chosen by Questore Pietro Caruso, chief of the Fascist police in Rome. Caruso had no reason to spare me, quite the contrary. But I later discovered that someone, somewhere, had a 'file' on him and that he was prepared to be accommodating to prevent its publication.

Between the four walls of my cell, I often thought about Bizzaro. I floated like an eagle on faraway roads. What country was he now trudging through, looking for a place where he could not be found, only to be found one day? He had been right. After the German invasion, conditions in the camps became brutal. The Risiera di San Sabba, known as Stalag 339, in Trieste, was as murderous as any concentration camp in occupied Poland. Prisoners were gassed using exhaust fumes from diesel engines. I had worked for these people. I had let their evil slide. And if I was better than all those who later whined and claimed that they had done nothing wrong, it was only because I did not whine and did not claim anything at all.

During my three years in prison, I received several visits from Pankratius Pfeiffer, a German priest of the Salvatorian order, nicknamed 'the Angel of Rome'. Pfeiffer had a crown of tousled white hair and wore the same round glasses as Pacelli and Francesco – one might almost think the Church had bought a job lot. He simply talked to me, but his voice could keep me warm for a week. Each time he left, he took with him a little more of my guilt, until one day I woke up and found that it was gone. There was still a residue, a little sediment at the bottom of a glass, but it no longer made my dreams swirl under blood-red skies. During those years, Pankratius negotiated the release of several prisoners and saved many Jews. Pope Pius XII would later be accused of not doing enough to save the Jews, of being too committed to the neutrality of the Vatican, but having lived amidst these tragedies, not far from the Holy See, I would argue that Pacelli worked actively, behind the scenes, to save as many people as he could. Few popes would have offered their own room at Castel Gandolfo to Jewish refugees. But Pacelli never spoke about it.

Not once did Viola visit me. I was grateful to her for that. Now I understood why she had kept me at a distance while in hospital. I will say no more about those years, because all prisons resemble each other. As do all their prisoners, guilty of the same crime: believing in a world that does not exist, and getting angry when they realise.

The *Vitaliani Pietà* was moved to the Sacra at an unknown date during the latter half of 1951. The Sacra was chosen precisely because it was isolated and had few if any visitors in those days – things have changed a lot since then, thinks Padre Vincenzo. Three layers of packing were used to protect the statue: a metal box enclosing two wooden crates. Despite the scandal – or perhaps because of it – the work was extraordinarily valuable, one of the few sculptures by Mimo Vitaliani to have survived the artist's almost preternatural ability to get himself into trouble.

The danger in transporting works of marble lies in the invisible micro-cracks that can shatter if the piece suffers any impact. In those days, works of art rarely travelled. And when they did, damage was not uncommon. A study was commissioned to assess the best way to protect the *Pietà*, and an American company, Koppers, supplied the prototype of a material called 'expandable polystyrene'. The same materials would be used to protect the other Michelangelo's *Pietà*, when it was sent to the New York World's Fair in 1964.

One day in 1951, the heavy door of an underground chamber was closed on Vitaliani's work, and its story ends there. All that followed was a series of increasingly strict security measures as rumours of its presence circulated. After the Laszlo Toth affair, a state-of-the-art alarm system was installed.

Padre Vincenzo puts away the last of the documents, replaces them in the safe and turns the key. The gears turn silently, activating cylinders and hinges. It once again looks like an antique wardrobe. Vincenzo hangs the key around his neck and flinches slightly as he turns towards the window. He hadn't noticed night drawing in. The office is glacial. Whenever he requests a proper heating system, he is invariably told that there is not enough money, which irritates him. Faith can warm the soul, but it has its limits.

Vincenzo switches off the light and descends the Staircase of the Dead. Within the thick walls of the abbey, there should be no noise, but he can still hear creaking, cracking, wheezing. Perhaps the dead are snoring. Vincenzo continues his descent, effortlessly finding his way through labyrinthine corridors, instinctively ducking his head to avoid a low arch, and enters the dying man's cell.

Four brothers are standing watching over Mimo Vitaliani. The doctor beckons him over, lifts the sculptor's eyelid from under the shock of white hair and flicks the beam of a pencil torch over his pupil – it does not contract.

'It won't be much longer now.'

'That's what you said this morning,' Vincenzo says a little more curtly than necessary.

He apologises with a shrug. Seeing that skin stretched taut over the facial bones, the slightly curled lips, those fitful breaths that chap and crack, he wishes it would end. If truth be told, Mimo Vitaliani is perhaps the closest thing he has ever had to a friend.

He turns to the monks and tells them he will keep vigil. 'Padre, from the way he is clinging to life, this could go on all night,' they protest, but he dismisses them with a smile. Mimo Vitaliani will leave when he leaves. Who knows what is going on under that slightly too large skull. Who knows if anything at all is going on.

Padre Vincenzo sits by the bed, takes the sculptor's burning hand and waits.

I was officially released at the end of April 1945. Mussolini had just been arrested, executed and his body hanged by its feet next to a petrol station in Milan, the very station where, a year earlier, the bodies of fifteen partisans massacred by Fascist troops had been publicly displayed. I was not released until a month later, since the country was in chaos and the paperwork took some time. Francesco was waiting outside the prison in a black limousine. His cassock was now adorned with red buttons; he wore a gold ring set with a sapphire on his right hand. Between Allied air raids, he had been elected cardinal. For a while, he put me up in one of the Vatican apartments, a studio that overlooked the roofs of a minor chapel and which, at noon, became a furnace as the sun was reflected off the zinc. Compared to my prison cell, it seemed immense. I had lost fifteen kilos. A few wits said that at least prison had its benefits.

Although the war was over, tensions in the country still ran high. The anti-Fascist purge was in full swing, and people were hunted down and summarily executed. Moderate anti-Fascists feared this civil war without a name might turn into a communist revolution. In order to address this, it was decided to give the people back their voice. No free elections had been held since 1921, so an election was set for 2 June 1946. A duly elected Constituent Assembly would take the reins of the country. Concurrently, there would be a referendum in which the Italian people would be asked to choose between a monarchy and a republic. Apathetically, I watched this tumult, dazzled by my zinc sun. Now that the dictatorship had fallen, I could stop playing politics for good. Or so I thought.

For many months, I lived like a recluse. The outside world seemed too big, too noisy. Little by little, old friends winkled me out. 'If this is how you are going to live, you should have stayed in prison,' said my Serbian princess, who had reinvented herself as a war photographer. The only thing worse than losing one's freedom is losing the taste for freedom. She dragged me to all the parties that mattered. And although I no longer enjoyed them, gradually I reacquired the taste, a scent of the new day, when dawn breaks and while the city sleeps. I was also surprised to discover that my star, which I thought had been extinguished, shone brighter than it ever had. I was the living embodiment of anti-Fascism. People asked my opinion on everything. But mostly, they asked if I had any space in my order book. I lied and said that it was full. I no longer felt the urge to sculpt.

When I had regained my strength, I went back to Pietra d'Alba, determined never to leave the village again. I arrived in March 1946, with the same waistline I had had thirty years earlier, but a head of grey hair. As he did every time I came home, Vittorio greeted me in the gravel courtyard outside the house. He was well into his forties but had not put back on the weight he lost after Anna left him. On the other hand, he was almost completely bald – which rather suited him. At seventy-three, my mother was still going strong, although she tired quickly. We did not talk much.

My friend had had the studio completely renovated. There was not the slightest trace of the barbarities inflicted on it. The windows had been changed, the walls were covered in fresh whitewash and the graffitied 'Bolshevik' and 'Jew Lover' had been obliterated.

I was exhausted by the journey. I would have to go visit the Orsini family, say hello to Emanuele, the mother of the twins, Dom Anselmo – but all that could wait. I dreamed of nothing but my bed. But news of my return had preceded me and spread like wildfire. Because that night, as I leaned out of the window, as I have to do to close the shutters with my short arms, I saw a red light glowing at the Villa Orsini. A warm, welcoming light I had not seen for twenty years, and one that I had ignored the last time it was lit.

'I'll be right there,' I whispered.

In the hollow trunk was a torn scrap of paper with a single scrawled sentence: *Waiting for you.*

I took the path to the cemetery, a little less sprightly than before. Though I had endlessly paced my cell, done my best to ward off inactivity and followed the advice of my fellow inmates, it would take months for me to regain my agility – or what remained of it at forty-two.

By force of habit – I remember thinking this word, *habit*, for I hadn't taken this path in what seemed like an eternity – I was first to arrive. It was a balmy evening; spring was approaching. It was a night of secret joys and pranks and lights that were turned off later. Five minutes after me, she appeared. I cannot describe the feeling that swept over me. The woman who stepped out of the forest was not the girl whose dreams of flight had been shattered at the foot of a fir tree, nor *avoccato* Campana's dutiful wife, nor the perfect little marchesa.

It was *Viola.*

I could tell by the way she walked, by the smirk that said she knew more than I, by the way her playful fingers were in constant movement, just waiting for the opportunity to point accusingly at someone or joyfully at the future. She came over to me and laid a gloved hand against my cheek. I gazed at her for a long time. A few threads of white were woven into her raven hair. There were tiny wrinkles I had never noticed in the corners of her eyes. Her cheekbones were more prominent, her chin more slender. We delayed uttering our first words, not knowing whether they would be banal or grandiose, simply so that we might savour them later. She slid her hand down my arm and clasped mine, and led me into the cemetery. I knew where we were going. Without a word, we lay down on the grave of Tommaso Baldi, and I swear I heard the little flautist sigh with relief.

'I met Bartolomeo Pagano,' I said.

'What's he like?'

'Tall.'

Overhead, the Milky Way flowed lazily. When you grow up, everything feels smaller except cemeteries. The western part, once wasteland, was now littered with new graves. The cypress trees had grown and, in our upside-down world, looked like huge green carrots planted in a field of stars.

'I still have trouble with time,' murmured Viola.

'What has time ever done to you? You're still as beautiful as ever.'

Viola didn't think to thank me. Not that she was indifferent to flattery, but she did not care about being beautiful.

But she was, or rather, she gave the impression of being beautiful. It was the same trick she used for changing into a bear – drawing the eye to where the illusionist wants it to be. I had been staring so intently at the she-bear I hadn't noticed it wasn't wearing the same dress. If you looked at Viola, all you saw were her eyes, and you forgot the long face inherited from her father and her lips that were a little too thin, and thought: *My God, she's beautiful!*

'Yesterday,' she said after a silence, 'I kissed my brother Virgilio, a handsome man in uniform heading off to war. He smelled of soap and ambergris. Tonight, my brother is a skeleton in a uniform that smells of mouldering dust. Yesterday was twenty-five years ago. Time does not pass at the same speed everywhere. Einstein is right.'

'You should tell him; it would make him happy.'

'Do you think so?' said Viola, in all seriousness.

I could not stop myself laughing, and for a minute she sulked, then got to her feet, dusting down her dress, which was covered in twigs and petals. 'Why don't you come to dinner tomorrow?'

'Oh, no,' I protested. 'What's going to happen this time?'

'Nothing is going to happen, Mimo. It's just dinner.'

'It's never *just* dinner with your family.'

'Don't be ridiculous. Will you walk me back to the villa? The roads are not very safe these days.'

While we walked, Viola brought me up to date with the

latest news. She had not been exaggerating when she said that the roads weren't safe, and had she told me earlier, I would have been less cavalier. Night was the preserve of marauding troops of ravenous creatures, self-proclaimed partisans hunting Fascists. In fact, most were small-time gangsters exploiting the power vacuum before the new elections to loot and pillage. It was rumoured that the Gambale family were in league with some of them. They were happy to fell or burn a few Orsini orange trees from time to time, while loudly insisting it was the work of roving gangsters. Stefano, leading a troop of men who enjoyed a little bare-knuckle fighting, would lurk in the Gambale valley and beat up members of the family, then claim that his men were not to blame, they had simply mistaken a Gambale for a robber.

Even in the darkness, I could see the fields had lost much of their splendour since the aqueduct was destroyed. True, they were neat and cultivated, a far cry from the neglect that had followed the droughts of the 1920s. But production was declining. Viola predicted a fall in the price of oranges, which, if she was right, would make matters worse. And Viola was always right.

As we parted, she turned to me. '*Sit felix occursus, optime Leo, nam totos tres annos te non vidi.* Goodnight, Mimo. I love the expression on your face when you don't understand what I'm saying.'

She walked on towards the villa, her shawl wrapped tightly around her shoulders, a sublime, heartbreaking figure limping through the January night.

'Viola!'

'Hmm?'

'*Well met, dear Lion, for I have not seen you these three years past.* You forced me to read that book by Erasmus where the lion and the bear have a conversation. You got it into your head that you were going to teach me Latin.'

Viola looked at me in surprise. 'Really? I don't remember…'

She let out that old laugh I remembered, hurled it at the moon, before disappearing through the postern door. Secretly delighted to be getting old, stiff and grey-haired and finally, finally, allowed to *forget* something.

When I came down to the kitchen the following morning, I was greeted by a young, bearded man in his twenties who was like Hercules. He stared at me kindly and laughed when I said nothing.

'It's me, Uncle Mimo. It's Zozo!'

It had only been five or six years since I last saw Vittorio and Anna's son, but the transformation from boy to man was spectacular. And it had also happened to me. This was why I was shocked to find my first grey hair. Change is gradual; it slyly whispers into your ear that nothing will change until it is too late.

Zozo was now helping his father in the workshop. He had come back from Genoa during the night, having been to visit his mother, whom he closely resembled. The same rounded cheeks, the same joyful glint in the eyes, though Anna's joy had faded.

I made my round of visits, ending with Dom Anselmo. Hale and hearty though he was over seventy, but where was the fiery, vaguely intimidating priest I had met when I first arrived? His skin was speckled with liver spots and his hands shook a little. I had blinked, and everyone had grown old.

'I am like this poor church,' he said, looking up at the peeling frescoes of the cupola. 'Full of draughts.'

That night, I went to the Villa Orsini for dinner. Only the Marchese, the Marchesa, Stefano, Viola and I were in attendance. The Marchese was the only one who had not changed since the day he first sat in a bath chair, never to get up, and uttered his last intelligible words: '*He's coming, he's coming.*' The startling features, the elongated head still crowned with a shock of hair, had weathered the passing years. Only his eyes were empty and rarely lit up. We talked about politics, about women's suffrage – 'What next?' sneered Stefano. 'Before you know it, we'll be letting horses vote!' – and the fact that one of the Gambale sons was standing in the forthcoming elections. He was roundly rebuked by the Marchesa in a surprising display of liberalism. While she could not imagine herself voting because, like most women, she understood nothing about politics, she was not opposed to the idea of some educated women voting. After all, a woman was no more stupid than a man.

'Especially if the man is you,' said Viola with a broad grin.

Stefano muttered something under his breath and drowned his irritation with a glass of wine. The Gambales were then cursed as an eternal obstacle to the development of the citrus groves.

I genuinely believed that this dinner would unfold without any trouble, that my life would finally be banal. But I had forgotten that the dining table, at the Villa Orsini as anywhere in Italy, from Sicilian palaces to the hovels of Genoa, was more than just a table: it was a stage. Tragedy was played out as farce. The more serious the subject, the more ridiculous it was.

Just before dessert, Viola announced: 'I will be standing in the elections. If elected, I will be your deputy at the Constituent Assembly.'

Stefano choked on the dessert wine that accompanied his second slice of *sacripantina*, tried to compose himself, flushed deep vermilion and pounded his fist on his chest. 'Is this a joke?'

'According to Decree No. 74/1946, I have the right to stand for election, and I intend to do so.'

It was an epic argument. The Marchesa, running low on liberalism, accused her daughter of having lost her mind. Her blue blood exempted her from having to endure the humiliation or – worse still – the vulgarity of an election.

Stefano choked, unable to understand how a woman, still less his sister, could aspire to public office. 'It's unthinkable! You have no political experience whatsoever.'

'How old are you?' said Viola calmly.

'How old? Forty-eight. What has my age got to do with anything?'

'In forty-eight years, you have lived through two world wars, both of them provoked and fought by the finest men in politics. So if that is what you mean by experience, forgive me for wanting to try a different approach.'

The shouting carried on. The Marchesa raised her voice, as did Stefano. Amid the deafening commotion, Viola sat smiling and unruffled, with that serene expression of the Virgin as painted by Fra Angelico. Henceforth, no storm would alter the course of her destiny. She had invited me to come tonight so that I would understand.

The next day, we were on the road. I had spent three years of my life living in slow motion. Suddenly the walls had crumbled, the stinging wind brought tears to my eyes, everything was moving so fast. Stefano had calmed down a little when I pointed out that his sister's candidacy would irritate the Gambales, who until now had faced no opposition. 'Oh, it's a phase – she'll get over it,' he said finally and went outside for a smoke.

Vittorio's son Zozo was our driver. We criss-crossed the region, knocking on every door. I must confess that, when Viola first announced her candidature, I had shared Stefano's scepticism. Or perhaps a milder version of it, since I knew his sister was capable of anything. I campaigned with her out of a sense of friendship, reminding myself that simply *wanting* to fly was not enough.

A month later, I knew that she would vin. Viola, who had never been involved in politics, was teaching the country a lesson. The local residents could scarcely believe their ears. Here was someone who talked about *them*, about *their* children. And, more astonishingly, about the future, that mysterious thing that was the preserve of the rich. About the possibility of doing more than eking out a life between the cradle and the grave, of moving to the city, getting an education. Of travelling. Initially, when we knocked on doors, we were greeted by dubious faces; by the time it came for us to leave, they almost refused to let us go. The son of the Gambales, whose campaign consisted of little more than getting up in the morning and scratching his balls, became angry. He had never had any political ambitions and had put his name forward only because some well-placed people had asked him to, since the region was short of candidates. But he had his pride, and that had suffered a blow when he realised that he risked being defeated. The raids by so-called partisans became more violent. A couple on their way to Lombardy were robbed and the woman assaulted. The police even bothered to show up, only to conclude that the culprits were nowhere to be found.

Often, at the end of the day, Viola and I would exchange a simple glance. We thought our lives had come to an end one evening in November 1920, when she jumped off a roof. But Viola's dreams, like the dreamer, were resilient.

'Tramontane, sirocco, libeccio, ponente, mistral. That's not hard, is it?' said Viola. 'There are only five winds here.'

'Tramontane, sirocco, libeccio... ponente, mistral.'

'Again.'

'Tramontane, sirocco, libeccio, ponente and mistral.'

All this because I was foolish enough to say: 'It's windy.' Viola had rapped me on the shoulder.

'Words have meaning, Mimo. To name something is to understand it. "It's windy" is meaningless. Are we talking about a wind that kills? A wind that sows? A wind that freezes plants or warms them? And what kind of deputy would I be if words had no meaning? I would be no different from the others.'

'All right, all right, I get it.'

'One last time, then.'

'Tramontane, sirocco, libeccio, ponente and mistral.'

I willingly indulged Viola's whims, if only to keep myself

busy while we were on the road. That day, Zozo was driving us to a village in the neighbouring Gambale valley. A man had come to see Viola that morning, cap in hand and decidedly awkward. It had taken half an hour before he dared speak, and then only after he had been relaxed by a little grappa. He had come to see her because people were saying she would be elected to represent the region, down in Rome, and the thing was, there was talk in the valley about building a motorway that would cut across his fields, and he wanted nothing to do with this motorway. An hour later, we were heading to his village.

Viola stood in the little square, while the old man rounded up a number of the villagers with the skill of a sheepdog. She pledged her support, promised that the motorway would not cut through their valley, then stayed a while to shake hands. On the way back, we stopped off in every village and hamlet, including the one where the Gambales lived. The atmosphere became tense when a man who had been watching the debate, leaning on a pitchfork, snarled: 'The motorway means progress! You're opposed to progress, aren't you?'

Viola calmed the commotion with a wave. 'A motorway is the opposite of progress. Yes, everything will go faster. But everything will go faster *elsewhere*. The villages in this valley will be like rocks thrown off a bridge. No one will stop here any more.'

This argument hit home, and Pitchfork left grumbling. When I went to bed that night, I started a habit, one that I have never given up – a superstitious habit perhaps. Before sinking into darkness and oblivion, I repeated *tramontane, sirocco, libeccio, ponente and mistral.*

They've killed Emanuele! They've killed Emanuele!

It was noon. We were on our way back from Viola's official investiture in Genoa. This banal journey had given her ten new ideas, including widening the road at several strategic points and a daily bus route linking Genoa, Savona and Pietra d'Alba. Presently, anyone who wanted to go there had to borrow a car, and it was not unusual to waste an hour stuck behind a donkey cart.

They've killed Emanuele! They've killed Emanuele!

Just before we reached the village, a car came speeding past in the opposite direction. In the back seat, a couple of people were hunched over what looked like a sprawling figure. Hardly had we reached the village square when the twins' mother almost threw herself in front of the car. Gaunt and dishevelled, she looked like a madwoman.

She stepped around the car and pounded on the window. 'They've killed Emanuele! They've killed my son!'

Pietra d'Alba is home to a unique species of small, dense truffle that grows late in the season and has an aroma so intense people say you don't need a dog to find them. A local farmer had been foraging for truffles near the Hanged Man's Oak when he heard screams. When it was silent once again and he felt able to leave the cover of the forest, he found Emanuele swinging from the largest branch, wearing a hussar's uniform. A sign around his neck read *Facist*, with a missing *s*. The so-called partisans who had hung him there had seen his uniform and, without a second thought, had arrested, tried and summarily executed him. Emanuele had launched into a panicked babble in his defence, but could not explain to the kangaroo court that the uniform was more than a century old and that they couldn't hang him because he hadn't finished delivering today's mail.

They've killed my son! They've killed my son!

But Emanuele was not just Emanuele. He was an *idea*. An incongruity, a little like me, an abnormality. Or perhaps the expression of a normality yet to come, the harbinger of a world in which people like him would have a voice and would harm others only by hugging them too hard. And it is a well-known fact that you cannot kill an idea. So they had not killed Emanuele.

Perhaps because, when the umbilical cord had strangled him during his difficult birth, he had learned to make do with a few atoms of oxygen, perhaps because the forager had found him very quickly after the crime and cut him down, Emanuele had survived. He came back from the hospital in Genoa a week later, smiling. Looking a little more bewildered, but the same. Only Vittorio reported a change – now even he found his brother difficult to understand.

No one called the police. This time, the men of the village took up arms. They scoured the forest for ten days and finally, at sunset, came across a troop of four starving men – starving and heavily armed – who claimed they were just passing through. No, they had heard nothing about the tragedy. They all offered their sympathy and made the sign of the cross. But one of them was wearing a highly ornate medal, the Order of the Iron Crown that Emanuele always wore with his hussar's uniform. The man said he had found it on the forest path. The sound of gunshots echoed around the mountains. The village men came back with the medal and offered no explanation. The medal was inscribed with the motto *Dio me la diede, guai chi la tocca* – God gave this to me; woe betide he who touches it. Emanuele cried when he got it back, though he was still distraught that his postbag hadn't been found. His assailants had dumped it in the forest when they realised it held nothing of value.

On the Sunday following the medal's return, Dom Anselmo took to the pulpit. He railed against the violence that was poisoning the world and had now infected Pietra d'Alba. He rebuked the villagers who had taken the law into their own hands, far from the eyes of man and those of God. There was a volley of protests, then others began to protest against the protestors, and all the while the priest carried on, trying to drown out the clamour. Finally, Viola rose to her feet and there was silence. She did not believe in God any more than she ever had, but she attended mass with her parents to support her father.

'Dom Anselmo is right,' she said firmly. 'If these murdered men were innocent, this was a crime.'

'Even if they weren't the ones who tried to kill Emanuele, they must have been guilty of something!' came a shout that was greeted by a scattering of applause.

From his pulpit, Dom Anselmo tried to restore order. Viola told me about it later, because I wasn't there.

'If they were guilty,' she replied, 'then we have institutions to try and punish them. It has been two thousand years since we lived in the Old Testament. And it has been a year since we lived in a dictatorship.'

A number of heads were bowed in contrition, but the dispute raged on. Dom Anselmo looked glum; he was out of his depth, and he felt somewhat annoyed by Viola's implicit comparison between the Old Testament and a dictatorship.

Then it happened. There was a loud snap that echoed around the church and silenced the congregation. By the time they looked up to see that the dome of San Pietro delle Lacrime had cracked, one of the stones had come loose. It plummeted into the transept crossing, smashing the pietà I had spent so much time studying. When they recovered from the shock, the parishioners ran out screaming. Fortunately, no one was hurt by the falling stone.

In an instant, Dom Anselmo recaptured all his youthful passion. He emerged from the church covered in dust, his lip curled, brandishing his fist. With the fervour of Savonarola excoriating Florence for its dissolute morals, he told the stunned villagers that God had sent them a sign, a sign of His wrath. Weary of the wars and crimes of men, the Lord had made this known by striking down His house. The time had come to atone. This time, no one dared protest.

Dom Anselmo blinked as though waking from a trance and stared in mild astonishment at these people who, for the first time in his fifty years as a priest, were really listening to him.

No one knew how news of the incident spread, but two world wars, in addition to slaughtering millions of men, had destroyed the slowness of the world. The following day, reporters arrived from Genoa. The day after, they came from Milan, and then from Rome. Francesco came home at once.

The Vatican briefly considered launching an investigation, in case this was indeed a miracle, but then they dug up the various petitions for funds sent by Dom Anselmo (all rejected) so that the church could be buttressed because there had been significant subsidence. The miracle was purely geological, but that did not rule out the possibility that this was a sign. A sign that, in the post-war era, a public relations exercise might not be a bad idea. Following a few discreet telephone calls, a line of credit was opened in the name of the parish of San Pietro delle Lacrime with the Istituto per le Opere di Religione, the Vatican bank.

Three days after the incident, Cardinal Francesco Orsini gathered with reporters beneath the cupola, riven by a crack almost a centimetre wide. The poor pietà had been destroyed.

'My friends, I come here as a man, as a priest and as a child of Pietra d'Alba. The Lord has sent us a sign. But the Almighty does not threaten. Ours is not a wrathful God. This is a sign calling for reconciliation. I therefore announce that, at the request of His Holiness Pope Pius XII, the Vatican will pay for the repairs to the cupola and all necessary work. I would also like to announce that we have commissioned Michelangelo Vitaliani, the sculptor who did so much for our family and for our country in opposing Fascist tyranny, to the point of sacrificing his own freedom, to create a new pietà for our church.'

I was there in the crowd, and I could do nothing to hide my

surprise. Viola stamped on my foot and signalled for me to keep my mouth shut. People crowded round to congratulate me. Needless to say, Francesco had not asked me anything, nor had I agreed to anything, but such details mattered little to villagers eager for reconciliation. I managed to avoid the reporters, who deduced from this that I was already in the midst of a feverish creativity and could not be disturbed. An hour later, I stumbled into the sacristy where Viola, the Orsini brothers and Dom Anselmo were waiting. From the village square came whoops of joy and the sound of shots being fired into the air.

'Reconciliation' was the only word on the villagers' lips. 'Reconciliation!' They hugged each other. After the years they had endured, it was difficult to blame them. But that did not stop me laying into Francesco.

'Don't you think you might have asked my opinion?'

'I'm sorry. I assumed you would be happy to contribute to the rebirth of this church.'

'This church you spent years ignoring because it didn't serve your ambitions?'

'Come on, Mimo, this is your anger talking. Or perhaps fatigue, because I can see no reason why you should be angry.'

'I'm angry because I am not a monkey. I don't sculpt to order.'

'Since we're talking about ambition, I think you'll find you've sculpted a lot of pieces to order in recent years.'

Dom Anselmo raised his hands and laid them on our shoulders. And we both bowed our heads, Francesco the cardinal and Mimo the artist, like two naughty boys caught red-handed.

'Come, brothers, we are all working towards the same thing. Let us forget who did or did not do what. Reconciliation means letting go of the past and looking to the future. Mimo, you were so critical of that pietà when you were a boy, remember? You said her arms were too long or something. Who better than you, a local boy, an artist of extraordinary talent, to offer us another?'

'You'll be well paid,' added Stefano, raising an eyebrow. 'They're loaded at the Istituto.'

'I'm sure that Mimo would not do this simply for the money,' said Francesco. 'Though you will be handsomely paid for your talent.'

'I think I have helped the Orsini family enough. Now we're even. Leave me in peace.' I turned to leave.

'Mimo.'

Viola had taken a step forward. She turned towards the priest. 'Dom Anselmo, could you give us a moment?'

'Of course.'

The priest left the sacristy, *his* sacristy, leaving me to the tender mercies of the Orsini siblings.

Viola looked at her brothers. 'Stop playing innocent patrons of the arts. All you care about is the family's glory.

And perhaps, Francesco, even the glory of your patron, Pius XII. So, yes, Mimo, you are right, my brothers are chiefly thinking of their own interests. But I am also asking you to accept this commission. If I am to change things, I first need to be elected. People know that the two of us are close. If you accept, I will benefit. For the first time in my entire life, what profits the Orsini family will profit me too.'

The two brothers took no offence at Viola's depiction. Stefano was far too surprised by her logic and Francesco, who knew perfectly well that his sister could reason as well as he did, was just pleased to know that they had won, because I could not refuse Viola anything.

'Very well,' I replied. 'I'll do your pietà.'

'You'll need stone,' said Francesco. 'A first-class block of marble. We can go to—'

'I already have the stone.'

They left in high spirits, Stefano for the villa, Francesco for Rome, while Viola joined the villagers still lingering in the square. A few minutes later, Dom Anselmo reappeared and found me sitting on a wooden chest with my head in my hands.

'Monsignor Orsini told me the good news. Thank you, Mimo.' Then he frowned. 'You don't look well.'

'I'm fine, Dom Anselmo, everything is fine.'

How could I tell him that I had gone blind?

I arrived in Florence by train two days later at 5.56 p.m. Almost exactly the same time I arrived on the day that Zio sold me. It wasn't winter this time, but spring, and my impression as I left the railway station and got off the train was very different. The city was captivating yet coy, reluctant to surrender herself even as she gave subtle clues – a sunset, a door ajar – encouraging the traveller to slip into her streets. Rome was a friend. Florence was my lover.

Metti was waiting for me at the station. Silently, we walked the same route we had long ago. In a corner of his studio, he pulled away a tarpaulin and released the block of Carrara marble I had entrusted to him, the one I had bought for *The New Man*. He had agreed to hide it just before I gave my speech to the Accademia.

I pressed my hand against it. The stone spoke to me. It was uniquely beautiful and dense. My instinct told me that it was perfect, that there were no hidden cracks that might ruin the work of the sculptor. A sculptor who would not be me. Because no matter how long I looked at it, I could see nothing. Or rather, I could see only the past, the dozens of statues I had already sculpted.

'You're blind, aren't you?' I heard Metti say softly behind me.

I kept my hand on the block, I didn't turn. 'I am.'

'This is what happened to me when I came back from the first war. I could have sculpted with one arm, I could have found a way, a different way of working. But I could no longer see anything. Just blocks of stone with nothing inside.'

'For the past decade all I have seen are blocks of stone with nothing inside. But that did not stop me from sculpting.'

'But you will not sculpt this pietà.'

'No. I have lied enough.'

'You will never sculpt again, will you?'

Finally, I turned around. And I uttered this word that frightened me less than I had thought it would.

'No.'

'Then what do you plan do about the pietà? The newspapers are already calling it the *Pietà Orsini*.'

'I'll ask Jacopo to do it, discreetly.'

'Jacopo?'

'My former assistant. He is working at a studio in Turin now, but I know he will accept. By the time he's finished, a year from now, no one will care who sculpted it. Can he come here and work in your studio?'

'No problem.'

With my left hand, I took his and shook it. 'Thank you. Goodbye, maestro.'

'Goodbye, Mimo.'

I spent a week in Florence, calling Francesco to tell him that I was preparing the block. If he sent someone to check –

and he might – they would confirm what I had said. Actually, the marble block had been prepared by my assistants in Rome when I first bought it. The rough edges had been polished away and the broad strokes of a triangular form sketched out. It would suit the pietà perfectly.

Before taking the train back to Pietra d'Alba, I stopped by the fairground. There was no longer a circus, only a half-completed eight-storey building, a concrete parallelepiped with tiny windows, like so many evil eyes.

There was only a month left before the elections. The summary justice meted out by the village men had had one positive effect: raids of marauders had stopped and the roads were safe again. Perhaps the men they had killed were guilty. Or perhaps this brutal act, unexpected in such bucolic surroundings, unexpected even by the men who had done it, had served to deter others.

Viola made the most of this to travel the length and breadth of her constituency. As summer approached, the days became long and languid. From these soft, citrus-scented nights, an explosion of *bambini* would be born.

I said nothing to Viola about my blindness. I said I would begin sculpting after the elections. I would tell her later; I knew she would understand. The road was calling us, endless and joyful. We would often sleep curled up next to each other in the back of the car, trusting Zozo's vigilance. We would leave at dawn and come back late at night. So, that week in May, we did not see the citrus groves become covered in dust from the plateau. A dust that was not whipped up by any wind – tramontane, sirocco, libeccio, ponente or mistral – but by the Fiat 2800 that came and went several times from the Villa Orsini.

E ver since the dome of San Pietro delle Lacrime had cracked, the Marchese hadn't been the same. Whenever he was brought to mass on Sundays, he would squirm in his bath chair, uttering long cries as he reached out his good arm towards the damaged fresco of the cupola, where the crack ran right between heaven and hell. What did he see there? The journey that lay ahead for him? Or the years of his youth, the undamaged cupola and fresco he had stared at so many times, the undamaged cupola and fresco beneath which he had dozed through countless masses, married his Marchesa, baptised his children, buried his eldest child? Or did he see this cupola as it was now, this fresco marred by a broad, black fissure?

The repairs had already begun. Experts were confident that the restoration would be virtually undetectable. A scaffold filled the transept, and mass was temporarily celebrated in a side chapel that was filled to overflowing. After the Marchese had interrupted several masses with his wailings, it was decided not to bring him to church. Dom Anselmo would come and give him communion every Sunday at the Villa Orsini.

A fortnight before the elections, Viola's mood suddenly changed. I had seen her plunge into troubled waters often enough to be concerned. She claimed that everything was fine, but I saw her eyes glaze over as she stared out the window as we drove. She no longer talked. And yet, when she was among what she called her 'future constituents', she was her old self again, cheerful and attentive. When she shook someone's hand, she found her voice. Only to slip back into melancholy as we drove home. One morning, as I went to fetch her, I saw her leaning on her cane. I pretended I had forgotten something and went back into the villa to confide my concerns to Stefano.

He simply shrugged. 'Probably that time of the month, if you know what I mean.'

As the elections drew nearer, we frequently came back to the car after knocking on doors in a village to find eggs had been thrown at the windscreen or a tyre had been slashed. Zozo was a tower of strength and always got us back on the road. Pietra d'Alba seemed to hold its breath in anticipation. On the roadsides and in the fields, the upheavals had abated. Labourers leaned on their pitchforks and watched us pass.

Perhaps they were wondering whether they preferred a king – Umberto had now succeeded his father, Vittorio Emanuele – to a republic, since the referendum would take place the same day.

Back at the studio, Vittorio told me that he was planning to spend two weeks in Genoa and would come back only to vote before going back down to the city. He and Anna had taken up the habit of going for long walks together, when seeing each other to drop off the children who were no longer children. When it was time to go their separate ways, there was always a brief awkward moment, a 'what if' that went unspoken. The purported reason for Vittorio's trip to Genoa was to get my mother and his (now firm friends) out of Pietra d'Alba for a while. His half-confessed aim was to win Anna back. Emanuele tagged along on this touristic and sentimental journey. He was afraid of being alone, because almost every night he dreamed of a gang of faceless men trying to hang him. A young man from the village would deliver the mail in his absence.

My mother wept when she left, shedding a few more violet tears, just as she had when she put me on a train in 1916. I had to remind her that she was only leaving for a fortnight and would only be an hour's drive away, but in Italy every journey is potentially legendary. Vittorio dropped me off in front of the church on the way, since I had promised Dom Anselmo that I would do a small repair to a sculpture in the portal that didn't need to be removed. Viola had stopped travelling anyway. There was only a week left before the elections. The die was cast.

I walked back to the studio. It was one of those wonderful spring evenings when the air smells of wisteria and jasmine, even when there is no wisteria or jasmine nearby. I had only just left the village and was heading down towards the plateau when a car pulled up beside me. The back door opened to reveal Francesco.

'Get in.'

'I thought you were in Rome.'

'Get in, Mimo.'

I did as I was told, convinced that he had seen through my charade. That he knew that I would not be sculpting his pietà, that I had decided to have someone else do it. But on the drive back to the villa he said nothing, he simply stared out of the window. His chauffeur dropped us off outside the gates of the Villa Orsini. Another car, a Fiat 2800, was parked there, bathed in the crimson twilight. Francesco put on his skullcap and led me into the dining room.

I stopped in the doorway, dumbstruck.

There were several people sitting at the table, which had not been laid for dinner: the Marchese, the Marchesa, Stefano and, facing them, old man Gambale sitting between his two sons. Francesco sat next to his brother and nodded to a seat at the end of the table.

'How is our pietà coming along?' he asked politely.

'It's coming along.'

Warily I sat down and stared at them in silence. The room smelled of beeswax mingled with a whiff of sweat coming from the Gambales, who had spent the day in their fields. From time to time, the Marchesa brought a handkerchief to her nose. But there was another, more acrid scent, the smell of the final act.

'We have asked you here,' Francesco said finally, 'to share some important news. The Orsini and the Gambale families are finally reconciled. It is a powerful symbol at the dawn of a new era.'

The Gambales nodded, with the economy of gesture and emotion typical of mountain men.

'Congratulations. I am very happy for you all, though I have never really understood what the feud was about.'

There was a long, slightly embarrassed silence, and then old father Gambale said in a gravelly voice: 'Whatever the reasons, I'm sure they were good.'

'The Gambale family has graciously agreed to cede us the land that separates our fields from our lake. So not only will we be able to rebuild the aqueduct and irrigate the citrus groves, but we can use half of the land to grow all-season lemon trees and late Valencia oranges, thereby increasing production by sixty per cent. On the other half, we will plant bergamot, which opens up the highly lucrative perfume market.'

'And in exchange?' I said.

'In exchange,' said Stefano, leaning forward, 'Viola will withdraw from the election.'

I got to my feet. Francesco glared at his brother, then made a gesture of appeasement. I sat down again, breathing heavily.

'There is a problem, Mimo. Now Orazio,' he nodded towards the elder Gambale son, 'is standing for election to the Constituent Assembly. He's doing so because a consortium of... shall we say, investors... is relying on him to support the projected motorway in the neighbouring valley.'

'And Viola is opposed to it,' I muttered. 'And Viola will win.'

Orazio growled and scratched his bearded cheek. He had the face of a thug – which he was – but his beady eyes glittered with intelligence.

'Viola will not win, because she will withdraw in favour of Orazio,' Francesco corrected me. 'Both our families will emerge stronger from this agreement.'

'What does Viola think?'

Stefano laughed and his brother sighed. 'You know what Viola is like. We had this discussion with her a week ago. She's adamant. You're our only chance of changing her mind.'

'Me? Why would I want to change her mind?'

There were a few surreptitious glances. Stefano opened his mouth to speak, but Francesco got in first. I think I already knew what he was going to say.

'Because the investors in question are people you do not want to cross. These are troubled but exciting times. The world is changing. No one can halt progress. We have to adapt to those changes.'

'Wait a minute, are you saying what I think you're saying?'

'There have been threats,' Francesco admitted.

For the first time, Orazio spoke. 'Not just threats. If your sister is elected…'

He traced a finger across his throat. There was a shocked silence, and even he seemed embarrassed.

'I need you to know that we have nothing to do with this,' said old father Gambale. 'We only agreed that Orazio would stand in exchange for a generous investment in our business. It is hardly our fault that Rome has suddenly decided that women can go into politics and that your sister has put herself forward. We wish her no ill, and we would never hurt her. We have a code. But these men…' He shook his head.

I was not completely naïve. I knew that the enforced unification of a country barely eighty years old would not come without its share of frustrations. And that illicit networks would spring up to exploit them. That the war and its repercussions offered them ample opportunity to further enrich themselves.

'So Campana was right, then. You really are a bunch of bastards.'

'This is an unfair trial. We love our sister and we will protect her. It is a delicate and complicated situation, but one that has a simple solution.'

I laughed. 'I'm sure that you've been planning this, in one form or another, since you were eight years old. Tell me something, Francesco, do you even believe in God?'

Behind his round glasses, Francesco looked away. Not out of cowardice, but because he was already looking further ahead than any of us. 'I believe in the Church, which amounts to the same thing. Unlike regimes and tyrants, the Church does not pass.'

'Because no one has ever come back to say whether it keeps its promises. You know something? I've had more than enough of your deranged family.'

Then, because in the thirty years I had known the Orsinis, I had learned a thing or two about turning a situation to my advantage, I said: 'I'm not sculpting your pietà. Find someone else.'

And because Francesco, in the thirty years he had known Mimo Vitaliani, had come to understand me, he simply said: 'You will find Viola in her room.'

The door was open. She was sitting at her desk, engrossed in a book, which she closed when she saw me. She was wearing a pair of oval horn-rimmed glasses that I had never seen before.

'I didn't know you needed glasses to read,' I said as I picked them up.

Viola said nothing, just stared at me curiously. I rested her glasses on the cover of the book, a leather book embossed with gold letters from of the family library. *An Essay Concerning Humane Understanding*, by John Locke. The only light in the room was the lamp by which she had been reading. Darkness softly crept over the walls, feeding on green, on paper flowers, fringes and tassels, a world of frills that was utterly unlike Viola and had not changed since I first smashed through the window of this room.

'I wondered when they would send you,' she said softly.

'Viola, I know what you're going to say—'

'If you know, let's not waste time. Go downstairs and tell them that you failed.'

She reopened her book.

'You don't understand. They will kill you. Or hurt you enough to make you give up. There is a lot of money at stake. Look, there might be another solution. You could still stand, but let them build their bloody motorway.'

Viola stared at me, she raised an eyebrow.

I got angry. 'I can't stay here to see that. I couldn't bear it. You have no idea what these men are capable of.'

She continued to stare at me in silence.

I angrily kicked a footstool and it rolled all the way to the bed. 'Jesus, can't you just be normal? Just normal for once in your life?'

A flicker of anger flashed across her face and quickly gave way to wrinkles of sadness.

'I'm sorry. I didn't mean to say that.'

'No, Mimo, it's true. My whole life, I have needed you in order to be normal. You're my centre of gravity, which is why you're not always funny. But there is something abnormal about me that even you can never cure. It is this: I am a woman and I don't give a damn.'

She was slipping away from me, I could feel it, she had always slipped away from me. I grabbed her hand and tried to hold on.

'Let's leave, Viola. I have had enough of this violence.'

'Leaving won't change anything. The worst form of violence is habit. The habit that means an intelligent woman like me – and I believe I am intelligent – is not allowed to decide for herself. Hearing them tell me this year after year, I started to think that perhaps they knew something I didn't, that they had a secret. The only secret is that they know nothing. This is the secret that my brothers and the Gambales and all the others are trying to protect.'

She was panting slightly, her cheeks were flushed, as though she had prepared her arguments – which she probably had.

'And if they kill you, what good will that do?'

'No one can hurt me any more. I have suffered everything. And do you know who hurt me the most? Myself. By trying to play their game. By convincing myself that they were right. When I jumped off that roof, Mimo, my fall did not last a few seconds. It lasted twenty-six years. But it is over now.'

She straightened up and added with a smile: '"I am a woman standing", as a girl I once knew would say.'

I was not remotely amused. And I no longer admired her. In that moment, my only weapon was fear.

'Viola, listen to me. I am not joking when I say that I would never allow anyone to hurt you. I would take a bullet for you if I could, and I wouldn't hesitate, but what would be the point since the next bullet would be for you. So I'm asking you... No, I'm begging you, one last time, to give up. Be reasonable. We will find a solution later. We always have.'

'And if I refuse?'

'Then I'll leave. I'll leave tonight. I mean it. You will never see me again.'

She nodded slowly. Then she took something that I initially thought was a bookmark and handed it to me. It was a sealed envelope. 'If anything should happen to me, I want you to read this. But not before. Swear it.'

'Viola...'

'Were you serious? Are you really going to leave?'

'If you don't change your mind, yes.'

'Then swear.'

I took the letter, feeling utterly defeated. 'I swear.'

She turned away and went back to her reading. During my years in Rome, I had spent many nights around the gambling tables, I had lost a lot, but I had also won a lot. I won when I was suicidal, when I was not afraid of anything. When you push a bet into the middle of the table, you have to do it casually, as though you are thinking about something else, as though winning doesn't matter. A lot of hardened players lost their arrogant smiles when I bluffed.

'Goodbye, Viola.'

I turned on my heel. Just as I was leaving, her voice stopped me.

'Mimo?' She brought two fingers to her temple in a salute. 'So long, Francese.'

Stefano and Francesco were waiting for me in the green vestibule downstairs.

I walked past without stopping. 'Fuck you all.'

Francesco's face darkened and he headed for the waiting car outside. A minute later, as I walked towards the main road, the car sped past in a cloud of dust and turned off towards Rome.

When I got back to the studio, I did not stop to think.

'We're leaving,' I said to Zozo.

'Leaving? Leaving for where?'

'I don't know. Anywhere.'

'I've never been to Milan...'

It was dark by the time I threw my trunk onto the back seat. Above our heads, the sky was filled with dark-bellied clouds illumined by intermittent flashes. We headed north. Before long, the thunderstorm broke, one of the last before summer, a raging storm that smelled of death and petitgrain. I hadn't changed my clothes. Viola's envelope still stuck out of the inside pocket of the jacket tossed next to my luggage. I picked it up, weighed it, tried to read through the paper – impossible given the darkness. After a long internal struggle, I put it back in my pocket then snatched it out again and ripped it open. A single sheet folded in three with a few lines in green ink.

My dear Mimo,

I knew you would not be able to wait very long, that you would open this letter in spite of your promise. I just wanted to tell you that I know. I know that every time you have betrayed me, in Florence, tonight when you asked me to stand down, and again now when you opened this letter, you have always done so out of love. I've never been angry with you, not really.

Your dear friend, Viola.

I burst out laughing, a nervous laugh that prompted a concerned look from Zozo in the rear-view mirror. We had just arrived in Pontinvrea. The lights of a taverna glowed bright and orange and welcoming in the storm.

'Stop there.'

'Here? What for?'

'To have a drink.'

Zozo parked in the square, under a plane tree. We had only twenty metres to walk, but arrived drenched to the skin. I ordered two beers and took a long draught of mine. An hour earlier, my anger had been a block of granite. Black, glossy, sharp-edged. But that had been an illusion, another of Viola's enchantments. The further we got from Pietra, the weaker the spell became, and the block of granite was revealed for what it truly was: a pile of sand. Hard though I tried to cling to it, the anger trickled through my fingers. After a second glass of beer, it was gone.

'We're not going to Milan, are we?'

I smiled at Zozo's disappointed expression. 'No.'

'Do you want me to drive you back now?'

'Why don't we get a bed for the night here? I'm cold and tired. We'll go back tomorrow morning. Why don't you have another beer?'

We went up to our room, a little tipsy, shortly after midnight on 1 June 1946. The taverna, a converted old rough-stone mill, overlooked the river. Zozo took one bed, I the other. I don't remember my dream, a heavy, fat dream in which I was trying to escape some nameless danger. There was a shot. Or an explosion.

When I opened my eyes, it was pitch dark. I was no longer in bed, but in the middle of the room, sprawled face down on the floor with a mouthful of dust. My hands were bleeding. Zozo was on all fours beside me, coughing violently. He tried to say something, shook his head and started coughing again. The air was as thick as plaster. I couldn't breathe. I needed to get out of there. Blood streamed into my eyes. I turned towards the window.

There was no window, no walls, just a vast expanse of night.

Mercalli scale

I – Imperceptible – only detectable by seismographs.

II – Very Weak – felt by persons at rest on upper floors or favourably placed.

III – Weak – tremor felt by few people, objects move and shake as though a small lorry has driven past. Many people do not recognise it as an earthquake.

IV – Light – tremor felt by most people, light fittings shaking, hanging objects sway as if a large lorry has driven past. Sensations are like a heavy truck striking a building.

V – Moderate – felt by nearly everyone, many awakened, some dishes and windows broken, unstable objects overturned.

VI – Strong – minor damage to buildings, shattered windows, trees and shrubs shaken, smaller bells ring.

VII – Very strong – difficult to keep one's balance, chimneys break, damage to buildings, water in puddles becomes cloudy, large bells ring.

VIII – Severe – partial collapse of some buildings, statues fall from their plinths, a few isolated victims.

IX – Violent – considerable damage, complete collapse of some buildings, underground pipes ruptured, numerous casualties.

X – Extreme – total collapse of many buildings, numerous casualties, cracks in the earth, bridges destroyed, damage to dams, railway tracks buckle.

XI – Catastrophic – whole towns devastated, huge number of victims, landslides, chasms, tidal waves, dykes breached, communications cut off.

XII – Cataclysmic – all buildings destroyed, landscape altered, ground undulates and the earth's crust shifts, very few survivors.

On 1 June 1946, at 3.42 a.m., an earthquake measuring XI on the Mercalli scale struck Pietra d'Alba and the surrounding areas. There were no fatalities in the taverna where we were staying. We were the only guests. The east façade, overlooking the river, completely collapsed, making it look like a doll's house. We did our best to calm the landlady, who was screaming hysterically in the street. Then Zozo started up the car. By five o'clock we were heading back to Pietra d'Alba. It had stopped raining.

The road was blocked in several places by fissures and landslides, which we managed to get past after considerable effort. Ten kilometres outside Pietra, the whole road had opened up over a span of twenty metres. We had to abandon the car, climb down to the riverbed and climb up the far bank. We walked in silence. We passed the little hamlet I had seen earlier that night. It was completely razed. There was not a sound, except a hen scurrying over the rubble.

Sometime in mid-afternoon, we were thrown to the ground by an aftershock. On the mountain slopes, on the other side of the road, a landslide traced a muddy brown line through the forest. Pine trees snapped like matchsticks.

We got to Pietra d'Alba shortly before sunset. Dirty, exhausted, caked in mud and dried blood. As we came to the plateau, Zozo began to cry. The air smelt of scorched stone. Nothing remained of the village except a small section of the church. The whole topography of the plateau had changed. It was bumpy, uneven and seemed to be leaning. I started to run, to run like hell along the broken road, cutting through the fields, spraining my ankle, falling and getting up again without feeling any pain. We passed the studio. The barn was a heap of broken planks, half the house had collapsed and, in the middle, where the water trough had been, the miraculous spring gushed like a geyser. I did not stop – Vittorio and my mother were safe in Genoa – and raced on to the Villa Orsini, past fields ploughed up by the hand of some mad god. I was greeted by the bear I had sculpted for Viola when I was sixteen. It had been hurled from its plinth beside the villa and lay near the gates, broken in two.

The Villa Orsini with its beautiful green curtains, the Villa Orsini with its frills and flounces and the parquet floors I had once dared to stain with my blood, no longer existed. Half of the ruin was covered by a mass of mud and trees. The forest behind the building had shifted, leaving a gaping wound, a gash that looked like a quarry. Only a hundred or so orange trees were still standing.

I hurled myself at the ruins, lifting what stones I could, trying to dislodge a beam. I felt Zozo's hand on my shoulder. I pushed him away, and I carried on until exhaustion finally overcame me. I tumbled, half-conscious, onto the rubble, splitting my forehead open.

Zozo put his jacket around my shoulders. 'Mimo... There's no point. We have to wait for the emergency services.'

I have no idea know how long it took them to get there, or how they got there. With nowhere to go, Zozo and I spent the night huddled together in a makeshift shelter made from planks propped on stones. For the first time since I first arrived on this plateau, there was utter silence. Not a chirrup from a bird or insect. Destruction makes no sound. During the night, there was a downpour. Then, suddenly, there they were. A phalanx of uniformed men, barking orders, cheering when they saw us, wrapping thick woollen blankets around shoulders in the pale dawn. Pietra d'Alba had never been pinker than that morning, as though the crushed and broken stone was exhaling the last breath of colour it had so long held inside.

Viola was the first to be found, shortly before noon. Her bedroom was on the top floor, in a part of the house that had not been covered by the landslide. As soon as I heard the screams, I set off running, despite the hands trying to hold me back. A fireman had just passed her to a colleague, standing next to a pile of rubble. The second fireman had taken her in his arms, bent down and laid her on the ground. Viola was naked and covered in dust. I knelt down beside her to touch her face, then pulled a tattered length of curtain over her body. The Orsinis had a curious pact with death: it took them without maiming them. Like her brother Virgilio, who had been found next to a crumpled train carriage, Viola was unmarked, except for a few scratches and the dramatic scars visible on her legs, arms and torso, thirty years after her flight. Scars that I had never seen. Only then did I realise what she had endured after her fall. Her right leg, below the knee, was a little twisted. But it was her face that struck me most. I had always thought her lips a little too thin, but I was wrong. They were full and opened onto a round smile now that she no longer had to grit her teeth. A lock of hair fell over the lifeless face and I brushed it aside with a finger. My broken Viola. Zozo wept for me.

Stefano and his mother were pulled from the rubble late that day, together with Silvio and the household staff. Surprisingly, the Marchese was never found. Zozo and I were driven down to Genoa, where we were greeted by Vittorio, Anna and our distraught mothers. I was forced to spend the night under observation in hospital because of my head injury. The following day, I immediately got dressed, walked past reception and down to the railway station.

If Filippo Metti was surprised to see me walking into his studio that evening with a bandage around my head, he did not show it. I went straight to my marble, pulled away the tarpaulin, grabbed the first chisel and hammer to hand and attacked it with all my strength. That night I finally wept splinters of stone. At around midnight, a plate of soup appeared and I ate distractedly, then went back to sculpting. An hour later, having barely started, I collapsed against the marble block.

Hands lifted me, voices whispered. They carried me up a staircase, a door creaked, and I was laid on a bed. A dry but gentle hand was laid on my forehead, before the footsteps faded. I had barely slept in three days; now at last I sank into the first oblivion I had experienced, into the room I would share with my old maestro for more than a year, now that I had regained my sight and could see my *Pietà*.

The earthquake claimed 472 lives. Almost the entire population of Pietra d'Alba, yet only a drop in the ocean compared to the 100,000 lives claimed by the Messina earthquake in 1908, or the 30,000 in Marsica in the Abruzzo in 1915, which also measured XI on the Mercalli scale. The twins, their mother and mine owed their lives to their trip to Genoa. The Orsini family was wiped out, with the exception of Francesco, who had left for Rome earlier that evening. Dom Anselmo and all the villagers gave their lives back to the rugged plateau on which they had been born. Experts later explained that the crack in the dome of San Pietro delle Lacrime had been a precursor to the quake, which should have been taken as a warning. The only person who had understood was the Marchese, but no one had understood *him*. A few months later, I was disturbed to read in a newspaper that a scientist, noticing significant seismic activity in the area, had written to warn the mayor of Pietra d'Alba. He received no reply. Part of me, the darkest and most poetic, wonders to this day if, by chance, that letter was not in the satchel stolen from Emanuele before he was hanged. Perhaps one day someone will discover it in a thicket, crumpled in the cracked leather mailbag, with its derisory warning.

The earthquake uncovered the remains of another village beneath ours, probably razed by a similar event, the memory of which was lost in the thirteenth century. No palace of pale gold or albino peoples, as Viola had imagined, but an admirably preserved network of underground passages in which little Tommaso Baldi and his flute would go astray five hundred years later. Ironically, the cemetery of Pietra d'Alba was the only place spared by the quake. There are some forces more powerful than magma.

In the absence of another candidate, Orazio Gambale was elected by the villages that had been spared. However, the projected motorway was abandoned after the Pietra incident – it would have been foolish to build a thoroughfare through such a dangerous valley. The A6, built in 1960, would pass much further west.

On 2 June 1946, my fellow citizens voted in favour of a republic. Umberto II went into exile and, for the first time, twenty-one women were elected to the Italian parliament.

———————

For more than a year, I did not set foot outside Florence. I sculpted all day and sometimes through the night, accepting help from no one except Metti. One morning he simply showed up and set to work, helping with anything that could be done single-handed. We simply nodded at each other. The Virgin emerged from the stone exactly as I had seen her, and then her son. Their hazy presence became clearer, more refined, more polished. One winter day in 1947, I stepped back to contemplate my work. It was freezing outside, the stove was not lit, but I was in shirtsleeves, bathed in sweat. Metti came into the studio with a boy of twelve or so carrying a suitcase and looking lost – a new apprentice. With his hand on the boy's shoulder, he silently approached.

The block I had been using to polish for several months fell from my stiff fingers. Metti circled the work. He touched the face of Mary, the infinite gentleness I had known, then the face of her son. He nodded slowly, several times. His left hand made an abortive movement towards his non-existent right arm. 'There are some losses from which it is impossible to recover.'

Of all the people who saw my Pietà, I think he was the only one who understood.

The boy stared at the work, his head raised, his mouth hanging open.

'Did you make this, signor?' he said fearfully.

He reminded me of myself once upon a time – in fact, we were the same height.

'You will do the same one day,' I promised.

'Oh no, signor, I don't think I would be able to.'

Metti and I exchanged a glance. Then I put my chisel in the boy's hand.

'Listen carefully. Sculpting is very simple. It is simply a matter of peeling away the layers of stories and unnecessary anecdotes until you reach the story that concerns everyone, you and me, this city, the whole country, the story that can no longer be sculpted away without losing something of itself. And that is when you have to stop. Do you understand?'

'No, signor.'

'Not "signor",' said Metti. 'You must call him "maestro".'

My *Pietà* was exhibited for the first time in Florence, in the Duomo itself. Francesco came to give a speech. He seemed more lugubrious. The tremor of the earth had robbed him of a lightness I had never noticed. At first, nothing happened. I avoided the press; the last photo of me was published in a local paper. Then came the first reactions, and they only continued to multiply. The *Pietà* was moved to the Vatican, but the situation further deteriorated. The rest is public knowledge. In a manner of speaking, of course. Only a few insiders truly know, and the Vatican hushed it up.

I was accorded the favour of living near her, at the Sacra, where they hid her. I had already lived a thousand lives; I did not want one more. I have spent the last forty years of my life here. Not as a monk, exactly, I confess. I would leave from time to time to visit my mother, my friends and sometimes even my Serbian princess. In each other's arms, we tried to forget, with varying degrees of success, our ageing bodies.

My mother, my sporadic mother, died in 1971 at the age of ninety-eight of a symphony in her throat. Her eyes had grown pale. They were no longer the intense mauve of twilight, but that of forget-me-nots. I got to the hospital just in time. She laid a hand on my cheek and whispered: 'My little man.'

Vittorio and Anna, now an elderly couple, still live near Genoa with Emanuele. It took the earth shaking to finally bring them together again, to move them towards each other. Zozo is now sixty-three; their daughter Maria is two years younger. They will be sad to get the phone call from Padre Vincenzo. *It's about your friend Mimo...*

The scandal triggered by my *Pietà*, which was inextricably tied to the name Orsini, did Francesco few favours. When Pope Pius XII died in 1958, he was passed over in favour of Angelo Roncalli, and he had no better luck in subsequent elections. He is now a red, stooped figure in councils and conclaves. But I think deep down he is happy that way.

With the exception of Metti, no one understood. I read the newspaper articles, the expert reports, the scientific and mystical ravings – all of them ridiculous. The professor who wrote a monograph about the *Pietà* came close to the truth in his own way, when he said that I had known the Virgin. That much is true. But, like all the others, he fell victim to the most beautiful trick Viola taught me when she turned into a bear.

Force the viewer to look where the magician wants them to look. Mary is not Viola. I used Anna's face for the Virgin, that expression of the purest gentleness from a village named Pietra d'Alba.

You have to look at Christ. Look at Viola. I sculpted her as I saw her that day, lying in the rubble, a body broken yet sublime, the twisted legs, the non-existent breasts, even more effaced by the fact that it is supine, the hair falling over the face. Yet, however androgynous, it is a woman lying there, with a woman's collarbones, a woman's chest, a woman's hips. Expecting to see a man, the eye sees a man, but all the other senses recognise a femininity that is all the more explosive for being all but invisible, her soaring flight cut short by the zealots who crucified her. Some viewers simply shrug and accept this. The more sensitive experience a visceral reaction not unlike desire, something inexplicable and incongruous to those who have not understood – in other words, to everyone. People looked to the devil, to science and what have you, when it was simply Viola. Viola whom I had unwittingly betrayed and denied so often it would make Saint Peter weep.

Yes, my brothers. That day, amid the rubble, I understood and I saw. You had commissioned a Pietà that would offer reconciliation. The Virgin weeping over the brutalised body of Christ. But this is the thing: if Christ truly is suffering, then, with all due respect, Christ is a woman.

I would like to know how it will happen. The passing over, the last breath. Will I leave mid-sentence? Words trailing off and then nothing, a magnificent silence and relief? Or will I have to be pinned down on this bed while my soul is ripped from my body?

Tramontane, sirocco, libeccio, ponente and mistral, I call you in the name of all the winds.

I loved my life, my life as coward, traitor and artist. And, as Viola taught me, you do not leave something you love without turning back. I can feel someone holding my hand. A brother, perhaps the Padre Vincenzo himself.

Tramontane, sirocco, libeccio, ponente and mistral, I call you by the name of all the winds.

Ah, Il Cornutto, Il Cornutto! Sing to us of leave takings. Let's sing a little song!

You should have seen Fra Angelico's frescoes in the blaze of a lightning flash...

Vincenzo raises his head, shivering in the chilly Piedmont morning. At first, he thinks he has been woken by the dawn, but day has just begun to break, painting a little pink upon the windowpane. Then he realises. The hand of the man he has been sitting with is feverishly clutching his. His breath is ragged, his eyes are open – they can no longer see.

Unthinkingly, Vincenzo touches the key that hangs around his neck. Later, he will go back down to the chamber to look at the *Pietà*. And he will visit her again and again, until he understands. Perhaps that is what the sculptor is trying to tell him before he takes his leave. *Look again.* Perhaps he has missed something, one of those tiny details from which revolutions are made.

The grip on his hand gently relaxes. A final swing of the pendulum, a final tick, the clock is about to stop. In the distance, the Alps are just emerging from the horizon. In the still dark sky, a point of light traces a lazy orbit.

Mimo Vitaliani, born into a world of birds, dies beneath the gaze of a satellite.

ACKNOWLEDGEMENTS

My thanks to Alexia Lazat-Lepage for helping me climb up on the rooftop, to Delphine Burton for the explosion of mimosa and forty-five years of friendship, to Samantha Bordais for her light.

Thanks also to Roland Baroni and Jean Gouny for the Latin lessons, the first scenes and Rome beneath the snow.